Yankee
WITCHES

Yankee WITCHES

Edited by Charles G. Waugh,
Martin H. Greenberg & Frank D. McSherry Jr.

Introduction by Frank D. McSherry, Jr.

Illustrated by Peter Farrow

Lance Tapley, Publisher

"All Souls'" by Edith Wharton. Copyright 1937 by D. Appleton-Century Co.; renewed © 1965 by William R. Tyler. Reprinted by permission of Watkins/Loomis Agency, Inc.

"Canavan's Back Yard" by Joseph Payne Brennan. © 1958 by Joseph Payne Brennan. Reprinted by permission of Kirby McCauley, Ltd.

"The Night Train to Lost Valley" by August Derleth. Copyright 1948 by *Weird Tales*. Reprinted by permission of the agent for the author's Estate, the Scott Meredith Literary Agency, Inc., 845 Third Avenue, New York NY 10022.

"A Message From Charity" by William M. Lee. © 1967 by Mercury Press, Inc. From *The Magazine of Fantasy and Science Fiction*. Reprinted by permission of the agent for the author's Estate, the Scott Meredith Literary Agency, Inc., 845 Third Avenue, New York NY 10022.

"The Fog on Pemble Green" by Shirley Barker. Copyright 1955 by Shirley Barker. Reprinted by permission of Harold Matson Co., Inc.

"The Three D's" by Ogden Nash. Copyright 1948 by The Hearst Corporation (originally appeared under the title "Victoria"). Reprinted courtesy of *Harper's Bazaar*.

"The Music Teacher" by John Cheever. © 1959 by John Cheever. Reprinted from *The Stories of John Cheever*, by permission of Alfred A. Knopf, Inc.

"Is the Devil a Gentleman?" by Seabury Quinn. Copyright 1948 by *Weird Tales*. Reprinted by permission of the agent for the author's Estate, the Scott Meredith Literary Agency, Inc., 845 Third Avenue, New York NY 10022.

"The Apprentice Sorcerer" by Stephen Rynas. Copyright 1953 by Stephen A. Rynas. Reprinted by permission of the author.

"The Thing on the Doorstep" by H. P. Lovecraft. Copyright 1937 by *Weird Tales*. Reprinted by permission of the agent for the author's Estate, the Scott Meredith Literary Agency, Inc., 845 Third Avenue, New York NY 10022.

"Just Another Working Mom" by Patricia B. Cirone. © 1988 by Patricia B. Cirone.

Illustrated by Peter Farrow
Designed by Lisa Lyons
Composed by G&G Laser Typesetting
Printed by Thomson-Shore, Inc.

Library of Congress Cataloging-in-Publication Data
Yankee Witches.
    1. Witchcraft—Fiction. 2. New England—Fiction.
3. Short stories, American—New England. I. Waugh, Charles. II. Greenberg, Martin Harry. III. McSherry, Frank D.
PS648.W5Y36 1988 813'.0872 88-2155
ISBN 0-912769-32-7

CONTENTS

INTRODUCTION

■ BY FRANK D. McSHERRY, JR. ■

The black candle gutters. In the gloom an aged woman with hate in her eyes thrusts a needle into the heart of a carefully carved wax doll—and, miles away, the man it resembles screams, grabs his chest, and falls dead.

The wrinkled hands move, weaving weird arabesques above the candle flame. The ancient voice mutters strange names— and a respectable citizen loses weight steadily and inexplicably until death. His wife miscarries. His cattle and orchards cease to bear, his fields lie sterile while his neighbors have rich harvests.

Surely such powers of darkness cannot exist.

Or can they?

It has long been whispered that a witch could do even more. She could change shape, becoming a giant wolf, or a cat that could kill babies by crouching on their chests and sucking the air from their lungs. She could suck blood from her victims like a vampire. She could change into a beautiful young woman of dazzling glamor. She could swallow her victims' souls. She could fly.

Whether today we believe that the witch was a figure of malice, a familiar of Satan, and a worker of spells; or whether we think she was a victim of prejudice, suspicion, and fear, we need to acknowledge our ancestors' beliefs. The annals of centuries abound with cases of men and women accused, and quite often convicted, of witchcraft. They were subjected to hideous tortures and impossible "tests": burning, drowning, flogging, being pierced by long pins, and hanging.

In New England, the nightmares of little girls got witches hanged. The worst outbreak of the terror in America took place in 1692. The female children of the household of the Rev. Samuel Parris of Salem, Massachusetts—his nine-year-old daughter Elizabeth and her eleven-year-old cousin Abigail—began to throw fits and make strange sounds like words in a "language" the Rev. Parris could not understand. The girls named people (mostly women) whom they saw in their fits, including Tituba, a half-Carib, half-black slave woman the Rev. Parris had brought from Barbados. The girls accused Tituba and others of witching them.

Arrested, Tituba confessed, telling the court how she flew on a broom to secret meetings at night in the hills, where a Black Mass was held, attended by many prominent members of the town. They ate red bread, she claimed, and drank red wine. A red rat spoke to her in a human voice, saying, "Serve me!" She signed a black book and swore to do mischief to children before a tall man from Boston who kept his face hidden.

Panic spread. Other arrests were made, one of a four- year-old girl. Before the witch fear subsided at year's end, twenty people had been executed, all but one by hanging.

(But compare this with the record of the Continent, where the witch fear ran for centuries, from the late 1500s to the early 1700s. In Germany alone, according to the *Encyclopedia of Witchcraft and Demonology*, at least a hundred thousand witches were executed.)

Ever since Salem, the witch has been a colorful character in New England lore and history, represented dramatically in fiction and fact, television, and films. Notable modern examples include Arthur Miller's famous play *The Crucible*, Marion Starkey's historical study *The Devil in Massachusetts*, and John Updike's novel *The Witches of Eastwick*.

The stories in this anthology of witchcraft in New England show the profound influence of the image of the witch on the American consciousness. They are by such noted authors as H. P.

Lovecraft, high priest of the macabre, whose fictitious, legend-haunted city of Arkham is really Salem; Edith Wharton, whose cool classical prose deals with a night of Black Mass and Sabbat horror; August Derleth, whose New Hampshire town is as familiar as your own back yard and as foreign as the moon; John Cheever, whose saturnine music teacher is a nightmare figure in the suburban landscape; Mary Wilkins Freeman, whose realistic background of colonial Massachusetts intensifies the icy horror of her tale; and there are many more.

Finding in witchcraft the potential for humor seems to be a twentieth-century phenomenon, and undoubtedly it is partly a product of our faith in science and modern psychology which tells us that there is a rational explanation for phenomena. If we can treat our fears lightly, the terror of Salem can become the sitcom of *Bewitched*, and authors such as Ogden Nash, William Lee, Stephen Rynas, and Patricia Cirone can have fun with the witch's legacy while preserving its age-old nature, as they do here.

The witch trials stopped in most countries in the first half of the 1700s (a little later in Germany, where the last trial and execution for witchcraft occurred in 1775). Yet does not the witch fear live on? Behind the masks of religious, racial, and sexual persecution, book burning, political "witch-hunts"—all too prevalent in the civilized world—the fear lives. . .and gives these stories, picked for their literary drama, a currency beyond their entertainment value.

Within recent years, some branches of science have begun to investigate the shadowy world of the para- and super-normal, of such eerie abilities as levitation, telepathy, and teleportation; and some of the findings suggest that these powers may be more than rumors.

ALL SOULS'

▪ BY EDITH WHARTON ▪

Q ueer and inexplicable as the business was, on the surface it appeared fairly simple—at the time, at least; but with the passing of years, and owing to there not having been a single witness of what happened except Sara Clayburn herself, the stories about it have become so exaggerated, and often so ridiculously inaccurate, that it seems necessary that someone connected with the affair, though not actually present—I repeat that when it happened my cousin was (or thought she was) quite alone in her house—should record the few facts actually known.

In those days I was often at Whitegates (as the place had always been called)—I was there, in fact, not long before, and almost immediately after, the strange happenings of those thirty-six hours. Jim Clayburn and his widow were both my cousins, and because of that, and of my intimacy with them, both families think I am more likely than anybody else to be able to get at the facts, as far as they can be called facts, and as anybody can get at them. So I have written down, as clearly as I could, the gist of the various talks I had with cousin Sara, when she could be got to talk—it wasn't often—about what occurred during that mysterious weekend.

I read the other day in a book by a fashionable essayist that ghosts went out when electric light came in. What nonsense! The

11

writer, though he is fond of dabbling, in a literary way, in the supernatural, hasn't even reached the threshold of his subject. As between turreted castles patrolled by headless victims with clanking chains, and the comfortable suburban house with a refrigerator and central heating where you feel, as soon as you're in it, *that there's something wrong*, give me the latter for sending a chill down the spine! And, by the way, haven't you noticed that it's generally not the high-strung and imaginative who see ghosts, but the calm matter-of-fact people who don't believe in them, and are sure they wouldn't mind if they did see one? Well, that was the case with Sara Clayburn and her house. The house, in spite of its age—it was built, I believe, about 1780—was open, airy, high-ceilinged, with electricity, central heating and all the modern appliances: and its mistress was—well, very much like her house. And, anyhow, this isn't exactly a ghost story and I've dragged in the analogy only as a way of showing you what kind of woman my cousin was, and how unlikely it would have seemed that what happened at Whitegates should have happened just there—or to her.

When Jim Clayburn died the family all thought that, as the couple had no children, his widow would give up Whitegates and move either to New York or Boston—for being of good Colonial stock, with many relatives and friends, she would have found a place ready for her in either. But Sara Clayburn seldom did what other people expected, and in this case she did exactly the contrary; she stayed at Whitegates.

"What, turn my back on the old house—tear up all the family roots, and go and hang myself up in a bird-cage flat in one of those new skyscrapers in Lexington Avenue, with a bunch of chickweed and a cuttlefish to replace my good Connecticut mutton? No, thank you. Here I belong, and here I stay till my executors hand the place over to Jim's next-of-kin—that stupid fat Presley boy. . . Well, don't let's talk about him. But I tell you what—I'll keep him out of here as long as I can." And she did—for being still in the early fifties when her husband died, and a muscular, resolute figure of a woman, she was more than a match for the fat

Presley boy, and attended his funeral a few years ago, in correct mourning, with a faint smile under the veil.

Whitegates was a pleasant hospitable-looking house, on a height overlooking the stately windings of the Connecticut River; but it was five or six miles from Norrington, the nearest town, and its situation would certainly have seemed remote and lonely to modern servants. Luckily, however, Sara Clayburn had inherited from her mother-in-law two or three old standbys who seemed as much a part of the family tradition as the roof they lived under; and I never heard of her having any trouble in her domestic arrangements.

The house, in Colonial days, had been foursquare, with four spacious rooms on the ground floor, an oak-floored hall dividing them, the usual kitchen extension at the back, and a good attic under the roof. But Jim's grandparents, when interest in the "Colonial" began to revive, in the early eighties, had added two wings, at right angles to the south front, so that the old "circle" before the front door became a grassy court, enclosed on three sides, with a big elm in the middle. Thus the house was turned into a roomy dwelling, in which the last three generations of Clayburns had exercised a large hospitality; but the architect had respected the character of the old house, and the enlargement made it more comfortable without lessening its simplicity. There was a lot of land about it, and Jim Clayburn, like his fathers before him, farmed it, not without profit, and played a considerable and respected part in state politics. The Clayburns were always spoken of as a "good influence" in the county, and the townspeople were glad when they learned that Sara did not mean to desert the place—"though it must be lonesome, winters, living all alone up there atop of that hill"—they remarked as the days shortened, and the first snow began to pile up under the quadruple row of elms along the common.

Well, if I've given you a sufficiently clear idea of Whitegates and the Clayburns—who shared with their old house a sort of reassuring orderliness and dignity—I'll efface myself and tell the tale, not in my cousin's words, for they were too confused and fragmentary, but as I built it up gradually out of her half-avowals and nervous reticences. If the thing happened at all—and I must leave you to judge of that—I think it must have happened in this way. . . .

• I •

The morning had been bitter, with a driving sleet—though it was only the last day of October—but after lunch a watery sun showed for a while through banked-up woolly clouds, and tempted Sara Clayburn out. She was an energetic walker, and given, at that season, to tramping three or four miles along the valley road, and coming back by way of Shaker's wood. She had made her usual round and was following the main drive to the house when she overtook a plainly dressed woman walking in the same direction. If the scene had not been so lonely—the way to Whitegates at the end of an autumn day was not a frequented one—Mrs. Clayburn might not have paid any attention to the woman, for she was in no way noticeable, but when she caught up with the intruder my cousin was surprised to find that she was a stranger—for the mistress of Whitegates prided herself on knowing, at least by sight, most of her country neighbors. It was almost dark, and the woman's face was hardly visible, but Mrs. Clayburn told me she recalled her as middle-aged, plain, and rather pale.

Mrs. Clayburn greeted her, and then added: "You're going to the house?"

"Yes, ma'am," the woman answered, in a voice that the Connecticut Valley in the old days would have called "foreign," but that would have been unnoticed by ears used to the modern multiplicity of tongues. "No, I couldn't say where she came from," Sara always said. "What struck me as queer was that I didn't know her."

She asked the woman, politely, what she wanted, and the woman answered: "Only to see one of the girls." The answer was natural enough, and Mrs. Clayburn nodded and turned off from the drive to the lower part of the gardens, so that she saw no more of the visitor then or afterward. And, in fact, a half hour later something happened which put the stranger entirely out of her mind. The brisk and light-footed Mrs. Clayburn, as she approached the house, slipped on a frozen puddle, turned her ankle, and lay suddenly helpless.

Price, the butler, and Agnes, the dour old Scottish maid whom Sara had inherited from her mother-in-law, of course knew exactly what to do. In no time they had their mistress stretched out on a lounge, and Dr. Selgrove had been called up from Norrington. When he arrived, he ordered Mrs. Clayburn to bed, did the necessary examining and bandaging, and shook his head over her ankle, which he feared was fractured. He thought, however, that if she would swear not to get up, or even shift the position of her leg, he could spare her the discomfort of putting it in plaster. Mrs. Clayburn agreed, the more promptly as the doctor warned her that any rash movement would prolong her immobility. Her quick imperious nature made the prospect trying, and she was annoyed with herself for having been so clumsy. But the mischief was done, and she immediately thought what an opportunity she would have for going over her accounts and catching up with her correspondence. So she settled down resignedly in her bed.

"And you won't miss much, you know, if you have to stay there a few days. It's beginning to snow, and it looks as if we were in for a good spell of it," the doctor remarked, glancing through the window as he gathered up his implements. "Well, we don't often get snow here as early as this, but winter's got to begin sometime," he concluded philosophically. At the door he stopped to add: "You don't want me to send up a nurse from Norrington? Not to nurse you, you know; there's nothing much to do till I see you again. But this is a pretty lonely place when the snow begins, and I thought maybe—"

Sara Clayburn laughed. "Lonely? With my old servants? You forget how many winters I've spent here alone with them. Two of them were with me in my mother-in-law's time."

"That's so," Dr. Selgrove agreed. "You're a good deal luckier than most people, that way. Well, let me see. This is Saturday. We'll have to let the inflammation go down before we can x-ray you. Monday morning, first thing, I'll be here with the x-ray man. If you want me sooner, call me up." And he was gone.

▪ II ▪

The foot at first had not been very painful; but toward the small hours Mrs. Clayburn began to suffer. She was a bad patient, like most healthy and active people. Not being used to pain she did not know how to bear it, and the hours of wakefulness and immobility seemed endless. Agnes, before leaving her, had made everything as comfortable as possible. She had put a jug of lemonade within reach, and had even (Mrs. Clayburn thought it odd afterward) insisted on bringing a tray with sandwiches and a thermos of tea. "In case you're hungry in the night, madam."

"Thank you, but I'm never hungry in the night. And I certainly shan't be tonight—only thirsty. I think I'm feverish."

"Well, there's the lemonade, madam."

"That will do. Take the other things away please." (Sara had always hated the sight of unwanted food "messing about" in her room.)

"Very well, madam. Only you might—"

"Please take it away," Mrs. Clayburn repeated irritably.

"Very good, madam." But as Agnes went out, her mistress heard her set the tray down softly on a table behind the screen which shut off the door.

"Obstinate old goose!" she thought, rather touched by the old woman's insistence.

Sleep, once it had gone, would not return, and the long black hours moved more and more slowly. How late the dawn came in November! "If only I could move my leg," she grumbled.

She lay still and strained her ears for the first steps of the servants. Whitegates was an early house, its mistress setting the example; it would surely not be long now before one of the women came. She was tempted to ring for Agnes, but refrained. The woman had been up late, and this was Sunday morning, when the household was always allowed a little extra time. Mrs. Clayburn reflected restlessly: "I was a fool not to let her leave the tea beside the bed, as she wanted to. I wonder if I could get up and get it?" But she remembered the doctor's warning, and dared not move.

Anything rather than risk prolonging her imprisonment. . . .

Ah, there was the stable clock striking. How loud it sounded in the snowy stillness! One—two—three—four—five. What? Only five? Three hours and a quarter more before she could hope to hear the door handle turned. . . . After a while she dozed off again, uncomfortably.

Another sound aroused her. Again the stable clock. She listened. But the room was still in deep darkness, and only six strokes fell. . . .She thought of reciting something to put her to sleep; but she seldom read poetry, and being naturally a good sleeper, she could not remember any of the usual devices against insomnia. The whole of her leg felt like lead now. The bandages had grown terribly tight—her ankle must have swollen. . . . She lay staring at the dark windows, watching for the first glimmer of dawn. At last she saw a pale filter of daylight through the shutters. One by one the objects between the bed and the window recovered first their outline, then their bulk, and seemed to be stealthily regrouping themselves, after goodness knows what secret displacements during the night. Who that has lived in an old house could possibly believe that the furniture in it stays still all night? Mrs. Clayburn almost fancied she saw one little slender-legged table slipping hastily back into its place.

"It knows Agnes is coming, and it's afraid," she thought whimsically. Her bad night must have made her imaginative, for such nonsense as that about the furniture had never occurred to her before. . . .

At length, after hours more, as it seemed, the stable clock struck eight. Only another quarter of an hour. She watched the hand moving slowly across the face of the little clock beside her bed. . .ten minutes. . .five. . .only five! Agnes was as punctual as destiny. . .in two minutes now she would come. The two minutes passed, and she did not come. Poor Agnes—she had looked pale and tired the night before. She had overslept herself, no doubt—or perhaps she felt ill, and would send the housemaid to replace her. Mrs. Clayburn waited.

She waited half an hour; then she reached up to the bell at the head of the bed. Poor old Agnes—her mistress felt guilty about waking her. But Agnes did not appear—and after a considerable interval Mrs. Clayburn, now with a certain impatience, rang again. She rang once; twice; three times— but still no one came.

Once more she waited; then she said to herself: "There must be something wrong with the electricity." Well—she could find out by switching on the bed lamp at her elbow (how admirably the room was equipped with every practical appliance!). She switched it on—but no light came. Electric current cut off; and it was Sunday, and nothing could be done about it till the next morning. Unless it turned out to be just a burnt-out fuse, which Price could remedy. Well, in a moment now someone would surely come to her door.

It was nine o'clock before she admitted to herself that something uncommonly strange must have happened in the house. She began to feel a nervous apprehension; but she was not the woman to encourage it. If only she had had the telephone put in her room, instead of out on the landing! She measured mentally the distance to be traveled, remembered Dr. Selgrove's admonition, and wondered if her broken ankle would carry her there. She dreaded the prospect of being put in plaster, but she had to get to the telephone, whatever happened.

She wrapped herself in her dressing gown, found a walking stick and, resting heavily on it, dragged herself to the door. In her bedroom the careful Agnes had closed and fastened the shutters, so that it was not much lighter there than at dawn; but outside in the corridor the cold whiteness of the snowy morning seemed almost reassuring. Mysterious things—dreadful things—were associated with darkness; and here was the wholesome prosaic daylight come again to banish them. Mrs. Clayburn looked about her and listened. Silence. A deep nocturnal silence in that day-lit house, in which five people were presumably coming and going about their work. It was certainly strange. . . . She looked out of the window, hoping to see someone crossing the court or coming along the drive. But no one was in sight, and the snow seemed to have the place to itself: a quiet, steady snow. It was still falling, with a businesslike regularity, muffling the outer world in layers on layers of thick white velvet, and intensifying the silence within. A noiseless world—were people so sure that absence of noise was what they wanted? Let them first try a lonely country house in a November snowstorm!

She dragged herself along the passage to the telephone. When she unhooked the receiver she noticed that her hand trembled.

She rang up the pantry—no answer. She rang again. Silence—more silence! It seemed to be piling itself up like the snow on the roof and in the gutters. Silence. How many people that she knew had any idea what silence was—and how loud it sounded when you really listened to it?

Again she waited: then she rang up "Central." No answer. She tried three times. After that she tried the pantry again. . . . The telephone was cut off then, like the electric current. Who was at work downstairs, isolating her thus from the world? Her heart began to hammer. Luckily there was a chair near the telephone, and she sat down to recover her strength—or was it her courage?

Agnes and the housemaid slept in the nearest wing. She would certainly get as far as that when she had pulled herself together. Had she the courage—? Yes, of course she had. She had always been regarded as a plucky woman; and had so regarded herself. But this silence—

It occurred to her that by looking from the window of a neighboring bathroom she could see the kitchen chimney. There ought to be smoke coming from it at that hour; and if there were she thought she would be less afraid to go on. She got as far as the bathroom and looking through the window saw that no smoke came from the chimney. Her sense of loneliness grew more acute. Whatever had happened belowstairs must have happened before the morning's work had begun. The cook had not had time to light the fire, the other servants had not yet begun their round. She sank down on the nearest chair, struggling against her fears. What next would she discover if she carried on her investigations?

The pain in her ankle made progress difficult; but she was aware of it now only as an obstacle to haste. No matter what it cost her in physical suffering, she must find out what was happening belowstairs—or had happened. But first she would go to the maid's room. And if that were empty— well, somehow she would have to get herself downstairs.

She limped along the passage, and on the way steadied herself by resting her hand on a radiator. It was stone-cold. Yet in that well-ordered house in winter the central heating, though damped down at night, was never allowed to go out, and by eight in the morning a mellow warmth pervaded the rooms. The icy chill of the pipes startled her. It was the chauffeur who looked after the heating—so he too was involved in the mystery, whatever it was, as well as the house servants. But this only deepened the problem.

• III •

At Agnes's door Mrs. Clayburn paused and knocked. She expected no answer, and there was none. She opened the door and went in. The room was dark and very cold. She went to the window and flung back the shutters; then she looked slowly around, vaguely apprehensive of what she might see. The room was empty but what frightened her was not so much its emptiness as its air of scrupulous and undisturbed order. There was no sign of anyone having lately dressed in it—or undressed the night before. And the bed had not been slept in.

Mrs. Clayburn leaned against the wall for a moment; then she crossed the floor and opened the cupboard. That was where Agnes kept her dresses; and the dresses were there, neatly hanging in a row. On the shelf above were Agnes's few and unfashionable hats, rearrangements of her mistress's old ones. Mrs. Clayburn, who knew them all, looked at the shelf, and saw that one was missing. And so was also the warm winter coat she had given to Agnes the previous winter.

The woman was out, then; had gone out, no doubt, the night before, since the bed was unslept in, the dressing and washing appliances untouched. Agnes, who never set foot out of the house after dark, who despised the movies as much as she did the wireless, and could never be persuaded that a little innocent amusement was a necessary element in life, had deserted the house on a snowy winter night, while her mistress lay upstairs, suffering and helpless! Why had she gone, and where had she gone? When she was undressing Mrs. Clayburn the night before, taking her orders, trying to make her more comfortable, was she already planning this mysterious nocturnal escape? Or had something—the mysterious and dreadful Something for the clue of which Mrs. Clayburn was still groping—occurred later in the evening, sending the maid downstairs and out of doors into the bitter night? Perhaps one of the men at the garage—where the chauffeur and gardener lived—had been suddenly taken ill, and someone had run up to the house for Agnes. Yes—that must be the explanation . . . . Yet how much it left unexplained.

Next to Agnes's room was the linen room; beyond that was the housemaid's door. Mrs. Clayburn went to it and knocked. "Mary!" No one answered, and she went in. The room was in the same immaculate order as her maid's, and here too the bed was unslept in, and there were no signs of dressing or undressing. The two women had no doubt gone out together—gone where?

More and more the cold unanswering silence of the house weighed down on Mrs. Clayburn. She had never thought of it as a big house, but now, in this snowy winter light, it seemed immense, and full of ominous corners around which one dared not look.

Beyond the housemaid's room were the back stairs. It was the nearest way down, and every step that Mrs. Clayburn took was increasingly painful; but she decided to walk slowly back, the whole length of the passage, and go down by the front stairs. She did not know why she did this; but she felt that at the moment she was past reasoning, and had better obey her instinct.

More than once she had explored the ground floor alone in the small hours, in search of unwonted midnight noises; but now it was not the idea of noises that frightened her, but that inexorable and hostile silence, the sense that the house had retained in full daylight its nocturnal mystery, and was watching her as she was watching it; that in entering those empty orderly rooms she might be disturbing some unseen confabulation on which beings of flesh and blood had better not intrude.

The broad oak stairs were beautifully polished, and so slippery that she had to cling to the rail and let herself down tread by tread. And as she descended, the silence descended with her—heavier, denser, more absolute. She seemed to feel its steps just behind her, softly keeping time with hers. It had a quality she had never been aware of in any other silence, as though it were not merely an absence of sound, a thin barrier between the ear and the surging murmur of life just beyond, but an impenetrable substance made out of the worldwide cessation of all life and all movement.

Yes, that was what laid a chill on her: the feeling that there was no limit to this silence, no outer margin, nothing beyond it. By this time she had reached the foot of the stairs and was limping across the hall to the drawing room. Whatever she found there, she was sure, would be mute and lifeless; but what would it be? The bodies of her dead servants, mown down by some homicidal maniac? And what if it were her turn next—if he were waiting for her behind the heavy curtains of the room she was about to enter? Well, she must find out—she must face whatever lay in wait. Not impelled by bravery—the last drop of courage had oozed out of her—but because anything, anything was better than to remain shut up in that snowbound house without knowing whether she was alone in it or not, "I must find that out, I must find that out," she repeated to herself in a sort of meaningless sing-song.

The cold outer light flooded the drawing room. The shutters had not been closed, nor the curtains drawn. She looked about her. The room was empty; and every chair in its usual place. Her armchair was pushed up by the chimney, and the cold hearth was piled with the ashes of the fire at which she had warmed herself before starting on her ill-fated walk. Even her empty coffee cup stood on a table near the armchair. It was evident that the servants had not been in the room since she had left it the day before after luncheon. And suddenly the conviction entered into her that, as she found the drawing room, so she would find the rest of the house; cold, orderly—and empty. She would find nothing, she would find no one. She no longer felt any dread of ordinary human dangers lurking in those dumb spaces ahead of her. She knew she was utterly alone under her own roof. She sat down to rest her aching ankle, and looked slowly about her.

There were the other rooms to be visited, and she was determined to go through them all—but she knew in advance that they would give no answer to her question. She knew it, seemingly, from the quality of the silence which enveloped her. There was no break, no thinnest crack in it anywhere. It had the cold continuity of the snow which was still falling steadily outside.

She had no idea how long she waited before nerving herself to continue her inspection. She no longer felt the pain in her ankle, but was only conscious that she must not bear her weight on it, and therefore moved very slowly, supporting herself on each piece of furniture in her path. On the ground floor no shutter had been closed, no curtain drawn, and she progressed without difficulty from room to room: the library, her morning room, the dining room. In each of them, every piece of furniture was in its usual place. In the dining room, the table had been laid for her dinner of the previous evening, and the candelabra, with candles unlit, stood reflected in the dark mahogany. She was not the kind of woman to nibble a poached egg on a tray when she was alone, but always came down to the dining room, and had what she called a civilized meal.

The back premises remained to be visited. From the dining room she entered the pantry, and there too everything was in irreproachable order. She opened the door and looked down the back passage with its neat linoleum floor covering. The deep silence accompanied her; she still felt it moving watchfully at her side, as though she were its prisoner and it might throw itself upon her if she attempted to escape. She limped on toward the kitchen. That of course would be empty too, and immaculate. But she must see it.

She leaned a minute in the embrasure of a window in the passage. "It's like the *Mary Celeste*—a *Mary Celeste* on *terra firma*," she thought, recalling the unsolved sea mystery of her childhood. "No one ever knew what happened on board the *Mary Celeste*. And perhaps no one will ever know what has happened here. Even I shan't know."

At the thought her latent fear seemed to take on a new quality. It was like an icy liquid running through every vein, and lying in a pool about her heart. She understood now that she had never before known what fear was, and that most of the people she had met had probably never known either. For this sensation was something quite different. . . .

It absorbed her so completely that she was not aware how long she remained leaning there. But suddenly a new impulse pushed her forward, and she walked on toward the scullery. She went there first because there was a service slide in the wall, through which she might peep into the kitchen without being seen; and some indefinable instinct told her that the kitchen held the clue to the mystery. She still felt strongly that whatever had happened in the house must have its source and center in the kitchen.

In the scullery, as she had expected, everything was clean and tidy. Whatever had happened, no one in the house appeared to have been taken by surprise; there was nowhere any sign of confusion or disorder. "It looks as if they'd known beforehand, and put everything straight," she thought. She glanced at the wall facing the door, and saw that the slide was open. And then, as she was approaching it, the silence was broken. A voice was speaking in the kitchen—a man's voice, low but emphatic, and which she had never heard before.

She stood still, cold with fear. But this fear was again a different one. Her previous terrors had been speculative, conjectural, a ghostly emanation of the surrounding silence. This was a plain everyday dread of evildoers. Oh, God, why had she not remembered her husband's revolver, which ever since his death had lain in a drawer in her room?

She turned to retreat across the smooth slippery floor but halfway her stick slipped from her, and crashed down on the tiles. The noise seemed to echo on and on through the emptiness, and she stood still, aghast. Now that she had betrayed her presence, flight was useless. Whoever was beyond the kitchen door would be upon her in a second. . . .

But to her astonishment the voice went on speaking. It was as though neither the speaker nor his listeners had heard her. The invisible stranger spoke so low that she could not make out what he was saying, but the tone was passionately earnest, almost threatening. The next moment she realized that he was speaking in a foreign language, a language unknown to her. Once more her terror was surmounted by the urgent desire to know what was going on, so close to her yet unseen. She crept to the slide, peered cautiously through into the kitchen, and saw that it was as orderly and empty as the other rooms. But in the middle of the carefully scoured table stood a portable wireless, and the voice she heard came out of it. . . .

She must have fainted then, she supposed; at any rate she felt so weak and dizzy that her memory of what next happened remained indistinct. But in the course of time she groped her way back to the pantry, and there found a bottle of spirits—brandy or whisky, she could not remember which. She found a glass, poured herself a stiff drink, and while it was flushing through her veins, managed, she never knew with how many shuddering delays, to drag herself through the deserted ground floor, up the stairs, and down the corridor to her own room. There, apparently, she fell across the threshold, again unconscious. . . .

When she came to, she remembered, her first care had been to lock herself in; then to recover her husband's revolver. It was not loaded, but she found some cartridges, and succeeded in loading it. Then she remembered that Agnes, on leaving her the evening before, had refused to carry away the tray with the tea and sandwiches, and she fell on them with a sudden hunger. She recalled also noticing that a flask of brandy had been put beside the thermos and being vaguely surprised. Agnes's departure, then, had been deliberately planned, and she had known that her mistress, who never touched spirits, might have need of a stimulant before she returned. Mrs. Clayburn poured some of the brandy into her tea, and swallowed it greedily.

After that (she told me later) she remembered that she had managed to start a fire in her grate, and after warming herself, had got back into her bed, piling on it all the coverings she could find. The afternoon passed in a haze of pain, out of which there emerged now and then a dim shape of fear—the fear that she might lie there alone and untended till she died of cold, and of the terror of her solitude. For she was sure by this time that the house was empty— completely empty, from garret to cellar. She knew it was so, she could not tell why; but again she felt that it must be because of the peculiar quality of the silence—the silence which had dogged her steps wherever she went and was now

folded down on her like a pall. She was sure that the nearness of any other human being, however dumb and secret, would have made a faint crack in the texture of that silence, flawed it as a sheet of glass is flawed by a pebble thrown against it. . . .

· IV ·

"Is that easier?" the doctor asked, lifting himself from bending over her ankle. He shook his head disapprovingly. "Looks to me as if you'd disobeyed orders—eh? Been moving about, haven't you? And I guess Dr. Selgrove told you to keep quiet till he saw you again, didn't he?"

The speaker was a stranger, whom Mrs. Clayburn knew only by name. Her own doctor had been called away that morning to the bedside of an old patient in Baltimore, and had asked this young man, who was beginning to be known at Norrington, to replace him. The newcomer was shy and somewhat familiar, as the shy often are, and Mrs. Clayburn decided that she did not much like him. But before she could convey this by the tone of her reply (and she was past mistress of the shades of disapproval) she heard Agnes speaking—yes, Agnes, the same, the usual Agnes, standing behind the doctor, neat and stern-looking as ever. "Mrs. Clayburn must have got up and walked about in the night instead of ringing for me, as she'd ought to," Agnes intervened severely.

This was too much! In spite of the pain, which was now exquisite, Mrs. Clayburn laughed. "Ringing for you? How could I, with the electricity cut off?"

"The electricity cut off?" Agnes's surprise was masterly. "Why, when was it cut off?" She pressed her finger on the bell beside the bed, and the call tinkled through the quiet room. "I tried that bell before I left you last night, madam, because if there'd been anything wrong with it I'd have come and slept in the dressing room sooner than leave you here alone."

Mrs. Clayburn lay speechless, staring up at her. "Last night? But last night I was all alone in the house."

Agnes's firm features did not alter. She folded her hands resignedly across her trim apron. "Perhaps the pain's made you a little confused, madam." She looked at the doctor, who nodded.

"The pain in your foot must have been pretty bad," he said.

"It was," Mrs. Clayburn replied. "But it was nothing to the horror of being left alone in this empty house since the day before yesterday, with the heat and the electricity off, and the telephone not working."

The doctor was looking at her in evident wonder. Agnes's sallow face flushed slightly, but only as if in indignation at an unjust charge. "But, madam, I made up your fire with my own hands last night—and look, it's smoldering still. I was getting ready to start it again just now, when the doctor came."

"That's so. She was down on her knees before it," the doctor corroborated.

Again Mrs. Clayburn laughed. Ingeniously as the tissue of lies was being woven about her, she felt she could still break through it. "I made up the fire myself yesterday—there was no one else to do it," she said, addressing the doctor, but keeping her eyes on her maid. "I got up twice to put on more coal, because the house was like a sepulcher. The central heating must have been out since Saturday afternoon."

At this incredible statement Agnes's face expressed only a polite distress; but the new doctor was evidently embarrassed at being drawn into an unintelligible controversy with which he had no time to deal. He said he had brought the x-ray photograper with him, but that the ankle was too much swollen to be photographed at present. He asked Mrs. Clayburn to excuse his haste, as he had all Dr. Selgrove's patients to visit besides his own, and promised to come back that evening to decide whether she could be x-rayed then, and whether, as he evidently feared, the ankle would have to be put in plaster. Then, handing his prescriptions to Agnes, he departed.

Mrs. Clayburn spent a feverish and suffering day. She did not feel well enough to carry on the discussion with Agnes; she did not ask to see the other servants. She grew drowsy, and understood that her mind was confused with fever. Agnes and the housemaid waited on her as attentively as usual, and by the time the doctor returned in the evening her temperature had fallen; but she decided not to speak of what was on her mind until Dr. Selgrove reappeared. He was to be back the following evening; and the new doctor preferred to wait for him before deciding to put the ankle in plaster—though he feared this was now inevitable.

▪ V ▪

That afternoon Mrs. Clayburn had me summoned by telephone, and I arrived at Whitegates the following day. My cousin, who looked pale and nervous, merely pointed to her foot, which had been put in plaster, and thanked me for coming to keep her company. She explained that Dr. Selgrove had been taken suddenly ill in Baltimore, and would not be back for several days, but that the young man who replaced him seemed fairly competent. She made no allusion to the strange incidents I have set down, but I felt at once that she had received a shock which her accident, however painful, could not explain.

Finally, one evening, she told me the story of her strange

weekend, as it had presented itself to her unusually clear and accurate mind, and as I have recorded it above. She did not tell me this till several weeks after my arrival; but she was still upstairs at the time, and obliged to divide her days between her bed and a lounge. During those endless intervening weeks, she told me, she had thought the whole matter over; and though the events of the mysterious thirty-six hours were still vivid to her, they had already lost something of their haunting terror, and she had finally decided not to reopen the question with Agnes, or to touch on it in speaking to the other servants. Dr. Selgrove's illness had been not only serious but prolonged. He had not yet returned, and it was reported that as soon as he was well enough he would go on a West Indian cruise, and not resume his practice at Norrington till the spring. Dr. Selgrove, as my cousin was perfectly aware, was the only person who could prove that thirty-six hours had elapsed between his visit and that of his successor; and the latter, a shy young man, burdened by the heavy additional practice suddenly thrown on his shoulders, told me (when I risked a little private talk with him) that in the haste of Dr. Selgrove's departure the only instructions he had given about Mrs. Clayburn were summed up in the brief memorandum: "Broken ankle. Have x-rayed."

Knowing my cousin's authoritative character, I was surprised at her decision not to speak to the servants of what had happened; but on thinking it over I concluded she was right. They were all exactly as they had been before that unexplained episode: efficient, devoted, respectful, and respectable. She was dependent on them and felt at home with them, and she evidently preferred to put the whole matter out of her mind, as far as she could. She was absolutely certain that something strange had happened in her house, and I was more than ever convinced that she had received a shock which the accident of a broken ankle was not sufficient to account for; but in the end I agreed that nothing was to be gained by cross-questioning the servants or the new doctor.

I was at Whitegates off and on that winter and during the following summer, and when I went home to New York for good early in October I left my cousin in her old health and spirits. Dr. Selgrove had been ordered to Switzerland for the summer, and this further postponement of his return to his practice seemed to have put the happenings of the strange weekend out of her mind. Her life was going on as peacefully and normally as usual, and I left her without anxiety, and indeed without a thought of the mystery, which was now nearly a year old.

I was living then in a small flat in New York by myself, and I had hardly settled into it when, very late one evening —on the last day of October—I heard my bell ring. As it was my maid's evening out, and I was alone, I went to the door myself, and on the threshold, to my amazement, I saw Sara Clayburn. She was wrapped in a fur cloak, with a hat drawn down over her forehead, and a face so pale and haggard that I saw something dreadful must have happened to her. "Sara," I gasped, not knowing what I was saying, "where in the world have you come from at this hour?"

"From Whitegates. I missed the last train and came by car." She came in and sat down on the bench near the door. I saw that she could hardly stand, and sat down beside her, putting my arm about her. "For heaven's sake, tell me what's happened."

She looked at me without seeming to see me. "I telephoned to Nixon's and hired a car. It took me five hours and a quarter to get here." She looked about her. "Can you take me in for the night? I've left my luggage downstairs."

"For as many nights as you like. But you look so ill—"

She shook her head. "No, I'm not ill. I'm only frightened— deathly frightened," she repeated in a whisper.

Her voice was so strange, and the hands I was pressing between mine were so cold, that I drew her to her feet and led her straight to my little guest room. My flat was in an old-fashioned building, not many stories high, and I was on more human terms with the staff than is possible in one of the modern Babels. I telephoned down to have my cousin's bags brought up, and meanwhile I filled a hot-water bottle, warmed the bed, and got her into it as quickly as I could. I had never seen her as unquestioning and submissive, and that alarmed me even more than her pallor. She was not the woman to let herself be undressed and put to bed like a baby; but she submitted without a word, as though aware that she had reached the end of her tether.

"It's good to be here," she said in a quieter tone, as I tucked her up and smoothed the pillows. "Don't leave me yet, will you—not just yet."

"I'm not going to leave you for more than a minute—just to get you a cup of tea," I reassured her; and she lay still. I left the door open, so that she could hear me stirring about in the pantry across the passage, and when I brought her the tea she swallowed it gratefully, and a little color came into her face. I sat with her in silence for some time; but at last she began: "You see it's exactly a year—"

I should have preferred to have her put off till the next morning whatever she had to tell me; but I saw from her burning eyes that she was determined to rid her mind of what was burdening it, and that until she had done so it would be useless to proffer the sleeping draft I had ready.

"A year since what?" I asked stupidly, not yet associating her precipitate arrival with the mysterious occurrences of the previous year at Whitegates.

She looked at me in surprise. "A year since I met that woman. Don't you remember—the strange woman who was coming up the drive the afternoon when I broke my ankle? I didn't think of it at the time, but it was on All Souls' eve that I met her."

Yes, I said, I remembered that it was.

"Well—and this is All Souls' eve, isn't it? I'm not as good as you are on church dates, but I thought it was."

"Yes. This is All Souls' eve."

"I thought so. . . . Well, this afternoon I went out for my usual walk. I'd been writing letters and paying bills and didn't start till late; not till it was nearly dusk. But it was a lovely clear evening. And as I got near the gate, there was the woman coming in—the same woman. . .going toward the house. . . ."

I pressed my cousin's hand, which was hot and feverish now. "If it was dusk, could you be perfectly sure it was the same woman?" I asked.

"Oh, perfectly sure, the evening was so clear. I knew her and she knew me; and I could see she was angry at meeting me. I stopped her and asked, 'Where are you going?' just as I had asked her last year. And she said, in the same queer half-foreign voice: 'Only to see one of the girls,' as she had before. Then I felt angry all of a sudden, and I said, 'You shan't set foot in my house again. Do you hear me? I order you to leave.' And she laughed. Yes, she laughed—very low, but distinctly. By that time it had got quite dark, as if a sudden storm was sweeping up over the sky, so that though she was so near me I could hardly see her. We were standing by the clump of hemlocks at the turn of the drive, and as I went up to her, furious at her impertinence, she passed behind the hemlocks, and when I followed her she wasn't there. . . .No! I swear to you she wasn't there. . . .And in the darkness I hurried back to the house, afraid that she would slip by me and get there first. And the queer thing was that as I reached the door the black cloud vanished, and there was the transparent twilight again. In the house everything seemed as usual, and the servants were busy about their work; but I couldn't get it out of my head that the woman, under the shadow of that cloud, had somehow got there before me." She paused for breath, and began again. "In the hall I stopped at the telephone and rang up Nixon and told him to send me a car at once to go to New York with a man he knew to drive me. And Nixon came with the car himself. . . ."

Her head sank back on the pillow and she looked at me like a frightened child. "It was good of Nixon," she said.

"Yes, it was very good of him. But when they saw you leaving—the servants, I mean. . . ."

"Yes. Well, when I got upstairs to my room I rang for Agnes. She came, looking just as cool and quiet as usual. And when I told her I was starting for New York in half an hour— I said it was on account of a sudden business call—well, then her presence of mind failed her for the first time. She forgot to look surprised, she even forgot to make an objection—and you know what an objector Agnes is. And as I watched her I could see a little secret spark of relief in her eyes, though she was so on her guard. And she just said, 'Very well, madam,' and asked me what I wanted to take with me. Just as if I were in the habit of dashing off to New York after dark on an autumn night to meet a business engagement! No, she made a mistake not to show any surprise—and not even to ask me why I didn't take my own car. And her losing her head in that way frightened me more than anything else. For I saw she was so thankful I was going that she hardly dared speak, for fear she should betray herself, or I should change my mind."

After that Mrs. Clayburn lay a long while silent, breathing less unrestfully; and at last she closed her eyes, as though she felt more at ease now that she had spoken, and wanted to sleep. As I got up quietly to leave her, she turned her head a little and murmured: "I shall never go back to Whitegates again." Then she shut her eyes and I saw that she was falling asleep.

I have set down above, I hope without omitting anything essential, the record of my cousin's strange experience as she told it to me. Of what happened at Whitegates that is all I can personally vouch for. The rest—and of course there is a rest—is pure conjecture; and I give it only as such.

My cousin's maid, Agnes, was from the isle of Skye, and the Hebrides, as everyone knows, are full of the supernatural—whether in the shape of ghostly presences, or the almost ghostlier sense of unseen watchers peopling the long nights of those stormy solitudes. My cousin, at any rate, always regarded Agnes as the—perhaps unconscious, at any rate, irresponsible—channel through which communications from the other side of the veil reached the submissive household at Whitegates. Though Agnes had been with Mrs. Clayburn for a long time without any peculiar incident revealing this affinity with the unknown forces, the power to communicate with them may all the while have been latent in the woman, only awaiting a kindred touch; and that touch may have been given by the unknown visitor whom my cousin, two years in succession, had met coming up the drive at Whitegates on the eve of All Souls'. Certainly the date bears out my hypothesis; for I suppose that, even in this unimaginative age, a few people still remember that All Souls' eve is the night when the dead can walk—and when, by the same token, other spirits, piteous or malevolent, are also freed from the restrictions which secure the earth to the living on the other days of the year.

If the recurrence of this date is more than a coincidence—and for my part I think it is—then I take it that the strange woman who twice came up the drive at Whitegates on All Souls' eve was either a "fetch," or else, more probably, and more alarmingly, a living woman inhabited by a witch. The history of witchcraft, as is well known, abounds in such cases, and such a messenger might well have been delegated by the powers who rule in these matters to summon Agnes and her fellow servants to a midnight "coven" in some neighboring solitude. To learn what happens at covens, and the reason of the irresistible fascination they exercise over the timorous and superstitious, one need only address oneself to the immense body of literature dealing with these mysterious rites. Anyone who has once felt the faintest curiosity to assist at a coven apparently soon finds the curiosity increase to desire, the desire to an uncontrollable longing, which, when the opportunity presents itself, breaks down all inhibitions; for those who have once taken part in a coven will move heaven and earth to take part again.

Such is my—conjectural—explanation of the strange happenings at Whitegates. My cousin always said she could not believe that incidents which might fit into the desolate landscape of the Hebrides could occur in the cheerful and populous Connecticut Valley; but if she did not believe, she at least feared—such moral paradoxes are not uncommon—and though she insisted that there must be some natural explanation of the mystery, she never returned to investigate it.

"No, no," she said with a little shiver, whenever I touched on the subject of her going back to Whitegates, "I don't want ever to risk seeing that woman again. . . ." And she never went back.

CANAVAN'S BACK YARD

▪ BY JOSEPH PAYNE BRENNAN ▪

I first met Canavan over twenty years ago, shortly after he had emigrated from London. He was an antiquarian and a lover of old books and so he quite naturally set up shop as a second-hand book dealer after he settled in New Haven.

Since his small capital didn't permit him to rent premises in the center of the city, he engaged combined business and living quarters in an isolated old house near the outskirts of town. The section was sparsely settled, but since a good percentage of Canavan's business was transacted by mail, it didn't particularly matter.

Quite often, after a morning spent at my typewriter, I walked out to Canavan's shop and spent most of the afternoon browsing among his old books. I found it a great pleasure, especially because Canavan never resorted to high-pressure methods to make a sale. He was aware of my precarious financial situation; he never frowned if I walked away empty-handed.

In fact he seemed to welcome me for my company alone. Only a few book buyers called at his place with regularity, and I think he was often lonely. Sometimes when business was slow, he would brew a pot of English tea and the two of us would sit for hours, drinking tea and talking about books.

Canavan even looked like an antiquarian book dealer—or

the popular caricature of one. He was small of frame, somewhat stoop-shouldered, and his blue eyes peered out from behind archaic spectacles with steel rims and square-cut lenses.

Although I doubt if his yearly income ever matched that of a good paperhanger, he managed to "get by" and he was content. Content, that is, until he began noticing his back yard.

Behind the ramshackle old house in which he lived and ran his shop, stretched a long desolate yard overgrown with brambles and high brindle-colored grass. Several decayed apple trees, jagged and black with rot, added to the scene's dismal aspect. The broken wooden fences on both sides of the yard were all but swallowed up by the tangle of coarse grass. They appeared to be literally sinking into the ground. Altogether the yard presented an unusually depressing picture and I often wondered why Canavan didn't clean it up. But it was none of my business; I never mentioned it.

One afternoon when I visited the shop, Canavan was not in the front display room and I therefore walked down a narrow corridor to a rear storeroom where he sometimes worked, packing and unpacking book shipments. When I entered the storeroom, Canavan was standing at the window, looking out at the back yard.

I started to speak and then for some reason didn't. I think what stopped me was the look on Canavan's face. He was gazing out at the yard with a peculiar intense expression, as if he were completely absorbed by something he saw there. Varying, conflicting emotions showed on his strained features. He seemed both fascinated and fearful, attracted and repelled. When he finally noticed me, he almost jumped. He stared at me for a moment as if I were a total stranger.

Then his old easy smile came back and his blue eyes twinkled behind the square spectacles. He shook his head. "That back yard of mine sure looks funny sometimes. You look at it long enough, you think it runs for miles!"

That was all he said at the time, and I soon forgot about it, but had I only known, that was just the beginning of the horrible business.

After that, whenever I visited the shop, I found Canavan in the rear storeroom. Once in a while he was actually working, but most of the time he was simply standing at the window looking out at that dreary yard of his.

Sometimes he would stand there for minutes completely oblivious to my presence. Whatever he saw appeared to rivet his entire attention. His countenance at those times showed an expression of fright mingled with a queer kind of pleasurable expectancy. Usually it was necessary for me to cough loudly, or shuffle my feet, before he turned from the window.

Afterward, when he talked about books, he would seem to be his old self again, but I began to experience the disconcerting feeling that he was merely acting, that while he chatted about incunabula, his thoughts were actually still dwelling on that infernal back yard.

Several times I thought of questioning him about the yard, but whenever words were on the tip of my tongue, I was stopped by a sense of embarrassment. How can one admonish a man for looking out of a window at his own back yard? What does one say and how does one say it?

I kept silent. Later I regretted it bitterly.

Canavan's business, never really flourishing, began to diminish. Worse than that, he appeared to be failing physically. He grew more stooped and gaunt, and though his eyes never lost their sharp glint, I began to believe it was more the glitter of fever than the twinkle of healthy enthusiasm which animated them.

One afternoon when I entered the shop, Canavan was nowhere to be found. Thinking he might be just outside the back door engaged in some household chore, I leaned up against the rear window and looked out.

I didn't see Canavan, but as I gazed out over the yard I was swept with a sudden inexplicable sense of desolation which seemed to roll over me like the wave of an icy sea. My initial impulse was to pull away from the window, but something held me. As I stared out over that miserable tangle of briars and brindle grass, I experienced what, for want of a better word, I can only call *curiosity*. Perhaps some cool, analytical, dispassionate part of my brain simply wanted to discover what had caused my sudden sense of acute depression. Or possibly some feature of that wretched vista attracted me on a subconscious level which I had never permitted to crowd up into my sane and waking hours.

In any case, I remained at the window. The long dry brown grass wavered slightly in the wind. The rotted black trees reared motionless. Not a single bird, not even a butterfly, hovered over the bleak expanse. There was nothing to be seen except the stalks of long brindle grass, the decayed trees, and scattered clumps of low-growing briary bushes.

Yet there was something about that particular isolated slice of landscape which I found intriguing. I think I had the feeling that it presented some kind of puzzle, and that if I gazed at it long enough, the puzzle would resolve itself.

After I had stood looking out at it for a few minutes, I experienced the odd sensation that its perspectives were subtly altering. Neither the grass nor the trees changed and yet the yard itself seemed to expand its dimensions. At first I merely reflected that the yard was actually much longer than I had previously believed. Then I had an idea that in reality it stretched for several acres. Finally I became convinced that it continued for an interminable distance and that if I entered it, I might walk for miles and miles before I came to the end.

I was seized by a sudden almost overpowering desire to rush out the back door, plunge into that sea of wavering brindle grass and stride straight ahead until I had discovered for myself just how far it did extend. I was, in fact, on the point of doing so—when I saw Canavan.

He appeared abruptly out of the tangle of tall grass at the near end of the yard. For at least a minute he seemed to be completely lost. He looked at the back of his own house as if he had never in his life seen it before. He was disheveled and obviously excited. Briars clung to his trousers and jacket, and pieces of grass were stuck in the hooks of his old-fashioned shoes. His eyes roved around wildly; he seemed about to turn and bolt back into the tangle from which he had just emerged.

I rapped loudly on the windowpane. He paused in a half turn, looked over his shoulder, and saw me. Gradually an expression of normalcy returned to his agitated features. Walking in a weary slouch, he approached the house. I hurried to the door and let him in. He went straight to the front display room and sank down in a chair.

He looked up when I followed him into the room. "Frank," he said in a half whisper, "would you make some tea?"

I brewed tea, and he drank it scalding hot without saying a word. He looked utterly exhausted; I knew he was too tired to tell me what had happened.

"You had better stay indoors for a few days," I said as I left.

He nodded weakly, without looking up, and bade me good-day.

When I returned to the shop the next afternoon, he appeared rested and refreshed but nevertheless moody and depressed. He made no mention of the previous day's episode. For a week or so it seemed as if he might forget about the yard.

But one day when I went into the shop, he was standing at the rear window and I could see that he tore himself away only with the greatest reluctance. After that, the pattern began repeating itself with regularity and I knew that that weird tangle of brindle grass behind his house was becoming an obsession.

Because I feared for his business, as well as for his fragile health, I finally remonstrated with him. I pointed out that he was losing customers; he had not issued a book catalog in months. I told him that the time spent in gazing at that witch's half acre he called his back yard would be better spent in listing his books and filling his orders. I assured him that an obsession such as his was sure to undermine his health. And finally I pointed out the absurd and ridiculous aspects of the affair. If people knew he spent hours in staring out of his window at nothing more than a miniature jungle of grass and briars, they might think he was actually mad!

I ended by boldly asking him exactly what he had experienced that afternoon when I had seen him come out of the grass with a lost, bewildered expression on his face.

He removed his square spectacles with a sigh. "Frank," he said, "I know you mean well. But there's something about that back yard—some secret—that I've got to find out. I don't know what it is exactly—something about distance and dimensions and perspectives, I think. But whatever it is, I've come to consider it—well, a challenge. I've got to get to the root of it. If you think I'm crazy, I'm sorry. But I'll have no rest until I solve the riddle of that piece of ground."

He replaced his spectacles with a frown. "That afternoon," he went on, "when you were standing at the window, I had a strange and frightening experience out there. I had been watching at the window and finally I felt myself drawn irresistibly outside. I plunged into the grass with a feeling of exhilaration, of adventure, of expectancy. As I advanced into the yard, my sense of elation quickly changed to a mood of black depression. I turned around, intending to come right out—but I couldn't. You won't believe this, I know—but I was lost! I simply lost all sense of direction and couldn't decide which way to turn. That grass is taller than it looks! When you get into it, you can't see anything beyond it.

"I know this sounds incredible—but I wandered out there for an hour. The yard seemed fantastically large once I got into that tangle of grass. It almost seemed to alter its dimensions as I moved, so that a large expanse of it lay always in front of me. I must have walked in circles. I swear I trudged miles!"

He shook his head. "You don't have to believe me. I don't expect you to. But that's what happened. When I finally found my way out, it was by the sheerest accident. And the strangest part of it is that once I got out, I felt suddenly terrified without the tall grass all around me and I wanted to rush back in again! This, in spite of the ghastly sense of desolation which the place aroused in me.

"But I've got to go back. I've got to figure the thing out. There's something out there that defies the laws of earthly nature as we know them. I mean to find out what it is. I think I have a plan and I mean to put it into practice."

His words stirred me strangely, and when I uneasily recalled my own experience at the window that afternoon, I found it difficult to dismiss his story as sheer nonsense. I did—half-heartedly—try to dissuade him from entering the yard again, but I knew even as I spoke that I was wasting my breath.

I left the shop that afternoon with a feeling of oppression and foreboding which nothing could remove.

When I called several days later, my worst fears were realized—Canavan was missing. The front door of the shop was unlatched, as usual, but Canavan was not in the house. I looked in every room. Finally, with a feeling of infinite dread, I opened the back door and looked out toward the yard.

The long stalks of brown grass slid against each other in the slight breeze with dry sibilant whispers. The dead trees reared black and motionless. Although it was late summer, I could hear neither the chirp of a bird nor the chirr of a single insect. The yard itself seemed to be listening.

Feeling something against my foot, I glanced down and saw a thick twine stretching from inside the door, across the scant cleared space immediately adjacent to the house and thence into the wavering wall of grass. Instantly I recalled Canavan's mention of a "plan." His plan, I realized immediately, was to enter the yard trailing a stout cord behind him. No matter how he twisted and turned, he must have reasoned, he could always find his way out by following back along the cord.

It seemed like a workable scheme, and I felt relieved. Probably Canavan was still in the yard. I decided I would wait for him to come out. Perhaps if he were permitted to roam around in the yard long enough, without interruption, the place would lose its evil fascinations for him, and he would forget about it.

I went back into the shop and browsed among the books. At the end of an hour I became uneasy again. I wondered how long Canavan had been in the yard. When I began reflecting on the old man's uncertain health, I felt a sense of responsibility.

I finally returned to the back door, saw that he was nowhere in sight, and called out his name. I experienced the disquieting sensation that my shout carried no further than the very edge of that whispering fringe of grass. It was as if the sound had been smothered, deadened, nullified as soon as the vibrations of it reached the border of that overgrown yard.

I called again, and again, but there was no reply. At length I decided to go in after him. I would follow along the cord, I thought, and I would be sure to locate him. I told myself that the thick grass undoubtedly did stifle my shout and possibly in any case Canavan might be growing slightly deaf.

Just inside the door, the cord was tied securely around the leg of a heavy table. Taking hold of the twine, I crossed the cleared area back of the house and slipped into the rustling expanse of grass.

The going was easy at first, and I made good progress. As I advanced, however, the grass stems became thicker and grew closer together and I was forced to shove my way through them.

When I was no more than a few yards inside the tangle, I was overwhelmed with the same bottomless sense of desolation which I had experienced before. There was certainly something uncanny about the place. I felt as if I had suddenly veered into another world—a world of briars and brindle grass whose ceaseless half-heard whisperings were somehow alive with evil.

As I pushed along, the cord abruptly came to an end. Glancing down, I saw that it had caught against a thorn bush, abraded itself and subsequently broken. Although I bent down and poked in the area for several minutes, I was unable to locate the piece from which it had parted. Probably Canavan was unaware that the cord had broken and was now pulling it along with him.

I straightened up, cupped my hands to my mouth and shouted. My shout seemed to be all but drowned in my throat by that dismal wall of grass. I felt as if I were down at the bottom of a well, shouting up.

Frowning with growing uneasiness, I tramped ahead. The grass stalks kept getting thicker and tougher and at length I needed both hands to propel myself through the matted growth.

I began to sweat profusely, my head started to ache, and I imagined that my vision was beginning to blur. I felt the same tense, almost unbearable oppression which one experiences on a stifling summer's day when a storm is brewing and the atmosphere is charged with static electricity.

Also, I realized with a slight qualm of fear that I had got turned around and didn't know which part of the yard I was in. During an objective half minute in which I reflected that I was actually worried about getting lost in someone's back yard, I almost laughed—almost. But there was something about the place which didn't permit laughter. I plodded ahead with a sober face.

Presently I began to feel that I was not alone. I had a sudden hair-raising conviction that someone—or something—was creeping along in the grass behind me. I cannot say with certainty that I heard anything, although I may have, but all at once I was firmly convinced that some creature was crawling or wriggling a short distance in my rear.

I felt that I was being watched and that the watcher was wholly malignant.

For a wild instant I considered headlong flight. Then, unaccountably, rage took possession of me. I was suddenly furious with Canavan, furious with the yard, furious with myself. All my pent-up tension exploded in a gust of rage which swept away fear. Now, I vowed, I would get to the root of the weird business. I would be tormented and frustrated by it no longer.

I whirled without warning and lunged into the grass where I believe my stealthy pursuer might be hiding.

I stopped abruptly; my savage anger melted into inexpressible horror.

In the faint brassy sunlight which filtered down through the towering stalks of brindle grass, Canavan crouched on all fours like a beast about to spring. His glasses were gone, his clothes were in shreds, and his mouth was twisted into an insane grimace, half smirk, half snarl.

I stood petrified, staring at him. His eyes, queerly out of focus, glared at me with concentrated hatred and without any faint glimmer of recognition. His gray hair was matted with grass and small sticks; his entire body, in fact, including the tattered remains of his clothing, was covered with them, as if he had grovelled or rolled on the ground like a wild animal.

After the first throat-freezing shock, I finally found my tongue.

"Canavan!" I screamed at him. "Canavan, for God's sake, don't you know me?"

His answer was a low throaty snarl. His lips twisted back from his yellowish teeth, and his crouching body tensed for a spring.

Pure terror took possession of me. I leaped aside and flung myself into that infernal wall of grass an instant before he lunged.

The intensity of my terror must have given me added strength. I rammed headlong through those twisted stalks, which before I had laboriously pulled aside. I could hear the grass and briar bushes crashing behind me, and I know that I was running for my life.

I pounded on as in a nightmare. Grass stalks snapped against my face like whips and thorns gashed me like razors, but I felt nothing. All my physical and mental resources were concentrated in one frenzied resolve: I must get out of that devil's field of grass and away from the monstrous thing which followed swiftly in my wake.

My breath began coming in great shuddering sobs. My legs felt weak and I seemed to be looking through spinning saucers of light. But I ran on.

The thing behind me was gaining. I could hear it growling and I could feel it lunge against the earth only inches back of my flying feet. And all the time I had the maddening conviction that I was actually running in circles.

At last when I felt that I must surely collapse in another second, I plunged through a final brindle thicket into the open sunlight. Ahead of me lay the cleared area at the rear of Canavan's shop. Just beyond was the house itself.

Gasping and fighting for breath, I dragged myself toward the door. For no reason that I could explain, then or afterwards, I felt absolutely certain that the horror at my heels would not venture into the open area. I didn't even turn around to make sure.

Inside the house I fell weakly into a chair. My strained breathing slowly returned to normal, but my mind remained caught up in a whirlwind of sheer horror and hideous conjecture.

Canavan, I realized, had gone completely mad. Some ghastly shock had turned him into a ravening bestial lunatic thirsting for the savage destruction of any living thing that crossed his path. Remembering the oddly focused eyes which had glared at me with a glaze of animal ferocity, I knew that his mind had not been merely unhinged—it had been totally destroyed. Death could be the only possible release.

But Canavan was still at least the shell of a human being, and he had been my friend. I could not take the law into my own hands.

With many misgivings I called the police and an ambulance.

What followed was more madness, plus an inquisitorial session of questions and demands which left me in a state of near nervous collapse.

A half dozen burly policemen spent the better part of an hour tramping through that wavering brindle grass without locating any trace of Canavan. They came out cursing, rubbing their eyes and shaking their heads. They were flushed, furious—and ill at ease. They announced that they had seen nothing and heard nothing except some sneaking dog which stayed always out of sight and growled at them at intervals.

When they mentioned the growling dog, I opened my mouth to speak, but thought better of it and said nothing. They were already regarding me with open suspicion, as if they believed my own mind might be breaking.

I repeated my story at least twenty times and still they were not satisfied. They ransacked the entire house. They inspected Canavan's files. They even removed some loose boards in one of the rooms and searched underneath.

At length they grudgingly concluded that Canavan had suffered total loss of memory after experiencing some kind of shock and that he had wandered off the premises in a state of amnesia shortly after I had encountered him in the yard. My own description of his appearance and actions they discounted as lurid exaggeration. After warning me that I would probably be questioned further and that my own premises might be inspected, they reluctantly permitted me to leave.

Their subsequent searches and investigations revealed nothing new and Canavan was put down as a missing person, probably afflicted with acute amnesia.

But I was not satisfied, and I could not rest.

Six months of patient, painstaking, tedious research in the files and stacks of the local university library finally yielded something which I do not offer as an explanation, nor even as a definite clue, but only as a fantastic near impossibility which I ask no one to believe.

One afternoon, after my extended research over a period of months had produced nothing of significance, the keeper of rare books at the university library triumphantly bore to my study niche a tiny crumbling pamphlet which had been printed in New Haven in 1695. It mentioned no author and carried the stark title, *Deathe of Goodie Larkins, Witche.*

Several years before, it revealed, an ancient crone, one Goodie Larkins, had been accused by neighbors of turning a missing child into a wild dog. The Salem madness was raging at the time, and Goodie Larkins had been summarily condemned to death. Instead of being burned, she had been driven into a marsh deep in the woods where seven savage dogs, starved for a fortnight, had been turned loose on her trail. Apparently her accusers felt that this was a touch of truly poetic justice.

As the ravening dogs closed in on her, she was heard by her retreating neighbors to utter a frightful curse:

"Let this lande I fall upon lye alle the way to Hell!" she had screamed. *"And they who tarry here be as these beastes that rende me dead!"*

A subsequent inspection of old maps and land deeds satisfied me that the marsh in which Goodie Larkins was torn to pieces by the dogs after uttering her awful curse originally occupied the same lot or square which now enclosed Canavan's hellish back yard!

I say no more. I returned only once to that devilish spot. It was a cold, desolate autumn day, and a keening wind rattled the brindle stalks in that unholy acre. I cannot say what urged me back; perhaps it was some lingering feeling of loyalty toward the Canavan I had known. Perhaps it was even some last shred of hope. But as soon as I entered the cleared area behind Canavan's boarded-up house, I knew I had made a mistake.

As I stared at the stiff waving grass, the bare trees, and the black ragged briar bushes, I felt as if I, in turn, were being watched. I felt as if something alien and wholly evil were observing me, and though I was terrified, I experienced a perverse, insane impulse to rush headlong into the whispering expanse. Again I imagined I saw that monstrous landscape subtly alter its dimensions and perspectives until I was staring toward a stretch of blowing brindle grass and rotted trees which ran for miles. Something urged me to enter, to lose myself in the lovely grass, to roll and grovel at its roots, to rip off the foolish encumbrances of cloth which covered me and run howling and ravenous, on and on, on and on. . . .

Instead, I turned and rushed away. I ran through the windy autumn streets like a madman. I lurched into my rooms and bolted the door.

I have never gone back since. And I never shall.

THE NIGHT TRAIN TO LOST VALLEY

▪ BY AUGUST DERLETH ▪

S omething about city lights in the dusk takes me back to
the old days when I was "on the road." A traveling
salesman for harnesses and leather goods—"drummers," we were
called then—certainly prosaic enough just past the turn of the
century. A curious thing, too, for lights were not too much a part
of that hill-country route in New Hampshire. Brighton to Hempfield to Dark Rock to Gale's Corners—and at last to Lost Valley,
on a little country train running out of Brighton on the spur to
Lost Valley and back, the train I had to take to make Lost Valley
and work back down to Brighton. And unique it was, surely, in
more ways than one—old-fashioned locomotive, coal car, and
seldom more than one coach with a baggage car.

I took the night train because there was no other. It went up
in the evening out of Brighton, and it came back next morning.
Strange, rugged country. Strange people, too—uncommonly
dark, and in many ways primitive—not backward, exactly, I
would never have called them that, but given to certain old ways
not frequently encountered even in the first decade of the century, when vestiges of the 1890s still lingered in widely scattered
areas of the country. But beautiful country, for all its strangeness:
that could not be gainsaid. Dark, brooding country, much
wooded, with startling vistas opening up before one's eyes on the

morning trip down out of Lost Valley.

I used to wonder why the spur had been run to Lost Valley, unless the town had given greater promise when the railroad was put through—a promise clearly never fulfilled, for it was small, its houses clustered close together, with many trees, even in its main street. The dusty roads, too, wound in and out among the trees. But, being in the heart of agricultural country, however sparsely settled, it supported a large harness shop, so that it was important to get into Lost Valley for the seasonal order.

The train used to wait on a siding in Brighton, steam up, ready to pull away. Sometimes, when people went down to Concord for an inauguration or for just a shopping trip, the single coach had to expand to two, and both were filled; but usually there were few people to make the trip all the way up to Lost Valley— about seventy miles or thereabouts, and quite often, considering the relatively few times I made the trip, I was the only passenger— sharing the train with the conductor, the brakeman, the engineer, and a fireman, with all of whom I grew quite friendly in the course of time, since the train's personnel did not change much in a decade.

The conductor, Jem Watkins, was an old fellow, lean and a little bent, with a sharp, wry humor which fitted in somehow with his small bright eyes and his thin goatee. I knew him better than the others, for often on the twenty-odd miles between Gale's Corners and Lost Valley, he came in and sat to talk. The brakeman did this too, on those occasions when I was the sole passenger. A tall, saturnine individual named Toby Colter, he never had much to say, but he could become enthusiastic about the weather, and he seemed to have an inexhaustible store of anecdotes concerning the weather in the vicinity of Lost Valley. Abner Pringle, the engineer, and Sib Whately, the fireman, I knew less well. I had a hailing knowledge of them, so to speak, and little more, but they were always friendly. They were all four hill-country men, all, in fact, from Lost Valley or its vicinity, and they were filled with the lore of that country.

Strange lore—strange with the strangeness of alliance to old things, to old customs long since forgotten. To what extent they were forgotten in Lost Valley I have since had more than one occasion to wonder, though there is not much doubt but that I would never have thought of any kinship at all between the town and the old customs if it had not been for my last trip to Lost Valley. It is always of that last trip and what happened that night that I come to think, finally, perplexed, unsure, and filled with a kind of amazed wonder still. Everything else—the trip up and back, the long talks with Jem Watkins and Toby Colter, the people of the town, the big orders placed in Lost Valley, even to a large extent the wild beauty of the scenery—ultimately falls into the general pattern of reminiscence, but not the last trip to Lost Valley.

Yet, vivid as it is, there is always an element of doubt. Did it, after all, really happen? Or was it a dream? For it had the quality of a dream, beyond question, and it had the hazy aftereffect of a dream. Things sometimes happen to a man which are so far out of the ordinary that he tends inevitably to discredit his senses. Conversely, dreams of such realism sometimes take place that a man deliberately seeks some supporting evidence to convince himself of their reality. Dream or reality, it does not matter. Something happened that night in Lost Valley, something of which the train and the men on it and I myself were an integral part, something which left in memory an abiding wonder and a chaotic confusion, and which might have had a meaning of which I have never cared—or dared—to think.

I knew it was to be my last trip, since I was going into office work; so that the event was in itself unusual. And then, too, the train—for once in the decade I had taken it— set out ahead of time. It was unprecedented, and if I had not been at the station in Brighton fully half an hour early, I would have missed the train and would have had to go to Lost Valley on the following day. I have often wondered whether what happened to me that night would have taken place the following night.

The early starting of the train was only the beginning of the curious events of that night. For one thing, when I waved at Abner Pringle, on my way past the locomotive to the single coach, I was startled to see an expression of almost ludicrous consternation upon his usually placid features, and he returned my wave with halfhearted reluctance. His reaction was so unexpected that before I had gone ten steps, I was convinced that I had imagined it. But I had not, for at sight of me, Jem Watkins likewise looked by turns unpleasantly surprised and dismayed.

"Mr. Wilson," he said in an uncertain voice.

"You don't look glad to see me, and that's a fact, Jem," I said.

"You're makin' the trip—tonight?"

I had climbed into the coach by this time, Jem Watkins after me, with his conductor's cap in one hand and the other scratching his head.

"I'm late this year, I know it," I said. "But I'm making the trip." I looked at him, and he at me; I could not get away from the conviction that I was the last person Jem Watkins expected or wanted to see. "But if you don't want to take me, Jem, why, say so."

Jem swallowed. The adam's apple of that scrawny neck moved up and down. "Couldn't you go up tomorrow?"

"Tonight," I said. "I'll tell you something. It's my last trip."

"Your last trip?" he echoed in a weak voice. "You mean—you're stayin' with us up there?"

"Well, no, not exactly. I've been transferred to the office. You'll have a new man hereafter, and I hope you'll treat him as nice as you always treated me."

Strangely, it seemed that the conductor was slightly mollified at the news that this was to be my last trip; I had thought, perhaps in some vanity, that he might regret it. Yet he was not wholly pleased, and perhaps nothing would have pleased him but that I descend and leave him and his train go along up to Lost Valley without me. Perhaps in other circumstances I might have done so, despite my feeling at a loss to account for my reception; but now, with promotion just ahead, I did not want to waste a minute in getting over with my last tasks as a salesman. So I settled myself, and tried to appear unconcerned about the curious way in which Jem Watkins stood there in the aisle of the coach, turning his hat in his hands, this way and that, and not knowing just what to say.

"The people up there are pretty busy this time of year," he said finally. "I don't know whether it wouldn't be best to send in by mail for your order from Mr. Darby."

"And miss saying goodbye to him?" I said. "Mr. Darby wouldn't like that."

Jem Watkins retreated, baffled, after a hurried look at his watch, and in a few moments the train pulled out of the station, just four minutes short of half an hour ahead of time. Since I was the only passenger, I knew Jem would be back; we had hardly gone two miles beyond Brighton, when he came walking into the car, and Toby Colter was with him, both of them looking uneasy and grim.

"We talked it over," said Jem slowly, while Toby nodded portentously, "and we kind of figured you might like to stay in Gale's Corners tonight and come in to Lost Valley in the morning."

I laughed at this; it seemed so ingenuous. "Come now, Jem, it's to Lost Valley I'm going, and no other place. Gale's Corners in the morning, remember? We've done it twice a year for ten years, and you've never thought of changing before."

"But this year you're late, Mr. Wilson," said Toby.

"That I am. And if I don't hurry now, I won't be back in Boston by the second. Let me see, it's April thirtieth today, and I've got to run into Gainesville before I head back to Boston. I can just make it."

"You won't see Mr. Darby tonight," said Jem.

"Why not?"

"Because he won't be there, that's why."

"Well, then I'll see him in the morning." But I thought with regret that I would not be sitting around that old-fashioned stove in the harness shop spending the evening in the kind of trivial talk which is the very stuff of life in country places.

Jem took my ticket and punched it, and Toby, after a baffled glance at me, left the car. Jem seemed resigned now. He sat looking out to the fleeting landscape; the last of the sun was drawing off the land, and out of the east, in the pockets among the hills, a blue and purple haze that was twilight was gathering. We were perhaps ten miles out of Brighton and already drawing near to Hempfield. And by that time I was filled with the strangeness of this ride—with everything about it, from the unexpected early start to the conductor's incredible attitude.

The country through which we were traveling was one of increasing wildness, and at this hour especially beautiful, for the last sunlight still tipped the hilltops, and the darkness of dusk welled up from the valleys, while the sky overhead was a soft blue of unparalleled clarity, against which the few small cirrus clouds were a startling white. It was that hour of the day during which the face of heaven and of earth changed with singular rapidity, so that in a few moments the clouds which had been white, were peach, and in a few more, crimson on the under side and old rose on top, and soon lavender, while the blue of the sky became dark overhead, and changed to aquamarine and amethyst above the lemon and turquoise of the afterglow. The train moved into the west, and I watched the ever-changing world outside the coach with a pleasure all the deeper and more appreciative for the knowledge that perhaps I would never again be viewing this particular scene.

The route to Lost Valley went steadily into hill country, and up to just beyond Gale's Corners by four miles or thereabouts, the railroad was an almost imperceptible up-grade; then, sixteen miles or so this side of Lost Valley, the down-grade began, though it was not the equivalent of the previous up-grade, so that clearly Lost Valley lay in a little pocket of the higher hills beyond Gale's Corners. We stopped briefly in Hempfield, apparently for the debouching of mail, and went on again without further interruption. I had made an effort to look out of the window to notice whether the station agent at Hempfield was at all surprised at the train's early arrival, but if he was, he did not show it. The conductor had leaned out of the window and passed the time of the evening with him, opining that it would be a clear night, and then again resumed his seat opposite me, from which he glanced at me with a kind of helpless dubiousness from time to time.

His unnatural uncommunicativeness troubled me eventually. "Jem," I said, "how has old Mrs. Perkins been? She was quite sick last time I was up."

"Oh, she's dead, Mr. Wilson," said Jem, nodding his head lugubriously. "Died in February."

"Too bad. And how's that crippled baby of Beales'?"

"Poorly, Mr. Wilson, poorly." He gave me a curious look just then, a very curious look, and for a moment I had the idea that he was about to say something; but evidently he thought better of it, for he did not speak, except to say, "Poorly," again.

"I'm sorry not to see Mr. Darby tonight," I went on. "I enjoy sitting around that stove with the old-timers who come in."

Jem said nothing.

"What would he be doing tonight?"

"Why, round about this time he finishes his winter work, as you'd ought to know, Mr. Wilson, and he's pretty busy tottin' up his books and gettin' things in order."

"That's so," I said, "but I've seen him at that earlier in April than this, and he never closed up shop for it then."

"Mr. Darby's gittin' old," said Jem, with unexpected vehemence.

Those were his last words until we were past Gale's Corners, and then he spoke only in answer to my perplexed comment that none of the station agents along the route had shown any surprise at the train's being almost three-quarters of an hour early, for it had accelerated its speed considerably since leaving Brighton.

"We're usually ahead of time this time of year," said Jem. And once more there was that curious, baffled glance—as if he thought I knew something I was not telling and wished that I would say it and clear the air.

Soon then we came into sight of Lost Valley—or what, in the gathering darkness, I knew to be Lost Valley: a cluster of lights, not many, for there were not more than thirty buildings in the hamlet, and it existed not so much because of the people who lived within its limits as it did because of those people back in the hills who did their trading there. Then we drew up at the station, and there was old Henry Pursley bent over the telegraph key with the yellow light of his lamp-lit room streaming out to the station platform: a cozy scene and one of pleasant warmth.

But I had no sooner stepped down from the train into the light than he looked up and saw me; and instead of the customary greeting I expected, his jaw dropped, and he sat staring at me, and then, accusingly, it seemed, at Jem. Only then did he greet me, soberly, and, coming out, spoke in a low voice to Jem, which sounded as if he were berating Jem for forgetting something. I went up along the street away from the station and seeing that Darby's Harness Shop was indeed dark, I crossed over to the one two-story house in town, that of the widowed Mrs. Emerson and her daughter, Angeline, where I was accustomed to staying. And there, too, I was greeted with the same consternation and surprise, and for a moment it seemed that for once the door of the house would be closed against me, but then Angeline, a tall dark girl with black eyes and a flamelike mark under one ear, opened the door and invited me in.

"You're late this spring, Mr. Wilson," she said.

I admitted it. "But it's my last trip," I explained, and told them why.

Mrs. Emerson looked at me shrewdly, "You've not eaten, Mr. Wilson. You look dissatisfied."

I felt dissatisfied and would have gone on to tell them why, if it were not that I felt they, too, would say nothing to me, for, after all, I was an outsider, and in all small towns, even in less secluded places, a man from "outside" does not gain the confidence of villagers for years, sometimes as many as twenty or more. I admitted that I had not eaten.

"Then you'll have to eat, Mr. Wilson."

"I wouldn't think of troubling you, thank you, Mrs. Emerson."

Mrs. Emerson, however, would hear of nothing but that Angeline must at once prepare food, and she herself brought me a bitter-tasting tea which, she said, she had brewed of bergamotte and mint; and it did have a minty aroma, though it tasted more bitter than minty, and I took the opportunity, when the women were both out of the sitting room for a moment, of pouring the brew into a pot containing a large fern, prayerfully hoping that no harm would come to the fern. I had drunk enough, in any case, to leave an unpleasant taste in my mouth, about which I complained to Mrs. Emerson as soon as she appeared, whereupon she immediately produced a piece of old-fashioned sweet chocolate.

"I thought might be you wouldn't care for it too much, but it's good for you just the same. But this'll take the taste of it away."

So it did. And the meal itself, which was a good and ample

one, did more—it made me realize that, what with all this rushing about of the day in Brighton and on the way there, I was tired. The hour was nine o'clock, and, while it was by no means late, it was to bed I wanted to go. Thereupon, with all the customary show of hospitality I had come to expect of my hostesses in the years past, I was shown to my room.

Once abed, I fell asleep with unusual alacrity.

From that point on, I cannot be sure that what happened was reality. It may have been dream. But there were subsequently certain disquieting factors, which, pieced together, pointed to conclusions wholly outside my small world—though I had never before realized how small the world was. What happened may have been a powerful, transcendent dream. It may not.

It began with my waking. I woke suddenly with a headache and the taste of Mrs. Emerson's bitter tea strong and hot in my mouth. Intending to go for water, I got up, put on my trousers, shoes, and shirt, and went downstairs, feeling my way in the dark. Before I reached the bottom of the stairs, I was aware of a commotion outside the house, and, pausing to look out, I saw an extraordinary movement of people in the direction of the railroad station, and then, peering up the street, I saw that the train—the night train to Lost Valley on which I had come—was standing, steam up, at the station. But, most strange of all, the people I saw were clad in conical hats and black cloaks; some of them carried torches, and some did not.

I turned and struck a match, and by its light I saw that a trunk under the stair had been thrown open, clothing taken out, and everything left as it was, as if someone had been in great haste to get away. Among the pieces there was a black cloak and a conical hat, which I divined to be the property of the late Mr. Emerson. I stood for a moment looking down at them; then the match went out.

What was it out there in the streets? Where were all these people going? Men, women, and children—it seemed as if the entire population of Lost Valley was deserting the town.

I reached down in the dark and touched the black cloak. I lifted it and set it on my shoulders, drawing it tight around my neck; it swathed me from neck to toe. I took up the conical hat and put it on and saw that it provided a kind of masking fold for the face as well.

Then, acting on an extraordinary impulse, I opened the door and went out to join the thronging people.

All were going to the train, and all were boarding the train. But the train was headed away from the only direction it could take out of Lost Valley, and it stood not quite at the station, but a little beyond it, and beyond the turntable where it customarily turned around to make the morning trip down to Brighton. The coach was not lit, but the light from the firebox and the glare of a half dozen torches held by men mounted on the locomotive made a weird illumination in a night dark save for the locomotive's headlight pointed to the woods ahead. And, looking in that direction, I was startled to see what must have been newly laid, but not new tracks, leading away into the dark hills beyond Lost Valley.

So much I saw before mounting into the unlit coach, which was crowded with silent people. Then nothing more. No light flared in the crowded coach. No one spoke. The silence was unbelievable, no human voice was heard save once the cry of a baby I could not see. Nor was the coach alone filled; so was the baggage car, and so, too, was the coal car. People clung to the train, from the locomotive to the rear platform —a great, silent throng, the entire population of Lost Valley, bent on a mission in the dead of night, for the hour surely approached midnight judging by the stars overhead, and the position of the gibbous moon which hung yellow low in the eastern sky. There was an extraordinary feeling of excitement, of tension, and of wonder in the coach, and I too began to feel it in the increased beating of my pulse, and in a kind of apprehensive exhilaration caught from my hooded and cloaked companions.

Without bell or whistle-sound, the train set out, drawing away from the deserted village into the dark hills. I tried to estimate how far we went—I thought not farther than seven miles. But we passed under arched trees of great age, through glens and narrow valleys, past murmurous brooks, past mourning whippoorwills and owls, into a veritable kingdom of night, before the train slowed to a stop, and at once everyone aboard began to get out, still wordless and tense. But this time the torchbearers took the lead, and certain others pushed up to be right behind them, while others waited patiently to fall into line, and I myself, fearful least some regular order be imposed upon the throng, waited until last, and then fell into step beside another hooded man, who, I felt sure, could be none other than Abner Pringle, for only he had such girth and height.

They did not go far, but, coming suddenly to an open space, the torchbearers alone went forward and ranged themselves below a stange stone image—or was it an image? The light flickered so and danced upon the stone there in the wood, I could not be sure; yet it seemed to be an image, and presently all were prostrate on the ground before the stone, and there remained, myself among them, until those who had walked directly behind the torchbearers rose and began a slow, rhythmic dancing, while another of them walked directly to the foot of the stone and began to chant in a voice I felt sure was Mr. Darby's. Latin, by the sound of it—but not pure Latin, for mixed with it was a gibberish I could not understand. Nor could I hear enough of the Latin to know what it was that was being said. A calling upon God, certainly. But what God? No Christian God in this place, for no Christian hand had touched the curious stone and the altarlike approach to it. If indeed it were an altar. Some hand had cut away the trees there, and someone had kept the grass down in that place. And there was something about the "fruits of the earth" and something more about "Ahriman" and something about the "Gift" (or "gifts") to come.

Then suddenly, a blue flame shone before the stone, and at sight of it the prostrate ones rose to their feet and began a wild dance to music coming from somewhere—a piping of fluted notes, which burst forth into the dark night like the startled voices of the forest's habitants themselves— music which grew wilder and wilder, as the dancers did, also—and I, too, for I was seized by a compulsion I could not struggle against, and I danced among them, sometimes alone, sometimes with someone— once, I am sure, with Angeline, in a wild, sensuous rout. The music mounted to a powerful crescendo, and on every side people screamed and chanted strange unintelligible words, and the dancing became more and more abandoned, until, as abruptly as it had begun, the music stopped.

At this instant, the celebrant before the stone stepped forward, bent and took up something there, tore away its covering, raised it high, whirling it thrice around his head, and dashed it to the stone, where its cry was stilled. What was it? What manner of creature had been sacrificed there? It seemed unfurred, unfeathered, too. White and unclothed. *A baby?*

A great sigh rose up. Then silence. The blue flame at the stone flickered, turned to green, to red, and began to subside.

The torchbearers started to file away from the stone, and the hooded celebrants waited to fall in line after them, though the master of the ceremony had been joined by two others, and all three were now bent about the base of the stone, while the others made their silent way back to the waiting train.

There we waited, again in unbroken silence, until all were once more on board, clinging to all sides of the train, filling every space. Then the train started up again, backing down to Lost Valley from which it had come away an hour or more before. How long I could not say. Time seemed to have no meaning in this eldritch night, but the moon was far higher than it had been. Two hours perhaps. Though it seemed incredible that we had been away so long.

I had wisely taken my place near to the door of the coach, so that I could make my escape quickly, get back to the house, remove my cloak and hood, and be in my room before Mrs. Emerson and Angeline returned. So I slipped away from the train and lost myself in the shadows. When the door opened and closed for the two women, I was once again in bed.

But had I ever left that bed?

I woke up tired, true. But I woke up to Lost Valley as I had always known it. When had my dream begun?

At the breakfast table, Mrs. Emerson asked whether the tea had agreed with me.

I told her it had not.

"Nor with me, either. It gave me a headache," she said. "And such a taste!"

"Well, nobody caught *me* drinking it," said Angeline.

I went over to the harness shop, and there was August Darby, just as hale and hearty as ever, just as friendly. A jovial fellow, fat-cheeked, Teutonic in his looks, with a full moustache and merry eyes.

"Heard you were in town last night. Man, why didn't you come to the house? I was there. Worked on my books till one o'clock," he said. His smile was fresh, guileless, innocent. "But today—I'm tired. I'm getting old."

He had a large order for me, and he made it larger before I left, after he found out he might not see me again.

I made a point of walking in the vicinity of the railroad station.

There were no tracks leading to the woods beyond the town. Nothing. There was no sign that any tracks had ever been there. The train was turned and waiting, and, seeing me go by, Jem Watkins called out, "Hey there, Mr. Wilson—you nearly ready?"

"Just about," I said.

I turned and went back into the village and stopped at Beales' house. I knocked on the door and Mrs. Beale came to answer, with her husband standing not far behind. Strange! He looked as if he had been crying. Red-eyed, bitter-mouthed. He stood a moment, and then was gone, backing away somewhere out of my sight.

"Hello, Mrs. Beale. How's the baby?"

She looked at me with a most extraordinary expression in her eyes. She glanced down, and I did, too. She was carrying folded baby clothes.

"Not well," she said. "Not well at all, Mr. Wilson. I'm afraid it won't be long."

"May I see her?"

She looked at me for a long moment. "I'm afraid not, Mr. Wilson. She's sleeping. It's been a hard time getting her to sleep."

"I'm sorry," I said.

I bade her goodbye and stepped away. But not before I had seen what she had been about when I knocked. Folding and wrapping baby clothes, a lot of them, and putting them away—not in a bureau—but in a trunk there in the front room.

I went over to the station and got into the train. From the window I took a last look at Lost Valley. When you come into a town as most drummers do, you take the town for granted, and sometimes you never notice things which other travelers might see at once. Like, for instance, churches. In ten years' time I had never noticed it—but now I did. There was no church of any kind in Lost Valley.

Anyone would say that is a small point—and it is. How many small points does it take to make a big one, I wonder? I ask myself how long it would take to lay seven miles of track, and I know it couldn't be done in a night. No, not in two nights. But then, it needn't be done in that time, not at all. Track could have been laid there for years, and all that needed to be done was perhaps a quarter of a mile from the station to just past the woods' edge out of sight. And afterwards, it could be taken up again, as easily, and stored away once more.

And in backward places like Lost Valley—little towns no one ever sees except such casual travelers like myself, and then but briefly, overnight—there are all kinds of primitive survivals, I understand. Perhaps even witchcraft or more ancient lore which has to do with human sacrifice to some dark alien god to propitiate him and thus assure the earth's fertility. Nobody knows what happens in such places. But most of them, unlike Lost Valley, have at least one church.

I remembered afterward that April thirtieth was Walpurgis Eve. And everyone along the Brighton–Lost Valley line seemed to understand that on that day the train set out earlier than its scheduled time. Could they know why? Not likely. For that matter, did I? I could not say with any sureness that I did.

Where does a dream begin? Where does it end? For that matter, what about reality? That too begins and ends. Plainly, on the way back, Jem Watkins and Toby Colter, for all their chattering talk, were tired. I could not imagine Jem's goatlike capering by torchlight. Nor Toby's clumsiness either. And Mr. Darby! Who else had a voice like him? None that I knew—but then, I did not know everyone in Lost Valley. Darby and Mrs. Emerson tired, too. But he had been up late working on his accounts, and she had spent a sleepless night because of bitter tea. Or had they?

Whose dream had I been in? Mine—or theirs?

Perhaps I would never have doubted that it was a dream had it not been for that visit I paid to the Beales. Even the sight of the baby clothes being folded and put away, set against that vivid memory of what had been flung in sacrifice against that silent stone thing in the woods, would not alone have given me the doubt I had. But on the way down, while Jem obligingly, as always, held the train at the stations, on the spur to Brighton, while I got out and got my orders from the local harness shops, I thought about it, and at last, getting back on the train at Hempfield for the final job to Brighton, I spoke about Beales' baby.

"I meant to call and see Beales' baby," I began.

Jem cut me off, loquaciously. "Good thing you didn't, Mr. Wilson. That poor little thing died in the night. You'd like to've upset them."

But at Beales' it had been sleeping less than two hours ago. Here in the sunny coach the baby in Jem's words was dead in the night. Was this, after all, the same dark train which played its part in some ancient woodland rite? A country train—worn locomotive, coal-car, baggage car, and creaking coach, making its run once daily up to Lost Valley, and once daily back. And in the night did it always rest quietly at the station at Lost Valley? Or did it, once a year, on Walpurgis Eve, make a secret sally into darkness?

I bade the train goodbye at Brighton. I said goodbye to Jem and Toby, Abner and Sib, who shook my hand as if I had been a lifelong friend. But somehow, I was never quite fully able to say goodbye to Lost Valley. It stayed just out of sight on the perimeter of consciousness, ready to reappear in the mind's eye at a moment's urging, at any casual thing that stirred memory. Like a country train on a little spur. Or masquerades and hooded things. Or city lights in the dusk.

I heard about Lost Valley indirectly once after that.

It was at a Cambridge party—one of those gatherings which include a wide variety of people. I was passing a little group on my way to the punchbowl, when I heard Lost Valley mentioned. I turned. I recognized the speaker: Jeffrey Kinnan, a brilliant young Harvard man, a sociologist, and I listened.

"Genetically, Lost Valley is most interesting. Apparently

there has been inbreeding there for generations. We should soon find an increasing number of degenerates in that vicinity. In genetics. . . ."

I walked away. Genetics indeed! Something that was old before Mendel was a mote in the cosmos. I could have spoken, too, but how could I be sure? Was it a dream or not? Certainly, wrapped up in his genetics, Kinnan would have called it a nightmare.

A MESSAGE FROM CHARITY

▪ BY WILLIAM M. LEE ▪

That summer of the year 1700 was the hottest in the memory of the very oldest inhabitants. Because the year ushered in a new century, some held that the events were related and that for a whole hundred years Bay Colony would be as torrid and steamy as the Indies themselves.

There was a good deal of illness in Annes Towne, and a score had died before the weather broke at last in late September. For the great part they were oldsters who succumbed, but some of the young were sick too, and Charity Payne as sick as any.

Charity had turned eleven in the spring and had still the figure and many of the ways of thinking of a child, but she was tall and strong and tanned by the New England sun, for she spent many hours helping her father in the fields and trying to keep some sort of order in the dooryard and garden.

During the weeks when she lay bedridden and, for a time, burning up with the fever, Thomas Carter and his good wife, Beulah, came as neighbors should to lend a hand, for Charity's mother had died abirthing and Obie Payne could not cope all alone.

Charity lay on a pallet covered by a straw-filled mattress which her father, frantic to be doing something for her and finding little enough to do beyond the saying of short fervent prayers, refilled with fresh straw as often as Beulah would allow. A few miles down Harmon Brook was a famous beaver pond where in winter the Annes Towne people cut ice to be stored under layers of bark and chips. It had been used heavily early in the summer, and there was not very much ice left, but those families with sickness in the home might draw upon it for the patient's comfort. So Charity had bits of ice folded into a woolen cloth to lay on her forehead when the fever was bad.

William Trowbridge, who had apprenticed in medicine down in Philadelphia, attended the girl, and pronounced her illness a sort of summer cholera which was claiming victims all up and down the brook. Trowbridge was only moderately esteemed in Annes Towne, being better, it was said, at delivering lambs and foals than at treating human maladies. He was a gruff and notional man, and he was prone to state his views on a subject and then walk away instead of waiting to argue and perhaps be refuted. Not easy to get along with.

For Charity he prescribed a diet of beef tea with barley and another tea, very unpleasant to the taste, made from pounded willow bark. What was more, all her drinking water was to be boiled. Since there was no other advice to be had, they followed it and in due course Charity got well.

She ran a great fever for five days, and it was midway in this period when the strange dreams began. Not dreams really, for she was awake though often out of her senses, knowing her father now and then, other times seeing him as a gaunt and frightening stranger. When she was better, still weak but wholly rational, she tried to tell her visitors about these dreams.

"Some person was talking and talking," she recalled. "A man or perchance a lad. 'Twas strange talk indeed, a porridge of the King's English and other words of no sense at all. And with the talk I did see some fearful sights."

"La, now, don't even think of it," said Dame Beulah.

"But I would fen both think and talk of it, for I am no longer afeared. Such things I saw in bits and flashes, as 'twere seen by a strike of lightning."

"Talk and ye be so minded, then. There's naught impious in y'r conceits. Tell me again about the carriages which traveled along with nary horse."

Annes Towne survived the Revolution and the War of 1812, and for a time seemed likely to become a larger, if not an important community. But when its farms became less productive and the last virgin timber disappeared from the area, Annes Towne began to disappear too, dwindling from twoscore of homes to a handful, then to none; and the last foundation had crumbled to rubble and been scattered a hundred years before it could have been nominated an historic site.

In time dirt tracks became stone roads, which gave way to black meanderings of macadam, and these in their turn were displaced by never-ending bands of concrete. The crossroads site of Annes Towne was cleared of brambles, sumac, and red cedar, and overnight it was a shopping center. Now, for mile on spreading mile the New England hills were dotted with ranch houses, saltboxes, and split-level colonial homes.

During four decades Harmon Brook had been fouled and poisoned by a textile bleach and dye works. Rising labor costs had at last driven the small company to extinction. With that event and increasingly rigorous legislation, the stream had come back to the extent that it could now be bordered by some of these prosperous homes and by the golf course of the Anniston Country Club.

With aquatic plants and bullfrogs and a few fish inhabiting its waters, it was not obvious to implicate the Harmon for the small outbreak of typhoid which occurred in the hot dry summer of 1965. No one was dependent on it for drinking water. To the discomfort of a local milk distributor, who was entirely blameless, indictment of the stream was delayed and obscured by the fact that the organisms involved were not a typical strain of *Salmonella typhosa*. Indeed they ultimately found a place in the American Type Culture Collection, under a new number.

Young Peter Wood, whose home was one of those pleasantly situated along the stream, was the most seriously ill of all the cases, partly because he was the first, mostly because his symptoms went unremarked for a time. Peter was sixteen and not highly communicative to either parents or friends. The Wood Seniors both taught, at Harvard and Wellesley, respectively. They were intelligent and well-intentioned parents, but sometimes a little offhand, and like many of their friends, they raised their son to be a miniature adult in as many ways as possible. His sports, tennis and golf, were adult sports. His reading tastes were catholic, ranging from Camus to Al Capp to science fiction. He had been carefully held back in his progress through the lower grades so that he would not enter college more than a year or so ahead of his age. He had an adequate number of friends and sufficient areas of congeniality with them. He had gotten a driver's license shortly after his sixteenth birthday and drove seriously and well enough to be allowed nearly unrestricted use of the second car.

So Peter Wood was not the sort of boy to complain to his family about headache, mild nausea, and other symptoms. Instead, after they had persisted for forty-eight hours, he telephoned for an appointment on his own initiative and visited the family doctor. Suddenly, in the waiting room, he became much worse, and was given a cot in an examining room until Dr. Maxwell was free to drive him home. The doctor did not seriously suspect typhoid, though it was among several possibilities which he counted as less likely.

Peter's temperature rose from 104° to over 105° that night. No nurse was to be had until morning, and his parents alternated in attendance in his bedroom. There was no cause for alarm, since the patient was full of wide-spectrum antibiotic. But he slept only fitfully with intervals of waking delirium. He slapped at the sheet, tossed around on the bed, and muttered or spoke now and then. Some of the talk was understandable.

"There's a forest," he said

"What?" asked his father.

"There's a forest the other side of the stream."

"Oh."

"Can you see it?"

"No, I'm sitting inside here with you. Take it easy, son."

"Some deer are coming down to drink, along the edge of Weller's pasture."

"Is that so?"

"Last year a mountain lion killed two of them, right where they drank. Is it raining?"

"No, it isn't. It would be fine if we could have some."

"It's raining. I can hear it on the roof." A pause. "It drips down the chimney."

Peter turned his head to look at his father, momentarily clear-eyed.

"How long since there's been a forest across the stream?"

Dr. Wood reflected on the usual difficulty of answering explicit questions and on his own ignorance of history.

"A long time. I expect this valley has been farmland since colonial days."

"Funny," Peter said. "I shut my eyes and I can see a forest. Really big trees. On our side of the stream there's a kind of a garden and an apple tree and a path goes down to the water."

"It sounds pleasant."

"Yeah."

"Why don't you try going to sleep?"

"Okay."

The antibiotic accomplished much less than it should have done in Peter's case, and he stayed very sick for several days. Even after diagnosis, there appeared no good reason to move him from home. A trained nurse was on duty after that first night, and tranquilizers and sedatives reduced her job to no more than keeping a watch. There were only a few sleepy communications from her young patient. It was on the fourth night, the last one when he had any significant fever, that he asked.

"Were you ever a girl?"

"Well, thanks a lot. I'm not as old as all that."

"I mean, were you ever inside a girl?"

"I think you'd better go back to sleep, young man."

He uttered no oddities thereafter, at least when there was anyone within hearing. During the days of his recovery and convalescence, abed and later stretched out on a chaise lounge on the terrace looking down toward Harmon Brook, he took to whispering. He moved his lips hardly at all, but vocalized each word, or if he fell short of this, at least put each thought into carefully chosen words and sentences.

The idea that he might be in mental communication with another person was not, to him, very startling. Steeped in the lore of science fiction whose heroes were, as like as not, adepts at telepathy, the event seemed almost as an expected outcome of his wishes. Many nights he had lain awake sending out (he hoped) a mental probe, trying and trying to find the trick, for surely there must be one, of making a contact.

Now that such a contact was established, he sought, just as vainly, for some means to prove it. How do you know you're not dreaming, he asked himself. How do you know you're not still delirious?

The difficulty was that his communication with Charity Payne could be by mental route only. Had there been any possibility for Peter to reach the girl by mail, by telephone, by travel and a personal visit, their rapport on a mental level might have been confirmed, and their messages cross-checked.

During their respective periods of illness, Peter and Charity achieved a communion of a sort which consisted at first of brief glimpses, each of the other's environment. They were not—then—seeing through one another's eyes, so much as tapping one another's visual recollections. While Peter stared at a smoothly plastered ceiling, Charity looked at rough-hewn beams. He, when his aching head permitted, could turn on one side and watch a television program. She, by the same movement, could see a small smoky fire in the monstrous stone fireplace, where water was heated and her beef and barley broth kept steaming.

Instead of these current images, current for each of them in their different times, they saw stored-up pictures, not perfect, for neither of them was remembering perfectly; rather like pictures viewed through a badly ground lens, with only the objects of principal interest in clear detail.

Charity saw her fearful sights with no basis for comprehension—a section of dual highway animated by hurtling cars and trucks and not a person, recognizable as a person, in sight; a tennis court, and what on earth could it be; a jet plane crossing the sky; a vast and many-storied building which glinted with glass and the silvery tracings of untarnished steel.

At the start she was terrified nearly out of her wits. It's all very well to dream, and a nightmare is only a bad dream after you waken, but a nightmare is assembled from familiar props. You could reasonably be chased by a dragon (like the one in the picture that St. George had to fight) or be lost in a cave (like the one on Parish Hill, only bigger and darker). To dream of things which have no meaning at all is worse.

She was spared prolongation of her terror by Peter's comprehension of their situation and his intuitive realization of what the experience, assuming a two-way channel, might be doing to her. The vignettes of her life which he was seeing were in no way disturbing. Everything he saw through her mind was within his framework of reference. Horses and cattle, fields and forest, rutted lanes and narrow wooden bridges were things he knew, even if he did not live among them. He recognized Harmon Brook because, directly below their home, there was an immense granite boulder parting the flow, shaped like a great bearlike animal with its head down, drinking. It was strange that the stream, in all those years, had neither silted up nor eroded away to hide or change the seaming of the rock, but so it was. He saw it through Charity's eyes and knew the place in spite of the forest on the far hill.

When he first saw this partly familiar, partly strange scene, he heard from somewhere within his mind the frightened cry of a little girl. His thinking at that time was fever-distorted and incoherent. It was two days later after a period of several hours of normal temperature when he conceived the idea—with sudden virtual certainty—these pastoral scenes he had been dreaming were truly something seen with other eyes. There were subtle perceptual differences between those pictures and his own seeing.

To his mother, writing at a table near the windows, he said, "I think I'm feeling better. How about a glass of orange juice?"

She considered. "The doctor should be here in an hour or so. In the meantime you can make do with a little more ice water. I'll get it. Drink it slowly, remember."

Two hundred and sixty-five years away, Charity Payne thought suddenly, "How about a glass of orange juice?" She had been drowsing, but her eyes popped wide open. "Mercy," she said aloud. Dame Beulah bent over the pallet.

"What is it, child?"

"How about a glass of orange juice?" Charity repeated.

"La, 'tis gibberish." A cool hand was laid on her forehead. "Would ye like a bit of ice to bite on?"

Orange juice, whatever that might be, was forgotten.

Over the next several days Peter Wood tried time and again to address the stranger directly, and repeatedly failed. Some of what he said to others reached her in fragments and further confused her state of mind. What she had to say, on the other hand, was coming through to him with increasing frequency. Often it was only a word or a phrase with a quaint twist like an historical novel, and he would lie puzzling over it, trying to place the person on the other end of their erratic line of communication. His recognition of Bear Rock, which he had seen once again through her eyes, was disturbing. His science-fiction conditioning led him naturally to speculate about the parallel worlds concept, but that seemed not to fit the facts as he saw them.

Peter reached the stage of convalescence when he could spend all day on the terrace and look down, when he wished, at the actual rock. There for the hundredth time he formed the syllables. "Hello, who are you?" and for the first time received a response. It was a silence, but a silence reverberating with shock, totally different in quality from the blankness which had met him before.

"My name is Peter Wood."

There was a long pause before the answer came, softly and timidly.

"My name is Charity Payne. Where are you? What is happening to me?"

The following days of enforced physical idleness were filled with exploration and discovery. Peter found out almost at once that, while they were probably no more than a few feet apart in their respective worlds, a gulf of more than a quarter of a thousand years stretched between them. Such a contact through time was a greater departure from known physical laws, certainly, than the mere fact of telepathic communication. Peter reveled in his growing ability.

In another way the situation was heartbreaking. No matter how well they came to know one another, he realized, they could never meet, and after no more than a few hours of acquaintance he found that he was regarding this naive child of another time with esteem and a sort of affection.

They arrived shortly at a set of rules which seemed to govern and limit their communications. Each came to be able to hear the other speak, whether aloud or subvocally. Each learned to perceive through the other's senses, up to a point. Visual perception became better and better, especially for direct seeing, while, as they grew more skillful, the remembered scene became less clear. Tastes and odors could be transmitted, if not accurately, at least with the expected response. Tactile sensations could not be perceived in the slightest degree.

There was little that Peter Wood could learn from Charity. He came to recognize her immediate associates and liked them, particularly her gaunt, weather-beaten father. He formed a picture of Puritanism which, as an ethic, he had to respect, while the supporting dogma evoked nothing but impatience. At first he exposed her to the somewhat scholarly agnosticism which prevailed in his own home, but soon found that it distressed her deeply and he left off. There was so much he could report from the vantage of 1965, so many things he would show her which did not conflict with her tenets and faith.

He discovered that Charity's ability to read was remarkable, though what she had read was naturally limited—the Bible from cover to cover, *Pilgrim's Progress*, several essays, and two of Shakespeare's plays. Encouraged by a schoolmaster who must have been an able and dedicated man, she had read and reread everything permitted to her. Her quite respectable vocabulary was gleaned from these sources and may have equaled Peter's own in size. In addition she possessed an uncanny word sense which helped her greatly in understanding Peter's jargon.

She learned the taste of bananas and frankfurters, chocolate ice cream and Coke, and displayed such an addiction to these delicacies that Peter rapidly put on some of the pounds he had lost. One day she asked him what he looked like.

"Well, I told you I am sixteen, and I'm sort of thin."

"Does thee possess a mirror?" she asked.

"Yes, of course."

At her urging and with some embarrassment he went and stood before a mirrored door in his mother's bedroom.

"Marry," she said after a dubious pause, "I doubt not thee is comely. But folk have changed."

"Now let me look at you," he demanded.

"Nay, we have no mirror."

"Then go and look in the brook. There's a quiet spot below the rock where the water is dark."

He was delighted with her appearance, having remembered Hogarth's unkind representations of a not much later period and being prepared for disappointment. She was in fact very much prettier by Peter's standards than by those of her own time, which favored plumpness and smaller mouths. He told her she was a beauty, and her tentative fondness for him turned instantly to adulation.

Previously Peter had had fleeting glimpses of her slim, smoothly muscled body, as she had bathed or dressed. Now, having seen each other face to face, they were overcome by embarrassment and both of them, when not fully clothed, stared resolutely into the corners of the room.

For a time Charity believed that Peter was a dreadful liar. The sight and sound of planes in the sky were not enough to convince her of the fact of flying, so he persuaded his father to take him along on a business flight to Washington. After she had recovered from the marvels of airplane travel, he took her on a walking tour of the Capitol. Now she would believe anything, even that the American Revolution had been a success. They joined his father for lunch at an elegant French restaurant and she experienced, vicariously, the pleasures of half of a half bottle of white wine and a chocolate eclair. Charity was by way of getting spoiled.

Fully recovered and with school only a week away, Peter decided to brush up his tennis. When reading or doing nothing in particular, he was always dimly aware of Charity and her immediate surroundings, and by sharpening his attention he could bring her clearly to the forefront of his mind. Tennis displaced her completely and for an hour or two each day he was unaware of her doings.

Had he been a few years older and a little more knowledgeable and realistic about the world, he might have guessed the peril into which he was leading her. Fictional villainy abounded, of course, and many items in the news didn't bear thinking about, but by his own firsthand experience, people were well intentioned and kindly, and for the most part they reacted to events with reasonable intelligence. It was what he expected instinctively.

A first hint of possible consequences reached him as he walked home from one of his tennis sessions.

"Ursula Miller said an ill thing to me today."

"Oh?" His answer was abstracted since, in all truth, he was beginning to run out of interest in the village gossip which was all the news she had to offer.

"Yesterday she said it was an untruth about the thirteen states. Today she avowed that I was devil-ridden. And Ursula has been my best friend."

"I warned you that people wouldn't believe you and you might get yourself laughed at," he said. Then suddenly he caught up in his thinking, "Good Lord—Salem."

"Please, Peter, thee must stop taking thy Maker's name."

"I'll try to remember. Listen, Charity, how many people have you been talking to about our—about what's been happening?"

"As I have said. At first to Father and Aunt Beulah. They did believe I was still addled from the fever."

"And to Ursula."

"Aye, but she vowed to keep it secret."

"Do you believe she will, now that she's started name-calling?"

A lengthy pause.

"I fear she may have told the lad who keeps her company."

"I should have warned you. Damn it, I should have laid it on the line."

"Peter!"

"Sorry. Charity, not another word to anybody. Tell Ursula you've been fooling—telling stories to amuse her."

"'Twould not be right."

"So what. Charity, don't be scared, but listen. People might get to thinking you're a witch."

"Oh, they couldn't."

"Why not?"

"Because I am not one. Witches are—oh, no, Peter."

He could sense her growing alarm.

"Go tell Ursula it was a pack of lies. Do it now."

"I must milk the cow."

"Do it now."

"Nay, the cow must be milked."

"Then milk her faster than she's ever been milked before."

On the Sabbath, three little boys threw stones at Charity as she and her father left the church. Obadiah Payne caught one of them and caned him, and then would have had to fight the lad's father save that the pastor intervened.

It was on the Wednesday that calamity befell. Two tight-lipped men approached Obadiah in the fields.

"Squire wants to see thy daughter Charity."

"Squire?"

"Aye. Squire Hacker. He would talk with her at once."

"Squire can talk to me if so be he would have her reprimanded. What has she been up to?"

"Witchcraft, that's what," said the second man, sounding as if he were savoring the dread news. "Croft's old ewe delivered a monstrous lamb. Pointy pinched-up face and an extra eye." He crossed himself.

"Great God!"

"'Twill do ye no good to blaspheme, Obadiah. She's to come with us now."

"I'll not have it. Charity's no witch, as ye well know, and I'll not have her converse with Squire. Ye mind the Squire's lecherous ways."

"That's not here nor there. Witchcraft is afoot again and all are saying 'tis your Charity at bottom of it."

"She shall not go."

First one, then the other displayed the stout truncheons they had held concealed behind their backs.

"'Twas of our own goodwill we told thee first. Come now and intrust thy daughter to go with us featly. Else take a clout on the head and sleep tonight in the gaol house."

They left Obie Payne gripping a broken wrist and staring in numbed bewilderment from his door stoop, and escorted Charity, not touching her, walking at a cautious distance to either side, to Squire Hacker's big house on the hill. In the village proper, little groups of people watched from doorways and, though some had always been her good friends, none had the courage now to speak a word of comfort.

Peter went with her each reluctant step of the way, counting himself responsible for her plight and helpless to do the least thing about it. He sat alone in the living room of his home, eyes closed to sharpen his reading of her surroundings. She offered no response to his whispered reassurances and perhaps did not hear them.

At the door her guards halted and stood aside, leaving her face-to-face with the grim-visaged squire. He moved backward step by step, and she followed him, as if hypnotized, into the shadowed room.

The squire lowered himself into a high-backed chair. "Look at me."

Unwillingly she raised her head and stared into his face.

Squire Hacker was a man of medium height, very broad in the shoulder, and heavily muscled. His face was disfigured by deep pock marks and the scar of a knife cut across the jaw, souvenirs of his earlier years in the Carib Islands. From the Islands he had also brought some wealth which he had since increased manyfold by the buying of land, share cropping, and money lending.

"Charity Payne," he said sternly, "take off thy frock."

"No. No, please."

"I command it. Take off thy garments, for I must search thee for witch marks."

He leaned forward, seized her arm, and pulled her to him. "If thee would avoid public trial and condemnation, thee will do as I say." His hands began to explore her body.

Even by the standards of the time, Charity regularly spent extraordinary hours at hard physical labor and she possessed a strength which would have done credit to many young men.

Squire Hacker should have been more cautious.

"Nay," she shouted and drawing back her arm, hit him in the nose with all the force she could muster. He released her with a roar of rage, then, while he was mopping away blood and tears with the sleeve of his ruffled shirt and shouting imprecations, she turned and shot out the door. The guards, converging, nearly grabbed her as she passed but, once away, they stood no chance of catching her and for a wonder none of the villagers took up the chase.

She was well on the way home and covering the empty road at a fast trot before Peter was able to gain her attention.

"Charity," he said, "Charity, you mustn't go home. If that s.o.b. of a squire had any influence with the court, you just fixed yourself."

She was beginning to think again and could even translate Peter's strange language.

"Influence!" she said. "Marry, he is the court. He is the judge."

"Ouch!"

"I wot well I must not be found at home. I am trying to think where to hide. I might have had trial by water. Now they will burn me for surety. I do remember what folk said about the last witch trials."

"Could you make your way to Boston and then maybe to New York—New Amsterdam?"

"Leave my home forever! Nay. And I would not dare the trip."

"Then take to the woods. Where can you go?"

"Take to—? Oh. To the cave, mayhap."

"Don't too many people know about it?"

"Aye. But there is another across the brook and beyond Tom Carter's freehold. I do believe none know of it but me. 'Tis very small. We must ford the brook just yonder, then walk that fallen tree. There is a trail which at sundown will be tromped by a herd of deer."

"You're thinking about dogs?"

"Aye, on the morrow. There is no good pack in Annes Towne."

"You live in a savage age, Charity."

"Aye," she said wryly. "'Tis fortunate we have not invented the bomb."

"Damn it," Peter said, "I wish we'd never met. I wish I hadn't taken you on the plane trip. I wish I'd warned you to keep quiet about it."

"Ye could not guess I would be so foolish."

"What can you do out here without food?"

"I'd liefer starve than be in the stocks, but there is food to be had in the forest, some sorts of roots and toadstools and autumn berries. I shall hide myself for three days, I think, then seek out my father by night and do as he tells me."

When she was safely hidden in the cave, which was small indeed but well concealed by a thicket of young sassafras, she said:

"Now we can think. First, I would have an answer from thy superior wisdom. Can one be truly a witch and have no knowledge of it?"

"Don't be foolish. There's no such thing as a witch."

"Ah well, 'tis a matter for debate by scholars. I do feel in my heart that I am not a witch, if there be such creatures. That book, Peter, of which ye told me, which recounts the history of these colonies."

"Yes?"

"Will ye look in it and learn if I came to trial and what befell me?"

"There'd be nothing about it. It's just a small book. But—"

To his parents' puzzlement, Peter spent the following morning at the Boston Public Library. In the afternoon he shifted his operations to the Historical Society. He found at last a listing of the names of women known to have been tried for witchcraft between the years 1692 and 1697. Thereafter he could locate only an occasional individual name. There was no record of any Charity Payne in 1700 or later.

He started again when the reading room opened next day, interrupting the task only momentarily for brief exchanges with Charity. His lack of success was cheering to her, for she overestimated the completeness of the records.

At close to noon he was scanning the pages of a photostatted doctoral thesis when his eye caught a familiar name.

"Jonas Hacker," it read. "Born Liverpool, England, date uncertain, perhaps 1659, was the principal figure in a curious action of law which has not become a recognized legal precedent in English courts.

"Squire Hacker, a resident of Annes Towne (cf. Anniston), was tried and convicted of willful murder and larceny. The trial was posthumous, several months after his decease from natural causes in 1704. The sentence pronounced was death by hanging which, since it could not be imposed, was commuted to forfeiture of his considerable estate. His land and other possessions reverted to the Crown and were henceforward administered by the Governor of Bay Colony.

"While the motivation and procedure of the court may have been open to question, evidence of Hacker's guilt was clear-cut. The details are these. . . ."

"Hey, Charity," Peter rumbled in his throat.

"Aye?"

"Look at this page. Let me flatten it out."

"Read it please, Peter. Is it bad news?"

"No. Good, I think." He read the paragraphs on Jonas Hacker.

"Oh, Peter, can it be true?"

"It has to be. Can you remember any details?"

"Marry, I remember well when they disappeared, the ship's captain and a common sailor. They were said to have a great sack of gold for some matter of business with Squire. But it could not be, for they never reached his house."

"That's what Hacker said, but the evidence showed that they got there—got there and never got away. Now here's what you must do. Late tonight, go home."

"I would fen do so, for I am terrible athirst."

"No, wait. What's your parson's name?"

"John Hix."

"Can you reach his house tonight without being seen?"

"Aye. It backs on a glen."

"Go there. He can protect you better than your father can

until your trial."

"Must I be tried?"

"Of course. We want to clear your name. Now let's do some planning."

The town hall could seat no more than a score of people, and the day was fair; so it was decided that the trial should be held on the common, in discomforting proximity to the stocks.

Visitors came from as far as twenty miles away, afoot or in carts, and nearly filled the common itself. Squire Hacker's own armchair was the only seat provided. Others stood or sat on the patchy grass.

The squire came out of the inn presently, fortified with rum, and took his place. He wore a brocaded coat and a wide-brimmed hat and would have been more impressive if it had not been for his still swollen nose, now permanently askew.

A way was made through the crowd then, and Charity, flanked on one side by John Hix, on the other by his tall son, walked to the place where she was to stand. Voices were suddenly stilled. Squire Hacker did not condescend to look directly at the prisoner, but fixed a cold stare on the minister; a warning that his protection of the girl would not be forgiven. He cleared his throat.

"Charity Payne, is thee willing to swear upon the Book?"

"Aye."

"No mind. We may forgo the swearing. All can see that ye are fearful."

"Nay," John Hix interrupted. "She shall have the opportunity to swear to her word. 'Twould not be legal otherwise." He extended a Bible to Charity, who placed her fingers on it and said, "I do swear to speak naught but the truth."

Squire Hacker glowered and lost no time coming to the attack. "Charity Payne, do ye deny being a witch?"

"I do."

"Ye do be one?"

"Nay, I do deny it."

"Speak what ye mean. What have ye to say of the monstrous lamb born of Master Croft's ewe?"

"I know naught of it."

"Was't the work of Satan?"

"I know not."

"Was't the work of God?"

"I know not."

"Thee holds then that He might create such a monster?"

"I know naught about it."

"In thy own behalf will thee deny saying that this colony and its neighbors will in due course make wars against our King?"

"Nay, I do not deny that."

There was a stir in the crowd and some angry muttering.

"Did ye tell Mistress Ursula Miller that ye had flown a great journey through the air?"

"Nay."

"Mistress Ursula will confound thee in that lie."

"I did tell Ursula that someday folk would travel in that wise. I did tell her that I had seen such travel through eyes other than my own."

Squire Hacker leaned forward. He could not have hoped for a more damning statement. John Hix's head bowed in prayer.

"Continue."

"Aye. I am blessed with a sort of second sight."

"Blessed or cursed?"

"God permits it. It cannot be accursed."

"Continue. What evil things do ye see by this second sight?"

"Most oftentimes I see the world as it will one day be. Thee said evil. Such sights are no more and no less evil than we see around us."

Hacker pondered. There was an uncomfortable wrongness about this child's testimony. She should have been gibbering with fear, when in fact she seemed self-possessed. He wondered if by some strange chance she really had assistance from the devil's minions.

"Charity Payne, thee had confessed to owning second sight. Does thee use this devilish power to spy on thy neighbors?"

It was a telling point. Some among the spectators exchanged discomfited glances.

"Nay, 'tis not devilish, and I cannot see into the doings of my neighbors—except—"

"Speak up, girl. Except what?"

"Once I did perceive by my seeing a most foul murder."

"Murder!" The squire's voice was harsh. A few in the crowd made the sign of the cross.

"Aye. To tell true, two murders. Men whose corpses do now lie buried unshriven in a dark cellar close onto this spot. 'Tween them lies a satchel of golden guineas."

It took a minute for the squire to find his voice.

"A cellar?" he croaked.

"Aye, a root cellar, belike the place one would keep winter apples." She lifted her head and stared straight into the squire's eyes, challenging him to inquire further.

The silence was ponderous as he strove to straighten out his thoughts. To this moment he was safe, for her words described every cellar in and about the village. But she knew. Beyond any question, she knew. Her gaze, seeming to penetrate the darkest corners of his mind, told him that, even more clearly than her words.

Squire Hacker believed in witches and considered them evil and deserving of being destroyed. He had seen and shuddered at the horrible travesty of a lamb in farmer Croft's stable yard, but he had seen like deformities in the Caribbee and did not hold the event an evidence of witchcraft. Not for a minute had he thought Charity a witch, for she showed none of the signs. Her wild talk and the growing rumors had simply seemed to provide the opportunity for some dalliance with a pretty young girl and possibly, in exchange for an acquittal, a lien upon her father's land.

Now he was unsure. She must indeed have second sight to have penetrated his secret, for it had been stormy that night five years ago, and none had seen the missing sailors near to his house. Of that he was confident. Further, shockingly, she knew how and where they lay buried. Another question and answer could not be risked.

He moved his head slowly and looked right and left at the silent throng.

"Charity Payne," he said, picking his words with greatest care, "has put her hand on the Book and sworn to tell true, an act, I opine, she could scarce perform, were she a witch. Does any person differ with me?"

John Hix looked up in startled hopefulness.

"Very well. The lambing at Master Croft's did have the taint of witchcraft, but Master Trowbridge has stated his belief that some noxious plant is growing in Croft's pasture, and 'tis at the least possible. Besides, the ewe is old and she has thrown runty lambs before.

"To quote Master Trowbridge again, he holds that the cholera which has afflicted us so sorely comes from naught but the drinking of bad water. He advises boiling it. I prefer adding a little rum."

He got the laughter he sought. There was a lessening of tension.

"As to second sight." Again he swept the crowd with his gaze. "Charity had laid claim to it, and I called it a devilish gift to test her, but second sight is not witchcraft, as ye well know. My own grandmother had it, and a better woman ne'er lived. I hold it to be a gift of God. Would any challenge me?

"Very well. I would warn Charity to be cautious in what she sees and tells, for second sight can lead to grievous disputations. I do not hold with her story of two murdered men, although I think that in her own sight she is telling true. If any have aught of knowledge of so dire a crime, I adjure him to step forth and speak."

He waited. "Nobody? Then, by the authority conferred on me by his Excellency the Governor, I declare that Charity Payne is innocent of the charges brought. She may be released."

This was not at all the eventuality which a few of Squire Hacker's cronies had foretold. The crowd had clearly expected a daylong inquisition climaxed by a prisoner to bedevil in the stocks. The Squire's about-face and his abrupt ending of the trial surprised them and angered a few. They stood uncertain.

Then someone shouted hurrah and someone else called for three cheers for Squire Hacker, and all in a minute the gathering had lost its hate and was taking on the look of a picnic. Men headed for the tavern. Parson Hix said a long prayer to which few listened, and everybody gathered around to wring Obie Payne's good hand and to give his daughter a squeeze.

At intervals through the afternoon and evening Peter touched lightly on Charity's mind, finding her carefree and happily occupied with visitors. He chose not to obtrude himself until she called.

Late that night she lay on her mattress and stared into the dark.

"Peter," she whispered.

"Yes, Charity."

"Oh, thank you again."

"Forget it. I got you into the mess. Now you're out of it. Anyway, I didn't really help. It all had to work out the way it did, because that's the way it had happened. You see?"

"No, not truly. How do we know that Squire won't dig up those old bones and burn them?"

"Because he didn't. Four years from now somebody will find them."

"No, Peter, I do not understand, and I am afeared again."

"Why, Charity?"

"It must be wrong, thee and me talking together like this and knowing what is to be and what is not."

"But what could be wrong about it?"

"That I do not know, but I think 'twere better you should stay in your time and me in mine. Goodbye Peter."

"Charity!"

"And God bless you."

Abruptly she was gone and in Peter's mind there was an emptiness and a knowledge of being alone. He had not known that she could close him out like this.

With the passing of days he became skeptical and in time he might have disbelieved entirely. But Charity visited him again. It was October. He was alone and studying, without much interest.

"Peter."

"Charity, it's you."

"Yes. For a minute, please, Peter, for only a minute, but I had to tell you. I—" She seemed somehow embarrassed. "There is a message."

"A what?"

"Look at Bear Rock, Peter, under the bear's jaw on the left side."

With that, she was gone.

The cold water swirled around his legs as he traced with one finger the painstakingly chiseled message she had left: a little girl message in a symbol far older than either of them.

THE SALEM WOLF

▪ BY HOWARD PYLE ▪

These things happened in the year when the witches were so malignant at Salem, and the trouble began over a crock of cider.

Deacon Graves and Jerusha and little Ichabod and old Patrick Duncan were in the cider-shed at the time. Granny Whitlow came to the cider-press, bringing with her a great stoneware crock, and she begged for a crockful of cider.

That was in October before she was hanged for a witch, and she was already in ill odor with all God-fearing men and women. It was known by many that she had an evil eye, and that her malignant soul was as black as a coal and fit for nothing but hell-fire.

Deacon Graves was a staunch professor and an upright believer in the gospel. "You'll get no cider here," says he. "Begone!" says he, "for I am a friend of God, and you are a friend of the devil."

Then up spoke old Patrick Duncan. He was born in Scotland and had fought in Poland with Douglas under King Karl Gustav of Sweden. It is known that the Scotch and Polish witches and warlocks are the worst in the world, and Patrick Duncan knew more about them and their ways than you could find in a book. "Master," says he, "you had best give her the cider, or else she'll maybe cast the evil eye on the whole pressing."

Then Granny Whitlow laughed very wickedly. "Do you speak of the evil eye?" says she. "Well, then, he may keep his cider, and he may take my black curse along with it," and with that she went out of the shed and left them. But she did not go far—only to the cow-house, and there sat down by the wall with her crock beside her.

By and by Patrick Duncan looked out from the door of the cider-shed and espied her where she sat. "Look, look, Master Graves!" says he. "Yonder sits the witch by the cow-house. Best drive her away, or else she will cast the evil eye upon the cattle."

So Deacon Graves went out to where Granny Whitlow sat and caught her by the arm, and lifted her to her feet, and says he: "Get you gone, witch! What mischief are you brewing here? Get you gone, I say!" Therewith, still holding her tight by the arm, he haled her down to the gate and thrust her out into the road. As he thrust her out she stumbled and fell, and her crock rolled into the ditch beside the road.

But she scrambled very quickly up from the dusty road, and so got to her feet. She spat upon the ground, and shook her fist at Deacon Graves (all skin and bone it was, and withered like a dead leaf). "Ah!" cries she, "would you treat me so! Well, then, you'll be sorry for this. For I curse you once!—I curse you twice!—I curse you thrice! And if I'm sorry today, may you be sorry tomorrow!"

Thus she said, and then she went away down the road, leaving her crock in the ditch where it had fallen.

That was how the trouble began, and that was how Granny Whitlow came to set the evil eye upon Deacon Graves—upon him and his. In less than a fortnight afterward the best cow was taken with hollow-horn, and though they bored holes in both horns with a gimlet, yet the poor beast died inside of four hours.

That was the first curse come true.

A week afterward the Deacon's fine gray mare was bogged in the ditch in the lower pasture, and sprung her shoulder so that she was never good for anything afterward.

That was the second curse come true.

But the third curse was bitter and black to the very bottom.

• II •

Deacon Graves had a daughter named Miriam. When she fell sick no one knew what ailed her. She grew very strange and wild, and if anybody asked her what ailed her she would maybe scream out, or fall to weeping, or else she would fall into a furious rage, as though seized with a frenzy.

She was a likely girl, with eyes as black as sloes, and black hair, and black eyebrows, and red cheeks, and red lips, and teeth as white as those of a dog. She was promised to Abijah Butler, the son of Aaron Butler the cordwainer, and he came up from town twice or thrice a week to court her.

He saw, as everybody else saw, that she was not as she had been, but was grown very strange and wild. For a while he kept his thoughts to himself, but at last things grew so dark that he spoke very plainly to the girl's father and mother about the matter. "'Tis my belief," says he, "that Granny Whitlow has bewitched her." And neither Deacon Graves nor Dame Graves could find any word to deny what he said.

One Sabbath day Abijah came out from town in the afternoon, and Miriam was in bed. Nothing seemed to ail her, but she would not get up out of bed, but lay there all day, staring at the ceiling and saying nothing. Then Abijah stood up, and he said: "It is high time to do something about this business. If I am to marry Miriam, I must first know what it is ails her."

Dame Graves says: "We none of us know what ails her. We've given her mustard, and sulphur, and boneset, and nothing does her any good."

"Well," says Abijah Butler, "what I said stays where I stuck it. Unless I know what is the matter with Miriam, all is off between us and I am away."

So Abijah Butler, and Deacon Graves, and Dame Graves, and Patrick Duncan, all four, went to the room where Miriam lay. There she was lying in bed and still as a log; but the moment they set foot in the room she cried out very loud and shrill, and snatched the coverlet over her head. Then she fell to shrieking and screaming as though she had gone mad, bidding them go away and let her lie in peace.

Deacon Graves went to the bedside and caught her very tight by the arm. "Be still!" says he. "Be still, or I will whip you!" and therewith she immediately fell silent, and lay trembling like any leaf.

Then Deacon Graves, still holding her tight by the arm, says to her, "What ails you?" And she said, speaking very weak and faint from under the bed coverlet. "Nothing ails me." Says he, "Tell me, are you bewitched?" and to that she said nothing. Then he says, "Tell me who has bewitched you?" but still she would say nothing. He says "Tell me who has bewitched you, or I will whip you."

At that she began crying under the coverlet, but still she would not say anything. Then Deacon Graves says, "Tell me, was it Granny Whitlow who bewitched you?" and at that she said "Yes."

After that they got the whole story from her by piecemeal. This was what she told them:

One day she was turning the bread in the oven. The kitchen door was open and a great black cat came running in. She struck the cat with the bread-peel, but the creature paid no heed to her, but ran around and around the room. Then she grew frightened of the cat and climbed up on the dough-trough. The cat ran around and around the kitchen so fast that her head spun. Then the cat was gone, and Granny Whitlow stood there in the kitchen looking at her. Granny Whitlow's eyes burned like live coals, and she said, "Move your arm!" and Miriam tried to move her arm and could not do so. Then Granny Whitlow said, "Move your other arm!" and Miriam could not move that either. She could not move a single hair but was like one in a dream, who tries to move and cannot. Then Granny Whitlow plucked three hairs out of her own head and came to Miriam where she sat on the dough-trough; and she tied the three hairs about the girl's little finger. "Now you are one of us," says she, and after that she went out of the kitchen, and Miriam came down from the dough-trough. Ever since that she had been bewitched.

This was the story she told, and after she had ended, her father tried to say something to her. At first he could not say anything, but could only swallow and swallow as though a nut was stuck in his throat. Then at last he says— speaking in a voice as dry as a husk, "Tell me, have you ever been to the Devil's Meeting House?"

At that Miriam began to cry out very loud from under the coverlet. Deacon Graves says, "Tell me the truth, or I will whip you!" Thereupon Miriam from under the coverlet said, "Yes— once or twice." He says, "Who took you?" and she says, "It was Granny Whitlow took me."

Then Deacon Graves says, "Let me see your hand." And the girl reached her hand out from under the coverlet. They all looked, and, lo! there was a ring of hair tied about her little finger.

Dame Graves took a pair of scissors and cut the hairs, and after that they all went out of the room and left her. They sat for a while together in the kitchen and were more happy than they had been for a long time, for they all thought that now that the hair ring was cut from her finger Miriam would be herself.

By and by Abijah Butler went home, and after he had gone, Dame Graves says to the Deacon: "You should not have asked Miriam about going to the Devil's Meeting House, and that before Abijah Butler. Who knows what he thinks! He might never come back again, and then where would we find another husband for the girl?" But Abijah Butler was wonderfully in love with Miriam, and even this, and worse than this, did not drive him away from her.

After that time, Miriam Graves was better for two or three days; then she became once more as wild as ever. By this they all knew either that the witchcraft had struck into her bones so that she could not rid herself of it, or else that she had been bewitched again. So a week or so after that (it was then about the middle of November) Deacon Graves went to town and saw Dominie Mather and told him the whole story from beginning to end, just as it was and without hiding anything.

When Granny Whitlow was tried for witchcraft, a great many things were testified against her that had never been known before.

A little girl named Ann Greenfield testified that she had one time been down in Bedloe's Swamp, and that she had there seen Granny Whitlow sitting at the root of a tree, stark and stiff as though she were dead. Little Ann said that she was very much afraid, but she did not run away. She said that she stood and looked at Granny Whitlow, and by and by she saw something that came running very fast. It looked like a mouse running very fast among the leaves. She said it ran to Granny Whitlow and run up her breast and into her mouth, and then Granny Whitlow came to life again and opened her eyes. The little girl said that Granny Whitlow did not see her, but rose and went somewhere into the swamp.

Another girl, named Mercy Nailor, testified that she had once seen Granny Whitlow riding across Fielding's Clearing in the dusk seated astride of a goat as black as coal. Mercy Nailor afterward withdrew her testimony and confessed that it was not true. But Ann Greenfield's testimony was true, and several other things that were testified were true, for they were never withdrawn.

Deacon Graves was in the crowd when Granny Whitlow rode to the gallows in the hangman's cart. She saw him where he stood and called out to him from the cart. "Ah, Deacon!" says she, "is that you? And so you have come to see me hanged, have you? Well, then, look to yourself. The third curse is still on you, and something worse than hanging will happen to you before the year is out."

Shortly after that she was hanged.

They all thought that, now Granny Whitlow was hanged, Miriam would be released from the witchcraft that tormented her, but she was not. Things went from bad to worse with her, for, by and by, they found that she would run away at night, no one knew whither. They set a watch upon her, but if they did but wink two or three times, lo! she would be gone.

God knows whither she went, but every time she ran away she would come back betwixt midnight and morning, all wild of face, but weak and wan as though she had ridden long and far. And always after such a time she would go straight to bed, and sleep, maybe, for a day and a night. Then she would wake and crave for something to eat, and when food was set before her she would eat, and eat, and eat like a wild creature that was starving.

· III ·

Early in the winter the Salem wolf appeared at that place. Such a thing as a wolf had not been seen at Salem for thirty years and more, and folks were slow to believe that it really was a wolf that killed the sheep or the young cattle or the swine that every now and then were found dead and part eaten in the morning.

But afterward everybody knew that it was a wolf; for one bright moonlit night Eli Hackett saw it as he was coming home from town meeting. A thin snow had fallen, and the night was wonderfully cold and clear and bright. Eli Hackett saw the wolf as plain as though it had been daylight. It ran across the corner of an open lot, and so back of the rope-walk. It appeared to be chasing something, and paid no heed to him, but ran straight on. And then he saw it again when it came out from behind the rope-walk—it ran across Widow Calder's garden-patch, and so into the clearing beyond.

After that several others saw the wolf at different times, and once it chased Dr. Wilkinson on a dark night for above a half mile, and into the very town itself. Then so many people saw the wolf that women and children were afraid to go out after nightfall, and even men would not go out without an axe or a club, or maybe a pistol in the belt. The wolf haunted the town for above a month, and a great many pigs and sheep and several calves were killed in that time.

Old Patrick Duncan and little Ichabod Graves slept together in the same bed in the attic. One night Patrick Duncan awoke, and found that little Ichabod was shaking his shoulder, and shaking it and shaking it.

Says Patrick Duncan: "What is it, child? What ails you?"

"Oh! Patrick Duncan," says the little boy. "Wake up! There is a great beast running about in the yard!"

"What is it you say?" says Patrick Duncan. "A great beast? Pooh! pooh! child; you have been dreaming. Go to sleep again."

"Oh, Patrick Duncan!" says the little boy. "Wake up, for I am not dreaming! There is indeed a great beast out in the yard. For first I heard it, and then I looked out of the window and saw it with my very eyes, and it is there running about in the moonlight."

Then Patrick Duncan got up and went to the window of the attic and looked out, and there he saw that what little Ichabod had said was true. For there was the wolf, and it was running around and around the yard in the snow, and he could see it in the moonlight as plainly as though it were upon a sheet of white paper.

The wolf ran around and around in a circle as though it were at play, and every now and then it would snap up a mouthful of snow and cast it into the air. And every now and then it would run its muzzle into the snow and plough through the crust as though in playful sport.

Patrick Duncan said, "Is the musket in the kitchen loaded?" And little Ichabod said: "Yes, for I saw father load it and prime it fresh a week ago come Sabbath evening. For there was fresh talk of the wolf just then." "Then bide you here," says Patrick Duncan, "and I'll go fetch it." So by and by he came, bringing the musket from the kitchen.

There was a broken pane in the attic window and an old stocking in the broken place. Patrick Duncan drew out the stocking very softly, and all the while the great beast played around and around in the snow in the yard below. Patrick Duncan put the musket out through the broken place in the window pane. He took long aim and then he fired. The musket bellowed like thunder, and the air was all full of gunpowder smoke. Patrick Duncan felt sure that he had killed the wolf, but when the gunpowder smoke cleared away, there lay the yard as bare and as empty as the palm of the hand.

The whole house was awakened by the sound of the musket. They all came into the kitchen, except Miriam, who did not come out of her room. They stood about the hearth listening to what Patrick Duncan and little Ichabod had to tell them about the wolf. Patrick Duncan said: "I took a sure and certain aim, and I don't see how I could have missed my shot.

"I could see the sight of the gun as plain as daylight, and it was pointed straight at the heart of the beast."

As they stood there talking about it all, the kitchen door opened of a sudden very softly and quietly. For a moment it stood ajar, and then someone came into the house as still as a ghost. It was Miriam, and she was clad only in her shift and petticoat. They all looked at her as though they had been turned to stone, but she did not appear to see them. She went straight across the kitchen and to her room, and they could hear the bedstead squeak as she got into bed.

Then Dame Graves began crying. "Alas!" says she, "Miriam walks in her sleep and we can't keep her abed. Suppose the wolf had caught her and killed her!"

The next day Miriam was churning in the kitchen. Patrick Duncan came in and found her there alone.

"I missed my aim last night, mistress," says he.

"So I hear tell," says she.

"I'll not miss it again," says he.

"Why not?" says she.

"Because," says he. "I am going to melt down this rix-dollar and cast it into a slug. I know this much," says he, "that sometimes a silver slug will go through a hide that will turn a lump of lead. So if ever you see the Salem wolf," says he, "just tell it that the next bullet I shoot at it will be made of silver."

Then the girl stopped churning, and said, "What concern is all this to me?"

"Well," says Patrick Duncan, "you know better than I do whether it concerns you or not."

After that, and for a while, no more was heard of the Salem wolf. It was said that Patrick Duncan's musket-shot had frightened the beast away, but Patrick knew better than that. He knew that it was the threat of the silver bullet that had driven it off.

Then after a while the wolf came back again, and more people saw it, and more sheep, and pigs, and some calves were found dead in the morning. Then came the worst of all, for one morning Ezra Doolittle was found dead in his own backyard, and his neck was all torn and rent by the savage wild beast.

That was the first that anyone suspected that this was no ordinary wolf, but a man-wolf that was running loose among them.

▪ IV ▪

Late one afternoon Abijah Butler came out from town. Deacon Graves was not at home, and so he went down to the barn where Patrick Duncan was milking. "Patrick Duncan," says he, "tell me, what do you think ails Miriam Graves?"

Patrick Duncan's cheek was lying close against the belly of the cow as he milked, and he did not lift his head. "Why do you ask me?" says he. "Go ask her father and her mother what ails her."

Abijah Butler says, "Her father is not at home."

"Well," says Patrick Duncan, "go ask her mother."

"So I will," says Abijah Butler, "but I want you to come with me."

"Well," says Patrick Duncan, "I will go with you when I finish milking the cow."

So after Patrick Duncan had finished his milking they went together to the house, and Dame Graves sat alone in the kitchen at her spinning. Abijah Butler went to her and began speaking, but Patrick Duncan stood by the bench at the window, where he had set the milk pail.

"Tell me," says Abijah Butler, "what is it ails Miriam?"

Dame Graves put her hand to the wheel and stopped it.

"You know what ails her as well as I do," says she, "for you heard what the girl said to her father."

"I heard what she said," says he, "but I fear me that worse even than witchcraft ails her. There are things said about her," says he, "that I can't bear to hear. So if I am to be her husband," says he, "I must know what ails her, or else I must break with her."

Then Dame Graves began crying and says she, "Don't you be hard with us, Abijah Butler. Nothing ails the girl, only that she walks in her sleep, and dreams she is awake."

Abijah Butler says, "Where is Miriam now?"

At that Dame Graves flung her apron over her head and cried out: "God knows where she is! She ran away half an hour ago!"

After that nobody spoke for a little while. Then Abijah Butler says, "Where is Deacon Graves?" And Dame Graves said, "He went to town with a load of potatoes. He'll be back by now, or in a little while."

Then up spoke old Patrick Duncan. "Best not wait till the night comes down," said he, "for the wolf will be out tonight."

Abijah Butler laughed, and he turned back his overcoat and showed that he had his axe hanging at his belt. He clapped his hand to the shining head of his axe, and says he:

"How now! Need I be afraid?"

Just then Patrick Duncan said of a sudden: "Yonder comes the sledge! Now you can talk to Deacon Graves himself."

Then in a moment he cries out: "How is this! The sledge is empty and the horse is running away!"

Thereafter, in a moment or two, the horse came running through the gate with the sledge behind it, and the sledge was empty and swung from this side to that. Thus the horse ran past the house with the empty sledge behind it, and so down to the barn. Abijah Butler and Patrick Duncan ran out of the house and down to the barnyard, and there they found the horse and the empty sledge. And the horse was all of a lather of sweat, and its eyes were starting, and it was trembling in every hair.

"God save us! The wolf!" cries Patrick Duncan. "Here is a bad business! Jump in quick, or we may be too late!"

So they both jumped into the sledge, and Patrick Duncan turned the horse about and drove away in a fury. And so they drove furiously down the road and toward the town.

Well, they had gone a little more than half a mile, when, all of a sudden, the horse stopped stock-still with a jerk that near threw them both out of the sledge. The poor creature stood with all four feet planted, and it snorted and snorted. The evening was then falling pretty fast, and Abijah Butler stood up in the sledge and looked. Then he cried out: "God of Mercy! What is that!" Then he cried out again: "God of Mercy! 'Tis Deacon Graves, and the wolf is at him!" With that he leaped out of the sledge into the snow, and even as he jumped he plucked the axe from his belt.

By now the horse was leaping and plunging as though it had gone mad and would dash both the sledge and itself to pieces, so that Patrick Duncan had all that he could do to hold it in check.

Abijah Butler ran through the snow as fast as he could to where the wolf was worrying the man in the middle of the road, and he yelled with all his might at the wolf as he ran.

The man lay in the snow and the wolf was worrying him this way and that. The man lay still and did not move, and the wolf worried at him as a wicked dog worries at a sheep. And it was so busy at what it was about that it paid no heed to Abijah Butler or to the plunging horse or to anything else.

It did not appear to be afraid and did not flee away, so that Abijah ran to it and caught it by the hair of its back and tried to drag it away from the man. And he yelled out: "Hell-hound! Let go!" and therewith he struck the beast a fearful blow upon the neck with the axe just where the neck joins the shoulder.

With that the wolf instantly let go the man, and whirled about several times in the road, howling and yelling. Then it leaped, yelling, over the wall, and ran away in a great circle across the field beyond. And as it ran, Abijah Butler saw it shake its head now and then, and whenever it shook its head he saw that the blood would sprinkle over the snow. Then in a moment or two it stopped yelling and ran very silently—only every now and then it would shake its head and sprinkle more blood upon the snow. So it ran into the woods, and they could not see it any longer.

They lifted up the Deacon and looked at his hurts, for there was still some light, and by it they could see how much harm he had suffered. He was cut and torn in shoulder and neck, and about the ears and head, but he was in a swoon and not dead, for he wore a fur coat, and the collar of the coat had saved him when the wolf worried at him. Old Patrick Duncan stayed by the wounded man, and Abijah Butler ran across the fields to the Buckners' farmhouse. In a little while he came running back with old Simeon Buckner and his two sons. Deacon Graves had not yet come fully out of his swoon, so they lifted him and laid him in the sledge, covering him over with the sheep pelts that were there.

Simeon Buckner and his two sons drove the sledge home very slowly, and Abijah Butler and old Patrick Duncan went on ahead to tell what had happened. Neither said a word to the other, but each looked down at his feet and walked through the snow in silence.

. V .

As they came near the house they saw that there were lights moving about within. As they kicked the snow off of their feet against the doorstep, the door was flung open, and there was Dame Graves standing on the doorsill. "Oh, Abijah Butler!" cries she. "Oh, Patrick Duncan! Come in quick, for Miriam has come back home and is sore hurt!"

Abijah Butler and Patrick Duncan looked at each other. They came into the house. Patrick Duncan took the candle from Dame Graves, and they all went into the room where Miriam lay. She lay in bed with a sheet drawn up to her chin, and the sheet was all stained red with blood.

Patrick Duncan came to the bedside and catched the sheet and pulled at it. Miriam tried to hold it, but he pulled it out of her hands and down over her shoulders. There was a great, terrible, deep wound in the girl's neck where the neck joins the shoulder, and the bed beneath her was all soaked red with blood.

Patrick Duncan cried out in a loud voice, "Where got you that hurt?"

Miriam said nothing, but only covered her face with both hands.

Patrick Duncan cried out in a still louder and more terrible voice, "Where got you that hurt?"

Upon that she began whimpering and whining just as a great dog would do, and she said, "Alas! I know not how I was hurt!"

Upon that Miriam screamed out of a sudden very loud, and she cried: "Torment me not and I will tell you all! I walked in my sleep, I walked out into the barn, and I walked on the haymow, and all the while I was asleep. I slipped from the haymow, and I fell on the scythe blade and cut my neck."

This was what she said, and she had evidence for it, for the next day they found that there was blood in the barn where the scythe hung in the corner under the haymow. But Patrick Duncan and many of the others said the blood was there because she had put on her shift and petticoat at the place before she went into the house.

They have not hanged any more witches since they pressed old Giles Corey to death. But God knows how such things as this are to be prevented unless the world is rid of such devil's crew.

As for Miriam Graves, her wound festered and she catched a burning fever and died of it on the sixth day after she had been hurt, at three o'clock in the afternoon. But Deacon Graves got well of his hurts.

Abijah Butler went to Providence in Rhode Island, where he joined business with his uncle, Justification Butler, and old Patrick Duncan went to Deerfield to drill a militia company, and was shot by an Indian who had hid in a clearing.

THE FOG ON PEMBLE GREEN

▪ BY SHIRLEY BARKER ▪

As he came onto Pemble Green he had to ride past the burying ground, at the right-hand side of the Boston Road and a little above it; and since the young minister's business was as much with the dead as with the living, he left his horse by the wall and climbed the rutted path that wound among the headstones. After a few steps he took off his tall black hat and carried it in his hand, not so much in reverence as in joyous response to the warm, blue weather—treacherously warm for a day in March—and to the sunshine on the drowned fields of Essex County. But he was not there to rejoice in the gentle season; he was there because a woman had died—because, her neighbors said, another woman had killed her.

The place he sought was not hard to find. It was near the top of the hill, where he could stand and look about him—a mile east to the wide curve of the sea, or to the woods and fields on the other three sides, or straight down into the town itself, a cluster of small houses about the common land, a low church, a flooded brook, and a water mill. Mistress Margery Reeve had been dead less than a month, he knew, and no turf covered the mound of clay and rubble they had heaped above her; but her gravestone was already set—a tall, rounded slate with a death's-head at the top.

Margery, wife of Stephen Reeve, it read, *Feb. 21, 1699. Aet. 18. Bewitched to Death.*

Thomas Warne, twenty-one years old, newly Master of Arts from Harvard College, copying manuscript to earn his bread while he further studied the body of Divinity with Mr. Cotton Mather, stood up straight and serious in the spring sunshine. The sea wind ruffled the fair hair on his forehead with no respect to the store of learning beneath it.

"Were you bewitched to death, Margery?" he asked aloud. "I do not believe it—I do not believe there be any witches, Margery."

Dame Margery did not answer him. He had not expected she would, but he wanted to wait a little before he went into the house where she used to live, and talked with the men and women who had known her; wanted to grow accustomed to the sharp, salt taste of the air in this eastern county where it was said to be as easy to see witches and other instruments of Satan as to see rabbits, where there had been such a hanging time about it scarce eight years ago. On every lip, in the tavern at Saugus where he had slept last night, he had heard two names—Margery Reeve and Joan Alder. The word had passed there that Mr. Haverley, the minister at Pemble Green where Margery died all in the short space between one noon and the next candlelighting, had sent to Boston to ask for advice and counsel from his brother ministers. No one in the tavern had guessed that the stranger, lodged there for one night only, was on his way to help Mr. Haverley. Perhaps not even the ministers in Boston knew that young Warne meant to be of what help he could to Joan Alder. Not that he had ever seen or known her—rather because he believed in her innocence, she being charged with a crime which to his mind no mortal could commit.

He sighed a little as he read again the crude, scraped letters— *Aet. 18.* How young she was! Then he strode down the hill and led his horse toward Pemble Common.

A group of children, slipping and sliding as they played tip-cat in the muddy road, pointed out Mr. Haverley's house, small, but with a wide chimney and decent gables, placed at the right of the church where the land sloped away to the brook and the mill with its clacking wheel. Not far from the mill, he noticed, as he crossed the minister's front yard, stood the most pretentious of the houses, tall and square, soundly built of red brick, with red turkey curtains in the windows. He tapped on the oak panels of Mr. Haverley's front door, and a sturdy, brown-faced servant maid opened it. A moment later he was seated in the study.

"Ah, yes." Mr. Haverley leaned forward in his greatchair and placed the tips of his fingers together while he stared at the younger man out of deepset, troubled eyes. "Mr. Warne. I heard you defend your thesis at the Commencement, I remember. A brilliant work, sir. I hope you can advise us here."

"I hope I can, Mr Haverley. Sometimes the stranger within the gates sees what too familiar eyes have overlooked. I have heard something from Mr. Mather of what happened, but not all, I think. Will you tell me, sir?"

The fire burned too brightly, Thomas thought, and the low-ceiled room was too warm. An odor of seething fish crept in from the passageway leading to the kitchen. He tugged the woolen scarf away from his throat, and then gave full attention to Mr. Haverley.

"It was sometime about a month ago, but the date I forget. Well after Candlemas it was, well after Candlemas, indeed, when I was called out about sunset by a servant of Dame Alice Reeve. She brought me the word that her son's wife, Margery, was violently ill and they had begun to fear her passing. I could hardly believe it then, for I had seen Margery no later than midday, and spoken with her that morning.

"It was warm, almost like late spring, for it has been an unseasonably mild winter, you know, unwholesomely mild. She had gone down the brook valley, she told me, to see if the willow catkins were yet in bud. She was singing to herself, and her steps were more like a dance than the gait of a sober matron, and instead of a seemly hood she wore a ribbon in her hair. I was forced to reprove her. Gaiety is a sin, as are the love of bright fabrics and a merry carriage. Was it to save us for this that Christ died? Ah, well, but you would know what happened. As I say, I met her by the green that morning and reproved her for her frivolity. Her eyes were laughing and her mouth bright and red. I saw upon her no mark of another world. I swear to you that on that morning she had the appearance of no illness of the flesh. She did not die a death of nature, Mr. Warne."

"That morning," Thomas said slowly, "she showed no illness and then at sunset they sent for you. You went, of course?"

"At once and in haste. I had known her since the day of her birth, when I prayed with her dying mother, Simon Hampstead's wife. He was our miller then, as now. And her husband's people I have always known. The greatest landowners hereabout. Dame Alice gives liberally to the church and to the poor. As I say, I went to their house. 'Tis but across the green. You must have marked it—of fine red brick?" The younger man nodded. "But when I arrived her sufferings were ended. The women were closing her eyes. Dame Alice, having labored to save her with whatever skill she had or could command among her neighbors, lay prostrate with shock and grief. Stephen, poor lad, had closeted himself."

"What course had her illness taken?" Thomas asked.

Mr. Haverley reached across his desk and pulled a small leather-bound book from a pile of other volumes near the huge inkpot. He thumbed the pages lingeringly.

"I have kept a careful record, sir, such as I keep for all deathbeds here. Since we have no doctor of physic, only women somewhat skilled in herbs and midwifery, and I myself let blood when I am applied to and deem it necessary—"

"A worthy habit, recordkeeping," said Thomas patiently, wishing he dared ask leave to take a pipe of tobacco.

"Ah, here it is! February 21st, 1699. Mrs. Margery Reeve. Taken about noonday in her husband's house, amongst a party of female company assembled for a quilting, with grievous sharp pains in her stomach region, followed by much vomiting of blood, four hours of agony, weakness, failure of the mortal senses, and then death."

He read it triumphantly, then fell silent.

"I see," said Thomas, thoughtfully. "Her death proceeded not from injury or attack, but from some cause within—an illness of nature or perhaps a poison—"

"Or from a work of Satan!" cried Mr. Haverley. "The town says it was by witchcraft. The whispers went out before her corpse was cold."

"Do you believe them, sir?"

The minister avoided the grave young eyes watching him.

"I—I do not know—" he said suddenly, helplessly. "I prayed God to instruct me. I have sought for evidence. But I cannot tell."

"And yet you hold a maid in gaol."

"No. Not in gaol, and not a maid either. We have confined the widow, Joan Alder, in an upper room at the Wheat Sheaf tavern until we know how to dispose of the case. We have no proof—but the whispers are all against her."

Thomas cleared his throat. "Mr. Haverley," he said, his eyes searching the eyes that would not meet his, "Mr. Mather has advised that we go forward with much caution in this matter. It is well known where whispers can lead. The Colony learned that at Salem years ago. The gaols were filled then, and your county in a panic, and many people were labeled firebrands of Hell and died on the gallows, many of whom it is now believed were innocent— as innocent as you or I. It must not happen again—in our time or any other time. I believe that if Mistress Reeve did not die a death of nature, she died from poison, since no other weapon could so work upon her from within."

Mr. Haverley was staring out of the window at the fine brick house.

"You may be right," he murmured. "I hope you are. But then we must needs find the poisoner. How will you proceed? How did Mr. Mather instruct you?"

"He did not instruct me. He prayed earnestly that God would do so. Tell me, why was the blame fixed on Widow Alder?"

"Why—why her name was in everyone's mouth."

"That does not answer me, sir."

Mr Haverley stood up and began to pace the floor, and Thomas noticed then that the wide pine boards were worn from many such pacings.

"No, it does not answer you. I suppose it was useless to hope—but I had done so. I had hoped that Dame Alice and her son might be spared further grievousness. She is of such piety and her gifts to the church—and he is but a youth. Do you feel you must speak with them?"

"Indeed I must. If Dame Alice is truly pious she will want

whatever sin there is in the matter rooted out. And as for her son, he is old enough to be a husband—and a widower. But do you not come to them over-soon? I had not mentioned them. I spoke of the accused. Was it the Reeve family who brought the charges against her?"

"Ah, no." The minister shook his head sadly. "I mention them because I must needs do so in order to tell you why Joan Alder is thought to have desired Margery's death. It is said that she would connive to marry with Stephen Reeve—he is a comely young man, with much land and a full purse."

Thomas Warne widened his eyes. He had the feeling that a thread was being put in his hand—not the thread he was looking for, but one that perhaps would lead somewhere.

"It is a story almost as old as the Fall of Man," he said slowly, "and as sad. Can you be sure it was not Stephen who sought Margery's death that he might have Joan? Joan is fair, I suppose?"

"She is—carnally fair," said the minister between his teeth.

"Has there ever been talk before of her casting spells or eyeing her neighbors' husbands?"

"I have not heard so."

"Was she known to have made any ill motion toward Mistress Margery? To curse her, or to quarrel with her, or attempt any of the uses of witchcraft."

"None such have been reported unto me."

"Has she ever been known to conduct herself unseemly with any man?"

"We do not have light on all her dark ways!" cried Mr. Haverley in exasperation.

Thomas Warne looked at him steadily. "Has she ever been known to conduct herself unseemly with any man?"

"No—but—"

"I shall visit her at the Wheat Sheaf," said Thomas, standing up, "but first I wish to speak with the husband and his mother. Will you accompany me there?"

Mr. Haverley rose with a sigh and put away his leather book. "I will do so," he answered austerely, "out of respect to Mr. Mather, but I cannot believe it is needful. I myself will vouch for them. Remember, they are of God's Elect, and they have suffered much."

"I shall remember," said Thomas, stepping out into the sunshine.

A few moments later he was seated on damask cushions deep in a wainscot chair, enjoying the hospitality of the brick house with the turkey red hangings. Dame Alice Reeve, a slight woman with sharp, high-boned features and graying locks, sat across the room on a straight chair, holding herself tense and prim while the servant handed round cakes and cherry brandy.

"Of course I understand your presence here, Mr. Warne, and we are hopeful that you will bring us light. Poor Margery's passing was a sad matter. We brood on it much, besides having it brought to our constant remembrance. But if there is a sink of evil here, the town must be cleansed of it. I labored to save the girl as if she were my own."

"So I have heard," said Thomas kindly. "Do you agree with Mr. Haverley that it was a death of violence and not some sudden illness come upon her?"

"Oh, sir, I do not know!" She drew a thin, bluish hand across her forehead. "It may have been her state. She had but newly told us that she was to bear a child in autumn."

"A child? I had not heard of that," said Thomas, turning to Mr. Haverley.

"Nor had I," said the minister sharply.

"I know. We have not spoken of it abroad. I think she had told no one but myself and Stephen. Her father and sister, perhaps. Have you consulted with them?"

"I have not, but I shall. Are such seizures common to women at that time? My mother was a midwife and I was brought up amongst lyings-in, but I never heard—"

"Oh, no, no," cried Dame Alice, hastily. "Not common, but still, such as might be. But no, sir. To tell you the truth, I do not think it was any mortal thing. I think it was for her wickedness that she was cut off. How it came about, I do not know. It may be that Satan called her home."

"You think she was wicked? That again I had not been told—"

"But I told you indeed," cried Mr. Haverley, flushing, "I told you how, on her very last day on earth, I had to reprove her for frivolity and unseemly carriage as she walked along the common."

"Gaiety, singing, and wearing ribbons in her hair! Did her wickedness consist of that?"

"They are certainly not the behavior of one of God's Elect," said the minister stubbornly.

Dame Alice nodded. "My daughter-in-law," she explained, "was not a godly woman. Her soul took no delight in the contemplation of its Lord, only in the things of this world. I did what I could to save her life, but all the while I strove at the bedside, I felt that I was being overwhelmed by a supernatural power. Her own sister watched with me and half a dozen other women. They can bear witness to what I did, how I used one healing measure after another until I had tried all to no avail."

"You believe that no mortal part had a hand then?"

Alice Reeve studied the tiny blue veins running under the skin of her tightly clenched hands.

"I did not say that," she murmured cautiously. "It is well known that Satan can only work upon man through other men, through men who have bound their souls to him and become his human instruments."

"You are thinking of Joan Alder. But you have not brought charges against her."

Dame Alice looked him straight in the eye. "It was not needful, Mr. Warne. The whole town has charged her. The whispers—"

"Who started the whispers?"

She flung out her hands in a helpless gesture.

"Ah, who can tell where whispers start? I have no proof that she injured Margery and none that she did not. But she is a giddy, carnal wench who should be warned out of town if nothing worse."

"Was she at your house that day when Margery fell ill?"

"Yes, she was there," Dame Alice admitted grudgingly.

"And others?"

"Many others—in and out all day."

"So any one of them could have done the hurt and you not known of it?"

"What sort of hurt?"

"Put herbs in Margery's food and drink—or a more active poison."

"They could—if it were the work of a poison."

"Do you know of any drugs or medicines that would bring about such an illness?"

"I? No."

"Do you, Mr. Haverley?"

The minister shook his head sadly.

"Then I should like to speak with Mr. Stephen Reeve."

Dame Alice clasped her hands. "Oh, no—not with Stephen!" she cried. "He has suffered enough! What more do you want to know? I will tell you all—anything you ask! Pray, do not trouble my son!"

"I am sorry," said Thomas Warne.

She bowed her head, rose, and stepped past him into a dim passageway crowded with heavy chests.

"Stephen!" she called, her voice tremulous.

Stephen came among them so swiftly that Thomas had the feeling that he had been close by and listening. It was true, as Mr. Haverley had said, that he was comely: tall and slight, with pale golden hair and warm gray eyes, a girl's mouth, and an uncertain chin. His mother put her hand on the sleeve of his velvet coat and drew him down beside her on a sofa.

"Stephen," she said, "this is Mr. Warne from Boston. It is unfortunate, but as you know, gossip has spread so wide that Mr. Haverley was loathe to proceed in avenging Margery's death until he was strengthened with other opinion."

Stephen Reeve looked downward at the toes of his well-made London boots. He did not look at his visitor or acknowledge the introduction. He waited, sucking his lower lip.

"Mr. Reeve," said Thomas slowly, reproaching himself inwardly because he could feel his own lip wanting to curl, "as I came into town I stopped by your wife's grave. I read on her stone that she was but eighteen years old. That is not an age for death—not for a girl who sings and wears ribbons in her hair and gathers willow catkins, a girl who is to bear a child."

Stephen Reeve turned white but his gaze did not lift. "No," he said.

"Mr. Reeve, what do you know of the way your wife died?"

"I—I—only know—how sweet she was—and how—! Poor Margery!"

He gulped, and stared miserably out of the window at the broad sweep of the fields, wet and black, waiting for the plow, dotted here and there with shocks of last year's Indian corn.

Thomas Warne rose. "I am sorry to trouble you further, Mr. Reeve, but one thing I must know. If you are not certain as to what caused the untimely taking off of your wife, why did you have the words *Bewitched to Death* cut on her gravestone?"

"I—I do not know that either. I cannot remember who advised me thus. There were so many besetting me, bemoaning her, trying to comfort me, making things worse—so many who had loved Margery. All the town seemed sure of the cause. I tell you, I do not know."

"I shall leave now to go and speak with the girl who is said to have had a reason for harming her, a girl who is carnally fair, Mr. Reeve. It is hinted that you may have found her so."

But Stephen Reeve looked at him dully, seeming to feel no thrust at all.

"Speak with whomever you will," he answered. "You cannot bring Margery back that way."

Murmuring his apologies, his thanks and farewells, Thomas stepped out through the wide front door and stood again at the edge of Pemble Common. He paused a moment under the leafless elms bare on the bright sky, waiting for the minister to join him, but Stephen had closed the door fast and it did not open again. A swinging golden sign on the front of the square house near the Boston Road told him that this was the Wheat Sheaf tavern, and when he entered, the host, a voluble, pot-bellied man in a leather apron, hastened to set out beef and beer. No, there'd be no trouble about his seeing the witch. Not that the poor girl was a witch, to his mind. 'Course, he had to keep her under lock and key because Constable said so, but that was better than sending her down to gaol in Salem Town. Oh, she was quiet enough. Ate what victuals he sent up and bothered nobody. Her husband? Henry Alder? No, there was nothing about his death to come in question. Got in a fight with a drunken Indian when he was up the country hunting deer last autumn, and the Indian shot first. No, there'd never been any talk before against Joan. How did he think young Mistress Reeve met her death? Why, eating spoiled meat, likely, or the hot, foreign spices from Salem market that the rich set such store by. It was women's gossip, the whole of it. If they was all kept as busy at home as his wife, they'd have no time to go clappering round amongst themselves causing trouble. He winked at Thomas, not noticing the tall hat which the young man still carried under his arm, not knowing he was talking to a minister.

It was a rather small iron key that the host gave to Thomas when he went upstairs, and it fitted an ill-hung lock on a rail pine door. He knocked gently and then called aloud.

"Mistress Alder! May I come in?"

"Who's to stop you?" cried out a warm, pulsing voice that in other circumstances might have been gay. Still Thomas waited.

"You are—if you will. But I hope you will not. I have come here to prove you are not a witch, Joan."

He heard her quick steps moving across the floor and then she called, "You must fetch the key. Or do you have it?"

"I have it."

He turned it slowly in the lock and swung the door open.

He had not fully realized what Mr. Haverley meant when he had said Joan was carnally fair, but now he saw and he agreed. She wore no ribbons or jewels, only an indifferent russet dress, and her chestnut hair hung loose on her shoulders; but if there was ever a woman better designed to put a man in mind of the things of the flesh, Thomas Warne had never seen one and he was not quite sure that he wanted to. Her eyes were warm and brown, and her person was of such a soft, ripe roundness everywhere. She was not bold, and she was not coy, she was simple and direct and somewhat defiant as she took a step toward him.

"So you think I am not a witch! Well now, praise God! Then the whole world has not gone mad, after all."

"No, it has not, but there are those who have, and we must find a way to make them sane again. I will tell you why I am here so you will see it is in no cause against you. We have heard in Boston of Mistress Reeve's strange death and that witchcraft was suspected and a woman accused. I have been sent to find out the truth of the matter."

She stood looking steadily at him. The room behind her was empty, save for a straw pallet and a broken table and sunlight pouring through a dormer window that looked out at the early afternoon, blue and golden on the burying hill.

After a long moment she said tensely, "Do—do you think you will find it?"

"I am not sure. I mean to try."

"You mean you will try for a witch? Throw me into a pond to see if I will float, and prick my flesh with needles to see if I will scream?"

"No. I shall not try you for a witch, for you are none. There are no witches, Joan. Many of us do not believe in them anymore. In time, no one will. But I want to find out how Margery died."

"Oh," she cried, "if only you would! Then they would suffer for it and I could go free! She was so merry, and so eager for life, and gay and brave and innocent, like a child!

"And so sweet to all! I cried in my pillow all that night it happened. And whoever did it—I hope they burn in Hell. I hope they burn in Hell forever. I hope—"

"Hush, do not curse them, Joan. There are the courts of law to punish sinners, and if they fail to do so, God will not fail. But you think someone is guilty therein? You do not think it was an illness only?"

She shook her head vehemently. "But it could not be! No one dies like that, with no ailing season! Not unless they be old. Not so quick, with such sharp, bloody pain."

"You were there?"

"Yes, I was there, and if you want to hear about it, it happened so: we met at noon at Mistress Reeve's house, and first we were to take food and drink and then to quilting. Dame Alice is a rich woman and not niggardly, and her servants went round and round the board with silver trays and baskets, and we took what we would."

"What did you eat yourself? If you try to think of that it may help you to remember what was served."

"What did I eat? Why, I, myself, took a bit of ham and corn cake, and pumpkin stewed with molasses and chopped walnuts, a handful of raisins, and a cup of spiced wine. I think that was all."

"Did you notice what Margery ate?"

Joan wrinkled her forehead. "No, I do not think so. She sat three places off. Meat, I think, but it need not have been ham, for there was turkey and venison as well. She asked me to pass her the pumpkin though; stewed with chopped walnut meats, as I told you, and I remember she complained because there was a sharp bit of nut shell in the serving she ladled up for herself. She laughed, and made a face, and spat it out in her napkin."

"Were any of the rest of you troubled so?"

"I do not know. No one remarked on it. I, myself, was not."

"Do you remember who sat beside her?"

"Yes. She sat between her mother-in-law and her own sister Sarah, and once Stephen came in from the study where he was working on his account books, and she fed him raisins with her fingers. You should have seen Sarah Hampstead's face! He courted her first, you know, and she felt so sure of him. But it was Margery he married."

Thomas sat still, looking at her. Did she know, he wondered, what she was telling him? Was her tongue innocent, or malicious and not too clever? If she kept on so, she would implicate everybody in town.

"I suppose," he said, "Mr. Haverley was there."

Joan opened her soft, bright eyes wider.

"Why, how did you know?" she cried. "He came in and stood behind Margery and Dame Alice and asked the blessing. Such a long blessing, and we had to keep our heads bowed! I got a crook in my neck. Oh, and one thing more, I remember—"

"What was that?"

"Why, Margery and Sarah! They came in together just before Mr. Haverley began to pray. They were late and made such a commotion sitting down. Margery had been to see her father and he'd made her take a dish of parsnips there, he was so proud to have them thawed this early from the ground. She feared it would spoil her appetite."

He stared at her, unsmiling. Suddenly she faltered, stopped, and caught her hand across her mouth.

"I—I see," she whispered through her fingers, "why you are looking at me so, why there is such—such a change of weather about you. I see! I've shown you how all of them, Alice and Stephen and Sarah and Simon Hampstead, how even Mr. Haverley could have poisoned her! But I was only telling you what happened!" Her voice broke.

"And it was you who handed her the pumpkin, Joan," he told her soberly, "stewed soft, and full of nut meats. It would disguise a poison well."

He locked the door behind him, returned the key to the host, and walked out on Pemble Green. Mr. Haverley was just coming away from the brick house. He hailed his younger colleague a little guiltily.

"I apologize, sir. But I felt my duty was to the mourning family. You had left them in an ill case, and much disturbed. Dame Alice weeps and Mr. Stephen hardly restrains himself from it. Are you any further with the business?"

"I think so. I have spoken with Joan Alder."

"Indeed? You think she is guilty then?"

Thomas stood very still, the sun warm on his bare head and the wet mud of the common land making a little sucking sound round his boot soles.

"Mr. Haverley, how do you suggest that Joan Alder killed Margery Reeve?"

"Why—why—through some subtlety of Satan's power—I do not know how. Witches, we know well, are but his instruments. He uses them as he will. He teaches them ways of doing we cannot detect. He—"

"You do not agree that Joan or someone else may have poisoned Margery in a mortal way with an earthly poison, that she was not slain by any supernatural means at all?"

"I cannot deny it. Satan may work in that way as well as in any other."

"I suppose you are right. I agree with you that any man's death at the hand of another man is Satan's work. But let us go and talk with her blood kin. We may find an answer there."

The two men walked silently to the small house under the willow trees, the home of Simon Hampstead, the miller. Simon himself opened the door when they knocked on it, a tall, bent man, his face red with rage and his small blue eyes burning.

Behind him stood his daughter Sarah, dark and thin, blotches of crimson anger on her cheeks and her mouth drawn tight. Plainly the two had been quarreling.

"Come in," stormed Simon. "I seen ye from the mill an' come to meet ye. Still stirring the mud, be ye, Parson, an' finding it fouler all the time, I don't doubt?"

"Goodman Hampstead," replied the minister in chilling tones, "we are here to seek light on the strange way of your daughter's passing. Do you not wish—"

"All's I wish is an end of the matter! If Margery got her death 'twas from the will of God. Let out that poor wench ye have locked in the tavern, an' forget the whole thing."

Even Thomas was shocked. "You sound like an unnatural father, Goodman Hampstead!" he exclaimed.

"And he is!" cried Sarah harshly. "That he is, indeed. Perhaps he killed her himself for all we know. He hated her! He always did!"

"Hold your tongue, wench, or it's yourself ye'll hang," roared her father, and Thomas could see a sudden ugly fear growing in the miller's narrow eyes. The red died away from his face and he turned, almost fawning, toward the ministers.

"'Tis true, I was never so fond of my younger girl as of Sarah here. But 'twas not out of nature. She came at the cost of her mother's life."

"That's a musty lie," Sarah told them. "You was fond of none of us, not even Mother in her time. But you hated Margery the worst because of Uncle William down in Salem Town. Because he had money and ships and never a child at all, and you think to have them when he is gone, but he had always favored Margery. And then she came that day and told us she was to bear. 'A son,' she said. 'Think how that will please Uncle William!' I saw the hate in your eyes when she said that. And she died before dark."

"Ye saw hate in my eyes!" he shouted, his temper running as untrammeled now as the brook that lashed past the little house. "An' what was the hate in my eyes 'side of the hate in yours when she stood up to marry Stephen Reeve? An' it wasn't me by her bedstead when she died! It was her dear loving sister!"

It was near an accusation and should have driven the sharp-tongued Sarah to greater fury, but instead she stopped, her mouth half open and her head thrown back. Her eyes softened and clouded, and then a look of recollection came into them, and with it a look of bewilderment.

"Yes, I was there," she whispered. "Dame Alice held a cup full of brandy and treacle and the maids were running with hot poultices. I sat on the edge of the counterpane and tried to hold Margery's hand, but she twisted so. 'Oh, Sarah, the little knives!' She kept saying. 'They cut me everywhere!' And then she doubled her body and held herself, and choked and shuddered, and then—and then, she was gone!"

"The little knives!" cried Mr. Haverley in triumph. "We must search again in the witch's house. We shall find a poppet in it—a poppet resembling Mistress Margery, made with some of her hair or nail parings, no doubt. A poppet stuck with knives, for that is the way witches work. You have helped us indeed, Sarah."

But Sarah had fallen, sobbing, on a three-legged stool beside the chimney. Her father stood near her, his chin sunk in the open collar of his tow shirt, and even he seemed to have no words any more. Silently the two ministers took their leave, but as he pulled the outer door shut behind him, Mr. Haverley began to speak.

"I shall have out the deacons and their wives, and we will tear the Alder house apart, beam and shingle, if need be. Will you aid us, Mr. Warne?"

"No," said Thomas, thoughtfully. "I understood you had searched the house before and found no ill evidence."

"And so we have, but from what the sister tells us now, 'tis plain we have not been thorough. You do not agree?"

"It would seem to me, sir," answered the young man slowly, "that the time has come to take counsel with God in this matter."

"You mean you would resort to the Scripture or to prayer?"

"To prayer, perhaps. In any case, I shall walk out into the fields a little, into the clear air. There is a fog on Pemble Green, Mr. Haverley, a fog of fear and suspicion, and somewhere in it, I do not know where, there is hate. I must pass beyond it for a time in order to summon to this matter thoughts that are my own and not the thoughts that others would think for me."

The minister shrugged. "Go where you will, and I pray that God may instruct you, as I feel he has already instructed me. Perhaps we may have tangible evidence for you when you return."

"Perhaps," said Thomas evenly, walking away, his head bent.

He plodded through the gray and yellow fields, along the flooding brooks that reflected the blue sky, and then the ruddy sunset, and then the emptiness of the early dark, and he did not wonder that Margery Reeve had died *Aet. 18.* With so many who wished her ill, he only wondered that she had lived as long as she had. And he asked himself questions and found no answers at all. Dame Alice had disapproved of her son's wife, but was that disapproval strong enough to cause her to bring about the girl's death? And Stephen himself seemed all dissolved away in grief, but was it honest grief or a shield he had devised to keep his own guilt from becoming known? Had he tired of Margery and desired Joan, newly free, or desired Sarah, his old love again? And as for Joan, knowing herself a tempting widow, had she with a bold stroke cut off the single life that stood between her and a rich young man?

Had Sarah Hampstead so abandoned herself to violence and passion, allowed her soul to become so corrupted with jealousy, that she could desire her sister's husband strongly enough to make her sister die? There had been violence and hatred in the house of the miller, stronger, or at least closer to the surface, than in any other spot on Pemble Green. Could a man slay two generations of his own flesh and blood to ensure himself an inheritance of money and ships? Yes, Thomas remembered, it had many times been done.

The young minister walked till the moon rose, round and white between the bare elm boughs, and lights sprang up in all the crooked little houses, and in from the fields and woods the men came trooping home. And he lived over in his mind every scene that had passed before his eyes that day, listened again to every word that every lip had spoken, and tried to make his way into the dark chambers that lie within the hearts of men. When he walked back to Pemble Green he thought he knew. He thought he knew, but he was not certain, and he pondered long and desperately on how a man may invoke the judgment of God. In the end he remembered a way the country folk have used through all the years—an old, simple way.

Mr. Haverley ushered him into his lamplit kitchen and the servant maid ladled up for them the seethed fish he had smelled cooking when he had come in at noon. They ate it with barley bread and drank mugs of dark, heavy cider, and the older man admitted disconsolately that they had found no poppets and no little knives, and he asked if God had seen fit to reveal His Truth to Thomas Warne.

"He has revealed to me a way to proceed," Thomas told him cautiously. "Is it here as in most of our towns, sir, that the entire congregation of the church can be readily assembled at the ringing of the bell?"

"Indeed, yes. It were necessary for our own defense if for no other reason. We have not yet forgotten the Indian wars."

"Then have the bell rung and have Mistress Alder brought from the Wheat Sheaf. Perhaps we cannot yet resolve this thing, but we can try."

Mr. Haverley hastened outside, his cloak flapping in the windy spring night, and Thomas waited a little till the bell in its low tower had been ringing for some moments and light shone out dimly through the diamond-shaped panes of Pemble Church. He waited till the thin voices and moving shadows that were the townspeople had all passed inside, leaving the common bare under the white moon. Then he, too, crossed the narrow strip of sodden grass and walked into the assembly, striding forward to take his place in a chair that Mr. Haverley motioned him to, at the left of the pulpit.

The clamor of the crowd died suddenly, and Thomas sat there for a moment facing them—the calm-faced wives wearing a sort of weathered beauty more becoming than fine garments, and the sturdy, blunt-featured men, used to earning their living by ploughing the fields or the sea. Alice Reeve sat in the front pew on the women's side, as became her goodly estate. Her face was pale and her eyes bright, and she wore a fur-edged mantle. Her son sat across the aisle from her, his jaw slack, his eyes dull and empty.

Searching further back in the crowd, Thomas marked Sarah Hampstead, upright as if a vise gripped her, her dark eyes burning in her white face. Her father, too, had come forth when the bell called him, but he did not meet the young minister's eyes or the eyes of any man. He did not lift his shaggy head. A stout man in a red coat, holding a constable's staff, crouched on a bench by the door, gripping the shapely wrist of Joan Alder who bent forward eagerly, her face full of hope rather than fear.

He turned then and looked across the pulpit into the troubled face of Mr. Haverley, and signaled him to address the congregation.

Mr. Haverley prayed briefly, and then Thomas stepped forward.

"My betters in Boston," he began, with a smile that he hoped was full of charming humility, "welcome always a call from the sister churches, from the golden branches of the one great, glowing candlestick that is the Church of Christ in Massachusetts. It is an opportunity for those of us who go forth among you not only to render aid but to reassure ourselves of the efficacy of the preaching you enjoy, to ascertain if you are instructed in all His Works as you have a right to be."

Out of the corner of his eye he could see Mr. Haverley start upright and grip the arms of his chair. He had expected that, but he went on.

"So I shall seek to try you tonight only with the simplest attribute of His glory, to know whether or not you be informed therein. I shall call upon each of you to repeat Our Lord's Prayer, and as I thus indicate, will you rise and do so, that I may bear the word back to Boston that holy uses are well known amongst you."

He did not look at Mr. Haverley as he pointed his finger here and there among the congregation, as the men and women of Pemble Green rose one by one and pronounced "Our Father," having been taught it at the cradleside and knowing it as well as they knew the names they bore. Finally he made an end, and then he paused and looked around him for a long moment.

"And now," he said, "we pass from this to another thing, yet we take the same road on our way. Certain among you have not yet returned me the prayer, because I have not yet called upon you. One of you, at least, will be unable to say it."

He did not look into any pair of eyes. He looked at the nail-studded door at the back of the room. He wanted no more foreknowledge than he had. He did not want the proof to break irrevocably upon him before it broke on the others.

"It is an old belief that came here from England with our grandfathers in the first ships, and from what older country it came into England, I do not know, that no witch, no instrument of Satan can repeat this prayer; that it will turn to meaningless syllables in the vile throat of such a one; that out of such cursed lips the sacred words shall not and cannot issue."

"But you told me," Joan Alder's voice rang clear as a chime from the back of the church, "you told me today when you came to see me at the Wheat Sheaf that you do not believe there are any witches. If there are no witches, how can such a thing be?"

Half the congregation turned toward her, and half bent forward to hear his reply.

"Indeed I said to you that there be no witches, Joan, and I do not believe there are. But there are Satan's instruments still. Anyone who kills another—by any means at all—is such an instrument. He need not do it by sorcery. He can do it as well with vicious herbs or sharp blade. If any living soul in this assembly has contrived the death of Margery Reeve, he is such an instrument, and he will not be able to utter the holy words of Our Lord."

He waited. For a moment silence held them, and then the benches creaked and the congregation settled back with a sigh of relief, once they had unwound the meaning of what he said. They had nothing to fear, for had they not already proved their innocence to him before they even knew what they did? But whom had he not yet called on? Heads turned and necks crooked. Simon Hampstead looked up, smiling bleakly. Dame Alice smiled too, frosty and secure in her rich cloak.

"Sarah Hampstead, will you repeat the Lord's Prayer?"

Sarah Hampstead stood up. "Our—Our Father—" she began tremulously, and broke off.

"Continue," he said evenly, "if you can."

"Our Father who art in Heaven, hallowed be Thy Name," gasped Sarah. Through to the end she gasped it, and then sat down and began to cry quietly into the folds of her cloak.

Thomas Warne let his eyes wander about the hushed room. Then he turned to Stephen Reeve. Stephen rose and answered straightforwardly in a toneless voice. He recited the prayer without missing a syllable. Then he too sat down.

"Simon Hampstead!" Thomas called sharply.

The miller stood up, scraping his rough boots on the pine floor. He looked boldly toward the pulpit, then lowered his head again like a bull about to charge.

"Our-Father-who-art-in-Heaven-hallowed-be-Thy-Name-Thy-Kingdom-come-Thy-Will-be-done—" He rushed through the prayer without halt or error and threw himself back into his seat.

And then Thomas called on Joan Alder.

Joan stood up and curtsied, and smiled all about her.

"Our Father who art in Heaven," she chanted sweetly, piously, her brown eyes cast down demurely. And the accused witch gave the Lord his own again, word for word. Then she smiled again, and dimpled toward the young man in the pulpit. She settled herself once more on the bench, cocked up her bright head at the constable, and ran out the tip of her saucy pink tongue.

"And now, Dame Alice Reeve," said Thomas blandly, smiling down at the thin, aristocratic woman in the fur-edged cape.

Dame Alice rose graciously. "I shall be glad to oblige you, sir," she answered, smoothing her skirts about her, lifting her head, and stepping away from the pew.

And everyone waited to listen to Dame Alice, because she was the town's great lady, and respected, if not loved. She would settle this Boston jackanapes who had been putting them through their paces like dancing bears. They waited and waited, and Dame Alice licked her lips and moved her throat, and gave forth no sound at all. But her face had gone pale, and then white, and her eyes were beginning to stare.

"The Lord's Prayer, Dame Alice. You can say it—if you are not an instrument of Satan!"

"I—I can say it," croaked Dame Alice, her voice breaking on

a high note—a sudden note of hysteria—and then dropping away. *"Nema reverof yrolg eht dna rewop—"*

She stopped in horror and bewilderment, her thin fingers plucking at her throat and mouth.

Thomas held up his hand. "Tell us what she is saying, Mr. Haverley, and what it means."

Mr. Haverley stood up, pale and swaying, gripping the tall, carved back of his pulpit chair.

"She is saying—she is saying—Oh, God help us, I have heard it done at the College as a student's jest—she is saying Our Lord's Prayer backwards! A sure mark of Satan! She is—she is—! Be gone, all of you! Sexton! Constable! Clear the church!"

Later they were alone, the three of them, Thomas and Mr. Haverley seated beside Alice Reeve where she crouched in her pew, shaken with mad, convulsive weeping. Her son Stephen was not with her. He had risen and gone with the others, without giving her a backward look. He must indeed, Thomas thought, have loved his wife Margery. Simon Hampstead had led his daughter away, his heavy arm gently supporting her, and Joan Alder had flirted her skirts a little, drooped her eyelashes, and walked off, a free woman.

"You knew," murmured Mr. Haverley across the woman's bent head. "You knew before she revealed herself, or rather, before God revealed her. You knew—but how?"

"When I walked through the fields and thought about it," answered Thomas simply, "I asked myself which one it could be, and I could not tell. And then I asked myself which ones it could *not* be."

"And then?"

"I thought first of the Hampsteads, and of the hatred and distrust that hung like wood smoke in their kitchen. And then I thought: Simon fears that Sarah may be the one, and since she is all he has left, he tried to shield her till she angered him too far. That was why he wished us to drop the matter. And Sarah burns with hatred for her father because she thinks the crime is his. And therefore, since each suspects the other, each must be innocent. That is clear, is it not?"

"Yes, yes, I should have seen that. But what was there to tell you it could not have been Mistress Joan?"

"Not Mistress Joan. She has a merry eye that roams everywhere and settles nowhere for long. There are too many young men in the world and they are too easy come by for her to risk her body and soul to make sure of one."

"Yes, of course. I fear we shall have trouble with her yet, trouble of another kind. And why did you dismiss Stephen?"

"Because he is not of sufficient valor to crush a caterpillar on a maize stalk. Not only does he lack the capacity for violence, but he lacks spirit and manliness, and then I asked myself why this was so."

"Still I do not see."

"There is a master in every house, sir, and in a house where the woman is master they will change natures in some if not in all, and we can look for wry things to fall about. Remember it was Dame Alice who spoke with us, who tried to shield him from our questions. It was Dame Alice who told us what she wished for us to know. Stephen may have suspected her. I think that he did, for he has not stayed to protest her innocence, though we have not had her own confession, even yet. I put it to you that it was Dame Alice who egged you on to condemn for witchcraft a girl she feared her son might turn to, now she had deprived him of his wife. You were guilty a little in this, since you permitted yourself to be led. Is that not so?"

"God forgive me," murmured the minister. "It is as you say. I trusted her piety, and I reverenced her too highly for her estate, and she led me as though my nose were looped with an iron ring."

Thomas turned to the hunched figure between them.

"Mistress Reeve," he asked steadily, "how did you do it, and why? Of what substance were your little knives?"

"They were of glass," she whispered. "Of glass, crushed fine. I broke out a tiny windowpane, high and unnoticed in the rear attic gable close to the chimney. I powdered it in the wooden mortar in the kitchen when the house was asleep. I sat by her at the table, and let it fall from my handkerchief into her pumpkin during grace. It was a long grace—I had asked Mr. Haverley to say a long grace—and I stirred it in well with a spoon."

"Why?"

She looked down and her mottled features turned a darker red.

"Do not tell us it was for her wickedness, for we will not believe."

She seemed to collapse upon herself then, and let her head hang limply like a crushed marigold on its stem.

"Why should I lie now?" she murmured. "He has turned from me, and thus I lose all. Very well. I did not kill her for her wickedness. I killed her that I might have my son again as he was before she came, close and sweet, always depending on me, always needing me, the way it was when he was a little boy. I could not bear to have him grow away from me into a man. I wanted him to be mine forever, mine only. I—I would kill her again for that."

Mr. Haverley coughed and stood up. "I think it is time we— but, Thomas, there is one thing more. How could you be so sure of the old belief, so sure that the instrument of Satan would falter in the prayer?"

Thomas looked down soberly at the disheveled head of Pemble Green's great lady.

"It was *her faith* I trusted rather than my own, sir. I depended on her belief that there are human instruments of Satan, and if I could convince her that she had become such an instrument, I felt she could not keep from revealing that she bore the mark. Perhaps—I would not be presumptuous enough to declare it, but it may be—perhaps God counseled me to proceed so. What are we, any of us, unless he gives us understanding of the dark ways of our neighbors' hearts? It is always therein that we must look, to try to illumine their darkness with His Light."

The two ministers walked out of the church side by side, Mr. Haverley to summon the constable to make an arrest for murder, not for witchcraft, and Thomas Warne to turn his back on Pemble Green from which the fog had now lifted.

THE WITCH SHEEP

· BY ALICE MORSE EARLE ·

I n the darkness of Christmas morning in the year 1811, old
Benny Nichols could not sleep. He was not thinking of Santa
Claus nor of Christmas gifts; he was watching for the first gray
dawn which marked his regular rising hour, and he tossed and
turned, wondering why he was so wakeful, until at last he rose in
despair and lighted a candle to discover how long he had to wait
before daybreak. To his amazement he found the hands of the old
clock pointing to the hour of nine, and as he stood shivering,
candle in hand, staring at the apparently deceitful, bland face, the
clock raised its voice and struck nine, loudly and brassily, as if to
prove that its hands and face told the truth. Benny then walked
quickly to the window, and saw that the apparent darkness and
length of the night came from a great wall of snow which covered
the entire window and which had nearly all fallen since the
previous sunset.

Keenly awake at once when he recognized the lateness of the
hour, the old man wakened his wife Debby, and bade her "hurry
up and git somethin' to eat. It's nine o'clock and we've had the
wust snowstorm ye ever see, and me a-layin' here in bed, and
them new sheep a-walkin' into the sea and gittin' drownded!"

Benny was a wizened-faced, dried-up old man, who was
shepherd of a large Narragansett farm which lay between Pender

135

Zeke's Corner and the bay. He knew well the danger that came to sheep in a heavy snowstorm. He had seen a great flock of a hundred timid, shrinking creatures retreat and cower one behind the other to shelter themselves from the fierce beating of the wind and sleet, until, in spite of his efforts, all were edged into the sea and lost, save a half-dozen whose throats were cut by him with a jackknife to save the mutton. Without waiting for any warm food, he cautiously opened the door to dig himself out.

"Ye can't go out, Benny Nichols, in them shoes," said Debby, firmly. "I told ye long ago they were half wore out—here, put on yer Sunday long-boots."

This suggestion was a bitter one to prudent Benny, who expected to have those boots for Sunday wear for the next ten years, just as he had for the past ten; and he knew well what a hard day's work he had before him, and how destructive it would prove to shoe leather. But Debby was firm, and, seizing the great boots from the nail on which they hung, she poured out the flaxseed with which they were always kept filled when they were not on Benny's feet. The old man pulled them on his shrivelled legs with a groan at Debby's extravagance, and then proceeded to dig out a path in the snow.

Benny had not seen such a snowstorm since the great "Hessian snowstorm" in the winter of 1778, when so many Hessian soldiers perished of cold and exposure. When he reached the surface and could look around him, he saw with satisfaction that the snow and wind had blown during the previous night *away* from the water, hence his sheep would hardly be drowned. He quickly discovered a strange-shaped bank of snow by the side of one of the great hay-ricks, so common throughout Narragansett, and he shrewdly suspected that some of his sheep were underneath the great drift. When he carefully searched with a rake-stale, this proved to be the case, and when he shovelled them out all in the mound were alive and well. In a snowdrift by the side of a high stone wall he found the remainder of his flock, save one, a fine little ewe of the creeper breed, the rarest and most valued of all his stock. As sheep-sheds at that time were unknown in Narragansett, the loss of sheep was great in the Christmas storm, and many cattle were frozen in the drifts.

One shepherd noted two weeks later that the hungry cattle he foddered never touched a full lock of hay that he had thrown on the top of a little hillock of snow near his rick. So he thrust at it with his hay-tines, and in so doing he lifted off a great shell of snow-crust, and there peered out of the whiteness the bronze, wrinkled face of the old squaw Betty Aaron, who was sitting bolt upright, frozen stiff, and dead, her chin resting on both hands, her elbows on her knees.

Benny was justly proud of his rescued flock, though he mourned the one sheep that was lost, and blamed himself for sleeping so late, saying, he "wouldn't have minded spoilin' his roast-meat boots if he could have found the creeper."

On the fourteenth day of January, Benny Nichols chanced to see in the snow, by the side of a hay-rick which stood a mile away from his home, a small hole about half an inch in diameter, which his practised eye recognized at once as a "breathing-hole," and which indicated that some living thing had been snowed in and was lying underneath. He broke away the covering of icy crust, and to his amazement saw a poor creature of extraordinary appearance, which he at first hardly could believe was his own lost creeper sheep. She was alive, but alas! in such a sorry plight.

The hungry sheep, in her three weeks' struggle against starvation, had eaten off every fibre of her own long wool that she could reach, and she lay bare and trembling in the cold air, too weak to move, too feeble to bleat either in distress or welcome. Old Benny wrapped the half-dead creature in the corner of his cloak and carried her home to Debby, who fairly shed tears at the sight of the poor naked skeleton of a sheep. Tenderly did the kind woman wrap the frozen ewe in an old flannel petticoat and feed her with warm milk, a few drops only at first, and then with much caution until the sheep was able to digest her ordinary food. In a week the creeper seemed as strong as ever, quickly gained the lost flesh, and could bleat both loud and long. And with returning health she grew active and mischievous, and was constantly thrusting her long black nose into the most unexpected and most unsuitable places, to the great distress of careful Debby, who longed to put her out of doors.

But the sheep's lost wool could not grow as quickly as did the fat on her ribs, and she could not be thrust out thus, naked and bare, in the winter air, so Debby decided to make for the little creature a false fleece. For this purpose she took an old blue coat which had once been worn by her son, and cut off the sleeves until they were the right length to cover the ewe's forelegs. She then sewed at the waist of the coat two sleeves from an old red flannel shirt; these were to cover Nanny's hind legs. And when Debby drew on the gay jacket and buttoned it up over the sheep's long backbone with the large brass coat-buttons, there never was seen such a comical, stunted, hind-side-foremost caricature of what is itself a caricature—an organ grinder's monkey.

When Benny carried the gayly dressed Nanny out to the enclosed yard, it was hard to tell which exhibition of feeling was the keenest—poor, unconscious, and absurd Nanny's delight in her freedom and her eager desire to take her place with her old companions, or the consternation and terror of the entire flock at the strange wild beast which was thus turned loose among them.

They ran from side to side, and crowded each other against the paling so unceasingly and so wildly, that Benny carried the unwilling ewe back to the kitchen.

At nightfall, however, Benny again placed Nanny in the open field with the sheep, thinking that they would gradually, throughout the darkness, become used to the presence of her little harlequin jacket, and allow her to graze by their side in peace.

That night two cronies of Benny's came from a neighboring farm to talk over that ever-interesting topic, the great snowstorm, and to buy some of his lambs. The three old men sat by the great fireplace in the old raftered kitchen in the pleasant glow from the blazing logs, each sipping with unction a mug of Benny's famous flip, while Debby rubbed with tallow the sadly stiffened long-boots that had been worn in the Christmas snow.

Suddenly a loud wail of distress rang in their ears, the door was thrust violently open, and in stumbled the breathless form of the tall, gaunt old Negro woman, Tuggie Bannocks. She was a relic of old slavery times, who lived on a small farm near the old Gilbert Stuart Mill on Petaquamscut River. They all knew her well. She had bought many a pound of wool from Benny to wash and card and spin into yarn, and she always helped Debby in that yearly trial of patience and skill—her soap-making. The old Negro woman had double qualifications to make her of use in this latter work: her long, strong arms could stir the soap untiringly for hours, and then she knew also how to work powerful charms— traditional relics of Voodooism—to make the soap always turn out a success.

Tuggie Bannocks sank upon the table by the fire, murmuring: "Tanks be to Praise! Tanks be to Praise!" and closed her eyes in speechless exhaustion. Debby took a half-crushed basket of eggs from the old woman's arm, drew off her red woollen mittens, and rubbed briskly her long, cold claws of hands. Benny had a vague rememberance of the old-time "emergency" saying, "feathers for fainters," and seized a turkey's wing that was in daily use as a hearth-brush, thrust it into the flames, and then held the scorching feathers under the old woman's nose until all the room were coughing and choking with the stifling smoke.

Spluttering and choking at the dense feather-smoke, Tuggie gasped out: "I ain't dead yit—I specks I shall be soon, though— 'cause I seen the old witch a-ridin'—I'se most scared to death" (then in a fainter voice)—"give me a mug of that flip." Startled, Benny quickly drew a great mug of home-brewed beer and gave it a liberal dash of Jamaica rum and sugar, then seized from the fire the red-hot "loggerhead" and thrust it seething into the liquid until the flip boiled and bubbled and acquired the burnt, bitter flavor that he knew Tuggie dearly loved. The old woman moaned and groaned as she lay on the tabletop, but watched the brewing of the flip with eager eye, and sat up with alacrity to drink it.

With many a shuddering sigh and many a glance behind her at the kitchen door, and crossing her fingers to ward off evil spirits she began: "Ye know, Miss Nichols, I told ye I was witch-rid by ole Mum Amey, an' this how I know I was. Ye see I was a-goin' to work a charm on her first off—not to hurt her none, jess to bother her a leetle—an' I jess put my project on the fire one night, an' it jess a-goin' to boil, an' in come her ugly, ole grinnin' face at the door, an' say she a-goin' to set with me a spell."

Mum Amey was a wrinkled half-breed Indian of fabulous age and crabbed temper.

"She walk over to the chimbly to light her pipe an' ask me what I a-cookin', an' I say Ise a-makin' glue, cause Ise afeard she see the rabbit's foot in the pot, an' I say it all done, an' yank the pot off the crane so she can't see into it. An' of course when I take the project off the fire afore it's worked, it break the charm; an' wuss still, I can't never try no project on her no more. Ole Mum Amey larf, an' say a-leerin' at me, that pot of glue won't never stick nothin' no more. An' ever sence that night I been witch-rid. Mornin's when I wakes up I sees marks of the bit in the corners of my mouth, where Mum Amey been a-ridin' me all over Boston Neck an' up the Ridge Hill till I so tired and stiff I can't hardly move. Ise been pinched in the night an' have my hair pulled. An' my butter won't come till I drop a red-hot horseshoe in the cream to drive her out. One day I jess try her to see if she a witch (though I know she one, 'cause I see her talkin' to a black cat); I drop a silver sixpence in her path, an' jess afore she get to it she turn an' go back, jess I know she would. No witch can't step over silver. An' now, Benny Nichols, I know for shore she's a witch, I see her jess now in the moonlight a-chasin' an' ridin' your sheep; an', shore's yer bawn, yer'll find some on 'em stone dead in the morning'—all on 'em mebbe!"

Benny looked wretched enough at this statement. Dearly as he loved his sheep and ready as he was to face physical discomfort and danger in their behalf, he was too superstitious to dare to go out in the night to rescue them and brave the witch.

"How did she look, Tuggie? And what did she do?" whispered awe-struck Debby.

"Oh, she was mons'ous fearsome to see! Witches don't never go in their own form when they goes to their Sabbaths. She was long an' low like a snake. She run along the groun' jess like a derminted yeller painter, a-boundin', an' leapin', an' springin', a-chasin' them pore sheeps—oh, how they run! With her old red an' blue blanket tied tight aroun' her—that's how I knowed her. An' she had big sparklin' gold dollars on her back—wages of the devil, I 'specks. Sometimes she jump in the air an' spread her wings an' fly awhile. Smoke an' sparks come outen her mouth an' nostrums! Big black horns stick outen her head! Lash her long black tail jess like the devil hisself!"

At this dramatic and breathless point in Tuggie's flip-nourished and quickly growing tale, credulous Debby, whose slow-working brain had failed to grasp all the vivid details in the black woman's fervid and imaginative description, interjected this gasping comment: "It must ha' been the devil or the creeper."

Benny jumped from his chair and stamped his foot, and at once burst into a loud laugh of intense relief, and with cheerful bravado began to explain animatedly to his open-mouthed cronies that of course anyone could see that Tuggie's sheep-chasing witch was only the creeper sheep in her new fleece, and he offered swaggeringly to go out alone to the field to bring the ewe in to prove it.

The old woman sprang to her feet, insulted and enraged at the jeering laughter and rallying jokes, and advanced threateningly toward him. Then, as if with a second thought, she stopped with a most malicious look, and in spite of Debby's conciliatory explanations and her soothing expressions "that it might have been Mum Amey after all," she thrust aside Benny's proffered mollification of a fresh mug of flip, seized her crushed basket, stalked to the door, and left the house muttering, vindictively: "High time to stop such unrageous goin's-on—dressin' up sheeps like devils—scarin' an ole woman to death an' breakin' all her aigs! Ole Tuggie Bannocks ain't forgot how to burn a project! Guess they won't larf at witches then!"

And surely enough—as days passed it could plainly be seen that the old woman had carried out her threat—for the chimney was "conjured"—was "salted." On windy nights the shepherd and his wife were sure they could hear Tuggie dancing and stamping on the roof, and she blew down smoke and threw down soot, and she called down the chimney in a fine high, shrieking voice: "I'll project ye, Benny; I'll project ye." And she burnt the cakes before the fire, and the roast upon the spit, and thrice she snapped out a blazing coal and singed a hole in Debby's best petticoat, though it was worn wrong side out as a saving-charm. And Benny could see, too, that the old ram was bewitched. The remainder of the flock soon became accustomed to the sight of Nanny's funny false fleece, but he always fled in terror at her approach. He grew thin and pale (or at any rate faded), and he would scarcely eat when Nanny was near. Debby despairingly tried a few feeble counter-charms, or "warders," but without avail. When sheep-shearing time came, however, and Nanny, shorn of her uncanny fleece and clothed in her own half-inch snowy wool, took her place with the other short-clipped members of the flock, the ram ceased to be "witch-rid"—the "project," the "conjure" was worked out. The ram grew fat and fiercely brave, and became once more the knight of the field, the lord of the domain, the patriarch, the potentate of his flock.

The story of Tuggie Bannocks's fright and her revengeful "project" spread far and wide on every farm from Point Judith to Pottawomat, and was told in later years by one generation of farmers to another. And as time rolled on and Nanny reared her lambs and they her grand-lambs, the creeper sheep were known and sold throughout Narragansett by the name of witch-sheep.

SILENCE

▪ BY MARY WILKINS FREEMAN ▪

At dusk Silence went down the Deerfield street to Ensign John Sheldon's house. She wore her red blanket over her head, pinned closely under her chin, and her white profile showed whiter between the scarlet folds. She had been spinning all day, and shreds of wool still clung to her indigo petticoat; now and then one floated off on the north wind. It was bitter cold, and the snow was four feet deep. Silence's breath went before her in a cloud; the snow creaked under her feet. All over the village the crust was so firm that men could walk upon it. The houses were half sunken in sharp, rigid drifts of snow; their roofs were laden with it; icicles hung from the eaves. All the elms were white with snow frozen to them so strongly that it was not shaken off when they were lashed by the fierce wind.

There was an odor of boiling meal in the air; the housewives were preparing supper. Silence had eaten hers; she and her aunt, Widow Eunice Bishop, supped early. She had not far to go to Ensign Sheldon's. She was nearly there when she heard quick footsteps on the creaking snow behind her. Her heart beat quickly, but she did not look around. "Silence," said a voice. Then she paused, and waited, with her eyes cast down and her mouth grave, until David Walcott reached her. "What do you out this cold night, sweetheart?" he said.

"I am going down to Goodwife Sheldon's," replied Silence. Then suddenly she cried out, wildly: "Oh, David, what is that on your cloak? What is it?"

David looked curiously at his cloak. "I see naught on my cloak save old weather stains," said he. "What mean you, Silence?"

Silence quieted down suddenly. "It is gone now," said she, in a subdued voice.

"What did you see, Silence?"

Silence turned toward him; her face quivered convulsively. "I have been seeing them everywhere all day. I have seen them on the snow as I came along."

David Walcott looked down at her in a bewildered way. He carried his musket over his shoulder and was shrugged up in his cloak; his heavy flaxen mustache was stiff and white with frost. He had just been relieved from his post as sentry, and it was no child's play to patrol Deerfield village on a day like that, nor had it been for many previous days. The weather had been so severe that even the French and Indians, lurking like hungry wolves in the neighborhood, had hesitated to descend upon the town and had stayed in camp.

"What mean you, Silence?" he said.

"What I say," returned Silence, in a strained voice. "I have seen blotches of blood everywhere all day. The enemy will be upon us."

David laughed loudly, and Silence caught his arm. "Don't laugh so loud," she whispered. Then David laughed again. "You be all overwrought, sweetheart," said he. "I have kept guard all the afternoon by the northern palisades, and I have seen not so much as a red fox on the meadow. I tell thee the French and Indians have gone back to Canada. There is no more need of fear."

"I have started all day and all last night at the sound of warwhoops," said Silence.

"Thy head is nigh turned with these troublous times, poor lass. We must cross the road now to Ensign Sheldon's house. Come quickly, or you will perish in this cold."

"Nay, my head is not turned," said Silence, as they hurried on over the crust, "the enemy be hiding in the forests beyond the meadows. David, they be not gone."

"And I tell thee they be gone, sweetheart. Think you not we should have seen their camp smoke had they been there? And we have had trusty scouts out. Come in, and my aunt, Hannah Sheldon, shall talk thee out of this folly."

The front windows of John Sheldon's house were all flickering red from the hearth fire. David flung open the door, and they entered. There was such a goodly blaze from the great logs in the wide fireplace that even the shadows in the remote corners of the large keeping-room were dusky red, and the faces of all the people in the room had a clear red glow upon them.

Goodwife Hannah Sheldon stood before the fire, stirring some porridge in a great pot that hung on the crane; some fair-haired children sat around a basket shelling corn, a slight young girl in a snuff-yellow gown was spinning, and an old woman in a quilted hood crouched in a corner of the fireplace, holding out her lean hands to the heat.

Goodwife Sheldon turned around when the door opened. "Good-day, Mistress Silence Hoit," she called out, and her voice was sweet, but deep like a man's. "Draw near to the fire, for in truth you must be near perishing with the cold."

"There'll be fire enough ere morning, I trow, to warm the whole township," said the old woman in the corner. Her small black eyes gleamed sharply out of the gloom of her great hood; her yellow face was all drawn and puckered toward the center of her shrewdly leering mouth.

"Now you hush your croaking, Goody Crane," cried Hannah Sheldon. "Draw the stool near to the fire for Silence, David. I cannot stop stirring, or the porridge will burn. How fares your aunt this cold weather, Silence?"

"Well, except for her rheumatism," replied Silence. She sat down on the stool that David placed for her, and slipped her blanket back from her head. Her beautiful face, full of a grave and delicate stateliness, drooped toward the fire, her smooth fair hair was folded in clear curves like the leaves of a lily around her ears, and she wore a high, transparent, tortoise-shell comb like a coronet in the knot at the back of her head.

David Walcott had pulled off his cap and cloak, and stood looking down at her. "Silence is all overwrought by this talk of Indians," he remarked presently, and a blush came over his weather-beaten blond face at the tenderness in his own tone.

"The Indians have gone to Canada," said Goodwife Sheldon, in a magisterial voice. She stirred the porridge faster; it was steaming fiercely.

"So I tell her," said David.

Silence looked up in Hannah Sheldon's sober, masterly face. "Goodwife, may I have a word in private with you?" She asked, in a half-whisper.

"As soon as I take the porridge off," replied Goodwife Sheldon.

"God grant it be not the last time she takes the porridge off!" said the old woman.

Hannah Sheldon laughed. "Here be Goody Crane in a sorry mind tonight," said she. "Wait till she have a sup of this good porridge, and I trow she'll pack off the Indians to Canada in a half hour!"

Hannah began dipping out the porridge. When she had placed generous dishes of it on the table and bidden everybody draw up, she motioned to Silence. "Now, Mistress Silence," said she, "come into the bedroom if you would have a word with me."

Silence followed her into the little north room opening out of the keeping-room, where Ensign John Sheldon and his wife Hannah had slept for many years. It was icy cold, and the thick fur of frost on the little windowpanes sent out sparkles in the candlelight. The two women stood beside the great chintz-draped and canopied bed, Hannah holding the flaring candle. "Now, what is it?" said she.

"Oh, Goodwife Sheldon!" said Silence. Her face remained quite still, but it was as if one could see her soul fluttering beneath it.

"You be all overwrought, as David saith," cried Goodwife Sheldon, and her voice had a motherly harshness in it. Silence had no mother, and her lover, David Walcott, had none. Hannah was his aunt, and loved him like her son, so she felt toward Silence as toward her son's betrothed.

"In truth I know not what it is," said Silence, in a kind of reserved terror, "but there has been all day a great heaviness of spirit upon me, and last night I dreamed. All day I have fancied I saw blood here and there. Sometimes, when I have looked out of the window, the whole snow hath suddenly glared with red. Goodwife Sheldon, think you the Indians and the French have in truth gone back to Canada?"

Goodwife Sheldon hesitated a moment, then she spoke up cheerily. "In truth have they!" cried she. "John said but this noon that naught of them had been seen for some time."

"So David said," returned Silence, "but this heaviness will not be driven away. You know how Parson Williams hath spoken in warning in the pulpit and elsewhere, and besought us to be vigilant. He holdeth that the savages be not gone."

Hannah Sheldon smiled. "Parson Williams is a godly man, but prone ever to look upon the dark side," said she.

"If the Indians should come tonight—" said Silence.

"I tell ye they will not come, child. I shall lay me down in that bed a-trusting in the Lord, and having no fear against the time I shall arise from it."

"If the Indians should come—Goodwife Sheldon, be not angered; hear me. If they should come, I pray you keep David here to defend you in this house, and let him not out to seek me. You know well that our house is musketproof as well as this, and it has long been agreed that they who live nearest, whose houses have not thick walls, shall come to ours and help us make defense. I pray you let not David out of the house to seek me, should there be a surprise tonight. I pray you give your promise for this, Goodwife Sheldon."

Hannah Sheldon laughed. "In truth will I give thee the promise, if it makes thee easier, child," said she. "At the very first war-screech will I tie David in the chimney-corner with my apron-string, unless you lend me yours. But there will be not war-screech tonight, nor tomorrow night, nor the night after that. The Lord will preserve His people that trust in Him. Today have I set a web of linen in the loom, and I have candles ready to dip tomorrow, and the day after I have a quilting. I look not for Indians. If they come I will set them to work. Fear not for David, sweetheart. In truth you should have a bolder heart, and you look to be a soldier's wife some day."

"I would I had never been aught to him, that he might not be put in jeopardy to defend me!" said Silence, and her words seemed visible in a white cloud at her mouth.

"We must not stay here in the cold," said Goodwife Sheldon. "Out with ye, Silence, and have a sup of hot porridge, and then David shall see ye home."

Silence sipped a cup of the hot porridge obediently, then she pinned her red blanket over her head. Hannah Sheldon assisted her, bringing it warmly over her face. "'Tis bitter cold," she said. "Now have no more fear, Mistress Silence. The Indians will not come tonight, but you come over tomorrow and keep me company while I dip the candles."

"There'll be company enough—there'll be a whole houseful," muttered the old woman in the corner; but nobody heeded her. She was a lonely and wretched old creature whom people sheltered from pity, although she was somewhat feared and held in ill repute. There were rumors that she was well versed in all the dark lore of witchcraft and held commerce with unlawful beings. The children of Deerfield village looked askance at her and clung to their mothers if they met her on the street, for they whispered among themselves that old Goody Crane rode through the air on a broom in the nighttime.

Silence and David passed out into the keen night. "If you meet my goodman, hasten him home, for the porridge is cooling," Hannah Sheldon called after them.

They met not a soul on Deerfield street and parted at Silence's door. David would have entered had she bidden him, but she wished him goodnight, and without a kiss, for Silence Hoit was chary of caresses. But tonight she called him back ere he was fairly in the street. "David," she called, and he ran back.

"What is it, Silence?" he asked.

She put back her blanket, threw her arms around his neck, and clung to him trembling.

"Why, sweetheart," he whispered, "what has come over thee?"

"You know—this house is made like—a fort," she said,

bringing out words in gasps, "and—there are muskets, and—powder stored in it, and—Captain Moulton, and his sons, and — John Carson will come, and make—a stand in it. I have—no fear should—the Indians come. Remember that I have no fear, and shall be safe here, David."

David laughed and patted her clinging shoulders. "Yes, I will remember, Silence," he said, "but the Indians will not come."

"Remember that I am safe here and have no fear," she repeated. Then she kissed him of her own accord, as if she had been his wife, and entered the house, and he went away, wondering.

Silence's aunt, Widow Eunice Bishop, did not look up when the door opened; she was knitting by the fire, sitting erect with her mouth pursed. She had a hostile expression, as if she were listening to some opposite argument. Silence hung her blanket on a peg; she stood irresolute a minute, then she breathed on the frosty window and cleared a space through which she could look out. Her aunt gave a quick, fierce glance at her, then she tossed back her head and knitted. Silence stood staring out of the little peephole in the frosty pane. Her aunt glanced at her again, then she spoke.

"I should think if you had been out gossiping and gadding for two hours, you had better get yourself at some work now," she said, "unless your heart be set on idling. A pretty housewife you'll make!"

"Come here quick, quick!" Silence cried out. Her aunt started, but she would not get up; she knitted, scowling. "I cannot afford to idle if other folk can," said she. "I have no desire to keep running to windows and standing there gaping, as you have done all this day."

"Oh, aunt, I pray you to come," said Silence, and she turned her white face over her shoulder toward her aunt, "there is somewhat wrong surely."

Widow Bishop got up, still scowling, and went over to the window. Silence stood aside and pointed to the little clear circle in the midst of the frost. "Over there to the north," she said, in a quick, low voice.

Her aunt adjusted her horn spectacles and bent her head

stiffly. "I see naught," said she.

"A red glare in the north!"

"A red glare in the north! Be ye out of your mind, wench! There be no red glare in the north. Everything be quiet in the town. Get ye away from the window and to your work. I have no more patience with such doings. Here have I left my knitting for nothing, and I just about setting the heel. You'd best keep to your spinning instead of spying out of the window at your own nightmares, and gadding about the town after David Walcott. Pretty doings for a modest maid, I call it, following after young men in this fashion!"

Silence turned on her aunt, and her blue eyes gleamed dark; she held up her head like a queen. "I follow not after young men," she said.

"Heard I not David Walcott's voice at the door? Went you not to Goodwife Sheldon's, where he lives? Was it not his voice—hey?"

"Yes, 'twas, and I had a right to go there an' I chose, and 'twas naught unmaidenly," said Silence.

"'Twas unmaidenly in my day," retorted her aunt; "perhaps 'tis different now." She had returned to her seat, and was clashing her knitting needles like two swords in a duel.

Silence pulled a spinning wheel before the fire and fell to work. The wheel turned so rapidly that the spokes were a revolving shadow. There was a sound as if a bee had entered the room.

"I stayed at home, and your uncle did the courting," Widow Eunice Bishop continued, in a voice that demanded response.

But Silence made none. She went on spinning. Her aunt eyed her maliciously. "I never went after nightfall to his house that he might see me home," said she. "I trow my mother would have locked me up in the garret, and kept me on meal and water for a week, had I done aught so bold."

Silence spun on. Her aunt threw her head back and knitted, jerking out her elbows. Neither of them spoke again until the clock struck nine. Then Widow Bishop wound her ball of yarn closer, and stuck in the knitting needles, and rose. "'Tis time to put out the candle," she said, "and I have done a good day's work, and feel need of rest. They that have idled cannot make it up by wasting tallow." She threw open the door that led to her bedroom, and a blast of icy confined air rushed in. She untied the black cap that framed her nervous face austerely, and her gray head, with its tight rosette of hair on the crown, appeared. Silence set her spinning wheel back, and raked the ashes over the hearth fire. Then she took the candle and climbed the stairs to her own chamber.

Her aunt was already in bed, her pale, white-frilled face sunk in the icy feather pillow; but she did not bid her goodnight: not on account of her anger; there was seldom any such formal courtesy exchanged between the women. Silence's chamber had one side sloping with the slope of the roof, and in it were two dormer windows looking toward the north. She set her candle on the table, breathed on one of these windows, as she had on the one downstairs, and looked out. She stood there several minutes, then she turned away, shaking her head. The room was very cold. She let down her smooth fair hair, and her fingers began to redden; she took off her kerchief; then she stopped, and looked hesitatingly at her bed, with its blue curtains. She set her mouth hard, and put on her kerchief. Then she sat down on the edge of her bed and waited. After a while she pulled a quilt from the bed and wrapped it around her. Still she did not shiver. She had blown out the candle, and the room was very dark. All her nerves seemed screwed tight like fiddle strings, and her thoughts beat upon them and made terrific waves of sound in her ears. She saw sparks and flashes like diamond fire in the darkness. She had her hands clinched tight, but she did not feel her hands nor her feet—she did not feel her whole body. She sat so until two o'clock in the morning. When the clock down in the keeping-room struck the hours, the peals shocked her back for a minute to her old sense of herself; then she lost it again. Just after the clock struck two, while the silvery reverberation of the bell tone was still in her ears, and she was breathing a little freer, a great rosy glow suffused the frosty windows. A horrible discord of sound arose without. Above everything else came something like a peal of laughter from wild beasts or fiends.

Silence arose and went downstairs. Her aunt rushed out of

her bedroom, shrieking, and caught hold of her. "Oh, Silence, what is it, what is it?" she cried.

"Get away till I light a candle," said Silence. She fairly pushed her aunt off, shovelled the ashes from the coals in the fireplace, and lighted a candle. Then she threw some wood on the smouldering fire. Her aunt was running around the room screaming. There came a great pound on the door.

"It's the Indians! It's the Indians! Don't let 'em in!" shrieked her aunt. "Don't let them in! Don't let them!" She placed her lean shoulder in her white bedgown against the door. "Go away! Go away!" she yelled. "You can't come in! O Lord Almighty, save us!"

"You stand off," said Silence. She took hold of her aunt's shoulders. "Be quiet," she commanded. Then she called out, in a firm voice, "Who is there?"

At the shout in response she drew the great iron bolts quickly and flung open the heavy nail-studded door. There was a press of frantic, white-faced people into the room; then the door was slammed to and the bolts shot. It was very still in the room, except for the shuffling rush of the men's feet, and now and then a stern, gasping order. The children did not cry; all the noise was without. The house might have stood in the midst of some awful wilderness peopled with fiendish beasts, from the noise without. The cries seemed actually in the room. The children's eyes glared white over their mothers' shoulders.

The men hurriedly strengthened the window shutters with props of logs, and fitted the muskets into the loopholes. Suddenly there was a great crash at the door, and a wilder yell outside. The muskets opened fire, and some of the women rushed to the door and pressed fiercely against it with their delicate shoulders, their white, desperate faces turning back dumbly, like a spiritual phalanx of defense. Silence and her aunt were among them.

Suddenly Widow Eunice Bishop, at a fresh onslaught upon the door, and a fiercer yell, lifted up her voice and shrieked back in a rage as mad as theirs. Her speech, too, was almost inarticulate, and the sense of it lost in a savage frenzy; her tongue stuttered over abusive epithets; but for a second she prevailed over the terrible chorus without. It was like the solo of a fury. Then louder yells drowned her out; the muskets cracked faster; the men rammed in the charges; the savages fell back somewhat; the blows on the door ceased.

Silence ran up the stairs to her chamber, and peeped cautiously out of a little dormer window. Deerfield village was roaring with flames, the sky and snow were red, and leaping through the glare came the painted savages, a savage white face and the waving sword of a French officer in their midst. The awful warwhoops and the death-cries of her friends and neighbors sounded in her ears. She saw, close under her window, the dark sweep of the tomahawk, the quick glance of the scalping-knife, and the red starting of caps of blood. She saw infants dashed through the air, and the backward-straining forms of shrieking women dragged down the street; but she saw not David Walcott anywhere.

She eyed in an agony some dark bodies lying like logs in the snow. A wild impulse seized her to run out, turn their dead faces, and see that none of them was her lover's. Her room was full of red light; everything in it showed distinctly. The roof of the next house crashed in, and the sparks and cinders shot up like a volcano. There was a great outcry of terror from below, and Silence hurried down. The Indians were trying to fire the house from the west side. They had piled a bank of brush against it, and the men had hacked new loopholes and were beating them back.

John Carson's wife clutched Silence as she entered the keeping-room. "They are trying to set the house on fire," she gasped, "and—the bullets are giving out!" The woman held a little child hugged close to her breast; she strained him closer. "They shall not have him, anyway," she said. Her mouth looked white and stiff.

"Put him down and help, then," said Silence. She began pulling the pewter plates off the dresser. "What be you doing with my pewter plates?" screamed her aunt at her elbow.

Silence said nothing. She went on piling the plates under her arm.

"Think you I will have the pewter plate I have had ever since I was wed, melted to make bullets for those limbs of Satan?"

Silence carried the plates to the fire; the women piled on wood and made it hotter. John Carson's wife laid her baby on the settle and helped, and Widow Bishop brought out her pewter spoons, and her silver cream-jug when the pewter ran low, and finally her dead husband's knee-buckles from the cedar chest. All the pewter and silver in Widow Eunice Bishop's house were melted down that night. The women worked with desperate zeal to supply the men with bullets, and just before the ammunition failed, the Indians left Deerfield village, with their captives in their train.

The men had stopped firing at last. Everything was quiet outside, except for the flurry of musket shots down on the meadow, where the skirmish was going on between the Hatfield men and the retreating French and Indians. The dawn was breaking, but not a shutter had been stirred in the Bishop house; the inmates were clustered together, their ears straining for another outburst of slaughter.

Suddenly there was a strange crackling sound overhead; a puff of hot smoke came into the room from the stairway. The roof had caught fire from the shower of sparks, and the staunch house that had withstood all the fury of the savages was going the way of its neighbors.

The men rushed up the stair, and fell back. "We can't save it!" Captain Isaac Moulton said, hoarsely. He was an old man, and his white hair tossed wildly around his powder-blackened face.

Widow Eunice Bishop scuttled into her bedroom and got her best silk hood and her gilt-framed looking glass. "Silence, get out the feather bed!" she shrieked.

The keeping-room was stifling with smoke. Captain Moulton loosened a window shutter cautiously and peered out. "I see no sign of the savages," he said. They unbolted the door, and opened it inch by inch, but there was no exultant shout in response. The crack of muskets on the meadow sounded louder; that was all.

Widow Eunice Bishop pushed forward before the others; the danger by fire to her household goods had driven her own danger from her mind, which could compass but one terror at a time. "Let me forth!" she cried; and she laid the looking glass and silk hood on the snow, and pelted back into the smoke for her feather bed and the best andirons.

Silence carried out the spinning wheel, and the others caught up various articles which they had wit to see in the panic. They piled them up on the snow outside, and huddled together, staring fearfully down the village street. They saw, amid the smouldering ruins, Ensign John Sheldon's house standing.

"We must make for that," said Captain Isaac Moulton, and they started. The men went before and behind, with their muskets in readiness, and the women and children walked between. Widow Bishop carried the looking glass; somebody had helped her to bring out her feather bed, and she had dragged it to a clean place well away from the burning house.

The dawn light lay pale and cold in the east; it was steadily overcoming the fire-glow from the ruins. Nobody would have known Deerfield village. The night before the sun had gone down upon the snowy slants of humble roofs and the peaceful rise of smoke from pleasant hearth fires. The curtained windows had gleamed out one by one with mild candlelight, and serene faces of white-capped matrons preparing supper had passed them. Now, on both sides of Deerfield street were beds of glowing red coals; grotesque ruins of doorposts and chimneys in the semblances of blackened martyrs stood crumbling in the midst of them, and twisted charred heaps, which the people eyed trembling, lay in the old doorways. The snow showed great red patches in the gathering light, and in them lay still bodies that seemed to move.

Silence Hoit sprang out from the hurrying throng, and turned the head of one dead man whose face she could not see. The horror of his red crown did not move her. She only saw that he was not David Walcott. She stooped and wiped off her hands in some snow.

"That is Israel Bennett," the others groaned.

John Carson's wife had been the dead man's sister. She hugged her baby tighter, and pressed more closely to her husband's back. There was no longer any sound of musketry on the meadows. There was not a sound to be heard except the wind in the dry trees and the panting breaths of the knot of people.

A dead baby lay directly in the path, and a woman caught it up, and tried to warm it at her breast. She wrapped her cloak around it, and wiped its little bloody face with her apron. "'Tis not dead," she declared, frantically. "The child is not dead!" She had not shed a tear nor uttered a wail before, but now she began sobbing aloud over the dead child. It was Goodwife Barnard's, and no kin to her; she was a single woman. The others were looking right and left for lurking savages; she looked only at the little cold face on her bosom. "The child breathes," she said, and hurried on faster that she might get succor for it.

The party halted before Ensign John Sheldon's house. The stout door was fast, but there was a hole in it, as if hacked by a tomahawk. The men tried it and shook it. "Open, open, Goodwife Sheldon!" they hallooed. "Friends! friends! Open the door!" But there was no response.

Silence Hoit left the throng at the door, and began clambering up on a slant of icy snow to a window which was flung wide open. The windowsill was stained with blood, and so was the snow.

One of the men caught Silence and tried to hold her back. "There may be Indians in there," he whispered, hoarsely.

But Silence broke away from him, and was in through the window, and the men followed her, and unbolted the door for the women, who pressed in wildly, and flung it to again. A child who was among them, little Comfort Arms, stationed herself directly with her tiny back against the door, with her mouth set like a soldier's, and her blue eyes gleaming fierce under her flaxen locks. "They shall not get in," said she. Somehow she had gotten hold of a great horse-pistol, which she carried like a doll.

Nobody heeded her, Silence least of all. She stared about the room, with her lips parted. Right before her on the hearth lay a little three-year-old girl, Mercy Sheldon, her pretty head in a pool of blood, but Silence cast only an indifferent glance when the others gathered about her, groaning and sighing.

Suddenly Silence sprang toward a dark heap near the pantry door, but it was only a woman's quilted petticoat.

The spinning wheel lay broken on the floor, and all the simple furniture was strewn about wildly. Silence went into

Goodwife Sheldon's bedroom, and the others followed her, trembling, all except little Comfort Arms, who stood unflinchingly with her back pressed against the door, and the single woman, Grace Mather; she stayed behind and put wood on the fire, after she had picked up the quilted petticoat, and laid the dead baby tenderly wrapped in it on the settle. Goodwife Sheldon's bedroom was in wild disorder. A candle still burned, although it was very low, on the table, whose linen cover had great red fingerprints on it. Goodwife Sheldon's decent clothes were tossed about on the floor; the curtains of the bed were half torn away. Silence pressed forward unshrinkingly toward the bed; the others, even the men, hung back. There lay Goodwife Sheldon dead in her bed. All the light in the room, the candlelight and the low daylight, seemed to focus upon her white, frozen profile propped stiffly on the pillow, where she had fallen back when the bullet came through that hole in the door.

Silence looked at her. "Where is David, Goodwife Sheldon?" said she.

Eunice Bishop sprang forward. "Be you clean out of your mind, Silence Hoit?" she cried. "Know you not she's dead? She's dead! Oh, she's dead, she's dead! And here's her best silk hood trampled underfoot on the floor!" Eunice snatched up the hood, and seized Silence by the arm, but she pushed her back.

"Where is David? Where is he gone?" she demanded again of the dead woman.

The other women came crowding around Silence then, and tried to soothe her and reason with her, while their own faces were white with horror and woe. Goodwife Sarah Spear, an old woman whose sons lay dead in the street outside, put an arm around the girl, and tried to draw her head to her broad bosom.

"Mayhap you will find him, sweetheart," she said. "He's not among the dead out there."

But Silence broke away from the motherly arm and sped wildly through the other rooms, with the people at her heels, and her aunt crying vainly after her. They found no more dead in the house; naught but ruin and disorder, and bloody footprints and handprints of savages.

When they returned to the keeping-room, Silence seated

herself on a stool by the fire, and held out her hands toward the blaze to warm them. The daylight was broad outside now, and the great clock that had come from overseas ticked; the Indians had not touched that.

Captain Isaac Moulton lifted little Mercy Sheldon from the hearth and carried her to her dead mother in the bedroom, and two of the older women went in there and shut the door. Little Comfort Arms still stood with her back against the outer door, and Grace Mather tended the dead baby on the settle.

"What do ye with that dead child?" a woman called out roughly to her.

"I tell ye 'tis not dead; it breathes," returned Grace Mather; and she never turned her harsh, plain face from the dead child.

"And I tell ye 'tis dead."

"And I tell ye 'tis not dead. I need but some hot posset for it."

Goodwife Carson began to weep. She hugged her own living baby tighter. "Let her alone!" she sobbed. "I wonder our wits be not all gone." She went sobbing over to little Comfort Arms at the door. "Come away, sweetheart, and draw near the fire," she pleaded, brokenly.

The little girl looked obstinately up at her. "They shall not come in again."

"No more shall they, and the Lord be willing, sweet. But, I pray you, come away from the door now."

Comfort shook her head, and she looked like her father as he fought on the Deerfield meadows.

"The savages are gone, sweet."

But Comfort answered not a word, and Goodwife Carson sat down and began to nurse her baby. One of the women hung the porridge-kettle over the fire; another put some potatoes in the ashes to bake. Presently the two women came out of Goodwife Sheldon's bedroom with grave, strained faces and held their stiff blue fingers out to the hearth fire.

Eunice Bishop, who was stirring the porridge, looked at them with sharp curiosity. "How look they?" she whispered.

"As peaceful as if they slept," replied Goodwife Spear, who was one of the women.

"And the child's head?"

"We put on her little white cap with the lace frills."

Eunice stirred the bubbling porridge, scowling in the heat and steam; some of the women laid the table with Hannah Sheldon's linen cloth and pewter dishes, and presently the breakfast was dished up.

Little Comfort Arms had sunk at the foot of the nail-studded door in a deep slumber. She slept at her post like the faithless sentry whose slumbers the night before had brought about the destruction of Deerfield village. Goodwife Spear raised her up, but her curly head drooped helplessly.

"Wake up, Comfort, and have a sup of hot porridge," she called in her ear.

She led her over to the table, Comfort stumbling weakly at arm's-length, and set her on a stool with a dish of porridge before her, which she ate uncertainly in a dazed fashion, with her eyes filming and her head nodding.

They all gathered gravely around the table, except Silence Hoit and Grace Mather. Silence sat still, staring at the fire, and Grace had dipped out a little cup of the hot porridge and was trying to feed it to the dead baby, with crooning words.

"Silence, why come you not to the table?" her aunt called out.

"I want nothing," answered Silence.

"I see not why you should so set yourself up before the others, as having so much more to bear," said Eunice, sharply. "There is Goodwife Spear, with her sons unburied on the road yonder, and she eats her porridge with good relish."

John Carson's wife set her baby on her husband's knee and carried a dish of porridge to Silence.

"Try and eat it, sweet," she whispered. She was near Silence's age.

Silence looked up at her. "I want it not," said she.

"But he may not be dead, sweet. He may presently be home. You would not he should find you spent and fainting. Perchance he may have wounds for you to tend."

Silence seized the dish and began to eat the porridge in great spoonfuls, gulping it down fast.

The people at the table eyed her sadly and whispered, and they also cast frequent glances at Grace Mather bending over the dead baby. Once Captain Isaac Moulton called out to her in his gruff old voice, which he tried to soften, and she answered back, sharply: "Think ye I will leave this child while it breathes, Captain Isaac Moulton? In faith I am the only one of ye all who has regard to it."

But suddenly, when the meal was half over, Grace Mather arose and gathered up the little dead baby, carried it into Goodwife Sheldon's bedroom, and was gone some time.

"She has lost her wits," said Eunice Bishop. "Think you not we should follow her? She may do some harm."

"Nay, let her be," said Goodwife Spear.

When at last Grace Mather came out of the bedroom, and they all turned to look at her, her face was stern but quite composed. "I found a little clean linen shift in the chest," she said to Goodwife Spear, who nodded gravely. Then she sat down at the table and ate.

The people, as they ate, cast frequent glances at the barred door and the shuttered windows. The daylight was broad outside, but there was no glimmer of it in the room, and the candles were lighted. They dared not yet remove the barricades, and the muskets were in readiness: the Indians might return.

All at once there was a shrill clamor at the door, and men sprang to their muskets. The women clutched each other, panting.

"Unbar the door!" shrieked a quavering old voice. "I tell ye, unbar the door! I be nigh frozen a-standing here. Unbar the door! The Indians are gone hours ago."

"'Tis Goody Crane!" cried Eunice Bishop.

Captain Isaac Moulton shot back the bolts and opened the door a little way, while the men stood close at his back, and Goody Crane slid in like a swift black shadow out of the daylight.

She crouched down close to the fire, trembling and groaning, and the women gave her some hot porridge.

"Where have ye been?" demanded Eunice Bishop.

"Where they found me not," replied the old woman, and there was a sudden leer like a light in the gloom of her great hood. She motioned toward the bedroom door.

"Goody Sheldon sleeps late this morning, and so doth

Mercy," said she. "I trow she will not dip her candles today."

The people looked at each other; a subtler horror than that of the night before shook their spirits.

Captain Isaac Moulton towered over the old woman on the hearth. "How knew you Goodwife Sheldon and Mercy were dead?" he asked, sternly.

The old woman leered up at him undauntedly; her head bobbed. There was a curious grotesqueness about her blanketed and hooded figure when in motion. There was so little of the old woman herself visible that motion surprised, as it would have done in a puppet. "Told I not Goody Sheldon last night she would never stir porridge again?" said she. "Who stirred the porridge this morning? I trow Goody Sheldon's hands be too stiff and too cold, though they have stirred well in their day. Hath she dipped her candles yet? Hath she begun on her weaving? I trow 'twill be a long day ere Mary Sheldon's linen-chest be filled, if she herself go a-gadding to Canada and her mother sleep so late."

"Eat this hot porridge and stop your croaking," said Goodwife Spear, stooping over her.

The old woman extended her two shaking hands for the dish. "That was what she said last night," she returned. "The living echo the dead, and that is enough wisdom for a witch."

"You'll be burned for a witch yet, Goody Crane, an' you be not careful," cried Eunice Bishop.

"There is fire enough outside to burn all the witches in the land," muttered the old woman, sipping her porridge. Suddenly she eyed Silence sitting motionless opposite. "Where be your sweetheart this fine morning, Silence Hoit?" she inquired.

Silence looked at her. There was a strange likeness between the glitter in her blue eyes and that in Goody Crane's black ones.

The old woman's great hood nodded over the porridge-dish. "I can tell ye, Mistress Silence," she said thickly, as she ate. "He is gone to Canada on a moose-hunt, and unless I be far wrong, he hath taken thy wits with him."

"How know you David Walcott is gone to Canada?" cried Eunice Bishop; and Silence stared at her with her hard blue eyes.

Silence's soft fair hair hung all matted like uncombed flax over her pale cheeks. There was a rigid, dead look about her girlish forehead and her sweet mouth.

"I know," returned Goody Crane, nodding her head. The women washed the pewter dishes, set them back on the dresser, and swept the floor. Little Comfort Arms had been carried upstairs and laid in the bed whence poor Mary Sheldon had been dragged and haled to Canada. The men stood talking near their stacked muskets. One of the shutters had been opened and the candles put out. The winter sun shone in the window as it had shone before, but the poor folk in Ensign Sheldon's keeping-room saw it with a certain shock, as if it were a stranger. That morning their own hearts had in them such strangeness that they transferred it like motion to all familiar objects. The very iron dogs in the Sheldon fireplace seemed on the leap with tragedy, and the porridge-kettle swung darkly out of some former age.

Now and then one of the men opened the door cautiously and peered out and listened. The reek of the smouldering village came in at the door, but there was not a sound except the whistling howl of the savage north wind, which still swept over the valley. There was not a shot to be heard from the meadows. The men discussed the wisdom of leaving the women for a short space and going forth to explore, but Widow Eunice Bishop interposed, thrusting her sharp face in among them.

"Here we be," scolded she, "a passel of women and children, and Hannah Sheldon and Mercy a-lying dead, and me with my house burnt down, and nothing saved except my silk hood and my looking glass and my feather bed, and it's a mercy that's not all smooched, and you talk of going off and leaving us!"

The men looked doubtfully at one another; then there was the hissing creak of footsteps on the snow outside, and Widow Bishop screamed. "Oh, the Indians have come back!" she proclaimed.

Silence looked up.

The door was tried from without.

"Who's there?" cried out Captain Moulton.

"John Sheldon," responded a hoarse voice. "Who's inside?"

Captain Moulton threw open the door, and John Sheldon stood there. His severe and sober face was painted like an Indian's with blood and powder grime; he stood staring in at the company.

"Come in, quick, and let us bar the door!" screamed Eunice Bishop.

John Sheldon came in hesitatingly and stood looking around the room.

"Have you but just come from the meadows?" inquired Captain Moulton. But John Sheldon did not seem to hear him. He stared at the company, who all stood still staring back at him; then he looked hard and long at the doors, as if expecting someone to enter. The eyes of the others followed his, but no one spoke.

"Where's Hannah?" asked John Sheldon. Then the women began to weep.

"She's in there," sobbed John Carson's wife, pointing to the bedroom door—"in there with little Mercy, Goodman Sheldon."

"Is—the child hurt, and—Hannah a-tending her?"

The women wept and pushed each other forward to tell him, but Captain Isaac Moulton spoke out and drove the knife home like an honest soldier, who will kill if he must, but not mangle.

"Goodwife Sheldon lies yonder, shot dead in her bed, and we found the child dead on the hearthstone," said Isaac Moulton.

John Sheldon turned his gaze on him.

"The judgments of the Lord are just and righteous altogether," said Isaac Moulton, confronting him with stern defiance.

"Amen," returned John Sheldon. He took off his cloak and hung it up on the peg as he was used.

"Where is David Walcott?" asked Silence, standing before him.

"David, he is gone with the Indians to Canada, and the boys, Ebenezer and Remembrance."

"Where is David?"

"I tell ye, lass, he is gone with the French and Indians to Canada, and you need be thankful he was but your sweetheart, and ye not wed, with a half-score of babes to be taken too. The curse that was upon the women of Jerusalem is upon the women of Deerfield." John Sheldon looked sternly into Silence's white wild face. Then his voice softened. "Take heart, lass," said he. "Erelong I shall go to Governor Dudley and get help, and then after them to Canada, and fetch them back. Take heart, I will fetch thee thy sweetheart presently."

Silence returned to her seat in the fireplace. Goody Crane looked across at her. "He will come back over the north meadow," she whispered. "Keep watch over the north meadow; but 'twill be a long day ere ye see him."

Silence paid seemingly little heed. She paid little heed to Ensign John Sheldon relating how the French and Indians, with Hertel de Rouville at their head, were on the road to Canada with their captives; of the fight on the meadow between the retreating foe and the brave band of Deerfield and Hatfield men, who had made a stand there to intercept them; how they had been obliged to cease firing because the captives were threatened; and the pitiful tale of Parson John Williams, two of whose children were killed, dragged through the wilderness with the others, and his sick wife.

"Had folk listened to him, we had all been safe in our good houses with our belongings," cried Eunice Bishop.

"They will not drag Goodwife Williams far," said Goody Crane, "nor the babe at her breast. I trow well it hath stopped wailing ere now."

"How know you that?" questioned Eunice Bishop, turning sharply on her.

But the old woman only nodded her head, and Silence paid no heed, for she was not there. Her slender girlish shape sat by the hearth fire in John Sheldon's house in Deerfield, her fair head showed like a delicate flower, but Silence Hoit was following her lover to Canada. Every step that he took painfully through pathless forests, on treacherous ice, and desolate snow fields, she took more painfully still; every knife gleaming over his head she saw. She bore his every qualm of hunger and pain and cold, and it was all the harder because they struck on her bare heart with no flesh between, for she sat in the flesh in Deerfield, and her heart went with her lover to Canada.

The sun stood higher, but it was still bitter cold; the blue frost on the windows did not melt, and the icicles on the eaves, which nearly touched the sharp snowdrifts underneath, did not drip. The desolate survivors of the terrible night began work among the black ruins of their homes. They cared as well as they might for the dead in Deerfield street, and the dead on the meadow where the fight had been. Their muscles were all tense with the cold, their faces seamed and blue with it, but their hearts were strained with a fiercer cold than that. Not one man of them but had one or more slain, with dead face upturned, seeking his in the morning light, or on that awful road to Canada. Ever as the men worked they turned their eyes northward and met grimly the icy blast of the north wind, and sometimes to their excited fancies it seemed to bring to their ears the cries of their friends who were facing it also, and they stood still and listened.

Silence Hoit crept out of the house and down the road a little way, and then stood looking over the meadow toward the north. Her fair hair tossed in the wind, her pale cheeks turned pink, the wind struck full upon her delicate figure. She had come out without her blanket.

"David!" she called. "David! David! David!" The north wind bore down upon her, shrieking with a wild fury like a savage of the air; the dry branches of a small tree near her struck her in the face. "David!" she called again. "David! David!" She swelled out her white throat like a bird, and her voice was shrill and sweet and far-reaching. The men moving about on the meadow below, and stooping over the dead, looked up at her, but she did not heed them. She had come through a break in the palisades; on each side of her the frozen snowdrifts slanted sharply to their tops, and they glittered with blue lights like glaciers in the morning sun over those drifts the enemy had passed the night before.

The men on the meadow saw Silence's hair blowing like a yellow banner between the drifts of snow.

"The poor lass has come out bareheaded," said Ensign Sheldon. "She is near out of her mind for David Walcott."

"A man should have no sweetheart in these times, unless he would her heart be broke," said a young man beside him. He was hardly more than a boy, and his face was as rosy as a girl's in the wind. He kept close to Ensign Sheldon, and his mind was full of young Mary Sheldon travelling to Canada on her weary little feet. He had often, on a Sabbath day, looked across the meeting-house at her, and thought that there was no maiden like her in Deerfield.

Ensign John Sheldon thought of his sweetheart lying with her heart still in her freezing bedroom, and stooped over a dead Hatfield man whose face was frozen into the snow.

The young man, whose name was Freedom Wells, bent over to help him. Then he started.

"What's that?" he cried.

"'Tis only Silence Hoit calling David Walcott again," replied Ensign Sheldon.

The voice had sounded like Mary Sheldon's to Freedom. The tears rolled over his boyish cheeks as he put his hands into the snow and tried to dig it away from the dead man's face.

"David! David! David!" called Silence.

Suddenly her aunt threw a wiry arm around her. "Be you gone clean daft," she shrieked against the wind, "standing here calling David Walcott? Know you not he is a half-day's journey toward Canada an' the savages have not scalped him by the way? Standing here with your hair blowing and no blanket! Into the house with ye!"

Silence followed her aunt unresistingly. The women in Ensign Sheldon's house were hard at work. They were baking in the great brick oven, spinning, and even dipping poor Goodwife

Sheldon's candles.

"Bind up your hair, like an honest maid, and go to spinning," said Eunice, and she pointed to the spinning wheel which had been saved from her own house. "We that be spared have to work, and not sit down and trot our own hearts on our knees. There is scarce a yard of linen left in Deerfield, to say naught of woollen cloth. Bind up your hair!"

And Silence bound up her hair and sat down by her wheel meekly, and yet with a certain dignity. Indeed, through all the disorder of her mind, that delicate maiden dignity never forsook her, and there was never aught but respect shown her.

As time went on, it became quite evident that although the fair semblance of Silence Hoit still walked the Deerfield street, sat in the meeting-house, and toiled at the spinning wheel and the loom, yet she was as surely not there as though she had been haled to Canada with the other captives on that terrible February night. It became the general opinion that Silence Hoit would never be quite her old self again and walk in the goodly company of all her fair wits unless David Walcott should be redeemed from captivity and and restored to her. Then, it was accounted possible, the mending of the calamity which had brought her disorder upon her might remove it.

"Ye wait," widow Eunice Bishop would say, hetchelling flax the while as though it were the scalp-locks of the enemy—"ye wait. If once David Walcott show his face, ye'll see Silence Hoit be not so lacking. She hath a tenderer heart than some I could mention, who go about smiling when their nearest of kin lay in torment in Indian lodges. She cares naught for picking up a new sweetheart. She hath a steady heart that be not so easy turned as some. Silence was never a light hussy, a-dancing hither and thither off the bridle path for a new flower on the bushes. And, for all ye call her lacking now, there be not a maid in Deerfield does such a day's task as she."

And that last statement was quite true. All the Deerfield women, the matrons and maidens, toiled unceasingly, with a kind of stern patience like that which served their husbands and lovers in the frontier cornfields, and which served all the dauntless border settlers, who were forced continually to rebuild after destruction, like wayside ants whose nests are always being trampled underfoot. There was need of unflinching toil at wheel and loom, for there was great scarcity of household linen in Deerfield, and Silence Hoit's shapely white maiden hands flinched less than any.

Nevertheless, many a day, in the morning when the snowy meadows were full of blue lights, at sunset when all the snow levels were rosy, but more particularly in wintry moonlight when the country was like a waste of silver, would Silence Hoit leave suddenly her household task, and hasten to the terrace overlooking the north meadow, and shriek out: "David! David! David Walcott!"

The village children never jeered at her, as they would sometimes jeer at Goody Crane if not restrained by their elders. They eyed with a mixture of wonder and admiration Silence's beautiful bewildered face, with the curves of gold hair around the pink cheeks, and the fretwork of tortoiseshell surmounting it. David Walcott had given Silence her shell comb, and she was never seen without it.

Many a time when Silence called to David from the terrace of the north meadow, some of the little village maids in their homespun pinafores would join her and call with her. They had no fear of her, as they had of Goody Crane.

Indeed, Goody Crane, after the massacre, was in worse repute than ever in Deerfield. There were dark rumors concerning her whereabouts upon that awful night. Some among the devout and godly were fain to believe that the old woman had been in league with the powers of darkness and their allies the savages, and had so escaped harm. Some even whispered that in the thickest of the slaughter, when Deerfield was in the midst of that storm of fire, old Goody Crane's laugh had been heard, and one, looking up, had spied her high overhead riding her broomstick, her face red with the glare of the flames. The old woman was sheltered under protest, and had Deerfield not been a frontier town, and graver matters continually in mind, she might have come to harm in consequence of the gloomy suspicions concerning her.

Many a night after the massacre would the windows fly up

and anxious faces peer out. It was as if the ears of the people were tuned up to the pitch of the Indian warwhoops, and their very thoughts made the nights ring with them.

The palisades were well looked to; there was never a slope of frozen snow again to form foothold for the enemy, and the sentry never slept at his post. But the anxious women listened all winter for the warwhoops, and many a time it seemed they heard them. In the midst of their nervous terror it was often a sore temptation to consult old Goody Crane, since she was held to have occult knowledge.

"I'll warrant old Goody Crane could tell us in a twinkling whether or no the Indians would come before morning," Eunice Bishop said one fierce windy night that called to mind the one of the massacre.

"Knowledge got in unlawful ways would avail us naught," returned Goodwife Spear. "I trow the Lord be yet able to protect His people."

"I doubt not that," said Eunice Bishop, "but I would like well to know if I had best bury my hood and my spinning wheel and looking glass in a snowdrift tonight. I have no mind the Indians shall get them. I warrant she knows well."

But Eunice Bishop did not consult Goody Crane, although she watched her narrowly and had a sharp ear to her mutterings as she sat in the chimney-corner. Eunice and Silence were living in John Sheldon's house, as did many of the survivors for some time after the massacre. It was the largest house in the village, and most of its original inhabitants were dead or gone into captivity. The people all huddled together fearfully in the few houses that were left, and the women's spinning wheels and looms jostled each other.

As soon as the weather moderated, the work of building new dwellings commenced, and went on bravely with the advance of the spring. The air was full of the calls of spring birds and the strokes of axes and hammers. A little house was built on the site of their old one for Widow Bishop and Silence Hoit. Widow Sarah Spear also lived with them, and Goody Crane took frequent shelter at their fireside. So they were a household of women, with loaded muskets at hand, and spinning wheels and looms at full hum. They had but a scanty household store, although Widow Bishop tried in every way to increase it. Several times during the summer she took perilous journeys to Hatfield and Squakheak, for the purpose of bartering skeins of yarn or rolls of wool for household articles. In December, when Ensign Sheldon with young Freedom Wells went down to Boston to consult with Governor Dudley concerning an expedition to Canada to redeem the captives, Widow Eunice Bishop, having saved a few shillings, burdened him with a commission to purchase for her a new cap and a pair of bellows. She was much angered when he returned without them, having quite forgotten them in his press of business.

On the day when John Sheldon and Freedom Wells started upon their terrible journey of three hundred miles to redeem the captives, Eunice Bishop scolded well as she spun by her hearth fire.

"I trow they will bring back nobody," said she, her nose high in the air, and her voice shrilling over the drone of the wheel; "an' they could not do the bidding of a poor lone widow-woman, and fetch her the cap and bellows from Boston, they'll fetch nobody home from Canada. I would I had ear of Governor Dudley. I trow men with minds upon their task would be sent." Eunice kept jerking her head as she scolded and spun like a bee angry with its own humming.

Silence sat knitting and paid no heed. She had paid no heed to any of the talk about Ensign Sheldon's and Freedom Wells's journey to Canada. She had not seemed to listen when Widow Spear had tried to explain the matter to her. "It may be, sweetheart, if it be the will of the Lord, that they will bring David back to thee," she had said over and over, and Silence had knitted and made no response.

She was the only one in Deerfield who was not torn with excitement and suspense as the months went by, and the only one unmoved by joy or disappointment when in May John Sheldon and Freedom Wells returned with five of the captives. But David Walcott was not among them.

"Said I not 'twould be so? scolded Eunice Bishop. "Knew I not 'twould be so when they forgot to get the cap and the bellows in

Boston? The one of all the captives that could have saved a poor maid's wits they leave behind. There's Mary Sheldon come home, and she a-coloring red before Freedom Wells, and everybody in the room a-seeing it. I trow they might have done somewhat for poor Silence," and Eunice broke down and wailed and wept, but Silence shed not a tear. Before long she stole out to the terrace and called "David! David! David!" over the north meadow, and strained her blue eyes toward Canada and held out her fair arms, but it was with no new disappointment and desolation.

There was never a day nor a night that Silence called not over the north meadow like a spring bird from the bush to her absent mate, and people heard her and sighed and shuddered.

One afternoon in the last of the month of June, as Silence was thrusting her face between the leaves of a wild cherry tree and calling "David! David! David!" David himself broke through the thicket and stood before her. He and three other young men had escaped from their captivity and come home, and the four, crawling half dead across the meadow, had heard Silence's voice from the terrace above, and David, leaving the others, had made his way to her.

"Silence!" he said, and held out his poor arms, panting.

But Silence looked past him. "David! David! David Walcott!" she called.

David could scarely stand for trembling, and he grasped a branch of the cherry tree to steady himself, and swayed with it.

"Know—you not—who I am, Silence?" he said.

But she made as though she did not hear, and called again, always looking past him. And David Walcott, being near spent with fatigue and starvation, wound himself feebly around the trunk of the tree, and the tears dropped over his cheeks as he looked at her; and she called past him, until some women came and led him away and tried to comfort him, telling him how it was with her, and that she would soon know him when he looked more like himself.

But the summer wore away and she did not know him, although he constantly followed her beseechingly. His elders ever reproved him for paying so little heed to his work in the colony. "It is not meet for a young man to be so weaned from usefulness by grief for a maid," said they. But David Walcott would at any time leave his reaping-hook in the corn and his axe in the tree, leave aught but his post as sentry, when he heard Silence calling him over the north meadow. He would stand at her elbow and say, in his voice that broke like a woman's: "Here I am, sweetheart, at thy side. I pray thee turn thy head." But she would not let her eyes rest upon him for more than a second's space, turning them ever past him toward Canada, and calling in his very ears with a sad longing that tore his heart: "David! David! David!" It was as if her mind, reaching out always and speeding fast in search of him, had gotten such impetus that she passed the very object of her search and knew it not.

Now and then would David Walcott grow desperate, fling his arms around her, and kiss her upon her cold delicate lips and cheeks as if he would make her recognize him by force; but she would free herself from him with a passionless resentment that left him helpless.

One day in autumn, when the borders of the Deerfield meadows were a smoky purple with wild asters, and goldenrods flashed out like golden flames in the midst of them, David Walcott had been pleading vainly with Silence as she stood calling on the north terrace. Suddenly he turned and rushed away, and his face was all convulsed like a weeping child's. As he came out of the thicket he met the old woman Goody Crane and would fain have hidden his face from her, but she stopped him.

"Prithee stop a moment's space, Master David Walcott," said she.

"What would you?" David cried out in a surly tone, and he dashed the back of his hand across his eyes.

"'Tis full moon tonight," said the old woman, in a whisper. "Come out here tonight when the moon shall be an hour high, and I promise ye she shall know ye."

The young man stared at her.

"I tell ye Mistress Silence Hoit shall know ye tonight," repeated the old woman. Her voice sounded hollow in the depths of her great hood, which she donned early in the fall. Her eyes in the gloom of it gleamed with a small dark brightness.

"I'll have no witch-work tried on her," said David, roughly.

"I'll try no witch-work but mine own wits," said Goody Crane. "If they would hang me for a witch for that, then they may. None but I can cure her. I tell ye, come out here tonight when the moon is an hour high. And mind ye wear a white sheep's fleece over your shoulders. I'll harm her not so much with my witch-work as ye'll do with your love, for all your prating."

The old woman pushed past him to where Silence stood calling, and waited there, standing in the shadow cast by the wild cherry tree until she ceased and turned away. Then she caught hold of the skirt of her gown, and David stood, hidden by the thicket, listening.

"I prithee, Mistress Silence Hoit, listen but a moment," said Goody Crane.

Silence paused, and smiled at her gently and wearily.

"Give me your hand," demanded the old woman.

And Silence held out her hand, flashing white in the green gloom, as if she cared not.

The old woman turned the palm, bending her hooded head low over it. "He draweth near!" she cried out suddenly. "He draweth near, with a white sheep's fleece over his shoulders! He cometh through the woods from Canada. He will cross the meadow when the moon is an hour high tonight. He will wear a white sheep's fleece over his shoulders, and ye'll know him by that."

Silence's wandering eyes fastened upon her face. The old woman caught hold of her shoulders and shook her to and fro. "David! David! David Walcott!" she screamed. "David Walcott with a white sheep's fleece on his back! On the meadow! Tonight when the moon's an hour high! Be ye out here tonight, Silence Hoit, if ye'd see him a-coming down from the north!"

Silence gasped faintly when the old woman released her and went muttering away. Presently she crept home, and sat down with her knitting-work in the chimney-place.

When Eunice Bishop hung on the porridge-kettle, Goody Crane lifted the latchstring and came in. It was growing dusky, but the moon would not rise for an hour yet. Goody Crane sat opposite Silence, with her eyes fixed upon her, and Silence, in spite of herself, kept looking at her. A gold brooch at the old woman's throat glittered in the firelight, and that seemed to catch Silence's eyes. She finally knitted with her eyes fixed upon it.

She scarcely took her eyes away when she ate her supper; then she sat down to her knitting and knitted, and gazed, in spite of herself, at the gold spot on the old woman's throat.

The moon arose; the tree branches before the windows tossed half in silver light; the air was shrill with crickets. Silence stirred uneasily, and dropped stitches in her knitting-work. "He draweth near," muttered Goody Crane, and Silence quivered.

The moon was a half-hour high. Widow Bishop was spinning, Widow Spear was winding quills, and Silence knitted. "He draweth near," muttered Goody Crane.

"I'll have no witchcraft!" Silence cried out, suddenly and sharply. Her aunt stopped spinning, and Widow Spear started.

"What's that?" said her aunt. But Silence was knitting again.

"What meant you by that?" asked her aunt, sharply.

"I have dropped a stitch," said Silence.

Her aunt spun again, with occasional wary glances. The moon was three-quarters of an hour high. Silence gazed steadily at the gold brooch at Goody Crane's throat.

"The moon is near an hour high. You had best be going," said the old woman, in a low monotone.

Silence arose directly.

"Where go you at this time of night?" grumbled her aunt.

But Silence glided past her.

"You'll lose your good name as well as your wits," cried Eunice. But she did not try to stop Silence, for she knew it was useless.

"A white sheep's fleece over his shoulders," muttered Goody Crane as Silence went out of the door; and the other women marvelled what she meant.

Silence Hoit went swiftly and softly down Deerfield street to her old haunt on the north meadow terrace. She pushed in among the wild cherry trees, which waved, white with the moonlight, like ghostly arms in her face. Then she called, setting her face toward Canada and the north: "David! David! David!" But her voice had a different tone in it, and it broke with her heart-beats.

David Walcott came slowly across the meadow below; a white fleece of a sheep thrown over his back caught the moonlight. He came on, and on, and on; then he went up the terrace to Silence. Her face, white like a white flower in the moonlight, shone out suddenly close before him. He waited a second, then he spoke. "Silence!" he said.

Then Silence gave a great cry and threw her arms around his neck, and pressed softly and wildly against him with her wet cheek to his.

"Know you who 'tis, sweetheart?"

"Oh, David, David!"

The trees arched like arbors with the weight of the wild grapes, which made the air sweet; the night insects called from the bushes; Deerfield village and the whole valley lay in the moonlight like a landscape of silver. The lovers stood in each other's arms, motionless, and seemingly fixed as the New England flora around them, as if they too might reappear hundreds of springtimes hence, with their loves as fairly in blossom.

THE THREE D'S

▪ BY OGDEN NASH ▪

Victoria was an attractive new girl at the Misses Mallisons' Female Seminary—such an attractive new girl, indeed, that it is a pity she never grew to be an old girl. Perhaps she would have, if the Misses Mallison had established their seminary a little closer to Newburyport—or at least a little farther from Salem.

Victoria was good enough at games and not too good at lessons; her mouth was wide enough to console the homely girls and her eyes bright enough to include her among the pretty ones; she could weep over the death of a horse in a story and remain composed at the death of an aunt in the hospital; she would rather eat between meals than at them; she wrote to her parents once a week if in need of anything; and she truly meant to do the right thing, only so often the wrong thing was easier.

In short, Victoria was an ideal candidate for The Three D's, that night-blooming sorority which had, like the cereus, flourished after dark for many years, unscented by the precise noses of the Misses Mallison.

So felt The Three D's, so felt Victoria, and the only obstacle to her admission lay in the very title of the club itself, which members knew signified that none could gain entrance without the accomplishment of a feat Daring, Deadly, and Done-never-before. Victoria was competent at daring feats, unsurpassable at deadly feats, but where was she to discover a feat done-never-before?

Of the present membership, Amanda had leaped into a cold bath with her clothes on, Miranda had climbed the roof in her nightgown to drop a garter snake down the Misses Mallisons' chimney, Amelia had eaten cold spaghetti blindfolded thinking it was worms, and Cordelia had eaten worms blindfolded thinking they were cold spaghetti. What was left for Victoria?

It was Amanda who, at a meeting of the Steering Committee, wiped the fudge from her fingers on the inside of her dressing gown and spoke the name of Eliza Catspaugh.

"Who was she?" asked Miranda, pouring honey on a slice of coconut cake.

"A witch," said Amanda.

"She was burned," said Amelia.

"Hanged," said Cordelia.

"And she couldn't get into the churchyard, so they buried her in the meadow behind the old slaughterhouse," said Amanda.

"The gravestone is still there," said Amelia. "Oh, bother, the cake's all gone! Never mind, I'll eat caramels."

"There's writing on it, too," said Cordelia, who was not hungry, "but you can't read it in the daytime, only by moonlight."

"I'd forgotten how good currant jelly is on marshmallows," said Amanda. "The Three D's must tell Victoria about Eliza Catspaugh."

Late next evening Victoria took her pen in hand. *Dear Father and Mother*, she wrote, *I hope you are well. I am doing well in algebra but Miss Hattie is unfair about my French ireguler verbs. I am doing well in grammar but Miss Mettie has choosen me to pick on. Dear Father, everybody elses Father sends them one dollar every week. I have lots of things to write but the bell is wringing for supper. Lots of love, your loveing daughter, Victoria.*

Victoria knew that in ten minutes Miss Hattie Mallison would open the door slightly, peer at the bed, murmur, "Good night, Victoria, sweet dreams," and disappear. It took Victoria seven minutes to construct a dummy out of a mop, a nightgown, and several pillows and blankets. As she lowered herself to the ground she heard the door open, heard Miss Hattie's murmur, heard the door close.

The soaring moon ran through Victoria as she marched, as she skipped, as she pranced toward the old slaughterhouse. She had for company her high moon-spirits and her long shadow—the shadow which was a Victoria that no Miss Mallison could ever cage. "No girl has ever had a taller, livelier companion than my shadow," thought Victoria, and she breathed deeply and spread her arms, and her shadow breathed with her and spread crooked arms up the walls and across the roof of the slaughterhouse.

The moon grew brighter with each burr that Victoria struggled against on her way across the meadow that had been abandoned to burrs, the meadow where no beasts fed, the meadow where Victoria's shadow strengthened at each proud and adventurous step.

Where the burrs grew thickest, where her loyalty to The Three D's wore the thinnest, she came upon the gravestone. How hard the moon shone as Victoria leaned against the crooked slab, perhaps to catch her breath, perhaps to stand on one foot and pluck the burrs off. When the stone quivered and rocked behind her, and the ground trembled beneath her feet, she bravely remembered her purpose: that at midnight, in the moonlight, she was to prove herself a worthy companion of Amanda and Miranda, Amelia and Cordelia. Unwillingly she turned, and willfully she read the lines which the rays of the moon lifted from the stone so obscured by rain and moss.

Here Waits
ELIZA CATSPAUGH
Who touches this stone
on moonlight meadow
shall live no longer
than his shadow.

The job of memorizing was done, the initiation into The Three D's handsomely undergone. "Gracious, is that all there is to it?" thought Victoria, and set out for the seminary.

It was natural that she should hurry, so perhaps it was natural that she did not miss the exuberant shadow which should have escorted her home. The moon was bright behind Victoria—who can tell how she forgot there should have been a shadow to lead the way?

But there was no shadow—her shadow had dwindled as she ran, as though Victoria grew shorter, or perhaps the moon grew more remote. And if she did not miss her shadow, neither did she hear or see whatever it may have been that rustled and scuttled past her and ahead of her.

"I hope my dear little dummy is still there," thought Victoria as she climbed through the window. "I hope Miss Hattie hasn't been unfair and shaken me."

She tiptoed across the room in the dark to the bed and bent to remove the dummy. But as she reached down, the dummy, which was no longer a dummy, reached up its dusty fingers first. . .

THE MUSIC TEACHER

· BY JOHN CHEEVER ·

I t all seemed to have been arranged—Seton sensed this
when he opened the door of his house that evening and
walked down the hall into the living room. It all seemed to have
been set with as much care as, in an earlier period of life, he had
known girls to devote to the flowers, the candles, and the records
for the phonograph. This scene was not arranged for his pleasure,
nor was it arranged for anything so simple as reproach. "Hello,"
he said loudly and cheerfully. Sobbing and moaning rent the air.
In the middle of the small living room stood an ironing board. One
of his shirts was draped over it, and his wife, Jessica, wiped away
a tear as she ironed. Near the piano stood Jocelin, the baby. Jocelin
was howling. Sitting in a chair near her little sister was Millicent,
his oldest daughter, sobbing and holding in her hands the pieces
of a broken doll. Phyllis, the middle child, was on her hands and
knees, prying the stuffing out of an armchair with a beer-can
opener. Clouds of smoke from what smelled like a burning leg of
lamb drifted out of the open kitchen door into the living room.

He could not believe that they had passed the day in such
disorder. It must all have been planned, arranged— including the
conflagration in the oven—for the moment of his homecoming.
He even thought he saw a look of inner tranquillity on his wife's
harassed face as she glanced around the room and admired the

185

effectiveness of the scene. He felt routed but not despairing and, standing on the threshold, he made a quick estimate of his remaining forces and settled on a kiss as his first move; but as he approached the ironing board his wife waved him away, saying, "Don't you come near me. You'll catch my cold. I have a terrible cold." He then got Phyllis away from the armchair, promised to mend Millicent's doll, and carried the baby into the bathroom and changed her diapers. From the kitchen came loud oaths as Jessica fought her way through the clouds of smoke and took the meat out of the stove.

It was burned. So was almost everything else—the rolls,the potatoes, and the frozen apple tart. There were cinders in Seton's mouth and a great heaviness in his heart as he looked past the plates of spoiled food to Jessica's face, once gifted with wit and passion but now dark and lost to him. After supper he helped with the dishes and read to the children, and the purity of their interest in what he read and did, the power of trust in their love, seemed to make the taste of burned meat sad as well as bitter. The smell of smoke stayed in the air long after everyone but Seton had gone up to bed. He sat alone in the living room, recounting his problems to himself. He had been married ten years, and Jessica still seemed to him to possess an unusual loveliness of person and nature, but in the last year or two something grave and mysterious had come between them. The burned roast was not unusual; it was routine. She burned the chops, she burned the hamburgers, she even burned the turkey at Thanksgiving, and she seemed to burn the food deliberately, as if it was a means of expressing her resentment toward him. It was not rebellion against drudgery. Cleaning women and mechanical appliances— the lightening of her burden—made no difference. It was not, he thought, even resentment. It was like some subterranean sea change, some sexual campaign or revolution stirring—unknown perhaps to her—beneath the shining and common appearance of things.

He did not want to leave Jessica, but how much longer could he cope with the tearful children, the dark looks, and the smoky and chaotic house? It was not discord that he resisted but a threat to the most healthy and precious part of his self-esteem. To be long-suffering under the circumstances seemed to him indecent. What could he do? Change, motion, openings seemed to be what he and Jessica needed, and it was perhaps an indication of his limitations that, in trying to devise some way of extending his marriage, the only thing he could think of was to take Jessica to dinner in a restaurant where they had often gone ten years ago, when they were lovers. But even this, he knew, would not be simple. A point-blank invitation would only get him a point-blank, bitter refusal. He would have to be wary. He would have to surprise and disarm her.

This was in the early autumn. The days were clear. The yellow leaves were falling everywhere. From all the windows of the house and through the glass panes in the front door, one saw them coming down. Seton waited for two or three days. He waited for an unusually fine day, and then he called Jessica from his office, in the middle of the morning. There was a cleaning woman at the house, he knew. Millicent and Phyllis would be in school, and Jocelin would be asleep. Jessica would not have too much to do. She might even be idle and reflective. He called her and told her—he did not invite her—to come to town and to have dinner with him. She hesitated; she said it would be difficult to find someone to stay with the children; and finally she succumbed. He even seemed to hear in her voice when she agreed to come a trace of the gentle tenderness he adored.

It was a year since they had done anything like dining together in a restaurant, and when he left his office that night and turned away from the direction of the station he was conscious of the mountainous and deadening accrual of habit that burdened their relationship. Too many circles had been drawn around his life, he thought; but how easy it was to overstep them. The restaurant where he went to wait for her was modest and good—polished, starched, smelling of fresh bread and sauces, and in a charming state of readiness when he reached it that evening. The hat-check girl remembered him, and he remembered the exuberance with which he had come down the flight of steps into the bar when he was younger. How wonderful everything smelled. The bartender had just come on duty, freshly shaved and in a white coat. Everything seemed cordial and ceremonious. Every surface was shining, and the light that fell onto his shoulders was the light that had fallen there ten years ago. When the headwaiter stopped to say good evening, Seton asked to have a bottle of wine—*their* wine—iced. The door into the night was the door he used to watch in order to see Jessica come in with snow in her hair, to see her come in with a new dress and new shoes, to see her come in with good news, worries, apologies for being late. He could remember the way she glanced at the bar to see if he was there, the way she stopped to speak with the hat-check girl, and then lightly crossed the floor to put her hand in his and to join lightly and gracefully in his pleasure for the rest of the night.

Then he heard a child crying. He turned around toward the door in time to see Jessica enter. She carried the crying baby against her shoulder. Phyllis and Millicent followed in their worn snowsuits. It was still early in the evening, and the restaurant was not crowded. This entrance, this tableau, was not as spectacular as it would have been an hour later, but it was—for Seton, at least—powerful enough. As Jessica stood in the doorway with a sobbing child in her arms and one on each side of her, the sense was not that she had come to meet her husband and, through some breakdown in arrangements, had been forced to bring the children; the sense was that she had come to make a public accusation of the man who had wronged her. She did not point her finger at him, but the significance of the group was dramatic and accusatory.

Seton went to them at once. It was not the kind of restaurant one brought children to, but the hat-check girl was kindly and helped Millicent and Phyllis out of their snowsuits. Seton took Jocelin in his arms, and she stopped crying.

"The baby-sitter couldn't come," Jessica said, but she hardly met his eyes, and she turned away when he kissed her. They were taken to a table at the back of the place. Jocelin upset a bowl of olives, and the meal was as gloomy and chaotic as the burned suppers at home. The children fell asleep on the drive back, and Seton could see that he had failed—failed or been outwitted again. He wondered, for the first time, if he was dealing not with the shadows and mysteries of Jessica's sex but with plain fractiousness.

He tried again, along the same lines; he asked the Thompsons for cocktails one Saturday afternoon. He could tell that they didn't want to come. They were going to the Carmignoles'—everyone was going to the Carmignoles'—and it was a year or more since the Setons had entertained; their house had suffered a kind of social infamy. The Thompsons came only out of friendship, and they came only for one drink. They were an attractive couple, and Jack Thompson seemed to enjoy a tender mastery over his wife that Seton envied. He had told Jessica the Thompsons were coming. She had said nothing. She was not in the living room when they arrived, but she appeared a few minutes later, carrying a laundry basket full of wash, and when Seton asked her if she wouldn't have a drink, she said that she didn't have time. The Thompsons could see that he was in trouble, but they could not stay to help him—they would be late at the Carmignoles'. But when Lucy Thompson had got into the car, Jack came back to the door and spoke to Seton so forcefully—so clearly out of friendship and sympathy—that Seton hung on his words. He said that he could see what was going on, and that Seton should have a hobby—a specific hobby; he should take piano lessons. There was a lady named Miss Deming and he should see her. She would help. Then he waved goodbye and went down to his car. This advice did not seem in any way strange to Seton. He was desperate and tired, and where was the sense in his life? When he returned to the living room, Phyllis was attacking the chair again with the beer-can opener. Her excuse was that she had lost a quarter in the upholstery. Jocelin and Millicent were crying. Jessica had begun to burn the evening meal.

They had burned veal on Sunday, burned meat loaf on Monday, and on Tuesday the meat was so burned that Seton couldn't guess what it was. He thought of Miss Deming and decided she might be a jolly trollop who consoled the men of the neighborhood under the guise of giving music lessons. But when he telephoned, her voice was the voice of a crone. He said that Jack Thompson had given him her name, and she said for him to come the next evening at seven o'clock. As he left his house after supper on Wednesday, he thought that there was at least some therapy in getting out of the place and absorbing himself in something besides his domestic and business worries. Miss Deming lived on Bellevue Avenue, on the other side of town. The house numbers were difficult to see, and Seton parked his car at the curb and walked, looking for the number of her house.

It was an evening in the fall. Bellevue Avenue was one of those back streets of frame houses that are irreproachable in their demeanor, their effect, but that are ornamented, through some caprice, with little minarets and curtains of wooden beading, like a mistaken or at least a mysterious nod to the faraway mosques and harems of bloody Islam. This paradox gave the place its charm. The street was declining, but it was declining gracefully; its decay was luxuriant, and in the back yards roses bloomed in profusion, and cardinals sang in the fir trees. A few householders were still raking their lawns. Seton had been raised on just such a street, and he was charmed to stumble on this fragment of his past. The sun was setting—there was a show of red light at the foot of the street—and at the sight of this he felt a pang in his stomach as keen as hunger, but it was not hunger, it was simple aspiration. Oh to lead an illustrious life!

Miss Deming's house had no porch, and may have needed paint more than the others, although he could not tell for sure, now that the light had begun to fade. A sign on the door said: KNOCK AND COME IN. He stepped into a small hallway, with a staircase and a wooden hatrack. In a farther room he saw a man as old as himself bent over the piano keys. "You're early," Miss Deming called out. "Please sit down and wait."

She spoke with such deep resignation, such weariness, that the tone of her voice seemed to imply to Seton that what he waited for would be disgusting and painful. He sat down on a bench, under the hatrack. He was uncomfortable. His hands sweated, and he felt painfully large for the house, the bench, the situation. How mysterious was this life, he thought, where his wife had hidden her charms and he was planning to study the piano. His discomfort got so intense that he thought for a moment of fleeing. He could step out of the door, into Bellevue Avenue, and never come back again. A memory of the confusion at home kept him where he was. Then the thought of waiting as a mode of eternity attacked him. How much time one spent waiting in dentists' and doctors' anterooms, waiting for trains, for planes, waiting in front of telephone booths and in restaurants. It seemed that he had wasted the best of his life in waiting, and that by contracting to wait for piano lessons he might throw away the few vivid years that were left to him. Again he thought of escaping, but at that moment the lesson in the other room came to an end. "You've not been practicing enough," he heard Miss Deming say crossly. "You have to practice an hour a day, without exception, or else you'll simply be wasting my time." Her pupil came through the little hall with his coat collar turned up so that Seton couldn't see his face. "Next," she said.

The little room with the upright piano in it was more cluttered than the hall. Miss Deming hardly looked up when he came in. She was a small woman. Her brown hair was streaked with gray, braided, and pinned to her head in a sparse coronet. She sat on an inflated cushion, with her hands folded in her lap, and moved her lips now and then with distaste, as if something galled her. Seton blundered onto the little piano stool. "I've never taken piano lessons," he said. "I once took cornet lessons. I rented a cornet when I was in high school—"

"We'll forget about that," she said. She pointed out middle C and asked him to play a scale. His fingers, in the bright light from the music rack, looked enormous and naked. He struggled with his scale. Once or twice, she rapped his knuckles with a pencil; once or twice, she manipulated his fingers with hers, and he had a vision of her life as a nightmare of clean hands, dirty hands, hairy hands, limp and muscular hands, and he decided that this might account for her feeling of distaste. Halfway through the lesson, Seton dropped his hands into his lap. His irresolution only made her impatient, and she placed his hands back on the keys. He wanted to smoke, but on the wall above the piano there was a large sign that forbade this. His shirt was wet when the lesson ended.

"Please bring the exact change when you come again. Put the money in the vase on the desk," she said. "Next." Seton and the next pupil passed each other in the doorway, but the stranger averted his face.

The end of the ordeal elated Seton, and as he stepped out into the darkness of Bellevue Avenue he had a pleasant and silly image of himself as a pianist. He wondered if these simple pleasures were what Jack Thompson had meant. The children were in bed when he got home, and he sat down to practice. Miss Deming had given him a two-handed finger drill with a little melody, and he went over this again and again for an hour. He practiced every day, including Sunday, and sincerely hoped when he went for his second lesson that she would compliment him by giving him something more difficult, but she spent the hour criticizing his phrasing and fingering, and told him to practice the drill for another week. He thought that at least after his third lesson he would have a change, but he went home with the same drill.

Jessica nether encouraged him nor complained. She seemed mystified by this turn of events. The music got on her nerves, and he could see where it would. The simple drill, with its melody, impressed itself even onto the memories of his daughters. It seemed to become a part of all their lives, as unwelcome as an infection, and as pestilential. It drifted through Seton's mind all during the business day, and at any sudden turn of feeling —pain or surprise—the melody would swell and come to the front of his consciousness. Seton had never known that this drudgery, this harrying of the mind was a part of mastering the piano. Now in the evening after supper when he sat down to practice, Jessica hastily left the room and went upstairs. She seemed intimidated by the music, or perhaps afraid. His own relationship to the drill was oppressive and unclear. Taking a late train one evening and walking up from the station past the Thompsons', he heard the same pestilential drill coming through the walls of their house. Jack must be practicing. There was nothing very strange about this, but when he passed the Carmignoles' and heard the drill again, he wondered if it was not his own memory that made it ring in his ears. The night was dark, and with his sense of reality thus shaken, he stood on his own doorstep thinking that the world changed more swiftly than one could perceive—died and renewed itself—and that he moved through the events of his life with no more comprehension than a naked swimmer.

Jessica had not burned the meat that night. She had kept a decent supper for him in the oven, and she served it to him with a timidity that made him wonder if she was not about to return to him as his wife. After supper, he read to the children and then rolled back his shirtsleeves and sat down at the piano. As Jessica was preparing to leave the room, she turned and spoke to him. Her manner was pleading, and this made her eyes seem larger and darker, and deepened her natural pallor. "I don't like to interfere," she said softly, "and I know I don't know anything about music, but I wonder if you couldn't ask her—your teacher—if she couldn't give you something else to practice. That exercise is on my mind so. I hear it all day. If she could give you a new piece—"

"I know what you mean," he said. "I'll ask her."

By his fifth lesson, the days had grown much shorter and there was no longer any fiery sunset at the foot of Bellevue Avenue to remind him of his high hopes, his longings. He knocked, and stepped into the little house, and noticed at once the smell of cigarette smoke. He took off his hat and coat and went into the living room, but Miss Deming was not on her rubber cushion. He called her, and she answered from the kitchen and opened the door onto a scene that astonished him. Two young men sat at the kitchen table, smoking and drinking beer. Their dark hair gleamed with oil and was swept back in wings. They wore motorcycle boots and red hunting shirts, and their manners seemed developed, to a fine point, for the expression of lawless youth. "We'll be waiting for you, lover," one of them said loudly as she closed the door after her, and as she came toward Seton he saw a look of pleasure on her face—of lightness and self-esteem— fade, and the return of her habitually galled look.

"My boys," she said, and sighed.

"Are they neighbors?" Seton asked.

"Oh, no. They come from New York. They come up and spend the night sometimes. I help them when I can, poor things. They're like sons to me."

"It must be nice for them," Seton said.

"Please commence," she said. All the feeling had left her voice.

"My wife wanted to know if I couldn't have something different—a new piece."

"They always do," she said wearily.

"Something a little less repetitious," Seton said.

"None of the gentlemen who come here have ever complained about my methods. If you're not satisfied, you don't have to come. Of course, Mr. Purvis went too far. Mrs. Purvis is still in the sanatorium, but I don't think the fault is mine. You want to bring her to her knees, don't you? Isn't that what you're here for? Please commence."

Seton began to play, but with more than his usual clumsiness. The unholy old woman's remarks had stunned him. What had he got into? Was he guilty? Had his instinct to flee when he first entered the house been the one he should have followed? Had he, by condoning the stuffiness of the place, committed himself to some kind of obscenity, some kind of witchcraft? Had he agreed to hold over a lovely woman the subtle threat of madness? The old crone spoke softly now and, he thought, wickedly. "Play the melody lightly, lightly, lightly," she said. "That is how it will do its work."

He went on playing, borne along on an unthinking devotion to consecutiveness, for if he protested, as he knew he should, he would only authenticate the nightmare. His head and his fingers worked with perfect independence of his feelings, and while one part of him was full of shock, alarm, and self-reproach, his fingers went on producing the insidious melody. From the kitchen he could hear deep laughter, the pouring of beer, the shuffle of motorcycle boots. Perhaps because she wanted to rejoin her friends—her boys—she cut the lesson short, and Seton's relief was euphoric.

He had to ask himself again and again if she had really said what he thought he heard her say, and it seemed so improbable that he wanted to stop and talk with Jack Thompson about it, until he realized that he could not mention what had happened; he would not be able to put it into words. This darkness where men and women struggled pitilessly for supremacy and withered crones practiced witchcraft was not the world where he made his life. The old lady seemed to inhabit some barrier reef of consciousness, some gray moment after waking that would be demolished by the light of day.

Jessica was in the living room when he got home, and as he put his music on the rack he saw a look of dread in her face. "Did she give you a piece?" she asked. "Did she give you something besides that drill?"

"Not this time," he said. "I guess I'm not ready. Perhaps next time."

"Are you going to practice now?"

"I might."

"Oh, not tonight, darling! Please not tonight! Please, please, *please* not tonight, my love!" and she was on her knees.

The restoration of Seton's happiness—and it returned to them both with a rush—left him oddly self-righteous about how it had come about, and when he thought of Miss Deming he thought of her with contempt and disgust. Caught up in a whirl of palatable suppers and lovemaking, he didn't go near the piano. He washed his hands of her methods. He had chosen to forget the whole thing. But when Wednesday night came around again, he got up to go there at the usual time and say goodbye. He could have telephoned her. Jessica was uneasy about his going back, but he explained that it was merely to end the arrangement, and kissed her, and went out.

It was a dark night. The Turkish shapes of Bellevue Avenue were dimly lighted. Someone was burning leaves. He knocked on Miss Deming's door and stepped into the little hall. The house was dark. The only light came through the windows from the street. "Miss Deming," he called. "Miss Deming?" He called her name three times. The chair beside the piano bench was empty, but he could feel the old lady's touch on everything in the place. She was not there—that is, she did not answer his voice—but she seemed to be standing in the door to the kitchen, standing on the stairs, standing in the dark at the end of the hall; and a light sound he heard from upstairs seemed to be her footfall.

He went home, and he hadn't been there half an hour when the police came and asked him to come with them. He went outside—he didn't want the children to hear—and he made the natural mistake of protesting, since, after all, was he not a most law-abiding man? Had he not always paid for his morning paper, obeyed the traffic lights, bathed daily, prayed weekly, kept his tax affairs in order, and paid his bills on the tenth of the month? There was not, in the broad landscape of his past, a trace, a hint of illegality. What did the police want with him? They wouldn't say, but they insisted that he come with them, and finally he got into the patrol car with them and drove to the other side of town, across some railroad tracks, to a dead-end place, a dump, where there were some other policemen. It was a scene for violence— bare, ugly, hidden away from any house, and with no one to hear her cries for help. She lay on the crossroads, like a witch. Her neck was broken, and her clothes were still disordered from her struggle with the great powers of death. They asked if he knew her, and he said yes. Had he ever seen any young men around her house, they asked, and he said no. His name and address had been found in a notebook on her desk, and he explained that she had been his piano teacher. They were satisfied with this explanation, and they let him go.

THE MIDNIGHT VOYAGE OF THE *SEAGULL*

• BY MRS. VOLNEY E. HOWARD •

It was a cold frosty night, in the savage month of January, when the moon and stars shone with uncommon brilliancy, and cast their icy beams over the thick carpet of snow that covered the streets and the country far about, that Horace Harden sat alone in his study, which opened to the street. The curtains were closely drawn, and a bright fire, roaring up the old-fashioned chimney, cast a blaze of light and cheerfulness over the room, with its massive oak furniture, its shelves of books, and a single oil painting (an heirloom) that hung opposite. Doctor Harden, as he was usually called, was seated at a table covered with books and papers, but he was not engaged in study. On what was he meditating? On his promising prospects? Or on the literary fame he had already won? No: he is meditating, with a look of deep despondency, upon a miniature which he had detached from a ribbon around his neck; let us glance at it—lovely, a very lovely girl! Who is she? Perchance the unfinished letter on the table before him will throw light upon the subject; let us use our privilege and look over his shoulder.

Dear George: I have but today received your most welcome letter. I am truly glad to hear of your arrival, though I acknowledge that a degree of selfishness had a share in my pleasure, as I

199

need a friendly heart to whom I can unburden my soul, and you have been from boyhood my only confidant. I have not now, as in former times, to tell you of my fond hopes, my lover's fears, and my efforts to obtain a competence, that I might offer it to my Sarah; you know long since that all my hopes seemed on the point of accomplishment. Competence, ay even wealth it may be termed in this country, is mine; Sarah's affections were, oh heavens! *are still*, mine; even her father consented to the marriage, and every obstacle seemed removed. Oh! what happiness it was when that consent was won, and I clasped her to my heart, exclaiming "Mine, my own, my beautiful!" Yes, it was bliss to sit and gaze into the depths of those dark eyes, and read the fond, the innocent love of the bashful girl, whose lips faltered in maiden modesty to make the avowal! Yes, it was bliss, and I was happy; but it was short-lived happiness, for the past year has been productive of frightful changes.

About a month after your departure, Mr. Carew, to the surprise of everybody, and of his daughter and myself in particular, after an excursion to Charlestown, Boston, and the vicinity, returned with another wife! No one doubted his right to wed if he wished; but the suddenness of the match, and the apparent unsuitableness of the lady, pained Sarah and myself. You recollect Mrs. Matte, the old French woman (as she was generally supposed), who resided in the outskirts of the town, on the path toward Lynn? I had heard it mentioned that her daughter had come to see her, but concluding that she was some poor person of her mother's class, with whom I could have nothing in common, I had forgotten her existence. Conceive then my astonishment on finding that she was the person selected by Mr. Carew to succeed his former excellent lady, to be the mother and companion of his beautiful daughter!

I had been absent for a day or two, and on my return hastened to Mr. Carew's. Sarah was alone in the usual sitting room; she had evidently been in tears, and in answer to my anxious inquiries, informed me of her father's marriage. I eagerly demanded what sort of a person his wife was, and how she behaved to Sarah. Her description of her mother-in-law was rather confused; I could only discover that she was an *oldish* woman, with fierce black eyes and a malicious look, dressed very gaily; very soft spoken, but in Sarah's opinion very deceitful. She had not treated Sarah ill; oh no, she had been there but two days, and called her, 'dear,' and 'her sweet girl,' and 'her charming daughter,' perpetually; but to Sarah's fancy all was hollow beneath this show of kindness; too much parade, too much officiousness. She was not vulgar, though there was a fussiness about her that showed, in Sarah's opinion, that she had not been accustomed to her present station in society.

I painted to myself a florid, buxom widow, of a station just above poverty, gaudily dressed and proud of her new importance, and was deliberating on what I should say to Mr. Carew, when the door opened and in glided the new Madam Carew. Suppose then my surprise at beholding one of the most elegant women I had ever seen, richly dressed it is true, but with the utmost taste and propriety, who, approaching with an air of the most winning kindness and suavity, said,

"Is your headache any better, my dear Miss Carew? I have been looking for these drops. They are excellent for a headache. Nay, do not refuse to gratify me by accepting such a trifle. I assure you they will relieve you immediately."

She forced into Sarah's hand a beautiful vinaigrette, set in pearls, and turning to me, who had involuntarily risen and remained standing, she continued:

"Dr. Harden, I think? I have had the pleasure of meeting you before, though you, I see, have forgotten it. Pray, sit down, and do not make me feel myself an intruder, for the few minutes I shall stay."

There was nothing in the words, but the manner in which they were said gave me the idea of an old friend, though when or where we had met, I could not for my life recall. She remained, perhaps, half an hour conversing cheerfully and pleasantly on various subjects, and disclosing a richly stored memory and cultivated mind. She endeavored to draw Sarah into the conversation; but, though I aided her endeavors, to my mortification Sarah uttered nothing but monosyllables, and became sadder and sadder, till Mrs. Carew rising, and gracefully bidding us adieu, quitted the room. For the first time, I thought Sarah prejudiced and unjust. Her mother-in-law appeared to me totally different from her description. Even now she insisted that her description was correct; that though she might look young to me, she looked old to her, and disagreeable and malicious she was sure she was.

If I write so minutely, I shall fill a volume instead of a letter: but I have been more particular in this instance, as it was the first symptom of a—what shall I call it? *wandering of intellect* in my beloved Sarah. I saw but little of Sarah for a month or six weeks after the marriage of Mr. Carew. The duties of my profession called me at that time much into the country, and when I returned cold or wet of an evening, I felt too much exhausted to dress and enter into general society. Mr. Carew's house was constantly filled with company, so that the only interviews I had with Sarah were for a few minutes in the morning before I began my now daily journeys. At the end of a few weeks, however, I became more disengaged, and was delighted to feel that I could once more give a large portion of my time to my affianced bride. But a change had come over my daydream bliss. I observed an alteration in my Sarah, that did not appear to have as yet struck any other person, at least no one had mentioned it: She seemed to have become apathetic; the bright glance of intelligence which was wont to meet mine, became wandering and cold; she became silent, sullen, and variable in her temper; at times she would weep violently, but give no reason for it. In fact, she became totally altered, till by degrees her fine mind was entirely deranged and lost: not in the wild ravings of insanity, but oh, misery, in the dullness of idiocy!

I have sat by her for hours, endeavoring to awaken some gleam of intellect in that beautiful statue, and in despair at my ill success, have broken from her presence, and in the silence and darkness of my room, have thrown myself on the floor and howled in unutterable agony. I think I could better bear to see her dead, to know that the worst had come, than to see her suffer this living death that forms the dreadful obstacle between us! I can see her whenever I choose, for to her father, yes, and even to Mrs. Carew, I seem ever a welcome guest; yes, five minutes' walk will place me in her presence, but for what? but to torture my heart by seeing her who was—Heaven forgive me—my idol, degraded to a child, and not an intelligent one either, sitting on the carpet playing with baby's toys, or crouched in a corner of the sofa in hopeless, sullen despondency. It is a singular feature in her distemper that she neither raves nor prattles; she seems to have forgotten how to talk connectedly. Alas! it is more like the meetings of old for me to sit in my lonely office, and gaze on those sweet features as limned by the artist, in the miniature she gave me. In that I can still see that bright glance, that smile of peculiar sweet archness which has so long been a stranger to those beautiful lips.

I had been absent for a few days; and on my return, I went to Mr. Carew's; my visits have been so constant, that I have gradually omitted knocking; and as usual, I opened the door of the sitting room, and entered without ceremony. This room has, since Sarah's illness, been appropriated to her, and there, as usual, I found her, attended not by her old nurse, but by Mrs. Carew.

She is a singular, and I believe an amiable woman. It was not till lately that I became, as it were, acquainted with her. When she was first married to Mr. Carew, I was so much absorbed in Sarah, that though I thought her handsome and elegant, I suffered myself to be prejudiced against her by the evident dislike of my poor Sarah, whose dislike is, I suppose, very natural from an only child to a stepmother. (Or, perhaps, it was the aberration of her intellect, which, alas, had then commenced, which created such groundless enmity.) Contrary to my fears, Mrs. Carew seems really attached to Sarah, and watches over her as over a younger sister; for in spite of poor Sarah's expressions of *oldish*, she is a young and very attractive woman; nay, she may well be called beautiful, for she gains on the esteem every time one sees her. Indeed, she looks younger every day; and yet it is a rather singular fact, that at times, when I look at her suddenly, I receive the impression that she is old; but I suppose it is fancy, because she is the wife of an old man; for her magnificent black eyes are as brilliant as diamonds, and her red lip and roseate cheeks tell that the blood of youth is coursing through her veins. Her figure is regal, and her conversation and manners particularly fascinating. It is a brilliant mixture of masculine sense and information with feminine softness and delicacy. I like her society; it prevents my thoughts from resting too intensely on my suffering love; and I generally converse with her for most of the time I pass at her house. But Sarah, it is evident, dislikes her as much as ever, and shows it as much as her enfeebled state will admit.

Mrs. Carew was standing before her when I entered; she held a glass with a dark-colored liquid which she was persuading Sarah very earnestly to take; but just as I opened the door, Sarah with angry vehemence dashed the glass from her hand, exclaiming "I won't, I won't, I won't!" then springing from the sofa and looking wildly round, she screamed, "You may beat me, but I won't, I won't!" At this moment Mrs. Carew looked around, she had heard the opening of the door; her face was agitated and flushed, and *for a second looked old*; but instantly composing herself, she approached me and said with a sigh,

"This is a thankless office! She will not take her medicine, though you ordered it every day! I am compelled to disguise it every way to get her to swallow it, and you heard how she speaks to me! Me, who have done and borne so much for her sake, and— why should I not say it—for yours! Oh! could I but see her restored! But that I fear is hopeless! It is hereditary—there was madness in her mother's family!"

"But I am surprised to hear her speak," said I. "I have not heard her say so much for months!"

"Haven't you indeed?" exclaimed Mrs. Carew. "She *can* talk if she pleases; but her language and ideas are so—so debased, that I am thankful when she is silent. It is so distressing to hear indecent language and vulgar oaths from lips like hers!"

"Good Heavens!" cried I. "Mrs. Carew, do not distract me!"

"Distract *you*!" said she, in her most musical voice, her large dark eyes suffused with tears. "Is is not enough to distract *me*, to see you hanging over yonder hopeless maniac? wasting your young feelings, your rich love, over a senseless block! But what do I say—excuse me, Dr. Harden. In truth I am very foolish and almost worn out."

All this was said with a manner and air that I cannot describe their fascination; suffice it to say, that I led her to a seat, pressed her hand to my lips, and was about to seat myself by her, when Sarah stood before us, her eyes flashing, her lips open, her face, her very brow flushed! She pushed Mrs. Carew away, and seizing my wrist looked in my face in such a sad, strange manner that it cut me to the heart; and, George, as I glanced from her to Mrs. Carew, as I live I saw flit over her countenance the elvish malicious expression I had sometimes heard poor Sarah speak of! Sarah seemed striving to speak, but after a moment the animation faded away, her features assumed a woebegone expression, she passed her hand backward and forward over her forehead as if striving in vain to recollect something, shook her head faintly, and dropping my hand returned slowly to her accustomed seat. I could stay no longer, but rushed into the open air. Poor, poor Sarah, how is this to end? I cannot but hope, for she certainly *did* seem more animated—there *was* a change, and I need not tell you that any change from the dead sea of stupidity, must be for the better.

Thus far had our hero written; he was still gazing mournfully at the miniature, when a slight knock was heard, and, though it was late in the evening, Dr. Harden was not surprised, but rose and bade the applicant walk in. The door was slowly pushed open, and first the head and then the body of a man was introduced, who nodding his head to the doctor by way of bow, stood twisting his raccoon-skin cap into different shapes, and glancing his little peery gray eyes into every corner of the room.

"Well, Joe," said Dr. Harden, after waiting for his visitor to speak, "what is the matter, does anybody want to see me?"

"I—I—I—would be glad to, sir," answered Joe, with considerable effort.

"Very well, sit down then, and let us see what's the matter," good-naturedly responded the doctor.

But Joe remained immovable, his foot half-raised, his mouth open, and his eyes no longer darting about, but fixed on the spot where the pet kitten quietly and comfortably slept at one side of the fireplace. (While he is staring at the cat, let us take a survey of him. He is a young man, not more than eighteen or nineteen years old, a little above the middle size, and formed for strength and activity. He was enveloped in a large pea jacket, which met a pair of loose, thick reddish boots, and round his neck was tied a black silk handkerchief. The head belonging to this alluring person was decorated with a natural shock of coarse light hair, that seemed unconscious of the comb or brush, and stood forth independently in every direction, excepting into a queue. The face, though not rich in intellect, was by no means foolish, though there was that uncertain wavering expression that characterized those who, "unstable as water," can never excel.) Dr. Harden reiterated his request to Joe to sit down; but that worthy, depositing his cap upon the floor, with long careful strides, as light as his heavy fishing boots would allow, approached the unsuspecting cat, and seizing her with both hands, with a grin of mingled terror and delight, marched toward the door.

"Joe!" said Horace, "what ails you? Are you bewitched?"

"Don't, Doctor—d-don't!" exclaimed Joe, holding the cat at arms' length. "You know who's hearing you?"

"Why nobody, you goose," said Horace, laughing, "but you and the cat!"

"Cat!" stuttered Joe. "'Deed, Doctor, I only called 'cause I'm so bad with the rheumatiz, and you're powerful in curing that. Only, you see, I can't tell just how I feel when anybody's here— I wouldn't affront pussy, I'm sure, only jest let me put her out doors till I'm done."

He carried the cat out, all the way declaring that all he came for was to consult the doctor about his ailments, then closing the door he crept to the fire, and looking piteously up in the doctor's face, he whispered.

"I'm in an awful state, Doctor!"

"In an awful state, Joe? What in the name of common sense is the matter? The rheumatism is not very pleasant, but you need not make so much fuss about it. Why, be a man, Joe!"

"Oh Doctor!" whimpered Joe, "'tain't that, it's my poor soul I'm feared about! Oh dear! Oh dear!"

"Your soul, Joe?" cried Horace; "You had better go to the minister, but sit down and don't be a fool, or go and let the cat in first—hear how she is mewing."

"Oh Lord, Doctor, don't! Do let her stay out a little while, do now. I've got somethen to tell you, and maybe *she* would tell *them*," said Joe; then sinking his voice to a whisper, he went on, "I've somethen to tell you, but you must not tell nobody, or it will be my death, oh dear, oh dear!"

"What have you been about, Joe?" said the doctor sternly. "Have you been doing anything wrong?"

"No! No, sir!" cried Joe eagerly, but, dropping his voice, he went on, "that is—I didn't want to do any, I were forced to do what I did! but you see, Doctor, you must promise not to tell nobody if you want to do any good. I'm afeard to tell, and then agin I'm afeard I shall go out of my head if I don't tell."

Dr. Harden felt both curiosity and interest about poor Joe; he knew him for a good-natured, simple fellow, much attached to him in return for former kindness shown to Joe's mother when she was suffering both from sickness and poverty. Horace had not seen him for some time, and now beheld with some surprise his usual vacant, good-humored simper and lounging gait exchanged for an eager, suffering look and a nervous terrified manner. He concluded that someone had been playing some trick on his humble friend, and resolved to interfere in his favor.

"Sit down, Joe," said he. "I promise to keep your secret, unless you give me leave to disclose it, so sit down and let me hear all about it."

Drawing his chair as near to that of his patron as possible, Joe commenced his narration in the following words:

"You know, sir, how I'm cabin boy aboard of the *Seagull*, I suppose? Well, when we come home last vi'ge, about a month ago, the ship was brought alongside of Mr. Carew's wharf in winter harbor and jest lashed to the piles, and after she was unloaded Mr. Carew said how if I was a-mind to be faithful and take good care of the vessel, I mought stay aboard and keep her in order, pump her out you know, sir, and sich like, and get my grub at his house, and he'd allow me a trifle for wages; so mother was glad that I could be arning somethen in winter, though it was main lonesome to the old woman having me away all night, and a good part of the day."

"My good fellow," said Horace, utterly out of patience, "if you have nothing better than this to tell you had better go home, I—"

"Oh Doctor," said Joe in great alarm, "I have, sir, I have, only I wanted you to know all about it. Well, sir, I stayed aboard, and for some nights nothin disturbed me, till one Friday night, jest after I had turned in, I heard somebody call me, so I jumped up and ran on deck, and now sir you won't believe me, but it is as true as I'm sitting here, who should be standing on the wharf but Madam Carew! I was struck all on a heap, and stood rubbin my eyes, when she said, 'Help me on board, Joe;' so what could I do, sir?"

"Go on," said Horace, "I will talk with you about it by and by."

"Well, sir, I went and give her my hand, and she jumped aboard, and arter her come the sightest a cats ever you *did* see; as I stood a thinking what she wanted and what she was going to do with all them hannimals, says she, 'Joe, is not there a bible in the cabin?' 'Yes marm,' says I. 'Well,' says she, 'go and bring it up.' So I runs down and brung it up, wondering what she was going to do; so she told me to take it and throw it overboard. 'Why marm,' says I, 'tis the cappen's'; but she stamped her foot on the deck and looked at me with them great big black eyes of hern so fiercelike that I felt quite flabbergasted. So says she, 'Ain't I your owner's wife,' says she, 'and what's more, if you don't do just as I tell you you shall never see another sun.' She frightened me so that I was afeard to say no, and I did as she said, and as I throwed the blessed bible over the taffrail, as it struck water she laughed, and there was such a laughing all round that I thought there was a hundred folks there, and then I heard a kind of scrabbling, and I looked and seed ever so many things like cats, only they *warn't* cats, crawling aboard on all sides, and them was what was laughing! I was just thinking of jumping ashore and running home, when Madam Carew says, 'Joe! you're in my power, and all that will save you is to do just as I tell you. Cast off the ropes there,' and she pointed to stem and stern, and I *felt* that I must do her bidding, she looked so dreadful, so I did, and then she told me to go down below and stay till she called me; so I went down into the cabin, for I was glad to get out of the way of such queer-looking folks."

"*What* queer-looking folks, Joe?" said Horace, concluding some trick had been played on his humble friend, and determined to sift it.

"Why—Doctor—didn't I tell you? The cats—I mean the men and women that they turned out to be, all dressed mighty fine too, but queer somehow, and they made such noises and looked so at me that I made but one jump down the companionway, and it was a good while afore I dared to peep up to see what they were about. By Jings! it was a sight, Doctor! These queer sailors had got the old *Seagull* under weigh, and though there warn't a thimbleful of wind, the sails drawed, and she went snorting through the water, right down the bay!"

"Joe," said Horace in utter surprise, "you mean you dreamed all this, I presume? It was singular dream to be sure, still—"

"Oh no, Doctor," said Joe, fixing his earnest eyes on Horace's face, "twan't a dream! I be telling Heaven's truth sir! Did I ever tell you a lie?"

"No, Joe, not that I know of. Go on with your story!" answered Horace, who determined to hear the whole, and then form his opinion as to Joe's sanity.

"Well, Doctor, they were all quiet enough for some time, but after a while—Lord save us!—what a racket they did make! The shrouds was hung full on 'em and they were chasing one another about the deck like mad, and sometimes they were dancing, but I could not see who played, and I never heard sich tunes afore; it made my flesh all creep-creep so queerly! And all the time it grew warmer and warmer, till it was more like July than December! Well! at last somebody hollered something that I could not understand, and they all stopped their frolicking and huddled together on deck, and I was feared they'd catch me peeping and kill me, so I creeped down and lay down on the transom; so in a minute Madam Carew looked down the companionway and called me, and at first I did not answer, for I was afeard that they had found out I was a-watching them and was a-going to throw me overboard, but she said, 'he's a-laying there sound asleep! I told you he was a simpleton!' So when she called again I made believe to wake up and—"

"Well, well, Joe! Don't be quite so long in your story, my man!" said the doctor, who began to be interested in Joe's adventure; if it *was* a hoax, it was a bold one, and he was determined to find it out.

"I'm a-telling as fast as I can, Doctor. I ain't book larned like you, so I hopes you will put up with me."

Horace saw that the more he interrupted Joe, the more prosaic he would be, and resolved to let him go on in his own fashion.

"Well Doctor, she called me, so I made believe I'd been asleep, and jumped up the ladder and stood a-looking about, and there we was, close into land, but it warn't Salem, it were bright moonlight, and I could see as plain as day. There warn't no more vessels there, for there was only a little bit of beach and no harbor, and what kept the vessel steady I don't know, for she warn't anchored. Howsever, Madam Carew told me to hoist out the boat and row her ashore—well, you see, there warn't no boat aboard but an old wherry turned bottom-up amidships—so I told her how it would take two or three men to hoist that out, but she stamped her foot, and I jest took hold and turned it over, and then a heap of 'em catched hold and had it out afore you could wink, for somehow it seemed as if they could not do anything of that sort without I begun first. Well! then *she* told me to row her ashore, so I jumped in and she and another got in with me and I pulled ashore, and I heard a great splattering in the water, and Lord! there was a whole school of cats a-swimming arter for dear life!

Well! I almost dropped the oars, for cats, you know, be creeters that don't like the water no how! But it made no odds whether I rowed or not, for the wherry went dancing along and run up high and dry itself. So they got out and went up the bank, and Madam Carew told me to stay by the boat till she come back, and staring at me with her big eyes, she held up her finger and said if I did not mind her I was a dead man, for she'd got the power over me. Well! I was forced to stay till they come back, which they did in no great time, all loaded with marsh rosemary, and oh how green and pretty it looked!"

"Marsh rosemary! Green and pretty at this time of year, Joe!" cried the doctor, thinking he had discovered a discrepancy in Joe's narrative.

"Don't I tell you, sir," cried Joe, "that it warn't this time of year *there*, for the trees looked all green and full of leaves, and it was as warm as summer! And I had to pull off my pea jacket? It got warm very soon after we left the bay, and the brig cut through the water like a streak of chalk, though, as I told you, there was not a capful of wind."

"Well Joe," said Horace, "this is the strangest story; has not some person put all this in your mouth? I am afraid you are suffering yourself to be made the tool of some bad person!"

"And that's true enough," cried poor Joe, "the tool of the devil, I'm afraid! Oh Lord, what's that?"

Horace started and looked in the direction to which Joe's trembling finger pointed. It was his cat that, tired of remaining in the cold, had scrambled onto the window ledge, and pressing herself against the glass, gave token of her presence by a loud mew.

"It is my own poor cat," said he, "and as she is very useful I must insist on taking her in, as I will prove to you that *she* at least is no witch." So saying he opened the window, and taking the shivering grimalkin in his hand, placed her on the cover of the large bible that lay on a corner of the table. Puss stood very contentedly rubbing her head against her master's hand, till Joe was satisfied that she was a *bona fide* cat and nothing else, and turning away continued his tale of *diablerie*.

"Doctor, you must not be mad with me for being skeart! If you'd a-seen all I seed, you mought be a leetle skeery too! But howsever, to finish off, when they got down to the wherry they seemed in a great hurry, and all of 'em put their green stuff into the wherry, and Madam Carew says, 'Come Joe, row me on board.' So she and one more got in, and I rowed them on board, and t'others come like cats again, only I could not see how they did it, for one minute they was men and women standing on the beach, and the next—why—they were cats walloping in the water! Well, the woman as was with Madam Carew says to me, 'Joe, how do you like Bermuda?' and Madam Carew said, 'Hush, there is no need to let him know more than we are obliged to, and if he tells *that*, he shall never see another Friday!' Oh Doctor, I'm afeard that I am a dead man if you can't help me! I ain't got much more to tell: they got the boat aboard somehow, and we got home before daybreak, then Madam Carew offered me a crown, but I didn't want none of her money, then she laughed and said I should take it, so I took it and put it down in the fo'c's'le, and here they are, for I won't keep 'em any longer!"

So saying he put his hand in his trousers pocket and drew forth a dirty rag, from which he took three crowns and presented them to the doctor, who said "There are three crowns, you said she gave you but one."

"That's the first time, sir," answered Joe. "They been twice since that. I don't think they always go to one place, but 'tis always warm weather, and they bring on board marsh rosemary or whatever it is."

"What do they do with it?" said the doctor.

"The dear Lord knows, sir, they takes it away with them, and is very careful to pick up every sprig. I ain't dared to speak of it, but I'm growing sick, and if they go on so I shall die, I can't stand it."

"Why, what is there in it so frightful, Joe?" said Horace, wishing to gain every information possible before he made up his mind on the singular account given by the young sailor.

"Oh you don't know the feel of it, Doctor," cried Joe with an involuntary shudder, and pulling his chair still nearer to the doctor, while his pallid countenance, his sunken cheeks and a sort of hopeless expression in his eyes, convinced his hearer that if it was a trick, Joe was sincere in his belief of its reality.

"It is an awful feel, sir, to have your flesh creeping all over you, and your hair standing up from the roots, and a sort of faintiness as if there was something awful nigh you that you could not see, as I know there is when they are on board. You see Doctor, after the first time, they didn't order me down below, and feeling curious like, I stood sometimes on deck, and as they didn't say nothing to me I felt bolder. I wanted to find out who steered and give orders, for though I could see *them*, there was thick darkness all abaft the binnacle, nor was there any candle in the binnacle, so how they could see the compass puzzled me famously—so when they were all eating and drinking (and where they got their vittles and wine I don't know) I crept up towards the helm, but I could not go there, for my hair stood on end worser than ever, and a cold clammy sweat broke out over me, and I thought I should have swounded, and a strange low laugh burst out of the darkness and rang all over the ship!

"*All* was still in a minute, and I was so skeered that I dropped right down on the deck and crawled away on all fours till I got down below. It wan't a loud laugh, it was very low and sweet, but it rang all round, and it made my blood run cold, and I didn't get over it, for I shook and trembled as I sat in the cabin, and every creak the rudder gave I shuddered and felt my heart jump up in my throat! And Doctor, it is a fact, I feel worser *now* when they go away than while they are there, for how do I know if *what* steers, that I *can't see*, goes away too? And I don't like to go on the quarter-deck in the daytime even, and nights—oh I can't sleep! I lay shivering and listening for that terrible laugh till I am almost crazy! Oh Doctor, I shall die or go crazy!—I cannot stand it! I've just stole up here to tell you about it, but I must go back, though I'd rather be tied up and take a hundred lashes!"

"Well, cannot you get permission to leave the brig? The voyage is up, and I suppose you can quit and take another service if you like," said Horace, anxious to discover if there was anything behind the story for although he knew Joe to be an honest, though generally considered a dull boy, his story was of such momentous importance, involving as it did the life and character of many individuals, that he felt as if treading among precipices blindfold, and wished to be certain that he was not misled.

"Oh sir," answered Joe, "*she* would kill me, she said she would, and I know she will keep her word, for she is an awful woman! And sometimes when I open my eyes in the night, I think I see a pair of huge shining eyes looking at me! Oh how do I know but that she sees me now!"

This confession of Joe was none the less interesting to Dr. Harden; his heart thrilled with wild and mingled emotions as he reflected that this, if true, might be in some measure connected with the strange state of his beloved. He recollected circumstances that, though at the time only striking him as odd, he now viewed with other feelings. The singular circumstance of the uncertainty he had himself felt of the age of Mrs. Carew, that she looked old at one minute and young the next, as he remembered to have heard observed by others as well as himself. It was not the difference caused by the mysteries of the toilet; that was a common occurrence; but it was a sort of haziness that seemed to play over her countenance at the first moment of looking at her, which he had formerly attributed to some weakness in his own eyesight; but now!—Wild ideas thronged upon him till his brain whirled; he felt the awful responsibility he had incurred by becoming the depository of so dreadful a secret: if he buried it in his bosom he was accessory to their deeds, and consigned his beloved Sarah and poor Joe to destruction; while on the evidence of a simple fellow like his humble friend (selected by them probably for that very reason), he dared not accuse the wife of so rich and influential a man as Mr. Carew.

He questioned Joe if he knew any of the others who participated in these infernal pleasure parties; but Joe declared that, though at the *first glance* he thought he knew a good many of them, there seemed a sort of haze over them so that he could not say for certain. The longer Dr. Harden reflected the more difficult appeared his position; to accuse them without more responsible evidence than Joe's was not to be thought of, but how to obtain his evidence was the question.

At length an idea struck him, which though hazardous, was the only feasible means he could think of to ascertain the truth or falsehood of Joe's allegations; it was to take Joe's place on the ensuing Friday. It was a wild plan, and if Joe had spoken the truth, a dangerous one; but to a young man like Horace, of ardent temperament, high courage, and deep devotion to his lady-love, it was not without its allurements. The very excitement was not without its pleasure to a mind of eager inquiry, tied down hitherto to the dull daily routine of life in a small town, as Salem then was. The only difficulty was how he was to pass for Joe. As he looked at him he saw the impossibility of his own athletic form, manly step, and erect carriage passing for Joe's shambling, slouching, loosely made person, even if the face could be concealed. A child might detect the difference, much more a company of witches. How then could he contrive it? On further questioning Joe, he found that they never looked about the vessel. Whether it was that they relied on her being deserted, or that they had means of knowing that Joe alone was on board he knew not; but he determined to run the risk of concealing himself on board.

On mentioning his plan to Joe, the delight that beamed over the sailor's countenance, proved that he had told no wilful falsehood; Horace promised him to come down on Friday evening, and charged him to watch his words and even looks, that no suspicion might be entertained of their intentions. He also desired him to tie up his face as if for the toothache and wear it so for the short time that would intervene before their adventure, as this was Wednesday. Joe promised obedience, and suggested to the doctor to come well armed, as in case he was discovered, he might defend himself.

"Though I thinks myself," he continued, "that if they found you they would all turn to cats, and jump overboard."

"If that be the case," said Horace, "why don't they go where they wish, without a vessel?"

"Lord knows, sir," cried Joe, shaking his head. "Who knows what they can do, or what they cannot? I don't see what they want of *me*, and yet it sort a seems to me that if I didn't go, and *begin* as it were for them, they couldn't go themselves! I can't explain what I mean, but you'll see sir, if you keep your promise."

"That I certainly shall," said Horace, "and now my good boy, if go you must, you had better make no longer delay. We must be careful to attract no suspicion."

On Friday Horace, taking the precaution of arming himself to the teeth, as it is called, sallied forth, and by a circuitous route gained the wharf at which was the *Seagull*—he hoped without attracting any observation. It was the dinner hour of the primitive inhabitants of Salem, and he had not met a person on his way. Joe, who was on the watch, welcomed him with tears of joy, and opening a small stateroom, gave him the key, which he had rummaged out, and called his attention to an old fowling-piece and a cutlass which he had placed in it for fear that the doctor should have forgotten his arms. Joe's face was tied up as the doctor had recommended, and he now produced a pea jacket, an old hat, and boots like those he wore himself, which, with a forethought so entirely unexpected that it almost aroused the doctor's suspicions, he had provided. He immediately put them on, and tying a handkerchief similar to Joe's over his face, saw that his opportunities of observation would be much safer from the disguise.

He now entered into a consultation with Joe, who had risen considerably in his estimation, as to the method to be adopted for him to see without being seen. Now that he had entered the lion's den, a thousand things occurred to him which he had not thought of before. He regretted that he had not written something to leave behind him, but it was now too late. He questioned Joe over and over respecting their proceedings; but minutely as he questioned, Joe's account did not vary. In answer to a query whether any of them remained on board while the rest went to gather the marsh rosemary, which seemed the object of the voyage, Joe could give him little satisfaction. Joe could not see anybody on deck, but as the brig, though neither moored nor made fast in any manner, remained stationary, he argued that some controlling power *must* be there, and mentioned the helmsman, who or whatever he might be, that it was likely *that* remained in the vessel. He also added that he thought he had seen two fiery eyes once glowing through the darkness that on these occasions shrouded that part of the deck.

Do not accuse Horace of cowardice, he was as brave as most men, nor would he have shrunk from dangers of which he could calculate the nature or extent; this was a leap in the dark; no shouting comrades to witness his bravery and stimulate it by their own; no applauding spectators; alone—far from any friendly refuge—in the night—he had rashly undertaken to beard the dreadful beings of whom he had often heard, though but half believed till now.

Bracing his mind to the adventure, he proceeded to take such measures and give Joe such instructions, as he thought requisite for their safety. He charged him, if left with the boat as usual, to search for some live shellfish, of a kind that grew not in the waters of Salem, and some green leaves or twigs, and above all, some of the marsh rosemary, as "tokens true," of their perilous adventure. Joe promised obedience, and suggested that, as night was rapidly approaching, it would be better for the doctor to retire into the stateroom and conceal himself, which Horace immediately did, and lying down in the berth, he endeavored to arrange his thoughts, till, singular as it may seem, he dropped into a sound slumber. When he awoke, it was night, but he could feel that the brig was in motion, and surging through the waves with immense rapidity. He arose as softly as he could, and ventured to peep into the cabin; it was dark, except a pale unnatural light that gleamed down the companionway, and, as far as he could discover, it was empty. He ventured out and crept to the foot of the ladder, where he could hear the sound of many voices in high revelry on deck. While he stood listening, he heard the sound of approaching footsteps, and hastily retreated to the stateroom, till he saw Joe descend. I have already said that he wore a suit of old clothes, and a slouched hat, and now wishing to see all that he could without detection, he ascended the ladder.

It was a gay though fearful sight that presented itself to his astonished eyes; the vessel was lit up by a lambent flame that played about the masts and rigging, now spreading itself in a thousand brilliant forms and colors over the shrouds, then collecting into a huge globe on the highest spar, and anon darting in bright streams and fantastic shapes round the dark hull, illumining the blue waves and their feathery crests of white foam as the gallant brig dashed swiftly onward. The deck seemed filled with revellers of both sexes, though what it was precisely that employed them, he found it impossible to discover, the atmosphere being filled with a sort of thin, transparent haze or gas, that by its constant quivering motion rendered every object of a dreamy character. Though many of the faces as well as voices seemed familiar to him, he no sooner fixed his eyes upon any person than the lineaments became distorted, resembling a reflection in the water disturbed by dropping in a pebble.

While he remained gazing with fascinated eyes upon this, two females separated themselves from the crowd and approached the companionway. He slipped down, and giving a sign to Joe, ensconced himself again in his stateroom. The women descended into the cabin, and ordering Joe to leave it, they seated themselves very near to the door of the stateroom, through which Horace was peeping. He could now see distinctly, and easily recognized Mrs. Carew and the old woman who passed for her mother. After a moment's pause they resumed their conversation, the old woman saying,

"You don't seem to advance much in your scheme, yet you

have been nearly a year about it already!"

"No, not yet," answered Mrs. Carew, "he holds out stoutly, but my triumph will be the greater when I *do* succeed, which I *shall*, depend on it. He talks much with me, and I see that he is pleased and interested by my conversation. None of the women he sees can compete with me, but he yet clings to Sarah, though I did hope he would have been tired of her before now. Oh how I hate her! When he sits bending over her, and speaking in his rich sweet voice, I feel as if I could stab her with pleasure, and long to drug her next draught so deeply that it would put her to sleep for ever, instead of stupefying her!"

"Why don't you, then?" said the other, carelessly. "She would then be out of your way, and you might do as you pleased with her old doting father."

"Yes, but *now* Harden would grieve for her, and perhaps not come to a house that reminded him of his loss; and as I wish him to respect as well as admire me, I could not seek him elsewhere. No! I must disgust him with her. Surely he cannot much longer love a drivelling idiot! When that is accomplished, and he is in my toils, I will quickly get rid of her and her foolish old father. But *you*, methinks, are not keeping faith with me! You promised, out of all the roots and plants and herbs we have obtained so plentifully, to compound me a philter, that as a last resort might be used and force him to love me!"

"And so I can," said the old crone, "but you are so impatient! It is not every hour or time that this can be done. The moon and the constellations must be in favorable positions. You know too that from some foolish whim you wanted to gain his love without the philter. Pah! love from a boy like him for such as *you* and *I*! But I will make it for you before the moon has again waned. Yet I warn you again that it will not be the kind of love he had for Sarah! *We* cannot make *that*, but as far as wild passion will content you I can—"

"I don't care, so he loves me and none but me. But I will try my own arts first, and have that ready if they fail. But why should I talk to you about *love*, who have outlived all your womanly feelings but love of mischief!"

"Well, you say true enough—I can't comprehend why you

care about a man's *loving* you, at your age, too! But I'll help you, I have sworn it, and we are also compelled to assist each other in all mischief. Now let us go up. We are losing the fun, and it is little enough a poor old woman like me gets to make her merry!"

So saying, she led the way on deck, followed by her companion; leaving the concealed listener in a tumult of feelings, in which, however, *joy* predominated. Yes, *joy*, for was his Sarah yet to be saved? The love professed for him by Mrs. Carew filled him with disgust; a thousand circumstances corroborated the words he had overheard, and he felt an intense loathing of her, which in some degree extended to himself for having liked to converse with her. "And I have kissed her hand!" thought he, and he wiped his lips violently, as if to remove the contamination. Just then Joe came down to apprise him in a whisper that land was in sight, for the witches had assembled at the bows, and he should soon have to go on shore.

In a short time all was silent on deck, and he determined to venture up. With proper precautions he ascended the gangway, and eagerly fixed his eyes on the beautiful island that lay sleeping in placid loveliness before him. The bright tropical moon poured her silver light over hill and dale, and the air seemed loaded with perfumes. As he watched the wherry drawn up on the little beach or inlet, and Joe standing by its side—there, thought he, is the bright southern isle! Oh for a walk in its sweet orange groves! Never shall I see it again! So near, yet never to stand upon its verdant shores!

As he thus meditated a taunting laugh rang out, as it seemed, just beside him; he turned, but no one was there! The bright moonbeams poured a flood of light upon the deck; none but himself was there! But the feeling of unaccountable dread, that poor Joe had described, fell upon him, and it seemed to him that he *must* jump overboard; anything to escape from that dreadful vessel, and that unseen but not unfelt influence. He was a bold and skillful swimmer, he could easily reach the shore, where he and Joe could remain till some vessel would sail for their native land!

But the thought of his sweet Sarah, withering under the drugs of that she-fiend, restrained him, and rushing down to the stateroom he buried his face in the bedclothes and lay listening with inward shuddering for the dreadful laugh that he felt was not formed by earthly lip! It died away, but still he lay, every sense lost in that of hearing, but it came not again. He was roused by his own name whispered by Joe, who said, as he tried to pull a blanket over him: "For massy sake, Doctor, take keer! The door wide open and your legs a-sticking out! If they'd a-come down instead of me, now! There, here are a passel of shells I got, and here's some weeds and—oh massy! they're coming!" He darted out of the stateroom, pulling the door after him, and gained the ladder as the others came down.

Horace sprang from the berth, and with a pistol in each hand stood at the door ready to defend his life, if he found himself betrayed. He could see, through a hole cut in the panel, several women come down loaded with herbs, which they piled carefully upon the cabin table, then all departed but three, who, seating themselves, commenced a consultation. He could not distinguish their faces, but he recognized the now-hated voice of Mrs. Carew.

"I have no desire to go again," said she, "we have as much rosemary as we need."

"Then let this be the last voyage," said another, "for much as you vaunted the stupid obedience of your simple boy, I doubt him. There is a boldness, an alertness in his manners tonight that I have not noticed before."

"Yes," muttered the third in a shuddering whisper, "and I heard *our master* laugh tonight, and that ye know bodes mischief somewhere!"

"Ay?" said Mrs. Carew. "Then we will give tonight to yonder boy a glass of wine, with the drug you know of in it, and when they seek him, for he will hardly go to town again, he will be silent enough. Come, let us go on deck and prepare."

The demon women then ascended the steps, leaving Horace in the greatest anxiety for his humble friend. Fortunately, however, Joe came down soon after the women went on deck, and was instantly put on his guard by Harden, who advised him to button up his pea jacket, pull the handkerchief further over his mouth, and pretend to be drinking the wine but pour it into his collar. He cheered him with assurances of his protection and assistance, and finally succeeded in reassuring him.

I will not describe at length the anxiety of that, as it seemed to him, long, long night; repose was out of the question; thought chased thought through his troubled mind, like clouds driven through the sky by a fierce northeaster, precursor of an autumnal tempest. And to what a tempest did he look forward, consequent to his intended denunciation of the infamous Mrs. Carew and her pretended mother! If he substantiated his charge, these women would probably accuse their confederates, and into how many families would the hand of justice carry agony and disgrace! Though unable to designate any but the two we have mentioned, he had a dim perception that he knew them all, the voices, the faces, all seemed familiar; and how many of those, with whom he daily associated, might be implicated, he dreaded to imagine! He must expect a powerful opposition; all who were linked together in that dreadful band, supported by their relatives and friends, would be against him; his tale would be discredited by every means, obloquy would be poured upon his character, his motives would be questioned, his veracity impugned, and himself perhaps ruined!

As he looked at the shellfish given him by Joe, and at the handful of sea rosemary taken from the table by himself, and reflected that these were all the evidence he could bring, beside that of the simple Joe, to substantiate the wild and improbable accusation he must bring against some of the first families, he felt a sad and deep despondency creeping over his heart, palsying its high and noble impulses, and shrouding with gloom his hopes and expectations. One bright star shone through of his sweet Sarah! She was not a maniac or an idiot, he might save her; she might recover, and be his, and was not that happiness to dream of? While he was thus "chewing the cud of sweet and bitter fancies," the door of the stateroom was cautiously opened, and Joe crept in.

"We are amost home now," whispered he, "don't you hear the music I told you of?"

Horace roused himself, and was indeed aware of a strain of music so wildly sweet, so soft, so soothing, that he hardly dared to breathe, lest he should lose some of that melody!

"It always comes," said Joe, heedless of the signs for silence made impatiently by the doctor. "I thought I'd peep in to tell you that *she* offered me the wine, and I took it and made believe drink it as you told me, and she didn't suspect. So now I go to sleep— it always put me to sleep."

So saying, and suiting the action to the word by yawning hideously, Joe stole out of the stateroom, leaving Horace to enjoy the harmony unmolested. In a minute or two, to his surprise, he felt himself nodding; he endeavored to rouse himself by every method he could think of, but in vain, and his last effort was to crawl to the little door and lock it, when he sunk on the floor, and, entranced by the delicious tones that were gushing around him, without further resistance gave way to slumber. He was awakened by repeated knocking, and his name, first low, then louder and louder till the call became a shout, and the hammering against the door threatened to beat in its panels. He gathered himself up, and hardly knowing where he was, felt for the door and opened it, to the great delight of Joe, whose fears for his safety had rendered him almost desperate.

"Oh Doctor!" whispered the poor fellow, "I'm so glad to see you alive, if you did but know how skeered I been! I kinder thought she might have done something to you, as I couldn't make you hear. You need not look about you now, they have all been gone this hour, and I been trying to wake you for I don't know how long!"

It was as Joe said, all were gone but that individual and himself. Horace looked for the shellfish and rosemary, and found them safe; his mind was made up, and directing Joe to follow him, he bent his steps, not to his own lodging, but to the house of the clergyman, from whence messengers were soon dispatched for the selectmen and other leading citizens of Salem.

In a small room appropriated to his daughter, in the handsome mansion of Mr. Carew, were his wife and his daughter. Crouching in a corner of the room, her back smarting from the lash, that, wielded by no weak or unwilling hand, had left its livid welts on her beautiful arms and shoulders; her pale features working with internal emotion, and her white lips muttering words which she either dared not, or could not articulate, was the once lovely, indulged, and admired Sarah Carew. On a sofa opposite, her triumphant eyes gloating on the misery of her victim, and her scornful lips mocking at her agony, sat Mrs. Carew.

"So! my pretty Miss! You won't obey me, will you! This is the second time you have dashed the medicine from my hand; but you shall find, minion, that *I* am mistress! Yes—mutter and gibber like an idiot as you are, *as I have made you*—do you hear? Ay, you understand, but it shall not avail you! When she comes for whom I have sent, she will bring another, and together we will force it down your throat, and then see if your doctor will like his pretty mammit!"

A fiendish laugh followed this taunting speech, and she watched with delight its effects on her shuddering hearer—when the door opened, and the clergymen of that and the adjoining parish, the selectmen, the lawyers, and the other dignitaries of the town entered. In the rear of the party walked Dr. Harden, whose haggard and worn look marked his sense of the responsibility he had incurred, while his resolute eye spoke a determination to do and dare all, to punish vice and unmask hypocrisy.

Mrs. Carew rose and confronted her visitors with a look that quailed not, and was as haughty as their own; but Sarah no sooner saw Dr. Harden, then with a cry of delight she bounded forward and, catching him by the arm, muttered, "Don't let her whip me again!" and exhibited her arms now black where the whip had struck. The eyes of the assembly turned first upon the victim, and thence to Mrs. Carew, who colored with rage as she saw her hated step-daughter folded in the arms of her lover; and she exclaimed:

"Poor thing! how she contrived to mark herself so, I cannot tell! I have just come in to give her attendant an opportunity to breakfast, but the unfortunate girl is very violent sometimes! But what is your wish, gentlemen? Mr. Carew is away from home, shall I send for him?"

In a few words the clergymen informed her of the accusation

against her; she laughed contemptuously, and desired to know what proof they could possibly expect to find of such a crime, and how they dared accuse her of such wickedness. "Who was her accuser?" She turned her flashing eyes upon the doctor, with a glance of mingled rage and surprise; but rallying her faculties, she ordered a servant to go instantly for Mr. Carew, and, seating herself, bade them search, if they thought it fitting and proper, on the accusation of a villain, whose base designs upon herself she had scorned, and forbore complaint to her husband only at his abject entreaty and solemn promise of reformation.

They searched the house throughout, but without success. Every apartment was closely investigated, and they were joined by an officer who had been employed to apprehend the mother of Mrs. Carew, who assured them that no trace of rosemary or anything uncommon had been discovered at her house. Horace was in despair; his companions had evidently lost all faith in his story and looked at him with no pleasant countenances, as one who had by his dreams led them to offend the richest, the most influential man among them. They proceeded in a body to the room of Mrs. Carew, to which she had retired, and asked respectfully for admittance. The door was thrown open, and Mrs. Carew demanded:

"Have you any further insult to offer, gentlemen? Ye have already searched this chamber, or I mistake, but perhaps ye wish to search my pockets!"

"No, madam, no!" cried one of the gentlemen, "if we have offended, I deeply regret it, but on the information that was sworn to before us, we could do no otherwise. We have now to take our leave, with every feeling of—"

"What!" interrupted Horace, "are you really going to take no further notice of my allegations, sworn to so solemnly? Do you intend to search no more?"

"Search yourself, sir, if you think proper," said one of the selectmen, who from the first had been very backward in the business. "For my part, I must think that you dreamed the adventure!"

"I dreamed the shellfish and green rosemary too, I presume!" cried Horace. "But I will search once more."

Thus saying, he recommenced a search, examining the panels, and turning up the carpet with an air of desperate determination that alarmed Mrs. Carew, who angrily exclaimed:

"I am willing that the proper officers should search my house, if such is your will, but I will not consent that this wretch, who had no view but to insult me, should be allowed to carry his insolence further. I command him to leave my habitation, and I pray ye to understand, that though my husband had given way to these proceedings for once, he will neither forget nor forgive insult to me—his lawful wife!"

The rest of the party, struck with dismay at her covert threat, began to insist upon his leaving the room, but Horace, who had at that moment discovered a small crack in one of the panels, through which he fancied he inhaled the perfume of the rosemary, refused to stir, and endeavored to force the panel in spite of the now furious menaces of Mrs. Carew.

"It is in here, infamous woman, you know it well. So help me Heaven! I will not stir from hence till I am satisfied!"

Glancing round the room, he saw some billets of wood lying on the hearth, and seizing one, in spite of the opposition of those around him, who began to think that the whole was a falsehood, or perhaps an insane fancy, he dashed the billet at the concealed door, and the shock succeeded as he wished, a part of the paneling sliding back, and giving to view a private closet, heaped with tropical productions!

There was the green rosemary, the golden orange, and the fragrant pineapple, with a hundred other productions of those sunny isles where winter is unknown. All rushed to have a nearer view, but Horace, whose quick eye beheld Mrs. Carew hastening to the door.

"Secure the sorceress!" shouted he, and at the word, the officers of justice seized their victim, who with bitter laugh and flashing eyes, taunted them even then, and bade them beware of her vengeance!

In spite of her denunciations, she and the hag her mother were securely lodged in the jail, and orders given that no one but the magistrates should have access to them.

The tumult—the horror and dismay of the town of Salem and its vicinity, can better be imagined than described. All confidence was destroyed, and Horace was beset from morning to night with inquiries which he could not answer, relative to those whom he saw on the fatal voyage. He gave as much of his time as possible to the care of his dear Sarah, whose rapid amendment was hailed with delight by both father and lover.

After two or three days, a private message was conveyed, by the jailer, from the old woman to one of the magistrates, promising a full confession if her life was spared, and an hour after, another communication to the same effect, was received from Mrs. Carew. The magistrates and their associates immediately met in consultation, and it was determined that as the day was far advanced, on the morrow they would visit the prison, and from one of the prisoners elicit all the information they could, even by sparing her life.

They were saved the trouble. That evening at a late hour, three men, so muffled up that not a feature but their eyes were visible, handed to the jailer an order signed by the magistrates for admittance to the prisoners; and ordering him to keep watch on the outside of the jail during their conference, the men proceeded to the rooms of the two women. After half an hour, the men left the prison, ordering that the prisoners should not be disturbed till morning.

In the morning, when the keeper visited the cells to carry breakfast to their inmates, he found both the miserable women strangled on their beds! He instantly gave the alarm, and the whole populace flocked to the prison. The magistrates solemnly denied having given authority to anybody to see the prisoners, and pronounced the order a forgery. It was long before the people could settle down into their usual state of security, if indeed they ever did, and when, some years after, the "Salem Witchcraft," as it was called, broke out, much of the ferocity and credulity of the populace at that period may be traced to the impression left by the Midnight Voyage of the *Seagull*.

IS THE DEVIL
A GENTLEMAN?

• BY SEABURY QUINN •

I
t had been a day of strange weather, a day the calendar declared to be late April and the thermometer proclaimed to be March or November. From dawn till early dark the rain had spattered down, chill, persistent, deceptive, making it feel many degrees colder than it really was, but just at sunset it had cleared and a sort of angry yellow half-light had spilled from a sky of streaky black against a bank of blood-red clouds. Now, while the dying wind was groping with chill-stiffened fingers at the window-casings, a fire blazed on the sturdy hearth, its comforting rose glow a gleaming island in the gathering shadows, its reflection daubing ever-changing patterns on the walls and tightly drawn curtains.

"On such a night," the Bishop quoted inexactly as he helped himself to brandy, "mine enemy's dog, though he had bit me, I would not turn away from my door."

Dr. Bentley, rector of St. Chrysostom's, dropped a second lump of sugar in his coffee and said nothing. He knew the Bishop, and had known him since their student days. When he quoted Shakespeare he was really searching through the lumber rooms of memory for a story, and there were few who had a better store of anecdotes then the Right Reverend Richard Chauncey, missionary, soldier, preacher, and ecclesiastical executive, worldly man of God and Godly man of the world. He'd looked forward to Dick's coming down for confirmation, and had made a point of asking Kitteringson in to dinner. Kitteringson was all right, of course; good, earnest worker, a good preacher and a good churchman, but a trifle too—how should he put it?—too dogmatic. If you couldn't find it in the writings of the Fathers of the Church or the Thirty-nine Articles he was against a proposition, whatever it might be. A session with the Bishop would be good for him.

"Good stuff in the lad," thought Dr. Bentley as he studied his junior, covertly. A rather strong, intelligent face he had, but marked by asceticism, the face of one who might be either an unyielding martyr or a merciless inquisitor. Now he was leaning forward almost eagerly, and the firelight did things to his earnest face—made it look like one of those old medieval monks in the old masters' paintings.

"I've been wondering all day, sir," he told Bishop Chauncey, "what you meant when you told the confirmation class they should use common sense about religious prejudices. Surely, there may be no compromise with evil—"

"I shouldn't care to lay that down as a precept," the Bishop answered with a low chuckle. "We're told the devil can quote Scripture for his purposes; why shouldn't Christians make use of the powers of darkness in a proper cause?"

Young Dr. Kitteringson was aghast. "Make use of Satan?" he faltered. "Have dealings with the arch-fiend—"

"Precisely, son. Shakespeare might have been more truthful than poetical when he declared the Prince of Darkness is a gentleman."

"I can't conceive of such a thing!" the younger man retorted. "All our experiences tell us—"

"All?" cut in Bishop Chauncey softly, and the young rector fell hesitant before the level irony of his gaze. "How old are you, son?"

"Thirty-two, sir, but I've read the writings of the Fathers of the Church, and one and all they tell us that to compromise with evil is a sin against—" He stopped, a little abashed at the look of tolerant amusement on his senior's face, then: "Can you name even one case when compromise with evil didn't end disastrously for all concerned, sir?" he challenged.

"Yes, I think I can," the Bishop passed the brandy snifter back and forth beneath his nostrils, inhaled the bouquet of the old cognac appreciatively, then took a delicate, approving sip. "I think I can, son. Like you, I have to call upon my reading to sustain me, but unlike you I can't claim ecclesiastical authority for my writers. One of them, indeed, was an ancestor of mine, a great-grandfather several times removed."

The gloom that waited just beyond the moving edge of firelight seemed flowing forward, like a slowly rising, stagnant tide, and a blazing ember falling to the layer of sand beneath the burning logs sent a sudden shaft of light across the intervening shade, casting a quick shadow of the Bishop on the farther wall. An odd shadow it was, not like the rubicund, gray-haired church-man, but queerly elongated and distorted, so that it appeared to be the shade of a lean man with gaunt and predatory features, muffled in a cloak and leaning forward at the shoulders, like one intent—almost in the act of pouncing.

Kundre Maltby (said the Bishop, drawing thoughtfully at his cigar so its recurrent glow etched his face in alternate red highlight and black shadow) was a confessed witch, and witches, as you know, are those who have made solemn compact with the Evil One.

She was a Swedish girl—at least she claimed that she was Swedish—whom Captain Pelatiah Maltby had found somewhere in his travels, married, and brought back to Danby. Who she really was nobody knew.

Captain Maltby's ship, the *Bountiful Adventure*, came on her Easter Monday morning, clinging to a hatch-grating some twenty miles or so off the Madeira coast. He'd cleared from Funchal the night before, swearing that he'd never make the port again, for the Portuguese had celebrated Easter with an *auto da fé* at which a hundred condemned witches had been burned, and the sight of the poor wretches' sufferings sickened him. When he asked the castaway her name she told him it was Kundre, and said her ship had been the *Blenkinge* of Stockholm, wrecked three days before.

Maltby marveled at this information, for he had been in the Madeiras for a whole week, and there had been no storm, not even a light squall. But there the girl was, lashed to the floating hatch-top, virtually nude and all but dead with thirst and starvation. Moreover, she had very winning ways and more than a fair share of beauty, so Captain Maltby asked no further questions, but put in at New York and married her before he brought the *Bountiful Adventure* up the coast to Danby.

Their life together seems to have been ideal, possibly idyllic. He was a raw-boned, tough-thewed son of New England, hard as flint outside and practical as the multiplication tables within. But it was from such ancestry that Whittier and Holmes and Bryant and Longfellow sprang, and probably beneath his workaday exterior Pelatiah Maltby had a poet's soul. They had twin children, a boy and a girl. At Pelatiah's insistence the girl was named for her mother, but Kundre chose the name of Micah for the boy, for in the whole Scripture she liked best that Prophet's question, "What doth the Lord require of thee, but to do justly, and to love mercy, and to walk humbly with thy God?"

She took to transplantation like a hardy flower, and grew and flourished on New England soil. From all accounts she must have been a beauty in a heavy Nordic way, a true woman of the sea. Full six feet tall she was, and strong as any man, yet with all the gracious curves of womanhood. Her hair, they say, was golden. Not merely yellow, but that metallic shade of gold which, catching glints of outside light, seems to hold a light of its own. And her skin was white as sea-foam, and her eyes the bright blue-green of the ice of the fjords, and her lips were red as sunset on the ocean when a storm has blown itself away.

Prosperity came with her, too. The winds were always favorable to Captain Maltby's ship. He made the longest voyages in the shortest time. When other ships were set upon by tempests and battered till they were mere hulks, he came safely through the raving storms or missed them altogether, and his enterprises always prospered. Foreign traders sold him goods at laughably low prices, or bought the cargoes that he brought at prices that astonished him.

He brought back treasures from the far corners of the earth, silks from Cathay and Nippon, carved coral from the South Sea Isles, pearls from Java, diamonds from Africa, a comb of solid beaten gold from India—and the golden comb seemed pallid when she drew it through the golden spate of her loosed golden hair.

The neighbors were first amazed, then wondering, finally suspicious. Experience had taught them Providence dealt even-handedly with men and balanced its smiles with its frowns. Yet Pelatiah Maltby always won. He never had to drain a cup of vinegar to compensate him for the many heady cups of success he quaffed.

It was Captain Joel Newton who brought matters to a head. He and Captain Maltby had been rivals many years. His pew was just across the aisle from Maltby's in the meeting house. His wife sat where she could not help but see the worldly gew-gaws Maltby lavished on Kundre, and Abigail Newton's tongue had an edge like that of a new-filed adz, and her jealousy the bitter bite of acid. Joel Newton heard himself compared to Pelatiah Maltby, with small advantage, every Lord's Day after service, and, driven by the lash of a shrew's tongue, he determined to find the key to Maltby's constant success, and set himself deliberately to trail the *Bountiful Adventure* from one port to another.

Not that it helped him. The *Bountiful Adventure* outsailed him every trip, and when he came into a foreign berth he found that Maltby had been there before him, secured what trade there was, and sailed away.

They came face to face at last at Tamatave in Madagascar. Maltby had traded rum and salted fish and tobacco for a holdful of rich native silver, and the local traders had no thought of laying in new stocks for months. Newton's ship was loaded to capacity with just the wares that Maltby had disposed of so profitably, there was no market for his cargo, his food was running low, and ruin stared him in the face.

Both had taken more of the French wines the inn purveyed than was their custom. Maltby was flushed with success, Newton bitter with the mordancy of disappointment. "Had I a witch-woman for wife I'd always fare well, too," he told his rival.

"How quotha?" Maltby asked. "What meanest, knave? My

Kundre is the fairest, sweetest bloom—"

"As ever sank its taproots deep in hell," his rival finished for him. "Oh, don't ye think to fool us, Neighbor Maltby! We know what 'tis that always sends the fair winds at thy tail when others lie becalmed. We know what 'tis that makes the heathen take thy wares at such great prices, and pay thee ten times what thou'd hoped to get. Aye, and we know whence comes thy witch-mate, too–how the Papishers had burned a drove of warlocks in the Madeiras the day before ye found her floating in the ocean. She said her vessel had been wrecked three days before, but had there been a storm? Thou knowest well there had not. Did'st offer her free passage back to the islands, and did she take thy offer kindly?"

Now this was a poser, for Pelatiah had offered to set Kundre on shore at Funchal when he rescued her, and she had refused tearfully, and begged him to hold to his course.

"And why?" asked Captain Newton as he warmed to his task of denunication. "I'll tell ye why, my fine bucko—because she was a cursed witch who'd slipped between the Papist's fingers and made use of thee to ferry her to safety. Thinkest thou she loves thee? Faugh! While thou'rt away she wantons it with every man 'twixt Danby and old Salem Town—"

"Thou liar!" The scandalous words were like to have been Joel's last, for Pelatiah drew his hanger and made for him with intent to stab the slander down his throat with cold steel, but Joel was just a thought too quick.

Before his rival reached him he jerked a pistol from his waistband and let fly, striking Captain Maltby fairly in the chest. Afterwards he boasted that it was a silver bullet he had used, since, as everybody knew, witches, warlocks, and werebeasts were impervious to lead, but vulnerable to silver missiles.

However that might be Captain Maltby halted in mid-stride, and his hanger fell with a clatter from his unnerved hand. He hiccoughed once and tried to draw a breath that stopped before he had it in, sagged at the knees, fell on his side, and died. But with that last unfinished breath they say he whispered, "Kundre dearest, they have done for me and will for thee if so be that they can, God have thee in His keeping—"

Maltby, of course, was a Protestant, and the only Christian

cemetery in the town was Catholic. It was not possible a heretic should lie in consecrated ground, but the missionary priest took counsel with the rabbi of the little Jewish congregation and arranged to buy a grave-site in the Hebrew burying ground.

There was no ordained minister of his faith to do the final service for Maltby, so the priest and rabbi stood beside his grave, and one said Christian prayers in Latin , and the other Jewish prayers in Hebrew, while the grim-faced sailors from New England stood by and marveled at this show of charity in those they had been taught to hate, and responded with tear-choked "Amens" when prayers were done and time had come to heap the earth upon the body sewn in sailcloth in lieu of a coffin.

It was a Wednesday in mid-April when the killing took place, and Kundre, so the story goes, was sitting beside the brooklet that ran through her back-lot. The weather was unseasonably warm, and her children waded in the stream and searched for buds of ground-rose while she sunned and bleached the hair that was her greatest pride—or vanity, according to the neighbors' wives. Suddenly she raised her head like one who listens to a hail from far away, shook back her clouding hair and cupped one hand to her ear to sit there statue-still for a long moment. Then, with a cry that seemed to be the echo of her riven heartstrings breaking, she called out, "Pelatiah, Oh beloved!" and fell forward on her face beside the brooklet lying with her arms outstretched before her like a diver's when he strikes the water, while her great, heroically formed body twitched and jerked, and little dreadful moans came bubbling from her lips, like blood that wells and bubbles from a mortal wound.

Presently she rose and dried her eyes and went into the house where she laid away her gown of crisp blue linen and put on widow's weeds before she sought Ezekiel Martin the stonemason and ordered him to cut and set a gravestone in the village churchyard. You could see that tombstone now if you should go to Danby burying ground.

Now, you'll allow it would be cause for comment, even in these days when extra-sensory perceptions are taken as more or less established facts, for a woman to become aware of her husband's death halfway round the world from her at the very moment of its happening. The circumstances caused comment in mid-seventeeth century New England, too, but not at all of the same kind. Everybody dreaded sorcery and witchcraft then, and in every unexplained occurrence men saw Satan's ungloved hand. So when Kundre went forth in her mourning clothes, sorrowing dry-eyed at the empty grave where she had placed the tombstone, neighbors looked at her from beneath lowered lids, and when she went to divine service at the meeting house the tithing man went past her hurriedly, and hardly paused to hold the alms basin before her, though he knew it would be heavier by a gold piece minted with the symbol of King Charles' majesty when he withdrew it.

In August came the *Bountiful Adventure* with her ensign flying at half mast, and Captain Maltby's death was confirmed by the sorrowing seamen.

But what became of Captain Joel Newton and his ship the *Crystal Wave* nobody ever knew. He had set sail from Tamatave the same day he shot Maltby, for everyone agreed he had provoked the quarrel, and the commandant of the garrison threatened his arrest unless he drew his anchor from the harbor mud at once. The rest was silence. Neither stick nor spar nor broken bit of wreckage ever washed ashore to show the *Crystal Wave*'s fate, or that of Captain Joel Newton and the twenty seamen of his crew.

Voyages of a year or even two years were the rule those days, and it was not until King Charles had been beheaded and the Lord Protectory proclaimed that Abigail Newton descended from the "widow's watch" that topped her square-roofed house beside the harbor and changed her homespun gown of blue for one of black linsey woolsey, then sent for Zeke Martin the mason to cut and set a stone in Danby churchyard.

The twenty widows of the *Crystal Wave*'s crew also went in mourning, and bewailed their joint and several losses piteously. When they passed Kundre in the street they looked away, but when she'd gotten safely past they spit upon the ground and muttered "witch!" and "devil's-hag!"

Kundre was a Swedish woman, and though the good folk of Danby had small use for King James' politics and even less for his religion, they were with him to a man in his views on witchcraft. Moreover, they recalled how Scandinavian witches had raised storms and tempests to prevent the Princess Anne from reaching Scotland where her marriage to King James was to be solemnized, and some of the more learned in the village knew the legends of *Sangreal* and remembered that the temptress who all but kept the Holy Grail from Parsifal was named Kundry. There seemed little difference between her name and Kundre's. Kundry of the legend was a witch damned beyond redemption; might not Kundre—the strange outland woman who knew of her husband's death four months before the news came home—also be a potent witch?

It seemed entirely possible and even probable, and when the widowed Abigail met widowed Kundre in the village street and taxed her with destroying both the *Crystal Wave*'s master and crew by witchcraft something happened to confirm the worst suspicions.

"Thou art a wicked, devil-vowed, and wanton witch!" said Abigail in hearing of at least three neighbor women. "By thy vile arts thou raised a monstrous storm and sank the *Crystal Wave* and all her people in the ocean."

Kundre looked at her, and in her ice-blue eyes there seemed to kindle a slow light like that which the aurora borealis makes on winter nights. "Thy tongue is dipped in venom like a serpent's, Goody Newton," she replied in the deep voice which was her Nordic heritage. "It never wags except to hurt thy neighbors, so 'twere best thou never used it hereafter."

Whether from the look in Kundre's eyes, or from astonishment that anyone should dare to tell her to keep still we do not know, but it was amply attested that Abigail for once had no reply to make, and we find in the old town records of Danby that on the evening after this encounter she lost her power of speech completely. More, she lost the use of her tongue, for it swelled and swelled until she could not keep it in her mouth, and she could take no nourishment but liquids, and those with greatest difficulty.

In the light of present-day medical knowledge it would not be difficult to attribute her misfortune to that rare condition known as macroglossia or hypertrophy of the tongue, which doctors tell us is due to engorgement and dilation of the lymph channels. Most of us who have served in hospitals have seen such cases, where the swollen tongue hangs from the mouth and gives the patient a peculiarly idiotic look. But medicine was far from an exact science those days, and besides there was the testimony of the women who had seen the curse of silence laid on Abigail. Three hours after sunset Kundre was "spoken against" as a witch and duly lodged in Danby jail.

By the common law of England torture was forbidden to force a prisoner to accuse himself, but by the witchcraft statues of King James certain "tests" which differed from torture neither in degree nor kind were permitted. One of these was known as "swimming," for it was believed a witch's body was so buoyed up with evil that it could not sink in water.

Accordingly, upon the second day of her confinement Kundre was brought out to be "swum." Stripped to her shift they led her from the jail to the horse pond which served the village as reservoir and ornamental lake at once, forced her to sit cross-legged on the ground and tied her right thumb to her left great toe, her right great toe to her left thumb with heavy linen thread which had been waxed for greater strength, and to make it cut more deeply in the tender flesh. Then over her they dropped a linen bed-sheet, tumbled her all helpless as she was upon her side and tied the sheet's loose ends together, exactly as a modern housewife makes a laundry bundle ready. A rope was fastened to the knotted sheet and willing hands laid hold on to and dragged it out into the water.

Now here we have a choice between the natural and the supernatural. We have all seen the properties of wet cloth to retain the air and resist water. The device known as water wings with which so many children learn to swim is simply a cloth bladder wet before inflation, and as long as outside pressure is evenly applied it will support surprisingly large weights in calm water.

Perhaps it was as natural a phenomenon as this that kept the accused woman afloat on the calm surface of the village horse pond. Perhaps, again, it was something more sinister. At any rate, the sheeted bundle bobbed and floated on the quiet surface of the pool as easily as if it had been filled with cork, and a great shout went up from the spectators: "She swims! She swims! It is the judgment of just Heaven! She is a proven witch!"

Her trial lasted a full day, and people came from miles about to hear the evidence poured on her. Ezekiel Martin the stonemason told how she came to him and ordered him to cut the tombstone for a man whose limbs were scarcely stiff in death, though none could know that he had died until his ship came in full four months later.

There was no dearth of testimony concerning the fine winds and weather that had been her husband's portion since he married her, or concerning the storms that had plagued his rivals.

Abigail Newton stood up in court that all might see her swollen tongue, and though she could not speak, she went through an elaborate dumb-show of the way the curse had been laid on her. Less reticent, Flee-from-the-Wrath-to-Come Epsworth, Rebecca Norris, and Susan Clayton told under oath how they had seen and heard Kundre strike Abigail with speechlessness.

A tithe of such evidence would have been enough to hang her, and the jury took but fifteen minutes to deliberate upon their verdict, which, of course, was guilty.

Asked what she had to say in her defense before the court pronounced sentence, she made a seemly curtsey to the judge and answered without hesitation: "'Tis true I am a witch as ye have charged me. Long years agone my sire and dam made compact with the Prince of Evil and bound me by their covenant, but never have I used my power to hurt a living creature, brute or human. That I should wish my man to prosper was but natural. Thus far I used my power over wind and tides, but no farther. Whether Heaven punished Goodman Newton for the foul murder that he did on my poor man I cannot say. I know naught of the matter, nor did I lift a finger to bring Heaven's retribution on him. 'Vengeance is mine, I will repay,' saith the Lord!

"As for the swollen tongue of yon shrew, belike it is the malice of her black and jealous heart that bloats it. As to that I cannot answer. But hark ye, neighbors, if I had the power to release her I'd not use it. The town is better for her silence, as I wis ye all agree."

With that she made another curtsey to the judge and stood

there silent, waiting sentence: "Since, therefore, Goodwife Kundre Maltby hath by her own confession admitted she was justly tried and convicted, so let her on account of her bond with the Devil and on account of the witchcraft she hath practiced, be hanged by the neck until she be dead."

The usual formula in hanging cases was for the court to add, "and may God have mercy on thy soul," but such a sentiment seemed obviously out of place here, and the judge forbore to express it.

They carried out the sentence next day, and a mighty crowd was gathered for the spectacle. The members of the trained band were much put to it to control the rabble when the hangman drove his cart beneath the gallows tree and made the hemp fast to her neck.

She wore her widow's weeds to execution, and round her neck was clasped a slender chain of some base metal with a flat pendant like a coin hung from it. It was the only ornament she'd had when Pelatiah found her floating on the grating, and she had laid it by when they were married. Now, through a whim, perhaps, she chose to wear it at her death.

They'd let her children visit her in jail the night before, and she had sent the girl back for the bauble. "Look well on it, my sweet," she told the child when it was clasped about her neck. "The time may come when thou'lt have need of it, and if it comes thou shalt not cry for it in vain."

As the hangman bound her elbows to her sides before he slipped the noose beneath her chin she begged him, "Leave the worthless chain in place when thy grim task is done, good Peter Grimes. In my left shoe thou'lt find a golden sovereign hidden to repay thee for thy work. Take it and welcome, but if thou take'st the chain and pendant from me—a witch's curse shall be on thee."

Peter Grimes was a poor man, and the clothes a felon stood in when he died were part of his perquisites, but he had no stomach for a witch's curse, so when he found the gold piece in her shoe as she had promised he took it and was well pleased to leave the worthless chain in place.

She did not die easily, from all accounts. Her splendid body was too powerful, the tide of life ran too strong in her, so she dangled, quivering and writhing in the air a full five minutes, then Peter Grimes, perhaps in charity, perhaps because he wished to have the business over with and go home to his breakfast, seized her by the legs and dragged until the double burden of his weight and hers proved too much for the spinal column, and with a snapping like the cracking of a fire-dried stick her neck broke and her struggles ended.

They raised the stone that she had set above her husband's empty grave, scooped out a shallow opening beneath it and dropped her in, coffinless and without proper graveclothes. So, as the neighbors sagely said, she had outreached herself and ordered her own tombstone when by her wicked wizardry she had the tidings of her man's death at the instant it occurred.

And here again we are forced to make a choice between the natural and supernatural. That Kundre should have confessed she was guilty was not particularly important. We know that under heavy mental stress people will accuse themselves of almost any crime. There's hardly a sensational murder case in which the police don't have to deal with numerous entirely innocent self-accusers. That part of it is understandable.

What is more difficult to explain is that at the very moment Peter Grimes broke Kundre's neck the swelling in Abigail Newton's tongue began to subside, and by noon she had entirely regained the power of speech. Indeed, she regained it so fully that within six months she was twice sentenced to the ducking stool for public scoldings, and finally was forced to stand before the meeting house on the Sabbath with a muzzle on her face and a paper reading "Common Scold" hung by a string around her neck.

Not the least mystifying thing about the mystery of Kundre Maltby was the way her fortune disappeared. That she and Pelatiah had been rich was common knowledge, but when the assessors went to her house to take her property in custody they could find nothing of substantial value. Not a single gold or silver coin, nor yet a bit of jewelry could they turn up, though they searched the place from cellar to ridgepole and even knocked down several walls in quest of concealed hiding places. So, balked in the attempt to work a forfeiture of her fortune, they sold the house and land at public vendue, put the proceeds in the town treasury, and farmed the children out to be taught useful trades.

Micah was apprenticed at the rope-walk owned by Goodman Richard Belkton, Kundre took her place among the sewing maids of Goodwife Deborah Stiles, and except when in school or going, well chaperoned, to divine service at the meeting house, they never saw each other.

Their lot was not a happy one. We all know the sadistic cruelty of the young. The lad who goes to a new school today has a hard time until he's proved himself to be the equal of the class bully, or till the novelty of hazing him wears off. But Kundre and her brother had to face the taunts and insults of their classmates endlessly. No one wished to sit with them or share a hornbook with them. If, maddened by the spiteful things said of his mother, Micah fought his tormentor and came off winner, his victory was vociferously attributed to witchcraft. If he lost the fight the victor called on all to witness how Heaven had helped the right in overcoming evil.

Both were apt pupils, but their readiness in reading, ciphering, and writing caused no commendation from the school-ma'am. She too believed their aptitude infernally inspired and made no secret of it. So successful recitations were rewarded by an acid reference to their mother's compact with the Evil One. Failure brought a caning.

In all the dreary monotone of life the one highlight for Kundre was Hosea Newton. It may seem strange that the son of her mother's fiercest persecutor should prove her only friend, but it was no stranger than the contrast between Hosea and his mother. Where she was angular and acid and sharp-tongued he was inclined to plumpness, slow of speech, and even-tempered. When all the little girls drew their skirts back from Kundre as from diabolic pollution, he chose a seat beside her on the form, and shared his primer with her and, to the scandal of the class, often gave her tidbits from the ample luncheon which his mother packed for him each morning. When Charity Wilkins accused Kundre of stealing a new thimble from her he found the missing bauble concealed in Charity's pocket and pulled her hair until she admitted her fault. Charity's big brother Benjamin took up the lists for his sister, whereupon Hosea entered combat with enthusiasm and left Benjamin with a bloody nose and greatly chastened tongue.

But this little interlude of friendship had disastrous results. Goodwife Wilkins went to Abigail, who, horrified that her son had espoused the witch-child's cause, took him forthwith to Reverend Silas Middleton, who quoted Scriptual texts to him— "Evil communications corrupt good manners—" exhorted him, prayed over him, and finally caned him soundly.

After that Hosea had to content himself with smiling at Kundre over his primer. All speech between them was forbidden, and though the Reverend Middleton's precepts had made but small impression on Hosea, he had a vivid memory of the thrashing that accompanied them.

The quiet of the lazy years flowed over Danby like a placid river. In the harbor the tall ships shook out their wings and sped to the far corners of the earth and presently came back again with holds filled with strange merchandise. Or perhaps they did not come back, and the women put on mourning clothes and there were new stones in the churchyard, with empty graves beneath them. King Philip's War was fought and won and the settlers needed to fear Indian raids no longer. But in the main, life just went on and on. Its groove was deepened, but the course and pattern never changed.

Hosea Newton went away to Harvard College where he was to be trained for the ministry, Micah worked at the ropewalk, harboring black resentment in his heart, but not daring to give tongue to it; Kundre toiled in Goody Stiles' workroom from sunrise to sunset. She proved a clever needle-woman and her work was eagerly bought up, but she had no credit for it. Goodwife Stiles displayed the dresses proudly, and accepted compliments with modest grace, but she never told whose agile fingers fashioned them. In this she showed sound business sense, for many of her customers would have hesitated to wear garments made by a witch-child. And then—

One evening in late summer Kundre lay in Goodman Stiles' oat field. She had worked hard all day, her eyes and muscles ached, and she was so tired that she could have cried with it, but now she had a little respite. The earth felt warm and comforting to her cramped muscles, she seemed to draw vitality from it while a little breeze played through the bearded grain, making it rustle softly, like a bride's dress.

A bride's dress! Kundre thought. Other maids went to the meeting house or stood up in their own homes in stiff, rustling taffeta while the parson joined them to the men of their choice. Was she forever doomed to tread the earth in loneliness, to find no lover, no friend, even, in the whole world? It seemed a hard fate for a maid as well-favored as she.

Kundre knew that she had beauty. Unlike her mother, she was little; little and slender with gray eyes and a soft-lipped, rather sad smile. Her hair, despite the severe braids in which she wore it, was positively thrilling in its beauty.

Paler than her mother's, it had the sweet amber-gold of melted honey in dark lights and the vivid sheen of burnished silver when the sunshine fell on it. There was a sort of aristocratic fragility hinted at by her arched, slender neck and delicately cut profile, her hands were so slight that she wore child's mittens in cold weather; and the cast-off shoon of neighbors' half-grown daughters were too large for her, even when she wore the thickest woolen stockings.

But now she had kicked off the rough brogans and stripped the heavy cotton stockings off and drew her naked, gleaming feet up under her as she half sat, half lay upon the warm and friendly earth. She rested her elbow upon a bent knee, outlining her chin with her fingers as she looked toward the blue, distant hills. How would it seem, she wondered, to have someone look at her in friendship, speak a kindly word to her, perhaps—her pulses quickened at the daring thought—tell her she was beautiful?

A footstep sounded at the margin of the field and she crouched like a little partridge when it hears the hunter coming. If she were very still perhaps whoever came would pass her by unseeing. She had no wish to be seen. Since early childhood she had never known a friendly look or word except—The footsteps came still nearer, swishing through the nodding grain, and now she heard a man's voice humming softly:

Wish and fullfillment can severed
be ne'er,
Nor the thing prayed for come
short of the prayer—

"I crave thy pardon, mistress!" Unaware of Kundre crouching in her covert he had almost trodden on her. A flush suffused his face as he stepped backward hurriedly and almost lost his balance in the process.

"I had no business trespassing on Neighbor Stiles' land— why, Kundre, lass, is't truly thou? How lovely thou art grown!" he broke off in surprised delight and to her utter, blank amazement, dropped down to the ground beside her. "It must be full three years since I have seen thee," he added.

Kundre looked at him in wonder. At first it had been but a man she saw, and men, almost as much as women, were her natural enemies, for she had led an odd and hunted life, and like an animal knew the world of men and women only through the blows it dealt her. But as she looked into the smiling, friendly face she felt the blood flow into her cheeks and bring sudden warmth to her brow, for it was Hosea Newton sitting by her in the oat field, Hosea Newton's voice, all rich with friendly laughter, asked how she did, and—her heart beat so that she could hardly breathe— Hosea Newton had just said that she was lovely.

The years had been kind to him. Strongly made, wide-shouldered, he was still not burly, only big; and his face was undeniably handsome. He had a short upper lip and a square jaw with a dimple in it, blue eyes set wide apart beneath dark, curving brows, and lightly curling dark hair that fitted his well-formed head like a cap.

"Art glad to see me?" he asked frankly, and Kundre sat in thoughtful silence for a while before she answered softly.

"I am not sure, Hosea. In all the world thou art the only person who has spoken kindly to me since my mother—died— but once, I recollect, thou suffered for thy kindness to me. Now—"

"Now," he mimicked laughing, "I'll dare the parson or the elders to admonish me. I am my own man, Kundre, and think what thoughts I choose, say what I will, and go with whom I please.

"Aye," he added as she answered nothing, "I've thought a deal about things, Kundre, and what I think might not make pleasant hearing for the parson and the elders, or my mother, either. I've seen the Quakers whipped and hanged and branded for their faith's sake, seen helpless, innocent old women go tottering to the gallows tree for witchcraft that they never worked and could not work, and seen the men who call themselves God's ministers work lustily in Satan's vineyard."

"Thou thinkest, then—" she asked him with a quaver in her voice—"it may be possible my mother was no witch—"

"No more a witch than any other," he replied. "Though I speak of the flesh that bore me, I say that those who swore her life away are tainted with blood of innocence—why, Kundre, lass, what aileth thee?"

The girl had flung her arms about him and was sobbing out her heart against his shoulder. For almost twenty years she'd led a pariah's life, hounded, scorned, and persecuted, and the memory of her mother had been rubbed into her breaking heart like salt into a raw wound. Now here at last was one who had a kind word for her mother, who dared suggest she had not merited a felon's shameful death.

What happened then was like a chemical reaction in its spontaneity. It may have been that pity which is said to be akin to love inspired him to put his arms about her as she sobbed against his shoulder, but in the fraction of a heartbeat there was no questioning the emotion that possessed him. From him to her, and from her to him, there seemed to flow a mystic fluid—a sort of intangible soul-substance—that met and mingled like the waters of two rivers at their confluence and merged them into each other until they were not twain, but one.

It was an odd idyl, this romance of a man whose childhood had been spent in the house with a brawling woman and this woman whose whole life had been warped by hatred and suspicion. To say that they loved at first sight would not be accurate. Each had carried the image of the other in his heart since childhood, in each the thought of the other had been present constantly, not consciously, any more than they were conscious of the hearts that beat beneath their breasts, but always there, the greatest, most important, most vital thing in either of their lives. Now they were aware of it with blinding, dazzling suddenness. The glory of it almost stunned them.

Every evening when her work for Goody Stiles was done Kundre hurried to the oat field, and always he was there to greet her and come hurrying with uplifted hands to take her in his arms.

Judged by modern free-and-easy standards they were inhibited in their love-making. They hardly kissed at all, and when they did it was a chaste embrace which brother and sister might have exchanged. But she would put her hand in his and turn it till her soft palm rested on his and her little fingers made a soft and gentle pattern of his own, then rest her head against his shoulder till her gleaming hair was on his cheek, its perfume fresh and sweet as that of the green growing things about them.

I said theirs was an odd love. So it was. A love compounded partly of loneliness, partly of heart-hunger, partly of true, honest friendship; not without its moment of passion, but entirely without the savage, selfish hunger of passion; not lacking ecstacy, but with the ecstacy of love fulfilled, not satiated.

They did not talk much. There was small need of words, for that mysterious warm current, strong as a rising ocean tide, flowed constantly between them, fusing their two selves in one. And when they came to say good night the sweet pain of their parting was itself a compensation for the day-long separation facing them.

Then came catastrophe, as dreadful and as unexpected as a thunderbolt hurled from a cloudless sky. Her brother Micah ran away from his master. It was either flight or murder, for despite the expert way in which he did his work old Goodman Belkton found fault with him constantly, and his fellow prentices, not slow to take their cue from the master, taunted him with his mother's conviction and intimated that he used her devilish arts to make his handiwork the best the walk turned out.

Runaway apprentices were fair game for anyone, and Goodman Belkton offered a reward of two pounds for the stray's return, so when four sturdy louts saw Micah on the dock at Salem

Town, about to sign before the mast for a voyage to the Indies, they set on him and bound him with a length of rope and dragged him back to Danby.

But while they were still in Danby suburbs they had been set upon by a ferocious heifer that gored one of them sorely, knocked down another, and put them all so utterly to flight that their prisoner escaped and joined the ship to Salem before she sailed with the tide. They brought their wounded comrade into Danby, where, over sundry mugs of potent rum-and-water, they had a wondrous story to relate.

The cow that set on them had been no ordinary cow. It seemed but a demon beast whose nostrils breathed forth fiery flames, and which announced *in human words*, "I'll soon set thee free from this scum, my brother!"

This all happened in the early evening, but before it was too dark for them to see the demon beast go tearing off across a meadow when its fell work had been done and suddenly sit down upon the sod like a woman, straddle a long fence-rail like a witch that mounts a broom, and fly shrieking off across the sky toward Goodman Stiles' oat field.

And where had Kundre been while this was happening? Her mistress asked her point-blank, and point-blank she refused to answer. And there the matter might have rested, perhaps, if Jonathan Sawyer, a laborer on Goodman Williams' plantation, had not volunteered the information that at nine o'clock the night before he'd seen her hurrying from Stiles' oat field and heard her singing something not to be found in the hymn book.

It seemed hardly necessary for the constable to call a *posse comitatus* of trained bandsmen to arrest her, or to summon Parson Middleton to lend them spiritual assistance. But so he did, and with martial clank of sword and pike and musket, and with the Parson with his Book beneath his arm, they went to Goodwife Stiles' house and formally took Kundre into custody, bound her wrists together with the constable's spare bridle, put a horse's leading-strap about her neck, and marched her through the streets to Danby jail, where they lodged her with a double guard before the door.

Hosea Newton roused from a deep, dream-tormented sleep,

completely conscious, every faculty alert. His room was buried in a darkness blinding as a black cloak, for the moon had set long since, and a cloud-veil obscured the stars. Some instinct, some sentinel of the spirit that stands watch while we are sleeping, told him he was not alone, but he could see or hear nothing.

All day he'd raged through Danby Town like a madman, calling on the parson and the constable and even the high magistrate to intercede for Kundre. She was no witch, he vowed, but a sweet, pure maid who held his heart in the cupped palms of her little hands. The ruffians who had told the story of the demon heifer were a lot of drunken, craven liars, seeking to excuse their prisoner's escape with this wide tale. He'd prove it; he would range the countryside until he'd found the cow that bested them and lead her singlehanded to the pound for all to see she was a natural beast.

The parson and the constable and magistrate were sympathetic listeners, but one and all refused to help him in his trouble. The woman was a witch, the vowed and dedicated votary of Satan—like mother, like daughter. Could any natural beast bestride a fence rail and sail through the sky on it? "Poor boy, thou art bewitched by this vile whelp from Satan's kennels," they told him.

"But fear not, poor, befuddled lad, tomorrow we shall prove that thy infatuation is the devil's work, for on the town common at sunrise we shall prick the witchling with long pins until we find the devil's mark, and thou shalt see she is in very truth a servant of the Prince of Darkness."

He'd tried to see her in the jail, but the trained bandsmen turned him back. No one must see the witch until she had passed through the ordeal, even the turnkey was forbidden to go near her or to look into her cell. How should she eat and wherewith should she quench her thirst? Let Beelzebub her master see to that. They were Christian men and had no traffic with the servants of Satan.

Finally, worn out in body and in spirit, he had come home, refused his supper—could he take food while Kundre starved?— and thrown himself upon his bed, full-dressed, to fall into a sleep of utter exhaustion.

Desperate men make desperate plans, and Hosea was desper-

250 · SEABURY QUINN

ate. It did not matter to him whether she were good or bad or innocent or guilty—and accusation was equivalent to conviction—he would denounce himself as a wizard and hang with her upon the gallows tree. She should not go to that dark land beyond the grave alone.

What was it? Something stirred in the soft darkness of the room, a shadow moving in the shadows, a rat that came to forage in the dark?

He knew that it was none of these, for in the gloom that blotted out the outlines of the furniture he saw a gleam of light, or rather lightness, like a cloud of faintly luminous vapor swirling from an unseen boiling kettle.

Slowly it spread, wafting upward, and now he saw the outlines of a figure in it, and the blood churned in his ears, his throat grew tight, and at the pit of his stomach he seemed to feel a burning and a freezing, all at once.

"Who—what are thou?" he croaked hoarsely, and the sound of his own frightened voice was terrifying in the haunted darkness.

No answer came to his challenge, but the figure looming faintly in the mist-cloud seemed taking on a kind of substance. Now he could see it quite clearly, and the terror which engulfed him seemed to be an icy flood that paralyzed his heart and brain and muscles.

Yet notwithstanding his terror he felt a kind of admiration for the phantom. It was a woman, tall as a tall man, yet with a calm and regal beauty wholly feminine. Across the low white brow a spate of gold-hued hair fell flowing to her knees, and from the perfect contour of her face great eyes of zenith-blue looked at him under brows of startling blackness. She was dressed in widow's weeds; a chain and pendant of some dull, lackluster metal hung about her throat.

He knew her! He had been a little lad scarce eight years old when Goodman Stiles had raised him to his shoulder that he might see the hangman Peter Grimes work the court's sentence on Kundre Maltby, the witch-woman. With a sudden pang of recollection he recalled how he had thought it a great pity that so much beauty should be vowed to Satan and hanged upon the gallows tree and entombed in the earth.

"What—" by supreme effort he forced speech between palsied lips—"what wouldst thou with me, Kundre Malby?"

"Wilt take my help, Hosea Newton?" asked the specter, and her voice was cold and desolate as December storm-wind blowing over pine-capped hills.

Hosea hesitated in his answer, and well he might. The wraith, if wraith it were, was that of a condemned witch-woman, hanged for sorcery, and, presumably, made fast in hell. He might have been in advance of his time, but he was part and parcel of his generation, and since Deuteronomy was penned men had regarded witches as disciples of the Evil One.

To traffic with them was forbidden under pain of death and loss of soul. This was a witch's ghost, as dreadful as the witch herself, perhaps more dreadful, since she had burned in hell for twenty years, and he must make the choice of taking aid from her and bidding her begone. There was no middle course; he must hold true to all the teachings that had been instilled in him since infancy and bid her avaunt, or make compromise with Evil incarnate and put his soul in dreadful jeopardy—to what end? Did not the writings of the Fathers teach that Satan is the archdeceiver? Would he keep the compact offered by this messenger from hell?

Then came the thought of Kundre, little Kundre, starved and thirsting, languishing in prison till the morrow, when they'd strip her to her shift in sight of all the town and pierce her tender flesh with long, cruel pins—a thousand thousand years of burning hell would be a bargain-price to pay for her deliverance.

"Say on, O spirit of my Kundre's mother," he commanded. "I'll take the help thou offerest me, and pay the price thou asketh."

The phantom raised one white, almost transparent hand and loosed the medal from its neck. "Take this," it bade, and it seemed that its ghostly voice was stronger, warmer. "Hie with it to the jailhouse and cut away the bars that pen her in. Then fly across the border southward—my time is sped. I must e'en go!"

The voice stopped suddenly, as though a hand had been laid on the specter's throat, and like an April snowflake melting in the rising sun of spring, the faintly shining vision merged back in the darkness.

He could not say if it had been a vivid dream or if a visitant had come to him, but presently he rose and struck a flint-spark in his tinderbox and lit a tallow dip. There on the floor beside his bed lay a medallion of dull metal, not lead nor iron, but apparently a mixture of the two, fixed to a length of slender chain of the same sheenless substance. Curiously, he noted that his hands were soiled with fresh earth and his fingernails broken, as though he had been burrowing like a woodchuck. Yet he knew he had not left his chamber since he flung himself upon the bed and fell asleep.

Or had he? We may wonder. Might he not have been the victim of somnambulism, and risen to go scraping at the earth that covered Kundre Maltby's body in the churchyard, then, still asleep, come back with the mysterious medal? The thought did not occur to him, but in the light of modern psychological experiments we may entertain it.

At any rate he recognized the medallion and took it in his hand. It was quite plain on one side and engraved with characters he could not read upon the other. Its edge was rounded like that of a milled coin, and though it was no larger than a penny it weighed as much as a gold sovereign.

What was it that the ghost had ordered him to do? "Hie with it to the jailhouse and cut away the bars that pen her in."

With this dull piece of soft metal? He was about to fling the medal from him in disgust when the echo of the ghostly voice seemed coming to him through the candlelight-stained darkness, "Hurry, hurry, lover of the falsely accused, or it will be too late!"

He knew what cell they'd lodged her in, the same in which her mother languished twenty years ago. It was on the ground floor of the prison, and by standing on his tiptoes he could look through the barred window.

If they caught him skulking round the jailhouse—What matter? He was resolved to die with her, why not share prison with her ere they hanged him?

Danby jail loomed dimly, a darker darkness in the starless night, as Hosea approached it, treading noiselessly in stockinged feet. "Kundre," he whispered softly as he tapped upon the stone sill of her cell window. "Can'st hear me, dearest love?"

"Is't thou, my very dearest?" the girl's reply came to him through the formless darkness. "Oh, Hosea—" He heard her sobs, the small, sad sounds of utter misery, as her voice broke.

"Aye, heart o' mine, 'tis I, and I have come to tell thee that thou shalt not go alone—come closer, love, stretch out thy hands to me—"

"I cannot, dearest one; they've chained me to the wall as if I were a rabid cur—"

Hosea clenched his teeth in fury, and unthinking, drove his hand against the prison bars. It was the hand in which he clasped the witch's medal, and as it struck the bar he drew back with a startled exclamation. The heavy, hand-forged iron had melted from contact with the medal as if it had been tallow touched by flame.

In a minute he was sawing at the window bars with the mysterious coin, cutting them away as if they had been cheese. Silently he laid them on the turf outside the prison window; then, when he had an opening large enough to crawl through, let himself inside the cell and felt his way toward her.

They wasted no time in reunion or premature rejoicings. With her hand on his to guide it he pressed the witch's coin against the iron collar locked around her neck, and laid the fetter on the straw-strewn cell floor carefully, lest its clanking rouse the guard who waited in the corridor outside. Then, step by cautious step, he led her to the window.

Hand in hand they crept along the shadowed street until they reached the stable where his mother's horses stamped before their managers. In a moment he had saddled the best beast and let it out, swung her to the saddle-bow before him and set out toward the southern boundary of the town. They dared not trot or gallop lest the pounding of the horse's hoofs arouse the neighbors, but presently they reached the churchyard, and he drove his heels into the stallion's flanks.

"Wait, wait, my dear," she begged him as they passed the white-spired meeting house, "I would say farewell to my mother ere we shake the dust of Danby from our shoon forever."

"Aye," he conceded, lowering her to the ground. "That is but fitting, sweetling. We are indebted to thy mother for thy liberty tonight."

Together they walked to the grave, and while the girl knelt on the moss that rimmed the stone he looked down at her pensively. He wondered why his conscience did not trouble him. Tonight he had accepted diabolic aid, made compromise with Evil. Even now he had the witch-wife's medal in his pocket—he drew the flat metallic disc out to look at it. Should he take it with him or return it to the grave? he wondered, then wondered more at what was happening. The coin seemed straining at his fingers, as if a thin, invisible thread were pulling it, or it had volition of its own and sought release from his grasp.

But, strangely, the pull was all in one direction, toward the foot of Kundre Maltby's grave.

Wonderingly, he stepped in the direction of the tug, and noticed that it increased sharply, then seemed to bear straight down toward the earth.

He dropped upon his knees. The coin seemed guiding his

hand toward the tombstone, and, still marveling, he reached in the direction that it indicated. His fingers touched the long grass growing by the stone and found an opening like a woodchuck's burrow. Inside was something stiff and hard, yet slightly pliable, like old oiled leather.

He grasped the object, tugged at it and brought it out. It was a leather sack, well smeared with tallow, stiff with age and long entombment in the earth, but wholly intact. A wax seal held the cord and bound its mouth, but this crumbled as he touched it. Inside were several smaller sacks, some of soft buckskin, some of coarse linen, and in them were bright English sovereigns, round silver Spanish dollars, and gleaming articles of jewelry. The mystery of Kundre Maltby's lost fortune was solved. She had buried it beneath the stone that marked her husband's empty grave, and when they went to scoop the hollow to receive her body they had used only the upper portion of the grave.

Hosea chuckled as he realized what had happened. The diggers' spades had been within a hand's width of the treasure, yet none had suspected it.

Witchcraft? Perhaps, but very fortunate witchcraft for him and Kundre. A moment since, they had had nothing but the clothes they stood in and the stolen stallion; now they were rich. Their life would not be hard—if they could get away.

The night was tiring rapidly as they rode into the woodland. Long streaks of gray were showing in the eastern sky, small noises came to them, the chirp of crickets and the sleepy murmurs of awakening birds, but on and on they rode, secure in the knowledge that Danby jail had no bloodhounds to pursue them, and their escape could not be known till sunrise, for no one, jailor, or turnkey, or guard, would dare go near the witch's cell till full daylight.

The Newport Quakers greeted them hospitably, and when they found that they had money, offered them letters to the first citizens of Philadelphia.

In two days they took passage on a sloop bound for the Delaware, and, once on the high sea, were married by the master. So Kundre Maltby and Hosea Newton, children of seafaring Danby skippers, plighted troth upon the ocean, with the singing of the wind in the rigging for a wedding march, and the skirling mewl of seagulls for a prothalamium.

They were not the first, nor, unhappily, the last to be driven from their homes by ignorance and bigotry masquerading as religion, but in Philadelphia they found such peace and happiness as never could have been theirs in New England.

Their house stood on a tall hill overlooking the wide Schuylkill and the prosperous little Quaker city, and there their family multiplied until they had four sons and three daughters.

It was an evening in mid-April, the anniversary of her father's death at Captain Newton's hand, if she had known it, that Kundre stood with Hosea on the porch of their mansion and watched the lights of Philadelphia quench out against the darkness. Honora, their last-born daughter, had been christened in the afternoon, and now, all vestige of original sin washed from her, was slumbering as peacefully as any cherub in the nursery.

"Look, heart of mine," bade Kundre, "all those good folk go to their rest down yonder. They are a kind and gentle people, and I know their dreams are of a better world."

"Aye, dearest," he slipped an arm round her, "a better world, in truth. Not in some dim, misty Promised Land on t'other side of Jordan, but here in this same world we live in. There'll come a time, my sweet, when men with lofty dreams shall waken at a great tomorrow's dawn and find their dreams still there, and nothing vanished but the night."

The Bishop brought his story to a close and looked from Dr. Bentley to the younger clergyman with a quizzical twinkle in his eye. "I shan't ask you to pass judgment," he said. "Whether Hosea Newton should have scorned the witch's offer—or whether he received it, for that matter—are purely academic questions today. I'm pretty sure, though," he chuckled, "that if he had refused it I should not be here this evening."

"How's that, sir?" asked young Dr. Kitteringson.

"Well, you see, Hosea Newton was my great-grandfather, several times removed, and his wife, the witch's child, my ancestress. So was the witch, for that matter."

"And the witch's coin?" asked Dr. Kitteringson. "Do you know what became of it?"

"Yes," answered Bishop Chauncey. "Here it is." He thrust two fingers in his waistcoat pocket and produced a little metal disc which might have been silver, but wasn't, flat and plain on one side, marked with faint traces of old Nordic runes upon the other. "I've carried it as a lucky piece for years," he added. "My grandfather carried it all through the Civil War and never had a wound. My father had it with him at San Juan Hill and came off without a scratch. I lugged it through the Argonne and came out safely, but once when I left it on my dressing table in Paris I was run down by a taxicab before I had a chance to cross the street."

Dr. Kitteringson was handling the strange coin gingerly, half curiously, half fearfully. "You've tested it for magic powers?" he asked.

"Good gracious, no, son. I don't suppose it has any, and— good heavens, look!"

Young Dr. Kitteringson had taken up the fire shovel and drawn the coin's blunt edge across its gleaming brass bowl.

Where the medal touched the brass it cut a kerf as easily as if it had been pressed through softened tallow.

"Great Scott, Bishop—Dick!" exclaimed Dr. Bentley. "What do you think of that?"

The Bishop dropped the witch's coin back in his waistcoat pocket and held his glass out toward his host. His hand was shaking slightly, but his eyes and voice were steady. "I think I'd like another drop of brandy. Quickly, if you please," he answered.

THE APPRENTICE SORCERER

· BY STEPHEN RYNAS ·

F ive years to the day had passed since that Halloween night when I heard a crash on the roof, ran outside, and found Marilyn lying limp and pale on the lawn beside the shattered remnants of a broomstick. I carried her into my house. She never left. Somewhere along the way we found time to get married, with the aid of a forged birth certificate, and we lived happily together.

Of course there were the usual problems of adjustment faced by every couple. Writers are temperamental people, and occasionally I would stop in at a bar for a drink and get lost for several hours, but Marilyn never said a word of reproach when I finally came home somewhat worse for wear. On the other hand I soon got used to the idea that as the moon grew fatter in the sky she would get a little restless, and finally when a full moon hung above the house she would take her favorite broom and walk out into the night not to return until morning. I never asked questions. About the only thing I did was to quietly hang a green and a red light on the chimney so that there would be no more accidents.

Of course there were a few awkward moments, like the time our next-door neighbor, Mrs. Marx, walked in the open door and saw Marilyn at her housework. Both Marilyn and I dashed for the broom that was busily sweeping the living room by itself, and it took several hours and a half dozen cocktails to convince Mrs. Marx that she had not seen what she had.

And then there was the time shortly after her arrival when I heard through the backyard news service that cats were disappearing at a fast rate from the neighborhood. Marilyn and I had a long talk, and after that the cats disappeared from other sections of Brattleboro.

We had no children, but we were happy with each other. Marilyn was beautiful, and everyone liked her. She was very small, barely five feet, and slim, but her figure had the roundness of a mature woman. She had long raven black hair and the blackest eyes ever seen, while her skin was as white as milk.

Halloween, in a way, was our anniversary, but I knew that it would be unfair for me to expect her to remain home on this night, of all the nights of the year. Still, I waited up in the large easy chair in the living room, reading one of my own novels, my favorite reading matter, with a bottle of vermouth for company.

At three a.m. the front door opened. I glanced at my watch to check the time. It was much too early for Marilyn to be coming back.

But it was Marilyn, and I only had to take one look at her face to see that something was wrong. Even the way she trailed her broom after her bespoke depression. Then I saw that someone else was following her. As he came into the light of the living room I saw that in many ways he resembled Marilyn. He was small, about five and a half feet, slim, with the same jet hair and black brooding eyes. But his complexion was swarthy and he wore a small waved mustache and a pointed goatee. Over his shoulders there was slung a black cape. He was very handsome in a satanic fashion. Naturally I disliked him intensely at first sight.

"Ralph," Marilyn said, approaching my chair slowly. I could see tears in her eyes. "I must say goodbye. Sorcerer Bascombe has claimed me, according to the promise made by my parents, and I must go."

"Sit down Marilyn," I said. "Sit down, uh, Sorcerer Bascombe. Have a glass of vermouth, and let's talk this over."

"No Ralph," Marilyn said, tapping her small foot in vexation, a large tear brimming from her right eye and running down her cheek, "there is nothing to talk over. I must go, Sorcerer Bascombe has claimed me."

"Claimed you for what?" I asked.

"To be my wife," Sorcerer Bascombe said, stepping forward with a sardonic smile.

Seldom had I seen such perfect white teeth. I could not help but think what a pleasure it would be to push the toe of my shoe into them. "I believe that Marilyn and I are married," I said stiffly. "We have a paper somewhere around here to prove it. If you can wait a few weeks, I'll be glad to find it for you."

"Oh, you don't understand," Marilyn said, and now she was really crying, "that marriage didn't mean anything. We don't recognize it. It wasn't performed during a full moon in a graveyard by a duly accredited ghoul."

"So you see, she must go with me," Sorcerer Bascombe said in a smug voice.

"Surely," I said, "there must be something I can do. Talk to her parents or something."

"No," Marilyn sobbed, "my parents have made an agreement and, under the provisions of Section Two of the Combined Witches and Demons Code, cannot change it."

"Of course you can challenge me to a duel to the death for her," Sorcerer Bascombe said with a broad smile. I could see that the idea did not displease him.

"Oh no," Marilyn cried, and she looked at me pleadingly, "you can't do that."

"Why not?" I demanded, "I used to be pretty handy with my epee in college, and I still have my forty-five from the war."

"But don't you see," Marilyn wailed, and it did my heart good to see that she was suffering for me, "Sorcerer Bascombe is a Class A Sorcerer. He'd burn you to a crisp before you could even get near him. Please let me go with him now, for your own good."

"Suppose I did challenge you," I asked my saturnine rival, stalling for time, "when do we try and blow each other's brains out?"

"At the next full moon—that would be a week from now." Sorcerer Bascombe was licking his lips like a satisfied cat.

"And Marilyn stays put until the matter is decided?" I asked.

Marilyn looked from one of us to the other with wide, frightened eyes.

"Under the law, Marilyn stays put," Sorcerer Bascombe said. He was not unhappy about the thought. He had decided that it would be worth it to kill me off, and he was supremely confident that he could do it.

"All right," I said. "A week with Marilyn is worth more to me than a lifetime without her. Consider yourself challenged, Sorcerer Bascombe, and please withdraw as soon as possible to allow us to begin to enjoy our week uncontaminated by your repulsive presence."

"No, no, Ralph," Marilyn interrupted wildly. "You can't."

"I have," I said.

"He has," Sorcerer Bascombe said triumphantly, and faded out right there in the middle of the room.

"Is he gone?" I asked uneasily.

"He's gone," Marilyn said, distraught. "Oh why did you do it, you crazy scribbler? You haven't a chance."

"Shut your mouth, little one," I said, "and come here. We've got to cram a lifetime into a week."

And so we tried.

The next day I decided that I had no intention of going to slaughter without a fight, and I started prying into those things I had studiously ignored for the past five years.

"After all," I said to Marilyn, "I've found you to be a very material woman, solid and substantial, so I don't think there's anything supernatural about you at all. Try and tell me just how you do your stuff."

"I can't tell you much," Marilyn said thoughtfully. "However, I've learned something about your science, and all I can say is that we just naturally do these things. I can generate the energy to fly a broomstick just as you can eat sugar and turn its matter into energy to heat your body. No one can explain how it's done. You just do it. It's part of you. Sorcerer Bascombe," she said, tears coming into her eyes again, "can burn you to a crisp without even knowing how he's doing it, anymore than you know where the energy comes from to lift your arm."

Her mention of energy certainly gave me something to hang my hopes on. "Tell me," I asked excitedly, "do you ever have trouble doing your stuff? That is, when you are near a radio station or something? Or in daylight?"

"Why yes," she said, her eyes glowing as she realized that we were making progress. "Those new things they've put up, radar, really make flying pretty rocky. I don't know anyone who ever had an accident because of it, but everyone agrees that they make you work awfully hard to stay up."

I got up and started pacing restlessly around the room. "That's it," I said. "Don't you see, these things that you do must be the result of some sort of energy that you generate naturally and release in waves similar to radio or radar, if radar causes interference.

"Why sure," I added as another idea struck me, "don't you use figurines to operate on when the object of your dislike is not close at hand?"

"Yes," Marilyn replied, puzzled. "The figurine must be a pretty exact copy of the original made out of copper and several other metals according to a very precise formula."

"That fits," I said excitedly. "Don't you realize that all radio is based on the idea that your set is in tune with the station. Now when you make an exact replica of the victim, it is in tune with him. You shoot your waves into it and they are broadcast to the victim."

"Why Ralph," Marilyn said, the lovelight shining in her black eyes, "you're wonderful. What are you going to do now?"

"Oh that," I said like a punctured balloon. "I don't know. I guess I'll go down to the library and cram up on radio and radar and see what I come up with."

For the next five days I divided my time pretty evenly between Marilyn and endless volumes of technical books in the library. However, my first hopes of finding out how Bascombe did his stuff and building a machine to duplicate it were pretty well shattered. Our science was a thousand years away from discussing antigravity waves, much less giving hints on how to build

264 • STEPHEN RYNAS

equipment for it at home. Nor were there any handy little blueprints for death rays for the home craftsman. Only on the fifth day did I get a glimmer of hope. It was a very slim glimmer, but by that time I was in the mood to clutch at any straws floating about.

During all this time Marilyn had been wonderfully brave, and also wonderful in other more important ways. Women do like to be died for; it builds up their egos and is much more flattering than sending them flowers.

"Can you get in touch with Sorcerer Bascombe?" I asked her on the evening of the fifth day.

"Of course," she replied, but added a bit stiffly, "however, you know that under the codes you can't back out now."

"I don't want to back out. I just want to see friend Bascombe for a few moments," I reassured her. "Could you arrange it for tonight?"

"Certainly," she replied, giving me a warm smile.

Some fifteen minutes later, Sorcerer Bascombe in all his satanic splendor materialized in the center of the living room. "You wanted to see me?" he sneered.

"Yes," I replied.

He strutted up to me. "You know, once a challenge has been made, it can't be withdrawn," he said, sneering again. It was becoming monotonous.

"I know," I said quietly.

I don't know what he expected. He probably thought that I was going to plead for mercy, and he was prepared to cut a great figure before Marilyn's eyes.

"Well, what do you want?" He demanded, a slightly puzzled tone creeping into his voice.

"Why, to see you, of course," I answered simply.

"Well, you've seen me," he said, exasperated.

"So I have," I said, "now go away."

He turned red and shot me a look chock full of malevolence, then without saying another word he disappeared again. Only a puff of yellow smoke remained where he had been.

"And that," I said to Marilyn's puzzled eyes, "is that. Let's retire. Only forty-eight hours left."

The full moon threw eerie and distorted shadows across the green grass carpet of the graveyard. Things half seen in its cold light fluttered past me as I stumbled awkwardly toward the duelling ground. Marilyn led the way, walking confidently through that confusing city of stone. It was already a quarter to twelve. We stopped at a level place between two ornate Vermont marble mausoleums. Sorcerer Bascombe was already there. He smiled broadly when he saw me and threw his black cape back over his shoulders. I managed a weak smile in return.

I glanced at my watch. Five minutes to twelve. In five minutes I would be facing a Class A Champion Sorcerer with nothing more than an untested homemade gadget literally up my sleeves. For Marilyn could not help me with her witchcraft. If she tried, the umpires would take immediate and drastic action.

A little-red-riding-hood-type hood, completely empty as far as I could see, detached itself from the shadowy crowd that was thickening around us, and floated over to the other end of the grassy clearing where Sorcerer Bascombe was promenading up and down, exuding confidence.

"His second," Marilyn whispered to me.

I felt something like a five-pronged stick hit me sharply on the back, and I turned to look into the face of a grinning skeleton. At least I thought he was grinning, but I've had very little experience with skeletons, and maybe I misread his expression. In any case, he was showing a lot of teeth, and making no bones about it.

"Never say die," he said. His teeth clattered together unpleasantly on each word.

"I won't," I promised. " I can see why you might be somewhat sensitive about the subject."

"This is your second," Marilyn whispered urgently. "It is one minute to twelve—I must leave the grounds now."

We wound ourselves around each other and clung for a moment. I could taste the salty tears that ran down her cheeks to where our mouths pressed together.

The long skeleton hand of my second separated us. "Smile," I called to Marilyn as she backed away.

She managed a wan smile. I could see her black eyes and jet

hair fading into the darkness as she backed into the circle of spectators just as the clock on the church steeple began to slowly toll the hour.

On the twelfth crash of the hammer, Sorcerer Bascombe again threw his cape back over his shoulder and strode forward confidently. There was a cruel smile on his swarthy face. For the first time that night I felt real fear. I wasn't afraid to die, but there was a look on his face that warned me that he would not try to kill me cleanly, but would play with me as a cat with a mouse if he had the chance.

I moved forward slowly. When he was about three yards from me, Sorcerer Bascombe suddenly whipped up both hands, pointed them at me, and a look of intense concentration wiped the evil grin from his face.

This is it, I thought, and my heart almost stopped beating. With sudden decision I put down my head and charged. If I only could get my hands on him.

Something like an invisible tank stopped me cold with a bang, then ran right on over me leaving me pressed into the ground and feeling like a pancake. A wave of force, I guessed, would be the technical explanation.

A sound like a cavern of echoes rose from the crowd. I painfully groped my way to my feet and saw Sorcerer Bascombe, looking worse for wear, with his cape muddy and grass-stained, pulling himself stiffly up. There was a puzzled look on his face; the grin was gone.

He moved his hands up again, concentrated harder, and I could see that he intended to give it more power this time. I still had the breath pretty well knocked out of me, and I didn't have it in me to charge again. I just stood unsteadily on my feet and let him do his stuff.

This time a solid wall of wind picked me up and carried me back a good five yards through the air until I was stopped rather sharply by the open arms of a marble angel perched on the mausoleum behind me. After dropping on the sod, I crawled a little toward Sorcerer Bascombe before I could gather the strength to rise. Even then it was fifty-fifty whether I could make it or not. On a slowly spinning grassy clearing I could see Sorcerer Bascombe lifting his hands stiffly again. A look of desperation and fear covered his face, and blood was trickling down from a cut over his left eye. His cape was gone, ripped off his back. He concentrated for a long time, aiming carefully. This was it, full power with no brakes on. I groggily stared at him, wondering which of us was getting the worst of it, and if I could survive another blast.

It came. I can't say much about what happened. It was as though someone had hit me on the forehead with an invisible sledgehammer. One brief shock and it was all over. The last thing I saw was the face of Sorcerer Bascombe. It swelled up, large and terrible, then disappeared. I couldn't tell if it was going away—or if I was. I fought to hold the vision, but it was slipping. The cemetery flowed into a dizzying pool of swirling blackness that faded into nothingness.

I came to slowly. Each bone and muscle in my body had its individual ache. I tried to sit up and yelped as a dozen muscles protested violently. A small gentle hand pushed me down. I opened my eyes and was greeted by the sight of Marilyn's face above me. She was smiling happily, but there were undried tears in the corners of her eyes. I turned my aching neck slightly and saw that my head was resting on her lap. We were still in the grassy space in the cemetery, but the moon was gone, and the eastern sky was ablaze with the rising sun.

"That was quite a haymaker," I said, moving my left arm gingerly. "Who won?"

"You did, darling," Marilyn said, leaning down and kissing me. "They carried the remains of Sorcerer Bascombe away in a small basket. He won't be bothering us again."

"Well, that's that," I said in a businesslike tone that only quavered a little. I pulled myself up on to my feet, leaning heavily against Marilyn's small body.

Though a little unsteady, I could stand. With fumbling fingers I started pulling wires out of my sleeves and pants legs. There was quite a pile of them by the time I finished. I reached into the pocket of my jacket and pulled out the small copper image of Sorcerer Bascombe.

"So that's how you did it," Marilyn said, nodding her head slowly in comprehension.

"Yes," I said. "It was really quite simple. The only thing that surprised me was that it worked. You remember the day I asked Sorcerer Bascombe to come to the house. Well, I had a barrage of concealed cameras ready, and I took the pictures to old Ed Longly, that sculptor down the street, and he turned out a pretty good replica. All I had to do after that was to wire myself like a walking aerial with all leads to the image of your late suitor in my pocket. Every time Sorcerer Bascombe threw a bolt at me, he got it broadcast right back at him. After I saw it worked, my only worry was which of us was going to get the worst of it. It seems that he was."

"Oh darling," Marilyn said, throwing her arms around me, "I'm so happy. And do you know what else happened?"

"No," I said a little hesitantly.

"You've been recognized as a full-fledged Sorcerer on the basis of your victory over Bascombe, and now we'll be able to be married by a real ghoul, and ride by broomstick together, and go to all the meetings together, and everything. Isn't that wonderful?"

I answered by taking her in my arms and giving her a long kiss, then with a sigh I picked up my little pile of wires and pushed them into my pocket. I had a feeling that I would be needing them again.

THE THING ON THE DOORSTEP

BY H. P. LOVECRAFT

I t is true that I have sent six bullets through the head of my best friend, and yet I hope to show by this statement that I am not a murderer. At first I shall be called a madman—madder than the man I shot in his cell at the Arkham Sanitarium. Later some of my readers will weigh each statement, correlate it with the known facts, and ask themselves how I could have believed otherwise than I did after facing the evidence of that horror—that thing on the doorstep.

Until then I also saw nothing but madness in the wild tales I have acted on. Even now I ask myself whether I was misled—or whether I am not mad after all. I do not know—but others have strange things to tell of Edward and Asenath Derby, and even the stolid police are at their wits' ends to account for that last terrible visit. They have tried weakly to concoct a theory of a ghastly jest or warning by discharged servants, yet they know in their hearts that the truth is something infinitely more terrible and incredible.

So I say that I have not murdered Edward Derby. Rather have I avenged him, and in so doing purged the earth of a horror whose survival might have loosed untold terrors on all mankind. There are black zones of shadow close to our daily paths, and now and then some evil soul breaks a passage through. When that happens, the man who knows must strike before reckoning the consequences.

I have known Edward Pickman Derby all his life. Eight years my junior, he was so precocious that we had much in common from the time he was eight and I sixteen. He was the most phenomenal child scholar I have ever known, and at seven was writing verse of a sombre, fantastic, almost morbid cast which astonished the tutors surrounding him. Perhaps his private education and coddled seclusion had something to do with his premature flowering. An only child, he had organic weaknesses which startled his doting parents and caused them to keep him closely chained to their side. He was never allowed out without his nurse, and seldom had a chance to play unconstrainedly with other children. All this doubtless fostered a strange secretive inner life in the boy, with imagination as his one avenue of freedom.

At any rate, his juvenile learning was prodigious and bizarre; and his facile writings such as to captivate me despite my greater age. About that time I had leanings toward art of somewhat grotesque cast, and I found in this younger child a rare kindred spirit. What lay behind our joint love of shadows and marvels was, no doubt, the ancient, mouldering, and subtly fearsome town in which we lived—witch-cursed, legend-haunted Arkham, whose huddled, sagging gambrel roofs and crumbling Georgian balustrades brood out the centuries beside the darkly muttering Miskatonic.

As time went by I turned to architecture and gave up my design of illustrating a book of Edward's demoniac poems, yet our comradeship suffered no lessening. Young Derby's odd genius developed remarkably, and in his eighteenth year his collected nightmare lyrics made a real sensation when issued under the title *Azathoth and Other Horrors*. He was a close correspondent of the notorious Baudelairean poet Justin Geoffrey, who wrote *The People of the Monolith* and died screaming in a madhouse in 1926 after a visit to a sinister, ill-regarded village in Hungary.

In self-reliance and practical affairs, however, Derby was greatly retarded because of his coddled existence. His health had improved, but his habits of childish dependence were fostered by over-careful parents, so that he never travelled alone, made independent decisions, or assumed responsibilities. It was early seen that he would not be equal to a struggle in the business or professional arena, but the family fortune was so ample that this formed no tragedy. As he grew in years of manhood he retained a deceptive aspect of boyishness. Blond and blue-eyed, he had the fresh complexion of a child; and his attempts to raise a moustache were discernible only with difficulty. His voice was soft and light, and his unexercised life gave him a juvenile chubbiness rather than the paunchiness of premature middle age. He was of good height, and his handsome face would have made him a notable gallant had not his shyness held him to seclusion and bookishness.

Derby's parents took him abroad every summer, and he was quick to seize on the surface aspects of European thought and expression. His Poe-like talents turned more and more toward the decadent, and other artistic sensitivenesses and yearnings were half-aroused in him. We had great discussions in those days. I had been through Harvard, had studied in a Boston architect's office, had married, and had finally returned to Arkham to practice my profession—settling in the family homestead in Saltonstall Street, since my father had moved to Florida for his health. Edward used to call almost every evening, till I came to regard him as one of the household. He had a characteristic way of ringing the doorbell or sounding the knocker that grew to be a veritable code signal, so that after dinner I always listened for the familiar three brisk strokes followed by two more after a pause. Less frequently I would visit at his house and note with envy the obscure volumes in his constantly growing library.

Derby went through Miskatonic University in Arkham since his parents would not let him board away from them. He entered at sixteen and completed his course in three years, majoring in English and French literature and receiving high marks in everything but mathematics and the sciences. He mingled very little with the other students, though looking enviously at the "daring" or "Bohemian" set—whose superficially "smart" language and meaningless ironic pose he aped, and whose dubious conduct he wished he dared adopt.

What he did do was to become an almost fanatical devotee of subterranean magical lore, for which Miskatonic's library was and is famous. Always a dweller on the surface of fantasy and strangeness, he now delved deep into the actual runes and riddles left by a fabulous past for the guidance or puzzlement of posterity. He read things like the frightful *Book of Eibon*, the *Unaussprechlichen Kulten* of von Junzt, and the forbidden *Necronomicon* of the mad Arab Abdul Alhazred, though he did not tell his parents he had seen them. Edward was twenty when my son and only child was born, and seemed pleased when I named the newcomer Edward Derby Upton, after him.

By the time he was twenty-five Edward Derby was a prodigiously learned man and a fairly well-known poet and fantaisiste, though his lack of contacts and responsibilities had slowed down his literary growth by making his products derivative and over-bookish. I was perhaps his closest friend—finding him an inexhaustible mine of vital theoretical topics, while he relied on me for advice in whatever matters he did not wish to refer to his parents. He remained single—more through shyness, inertia, and parental protectiveness than through inclination—and moved in society only to the slightest and most perfunctory extent. When the war came both health and ingrained timidity kept him at home. I went to Plattsburg for a commission but never got overseas.

So the years wore on. Edward's mother died when he was thirty-four, and for months he was incapacitated by some odd psychological malady. His father took him to Europe, however, and he managed to pull out of his trouble without visible effects. Afterward he seemed to feel a sort of grotesque exhilaration, as if of partial escape from some unseen bondage. He began to mingle in the more "advanced" college set despite his middle age, and was present at some extremely wild doings—on one occasion paying heavy blackmail (which he borrowed of me) to keep his presence at a certain affair from his father's notice. Some of the whispered rumors about the wild Miskatonic set were extremely singular. There was even talk of black magic and of happenings utterly beyond credibility.

• II •

Edward was thirty-eight when he met Asenath Waite. She was, I judge, about twenty-three at the time and was taking a special course in mediaeval metaphysics at Miskatonic. The daughter of a friend of mine had met her before—in the Hall School at Kingsport—and had been inclined to shun her because of her odd reputation. She was dark, smallish, and very good-looking except for over-protuberant eyes; but something in her expression alienated extremely sensitive people. It was, however, largely her origin and conversation which caused average folk to avoid her. She was one of the Innsmouth Waites, and dark legends have clustered for generations about crumbling, half-deserted Innsmouth and its people. There are tales of horrible bargains about the year 1850, and of a strange element "not quite human" in the ancient families of the run-down fishing port—tales such as only old-time Yankees can devise and repeat with proper awesomeness.

Asenath's case was aggravated by the fact that she was Ephraim Waite's daughter—the child of his old age by an unknown wife who always went veiled. Ephraim lived in a half-decayed mansion in Washington Street, Innsmouth, and those who had seen the place (Arkham folk avoid going to Innsmouth whenever they can) declared that the attic windows were always boarded, and that strange sounds sometimes floated from within as evening drew on. The old man was known to have been a prodigious magical student in his day, and legend averred that he could raise or quell storms at sea according to his whim. I had seen him once or twice in my youth as he came to Arkham to consult forbidden tomes at the college library, and had hated his wolfish, saturnine face with its tangle of iron-gray beard. He had died insane—under rather queer circumstances—just before his daughter (by his will made a nominal ward of the principal) entered the Hall School, but she had been his morbidly avid pupil and looked fiendishly like him at times.

The friend whose daughter had gone to school with Asenath Waite repeated many curious things when the news of Edward's acquaintance with her began to spread about. Asenath, it seemed, had posed as a kind of magician at school; and had really seemed able to accomplish some highly baffling marvels. She professed to be able to raise thunderstorms, though her seeming success was generally laid to some uncanny knack at prediction. All animals markedly disliked her, and she could make any dog howl by certain motions of her right hand. There were times when she displayed snatches of knowledge and language very singular—and very shocking—for a young girl; when she would frighten her schoolmates with leers and winks of an inexplicable kind, and would seem to extract an obscene zestful irony from her present situation.

Most unusual, though, were the well-attested cases of her influence over other persons. She was, beyond question, a genuine hypnotist. By gazing peculiarly at a fellow student she would often give the latter a distinct feeling of *exchanged personality*—as if the subject were placed momentarily in the magician's body and able to stare half across the room at her real body, whose eyes blazed and protruded with an alien expression. Asenath often made wild claims about the nature of consciousness and about its independence of the physical frame—or at least from the life processes of the physical frame. Her crowning rage, however, was that she was not a man; since she believed a male brain had certain unique and far-reaching cosmic powers. Given a man's brain, she declared, she could not only equal but surpass her father in mastery of unknown forces.

Edward met Asenath at a gathering of "intelligentsia" held in one of the students' rooms, and could talk of nothing else when he came to see me the next day. He had found her full of the interests and erudition which engrossed him most and was in addition wildly taken with her appearance. I had never seen the young woman and recalled casual references only faintly, but I knew who she was. It seemed rather regrettable that Derby should become so upheaved about her; but I said nothing to discourage him, since infatuation thrives on opposition. He was not, he said, mentioning her to his father.

In the next few weeks I heard of very little but Asenath from young Derby. Others now remarked Edward's autumnal gallantry, though they agreed that he did not look even nearly his actual age, or seem at all inappropriate as an escort for his bizarre divinity. He was only a trifle paunchy despite his indolence and self-indulgence, and his face was absolutely without lines. Asenath, on the other hand, had the premature crow's feet which come from the exercise of an intense will.

About this time Edward brought the girl to call on me, and I at once saw that his interest was by no means one-sided. She eyed him continually with an almost predatory air, and I perceived that their intimacy was beyond untangling. Soon afterward I had a visit from old Mr. Derby, whom I had always admired and respected. He had heard the tales of his son's new friendship, and had wormed the whole truth out of "the boy." Edward meant to marry Asenath and had even been looking at houses in the suburbs. Knowing my usually great influence with his son, the father wondered if I could help to break the ill-advised affair off; but I regretfully expressed my doubts. This time it was not a question of Edward's weak will but of the woman's strong will. The perennial child had transferred his dependence from the parental image to a new and stronger image, and nothing could be done about it.

The wedding was performed a month later—by a justice of the peace, according to the bride's request. Mr. Derby, at my advice, offered no opposition, and he, my wife, my son, and I attended the brief ceremony—the other guests being wild young people from the college. Asenath had bought the old Crowninshield place in the country at the end of High Street, and they proposed to settle there after a short trip to Innsmouth, whence three servants and some books and household goods were to be brought. It was probably not so much consideration for Edward and his father as a personal wish to be near the college, its library, and its crowd of "sophisticates," that made Asenath settle in Arkham instead of returning permanently home.

When Edward called on me after the honeymoon I thought he looked slightly changed. Asenath had made him get rid of the undeveloped moustache, but there was more than that. He looked soberer and more thoughtful, his habitual pout of childish rebelliousness being exchanged for a look almost of genuine sadness.

I was puzzled to decide whether I liked or disliked the change. Certainly he seemed for the moment more normally adult than ever before. Perhaps the marriage was a good thing—might not the *change* of dependence form a start toward actual *neutralization*, leading ultimately to responsible independence? He came alone, for Asenath was very busy. She had brought a vast store of books and apparatus from Innsmouth (Derby shuddered as he spoke the name), and was finishing the restoration of the Crowninshield house and grounds.

Her home—in that town—was a rather disgusting place, but certain objects in it had taught him some surprising things. He was progressing fast in esoteric lore now that he had Asenath's guidance. Some of the experiments she proposed were very daring and radical—he did not feel at liberty to describe them—but he had confidence in her powers and intentions. The three servants were very queer—an incredibly aged couple who had been with old Ephraim and referred occasionally to him and to Asenath's dead mother in a cryptic way, and a swarthy young wench who had marked anomalies of feature and seemed to exude a perpetual odor of fish.

• III •

For the next two years I saw less and less of Derby. A fortnight would sometimes slip by without the familiar three-and-two strokes at the front door; and when he did call—or when, as happened with increasing infrequency, I called on him—he was very little disposed to converse on vital topics. He had become secretive about those occult studies which he used to describe and discuss so minutely, and preferred not to talk of his wife. She had aged tremendously since her marriage, till now—oddly enough—she seemed the elder of the two. Her face held the most concentratedly determined expression I had ever seen, and her whole aspect seemed to gain a vague, unplaceable repulsiveness. My wife and son noticed it as much as I, and we all ceased gradually to call on her—for which, Edward admitted in one of his boyishly tactless moments, she was unmitigatedly grateful. Occasionally the Derbys would go on long trips—ostensibly to Europe, though Edward sometimes hinted at obscurer destinations.

It was after the first year that people began talking about the change in Edward Derby. It was very casual talk, for the change was purely psychological; but it brought up some interesting points. Now and then, it seemed, Edward was observed to wear an expression and to do things wholly incompatible with his usual flabby nature. For example—although in the old days he could not drive a car, he was now seen occasionally to dash into or out of the old Crowninshield driveway with Asenath's powerful Packard, handling it like a master, and meeting traffic entanglements with a skill and determination utterly alien to his accustomed nature. In such cases he seemed always to be just back from some trip or just starting on one—what sort of trip, no one could guess, although he mostly favoured the Innsmouth road.

Oddly, the metamorphosis did not seem altogether pleasing. People said he looked too much like his wife, or like old Ephraim Waite himself, in these moments—or perhaps these moments seemed unnatural because they were so rare. Sometimes, hours after starting out in this way, he would return listlessly sprawled on the rear seat of the car while an obviously hired chauffeur or mechanic drove. Also, his preponderant aspect on the streets during his decreasing round of social contacts (including, I may say, his calls on me) was the old-time indecisive one—its irresponsible childishness even more marked than in the past. While Asenath's face aged, Edward's—aside from those exceptional occasions—actually relaxed into a kind of exaggerated immaturity, save when a trace of the new sadness or understanding would flash across it. It was really very puzzling. Meanwhile the Derbys almost dropped out of the gay college circle—not through their own disgust, we heard, but because something about their present studies shocked even the most callous of the other decadents.

It was in the third year of the marriage that Edward began to hint openly to me of a certain fear and dissatisfaction. He would let fall remarks about things "going too far," and would talk darkly about the need of "gaining his identity." At first I ignored such references, but in time I began to question him guardedly, remembering what my friend's daughter had said about Asenath's hypnotic influence over the other girls at school—the cases where students had thought they were in her body looking across the room at themselves. This questioning seemed to make him at once alarmed and grateful, and once he mumbled something about having a serious talk with me later.

About this time old Mr. Derby died, for which I was afterward very thankful. Edward was badly upset, though by no means disorganized. He had seen astonishingly little of his parent since his marriage, for Asenath had concentrated in herself all his vital sense of family linkage. Some called him callous in his loss—especially since those jaunty and confident moods in the car began to increase. He now wished to move back into the old family mansion, but Asenath insisted on staying in the Crowninshield house to which she had become well adjusted.

Not long afterward my wife heard a curious thing from a friend—one of the few who had not dropped the Derbys. She had been out to the end of High Street to call on the couple and had seen a car shoot briskly out of the drive with Edward's oddly confident and almost sneering face above the wheel. Ringing the bell, she had been told by the repulsive wench that Asenath was also out; but had chanced to look at the house in leaving. There, at one of Edward's library windows, she had glimpsed a hastily withdrawn face—a face whose expression of pain, defeat, and wistful hopelessness was poignant beyond description. It was—incredibly enough in view of its usual domineering cast—Asenath's; yet the caller had vowed that in that instant the sad, muddled eyes of poor Edward were gazing out from it.

Edward's calls now grew a trifle more frequent, and his hints occasionally became concrete. What he said was not to be believed, even in centuried and legend-haunted Arkham; but he threw out his dark lore with a sincerity and convincingness which made one fear for his sanity. He talked about terrible meetings in lonely places, of cyclopean ruins in the heart of the Maine woods beneath which vast staircases led down to abysses of nighted secrets, of complex angles that lead through invisible walls to other regions of space and time, and of hideous exchanges of personality that permitted explorations in remote and forbidden places, on other worlds, and in different space-time continua.

He would now and then back up certain crazy hints by exhibiting objects which utterly nonplussed me—elusively coloured and bafflingly textured objects like nothing ever heard of on earth, whose insane curves and surfaces answered no conceivable purpose and followed no conceivable geometry. These things, he said, came "from outside"; and his wife knew how to get them. Sometimes—but always in frightened and ambiguous whispers—he would suggest things about old Ephraim Waite, whom he had seen occasionally at the college library in the old days. These adumbrations were never specific, but seemed to revolve around some especially horrible doubt as to whether the old wizard were really dead—in a spiritual as well as corporeal sense.

At times Derby would halt abruptly in his revelations, and I wondered whether Asenath could possible have divined his speech at a distance and cut him off through some unknown sort of telepathic mesmerism—some power of the kind she had displayed at school. Certainly, she suspected that he told me things, for as the weeks passed she tried to stop his visits with words and glances of a most inexplicable potency. Only with difficulty could he get to see me, for although he would pretend to be going somewhere else, some invisible force would generally clog his motions or make him forget his destination for the time being. His visits usually came when Asenath was away—"away in her own body," as he once oddly put it. She always found out later—the servants watched his goings and comings—but evidently she thought it inexpedient to do anything drastic.

▪ IV ▪

Derby had been married more than three years on that August day when I got that telegram from Maine. I had not seen him for two months, but had heard he was away "on business." Asenath was supposed to be with him, though watchful gossip declared there was someone upstairs in the house behind the doubly curtained windows. They had watched the purchases made by the servants. And now the town marshal of Chesuncook had wired of the draggled madman who stumbled out of the woods with delirious ravings and screamed to me for protection. It was Edward—and he had been just able to recall his own name and address.

Chesuncook is close to the wildest, deepest, and least explored forest belt in Maine, and it took a whole day of feverish jolting through fantastic and forbidding scenery to get there in a car. I found Derby in a cell at the town farm, vacillating between frenzy and apathy. He knew me at once, and began pouring out a meaningless, half-incoherent torrent of words in my direction.

"Dan—for God's sake! The pit of the shaggoths! Down the six thousand steps. . .the abomination of abominations. . .I never would let her take me, and then I found myself there— Iä! Shub-Niggurath!—The shape rose up from the altar, and there were five hundred that howled—The Hooded Thing bleated 'Kamog! Kamog!'—that was old Ephraim's secret name in the coven—I was there, where she promised she wouldn't take me— A minute before I was locked in the library, and then I was there where she had gone with my body—in the place of utter blasphemy, the unholy pit where the black realm begins and the watcher guards the gate—I saw a shaggoth—it changed shape—I can't stand it— I'll kill her if she ever sends me there again—I'll kill that entity— her, him, it—I'll kill it! I'll kill it with my own hands!"

It took me an hour to quiet him, but he subsided at last. The next day I got him decent clothes in the village and set out with him for Arkham. His fury of hysteria was spent, and he was inclined to be silent, though he began muttering darkly to himself when the car passed through Augusta—as if the sight of a city aroused unpleasant memories. It was clear that he did not wish to go home; and considering the fantastic delusions he seemed to have about his wife—delusions undoubtedly springing from some actual hypnotic ordeal to which he had been subjected—I thought it would be better if he did not. I would, I resolved, put him up myself for a time; no matter what unpleasantness it would make with Asenath. Later I would help him get a divorce, for most assuredly there were mental factors which made this marriage suicidal for him. When he struck open country again Derby's muttering faded away, and I let him nod and drowse on the seat beside me as I drove.

During our sunset dash through Portland the muttering commenced again, more distinctly than before, and as I listened I caught a stream of utterly insane drivel about Asenath. The extent to which she had preyed on Edward's nerves was plain, for he had woven a whole set of hallucinations around her. His present predicament, he mumbled furtively, was only one of a long series. She was getting hold of him, and he knew that some day she would never let go. Even now she probably let him go only when she had to, because she couldn't hold on long at a time. She constantly took his body and went to nameless places for nameless rites, leaving him in her body and locking him upstairs—but sometimes she couldn't hold on, and he would find himself suddenly in his own body again in some far-off, horrible, and perhaps unknown place. Sometimes she'd get hold of him again and sometimes she couldn't. Often he was left stranded somewhere as I had found him—time and again he had to find his way home from frightful distances, getting somebody to drive the car after he found it.

The worst thing was that she was holding on to him longer and longer at a time. She wanted to be a man—to be fully human— that was why she got hold of him. She had sensed the mixture of fine-wrought brain and weak will in him. Some day she would crowd him out and disappear with his body—disappear to become a great magician like her father and leave him marooned in that female shell that wasn't even quite human. Yes, he knew about the Innsmouth blood now. There had been traffick with things from the sea—it was horrible. . . . And old Ephraim—he had known the secret, and when he grew old did a hideous thing to keep alive—he wanted to live forever—Asenath would succeed— one successful demonstration had taken place already.

As Derby muttered on I turned to look at him closely, verifying the impression of change which an earlier scrutiny had given me. Paradoxically, he seemed in better shape than usual—harder, more normally developed, and without the trace of sickly flabbiness caused by his indolent habits. It was as if he had been really active and properly exercised for the first time in his coddled life, and I judged that Asenath's force must have pushed him into unwonted channels of motion and alertness. But just now his mind was in a pitiable state; for he was mumbling wild extravagances about his wife, about black magic, about old Ephraim, and about some revelation which would convince even me. He repeated names which I recognized from bygone browsings in forbidden volumes, and at times made me shudder with a certain thread of mythological consistency—or convincing coherence—which ran through his maundering. Again and again he would pause, as if to gather courage for some final and terrible disclosure.

"Dan, Dan, don't you remember him—wild eyes and the unkempt beard that never turned white? He glared at me once, and I never forgot it. Now *she* glares that way. *And I know why!* He found it in the *Necronomicon*—the formula. I don't dare tell you the page yet, but when I do you can read and understand. Then you will know what has engulfed me. On, on, on, on—body to body to body—he means never to die. The life-glow—he knows how to break the link. . .it can flicker on a while even when the body is dead. I'll give you hints and maybe you'll guess. Listen, Dan—do you know why my wife always takes such pains with that silly backhand writing? Have you ever seen a manuscript of old Ephraim's? Do you want to know why I shivered when I saw some hasty notes Asenath had jotted down?

"Asenath—*is there such a person?* Why did they half-think there was poison in old Ephraim's stomach? Why do the Gilmans whisper about the way he shrieked—like a frightened child—when he went mad and Asenath locked him up in the padded attic room where—the other—had been? *Was it old Ephraim's soul that was locked in? Who locked in whom?* Why had he been looking for months for someone with a fine mind and a weak will?—Why did he curse that his daughter wasn't a son? Tell me, Daniel Upton—*what devilish exchange was perpetrated in the house of horror where that blasphemous monster had his trust-*

ing, weak-willed half-human child at his mercy? Didn't he make it permanent—as she'll do in the end with me? Tell me why that thing that calls itself Asenath writes differently off guard, *so that you can't tell its script from—"*

Then the thing happened. Derby's voice was rising to a thin treble scream as he raved, when suddenly it was shut off with an almost mechanical click. I thought of those other occasions at my home when his confidences had abruptly ceased—when I had half-fancied that some obscure telepathic wave of Asenath's mental force was intervening to keep him silent. This, though, was something altogether different— and, I felt, infinitely more horrible. The face beside me was twisted almost unrecognizably for a moment, while through the whole body there passed a shivering motion—as if all the bones, organs, muscles, nerves, and glands were readjusting themselves to a radically different posture, set of stresses, and general personality.

Just where the supreme horror lay, I could not for my life tell; yet there swept over me such a swamping wave of sickness and repulsion—such a freezing, petrifying sense of utter alienage and abnormality—that my grasp of the wheel grew feeble and uncertain. The figure beside me seemed less like a lifelong friend than like some monstrous intrusion from outer space—some damnable, utterly accursed focus of unknown and malign cosmic forces.

I had faltered only a moment, but before another moment was over my companion had seized the wheel and forced me to change places with him. The dusk was now very thick, and the lights of Portland far behind, so I could not see much of his face. The blaze of his eyes, though, was phenomenal; and I knew that he must now be in that queerly energized state—so unlike his usual self—which so many people had noticed. It seemed odd and incredible that listless Edward Derby—he who could never assert himself, and who had never learned to drive—should be ordering me about and taking the wheel of my own car, yet that was precisely what had happened. He did not speak for some time, and in my inexplicable horror I was glad he did not.

In the lights of Biddeford and Saco I saw his firmly set mouth, and shivered at the blaze of his eyes. The people were right—he did look damnably like his wife and like old Ephraim when in these moods. I did not wonder that the moods were disliked—there was certainly something unnatural in them, and I felt the sinister element all the more because of the wild ravings I had been hearing. This man, for all my lifelong knowledge of Edward Pickman Derby, was a stranger—an intrusion of some sort from the black abyss.

He did not speak until we were on a dark stretch of road, and when he did his voice seemed utterly unfamiliar. It was deeper, firmer, and more decisive than I had ever known it to be; while its accent and pronunciation were altogether changed—though vaguely, remotely, and rather disturbingly recalling something I could not quite place. There was, I thought, a trace of very profound and very genuine irony in the timbre—not the flashy, meaninglessly jaunty pseudo-irony of the callow "sophisticate," which Derby had habitually affected, but something grim, basic, pervasive, and potentially evil. I marvelled at the self-possession so soon following the spell of panic-struck muttering.

"I hope you'll forget my attack back there, Upton," he was saying. "You know what my nerves are, and I guess you can excuse such things. I'm enormously grateful, of course, for this lift home.

"And you must forget, too, any crazy things I may have been saying about my wife—and about things in general. That's what comes from overstudy in a field like mine. My philosophy is full of bizarre concepts, and when the mind gets worn out it cooks up all sorts of imaginary concrete applications. I shall take a rest from now on—you probably won't see me for some time, and you needn't blame Asenath for it.

"This trip was a bit queer, but it's really very simple. There are certain Indian relics in the north woods—standing stones and all that—which mean a good deal in folklore, and Asenath and I are following that stuff up. It was a hard search, so I seem to have gone off my head. I must send somebody for the car when I get home. A month's relaxation will put me on my feet."

I do not recall just what my own part of the conversation was, for the baffling alienage of my seatmate filled all my consciousness. With every moment my feeling of elusive cosmic horror increased, till at length I was in a virtual delirium of longing for the end of the drive. Derby did not offer to relinquish the wheel, and I was glad of the speed with which Portsmouth and Newburyport flashed by.

At the junction where the main highway runs inland and avoids Innsmouth, I was half-afraid my driver would take the bleak shore road that goes through that damnable place. He did not, however, but darted rapidly past Rowley and Ipswich toward our destination. We reached Arkham before midnight, and found the lights still on at the old Crowninshield house. Derby left the car with a hasty repetition of his thanks, and I drove home alone with a curious feeling of relief. It had been a terrible drive—all the more terrible because I could not quite tell why—and I did not regret Derby's forecast of a long absence from my company.

The next two months were full of rumors. People spoke of seeing Derby more and more in his new energized state, and Asenath was scarcely ever in to her callers. I had only one visit from Edward, when he called briefly in Asenath's car—duly reclaimed from wherever he had left it in Maine—to get some books he had lent me. He was in his new state and paused only long enough for some evasively polite remarks. It was plain that he had nothing to discuss with me when in this condition—and I noticed that he did not even trouble to give the old three-and-two signal when ringing the doorbell. As on that evening in the car, I felt a faint, infinitely deep horror which I could not explain; so that his swift departure was a prodigious relief.

In mid-September Derby was away for a week, and some of the decadent college set talked knowingly of the matter— hinting at a meeting with a notorious cult-leader, lately expelled from England, who had established headquarters in New York. For my part I could not get that strange ride from Maine out of my head. The transformation I had witnessed had affected me profoundly, and I caught myself again and again trying to account for the thing—and for the extreme horror it had inspired in me.

But the oddest rumors were those about the sobbing in the old Crowninshield house. The voice seemed to be a woman's, and some of the younger people thought it sounded like Asenath's. It was heard only at rare intervals, and would sometimes be choked off as if by force. There was talk of an investigation, but this was dispelled one day when Asenath appeared in the streets and chatted in a sprightly way with a large number of acquaintances— apologizing for her recent absence and speaking incidentally about the nervous breakdown and hysteria of a guest from Boston. The guest was never seen, but Asenath's appearance left nothing to be said. And then someone complicated matters by whispering that the sobs had once or twice been in a man's voice.

One evening in mid-October, I heard the familiar three- and-two ring at the front door. Answering it myself, I found Edward on the steps, and saw in a moment that his personality was the old one which I had not encountered since the day of his ravings on that terrible ride from Chesuncook. His face was twitching with a mixture of odd emotions in which fear and triumph seemed to share dominion, and he looked furtively over his shoulder as I closed the door behind him.

Following me clumsily to the study, he asked me for some whiskey to steady his nerves. I forebore to question him, but waited till he felt like beginning whatever he wanted to say. At length he ventured some information in a choking voice.

"Asenath has gone, Dan. We had a long talk last night while the servants were out, and I made her promise to stop preying on me. Of course I had certain—certain occult defences I never told you about. She had to give in, but got frightfully angry. Just packed up and started for New York— walked right out to catch the 8:20 in to Boston. I suppose people will talk, but I can't help that. You needn't mention that there was any trouble—just say she's gone on a long research trip.

"She's probably going to stay with one of her horrible groups of devotees. I hope she'll go west and get a divorce— anyhow, I've made her promise to keep away and let me alone. It was horrible, Dan—she was stealing my body—crowding me out—making a prisoner of me. I lay low and pretended to let her do it, but I had to be on the watch. I could plan if I was careful, for she can't read my mind literally, or in detail. All she could read of my planning was a sort of general mood of rebellion—and she always thought I was helpless. Never thought I could get the best of her. . .but I had a spell or two that worked."

Derby looked over his shoulder and took some more whiskey.

"I paid off those damned servants this morning when they got back. They were ugly about it and asked questions, but they went. They're her kind—Innsmouth people—and were hand and glove with her. I hope they'll let me alone—I didn't like the way they laughed when they walked away. I must get as many of Dad's old servants again as I can. I'll move back home now.

"I suppose you think I'm crazy, Dan—but Arkham history ought to hint at things that back up what I've told you—and what I'm going to tell you. You've seen one of the changes, too—in your car after I told you about Asenath that day coming home from Maine. That was when she got me—drove me out of my body. The last thing I remember was when I was all worked up trying to tell you *what that she-devil is*. Then she got me, and in a flash I was back at the house—in the library where those damned servants had me locked up—and in that cursed fiend's body. . .that isn't even human. . . . You know it was she you must have ridden home with—that preying wolf in my body—You ought to have known the difference!"

I shuddered as Derby paused. Surely, I *had* known the difference—yet could I accept an explanation as insane as this? But my distracted caller was growing even wilder.

"I had to save myself—I had to, Dan! She'd have got me for good at Hallow-mass—they hold a Sabbat up there beyond Chesuncook, and the sacrifice would have clinched things. She'd have got me for good—she'd have been I, and I'd have been she—forever—too late—My body'd have been hers for good—She'd have been a man, and fully human, just as she wanted to be—I suppose she'd have put me out of the way—killed her own ex-body with me in it, damn her, just as she did before—just as she, he, or it did before—" Edward's face was now atrociously distorted, and he bent it uncomfortably close to mine as his voice fell to a whisper.

"You must know what I hinted in the car—*that she isn't Asenath at all, but really old Ephraim himself*. I suspected it a year and a half ago, and I know it now. Her handwriting shows it when she goes off guard—sometimes she jots down a note in writing that's just like her father's manuscripts, stroke for stroke—and sometimes she says things that nobody but an old man like Ephraim could say. He changed forms with her when he felt death coming—she was the only one he could find with the right kind of brain and a weak enough will—he got her body permanently, just as she almost got mine, and then poisoned the old body he'd put her into. Haven't you seen old Ephraim's soul glaring out of that she-devil's eyes dozens of times—and out of mine when she had control of my body?"

The whisperer was panting and paused for breath. I said nothing; and when he resumed his voice was nearer normal. This, I reflected, was a case for the asylum, but I would not be the one to send him there. Perhaps time and freedom from Asenath would do its work. I could see that he would never wish to dabble in morbid occultism again.

"I'll tell you more later—I must have a long rest now. I'll tell you something of the forbidden horrors she led me into—some-

thing of the forbidden horrors that even now are festering in out-of-the-way corners with a few monstrous priests to keep them alive. Some people know things about the universe that nobody ought to know and can do things that nobody ought to be able to do. I've been in it up to my neck, but that's the end. Today I'd burn that damned *Necronomicon* and all the rest if I were librarian at Miskatonic.

"But she can't get me now. I must get out of that accursed house as soon as I can, and settle down at home. You'll help me, I know, if I need help. Those devilish servants, you know—and if people should get too inquisitive about Asenath. You see, I can't give them her address. . . . Then there are certain groups of searchers—certain cults, you know—that might misunderstand our breaking up. . .some of them have damnably curious ideas and methods. I know you'll stand by me if anything happens—even if I have to tell you a lot that will shock you. . . ."

I had Edward stay and sleep in one of the guest-chambers that night, and in the morning he seemed calmer. We discussed certain possible arrangements for his moving back into the Derby mansion, and I hoped he would lose no time in making the change. He did not call the next evening, but I saw him frequently during the ensuing weeks. We talked as little as possible about strange and unpleasant things, but discussed the renovation of the old Derby house, and the travels which Edward promised to take with my son and me the following summer.

Of Asenath we said almost nothing, for I saw that the subject was a peculiarly disturbing one. Gossip, of course, was rife; but that was no novelty in connection with the strange menage at the old Crowninshield house. One thing I did not like was what Derby's banker let fall in an over-expansive mood at the Miskatonic Club—about the checks Edward was sending to a Moses and Abigail Sargent and a Eunice Babson in Innsmouth. That looked as if those evil-faced servants were extorting some kind of tribute from him—yet he had not mentioned the matter to me.

I wished that the summer—and my son's Harvard vacation—would come, so that we could get Edward to Europe. He was not, I soon saw, mending as rapidly as I had hoped he would; for there was something a bit hysterical in his occasional exhilaration, while his moods of fright and depression were altogether too frequent. The old Derby house was ready by December, yet Edward constantly put off moving. Though he hated and seemed to fear the Crowninshield place, he was at the same time queerly enslaved by it. He could not seem to begin dismantling things, and invented every kind of excuse to postpone action. When I pointed this out to him he appeared unaccountably frightened. His father's old butler—who was there with other reacquired servants—told me one day that Edward's occasional prowlings about the house, and especially down cellar, looked odd and unwholesome to him. I wondered if Asenath had been writing disturbing letters, but the butler said there was no mail which could have come from her.

It was about Christmas that Derby broke down one evening while calling on me. I was steering the conversation toward next summer's travels when he suddenly shrieked and leaped up from his chair with a look of shocking, uncontrollable fright—a panic and loathing such as only the nether gulfs of nightmare could bring to any sane mind.

"My brain! My brain! God, Dan—it's tugging—from beyond—knocking—clawing—that she-devil—even now—Ephraim —Kamog! Kamog!—The pit of the shaggoths—Iä! Shub-Niggurath! The Goat with a Thousand Young! . . .

"The flame—the flame—beyond body, beyond life—in the earth—oh, God! . . ."

I pulled him back to his chair and poured some wine down his throat as his frenzy sank to a dull apathy. He did not resist, but kept his lips moving as if talking to himself. Presently I realized that he was trying to talk to me, and bent my ear to his mouth to catch the feeble words.

"Again, again—she's trying—I might have known—nothing can stop that force; not distance nor magic, nor death—it comes and comes, mostly in the night—I can't leave—it's horrible—oh, *God*, Dan, *if you only knew as I do just how horrible it is. . . .*"

When he had slumped down into a stupor I propped him with pillows and let normal sleep overtake him. I did not call a doctor, for I knew what would be said of his sanity and wished to give nature a chance if I possibly could. He waked at midnight, and I put him to bed upstairs, but he was gone by morning. He had let himself quietly out of the house—and his butler, when called on the wire, said he was at home pacing about the library.

Edward went to pieces rapidly after that. He did not call again, but I went daily to see him. He would always be sitting in his library, staring at nothing and having an air of abnormal listening. Sometimes he talked rationally, but always on trivial topics. Any mention of his trouble, of future plans, or of Asenath would send him into a frenzy. His butler said he had frightful seizures at night during which he might eventually do himself harm.

I had a long talk with his doctor, banker, and lawyer, and finally took the physician with two specialist colleagues to visit him. The spasms that resulted from the first questions were violent and pitiable—and that evening a closed car took his poor struggling body to the Arkham Sanitarium. I was made his guardian and called on him twice weekly—almost weeping to hear his wild shrieks, awesome whispers, and dreadful, droning repetitions of such phrases as "I had to do it—I had to do it—it'll get me—it'll get me—down there—down there in the dark— Mother! Mother! Dan! Save me—save me—"

How much hope of recovery there was, no one could say, but I tried my best to be optimistic. Edward must have a home if he emerged, so I transferred his servants to the Derby mansion, which would surely be his sane choice. What to do about the Crowninshield place with its complex arrangements and collections of utterly inexplicable objects I could not decide, so I left it momentarily untouched—telling the Derby household to go over and dust the chief rooms once a week, and ordering the furnace man to have a fire on those days.

The final nightmare came before Candlemas—heralded, in cruel irony, by a false gleam of hope. One morning late in January the sanitarium telephoned to report that Edward's reason had suddenly come back. His continuous memory, they said, was badly impaired; but sanity itself was certain. Of course he must remain some time for observation, but there could be little doubt of the outcome. All going well, he would surely be free in a week.

I hastened over in a flood of delight, but stood bewildered

when a nurse took me to Edward's room. The patient rose to greet me, extending his hand with a polite smile; but I saw in an instant that he bore the strangely energized personality which had seemed so foreign to his own nature— the competent personality I had found so vaguely horrible, and which Edward himself had once vowed was the intruding soul of his wife. There was the same blazing vision—so like Asenath's and old Ephraim's—and the same firm mouth; and when he spoke I could sense the same grim, pervasive irony in his voice—the deep irony so redolent of potential evil. This was the person who had driven my car through the night five months before—the person I had not seen since that brief call when he had forgotten the oldtime doorbell signal and stirred such nebulous fears in me—and now he filled me with the same dim feeling of blasphemous alienage and ineffable hideousness.

He spoke affably of arrangements for release—and there was nothing for me to do but assent, despite some remarkable gaps in his recent memories. Yet I felt that something was terribly, inexplicably wrong and abnormal. There were horrors in this thing that I could not reach. This was a sane person—but was it indeed the Edward Derby I had known? If not, who or what was it—and where was Edward? Ought it to be free or confined—or ought it to be extirpated from the face of the earth? There was a hint of the abysmally sardonic in everything the creature said— the Asenath-like eyes lent a special and baffling mockery to certain words about the early liberty earned by an *especially close confinement*! I must have behaved very awkwardly and was glad to beat a retreat.

All that day and the next I racked my brain over the problem. What had happened? What sort of mind looked out through those alien eyes in Edward's face? I could think of nothing but this dimly terrible enigma and gave up all efforts to perform my usual work. The second morning the hospital called up to say that the recovered patient was unchanged, and by evening I was close to a nervous collapse—a state I admit, though others will vow it colored my subsequent vision. I have nothing to say on this point except that no madness of mine could account for all the evidence.

• V •

It was in the night—after the second evening—that stark, utter horror burst over me and weighted my spirit with a black, clutching panic from which it can never shake free. It began with a telephone call just before midnight. I was the only one up, and sleepily took down the receiver in the library. No one seemed to be on the wire, and I was about to hang up and go to bed when my ear caught a very faint suspicion of sound at the other end. Was someone trying under great difficulties to talk? As I listened I thought I heard a sort of half-liquid bubbling noise—"glub. . . glub. . .glub"—which had an odd suggestion of inarticulate, unintelligible word and syllable divisions. I called "Who is it?" But the only answer was "glub. . .glub. . .glub-glub." I could only assume that the noise was mechanical; but fancying that it might be a case of a broken instrument able to receive but not to send, I added, "I can't hear you. Better hang up and try Information." Immediately I heard the receiver go on the hook at the other end.

This, I say, was just before midnight. When that call was traced afterward it was found to come from the old Crowninshield house, though it was fully half a week from the housemaid's day to be there. I shall only hint what was found at that house—the upheaval in a remote cellar storeroom, the tracks, the dirt, the hastily rifled wardrobe, the baffling marks on the telephone, the clumsily used stationery, and the detestable stench lingering over everything. The police, poor fools, have their smug little theories, and are still searching for those sinister discharged servants—who have dropped out of sight amidst the present furor. They speak of a ghoulish revenge for things that were done, and say I was included because I was Edward's best friend and adviser.

Idiots! Do they fancy those brutish clowns could have forged that handwriting? Do they fancy they could have brought what later came? Are they blind to the changes in that body that was Edward's? As for me, *I now believe all that Edward Derby ever told me.* There are horrors beyond life's edge that we do not suspect, and once in a while man's evil prying calls them just within our range. Ephraim— Asenath—that devil called them in, and they engulfed Edward as they are engulfing me.

Can I be sure that I am safe? Those powers survive the life of the physical form. The next day—in the afternoon, when I pulled out of my prostration and was able to walk and talk coherently— I went to the madhouse and shot him dead for Edward's and the world's sake, but can I be sure till he is cremated? They are keeping the body for some silly autopsies by different doctors— but I say he must be cremated. *He must be cremated—he who was not Edward Derby when I shot him.* I shall go mad if he is not, for I may be the next. But my will is not weak—and I shall not let it be undermined by the terrors I know are seething around it. One life—Ephraim, Asenath, and Edward—who now? I *will not* be driven out of my body. . . I *will not* change souls with that bullet-ridden lich in the madhouse!

But let me try to tell coherently of that final horror. I will not speak of what the police persistently ignored—the tales of that dwarfed, grotesque, malodorous thing met by at least three wayfarers in High Street just before two o'clock, and the nature of the single footprints in certain places. I will say only that just about two the doorbell and knocker waked me—doorbell and knocker both, plied alternately and uncertainly in a kind of weak desperation, *and each trying to keep to Edward's old signal of three-and-two strokes.*

Roused from sound sleep, my mind leaped into a turmoil. Derby at the door—and remembering the old code! That new personality had not remembered it. . .was Edward suddenly back in his rightful state? Why was he here in such evident stress and haste? Had he been released ahead of time, or had he escaped? Perhaps, I thought as I flung on a robe and bounded downstairs, his return to his own self had brought raving and violence, revoking his discharge and driving him to a desperate dash for freedom. Whatever had happened, he was good old Edward again, and I would help him!

When I opened the door into the elm-arched blackness a gust of insufferably fetid wind almost flung me prostrate. I choked in nausea, and for a second scarcely saw the dwarfed, humped figure on the steps. The summons had been Edward's, but who was this foul, stunted parody? Where had Edward had time to go? His ring had sounded only a second before the door opened.

The caller had on one of Edward's overcoats—its bottom almost touching the ground. On the head was a slouch hat pulled low, while a black silk muffler concealed the face. As I stepped unsteadily forward, the figure made a semi-liquid sound like that I had heard over the telephone—"glub. . . glub. . ."—and thrust at me a large, closely written paper impaled on the end of a long pencil. Still reeling from the morbid and unaccountable fetor, I seized the paper and tried to read it in the light from the doorway.

Beyond question, it was in Edward's script, but why had he written when he was close enough to ring—and why was the script so awkward, coarse, and shaky? I could make out nothing in the dim half light, so edged back into the hall, the dwarf figure clumping mechanically after but pausing on the inner door's threshold. The odor of this singular messenger was really appalling, and I hoped (not in vain, thank God!) that my wife would not wake and confront it.

Then, as I read the paper, I felt my knees give under me and my vision go black. I was lying on the floor when I came to, that accursed sheet still clutched in my fear-rigid hand. This is what it said.

"Dan—go to the sanitarium and kill it. Exterminate it. It isn't Edward Derby any more. She got me—it's Asenath—*and she has been dead three months and a half.* I lied when I said she had gone away. I killed her. I had to. It was sudden, but we were alone and I was in my right body. I saw a candlestick and smashed her head in. She would have got me for good at Hallow-mass.

"I buried her in the farther cellar storeroom under some old boxes and cleaned up all the traces. The servants suspected next morning, but they have such secrets that they dare not tell the police. I sent them off, but God knows what others of the cult will do.

"I thought for a while I was all right, and then I felt the tugging at my brain. I knew what it was—I ought to have remembered. A soul like hers—or Ephraim's—is half detached, and keeps right on after death as long as the body lasts. She was getting me—making me change bodies with her—seizing my body and putting me in that corpse of hers in the cellar.

"I knew what was coming—that's why I snapped and had to go to the asylum. Then it came—I found myself choked in the dark—in Asenath's rotting carcass down there in the cellar under the boxes where I put it. And I knew she must be in my body at the sanitarium—permanently, for it was after Hallow- mass, and the sacrifice would work even without her being there—sane and ready for release as a menace to the world. I was desperate, *and in spite of everything I clawed my way out.*

"I'm too far gone to talk—I couldn't manage to telephone— but I can still write. I'll get fixed up somehow and bring this last word and warning, *Kill that fiend* if you value the peace and comfort of the world. *See that it is cremated.* If you don't, it will live on and on, body to body forever, and I can't tell you what it will do. Keep clear of black magic, Dan, it's the devil's business. Goodbye—you've been a great friend. Tell the police whatever they'll believe—and I'm damnably sorry to drag all this on you. I'll be at peace before long—this thing won't hold together much more. Hope you can read this. *And kill that thing—kill it.*

Yours—Ed."

It was only afterward that I read the last half of this paper, for I had fainted at the end of the third paragraph. I fainted again when I saw and smelled what cluttered up the threshold where the warm air had struck it. The messenger would not move or have consciousness any more.

The butler, tougher-fibred than I, did not faint at what met him in the hall in the morning. Instead, he telephoned the police. When they came I had been taken upstairs to bed, but the—other mass—lay where it had collapsed in the night. The men put handkerchiefs to their noses.

What they finally found inside Edward's oddly assorted clothes was mostly liquescent horror. There were bones, too— and a crushed-in skull. Some dental work positively identified the skull as Asenath's.

JUST ANOTHER WORKING MOM

▪ BY PATRICIA B. CIRONE ▪

Carrie glanced out the window, saw Mrs. Trueglove huffing up the path like a small asthmatic locomotive, and winced. Could she pretend she wasn't home? . . . No, she had left the garage door open, ready for a quick run to the store, so her car was in plain sight. Damn!

With a sigh, Carrie rubbed her hands on her jeans and headed for the door, cursing Sylvia Braddock. Ever since her "dear friend" Sylvia had "let slip" — in apparently fifty different places — some words about Carrie's family heritage of witchcraft, a number of odd people had been beating on her door.

Including Mrs. Trueglove. Not content with spending three hours talking about her son's problem her first time with Carrie, she had visited two days later for yet another wasted hour. And now here she was again.

"Hello, Mrs. Trueglove."

"Hi, dear. I just wondered if you had had a chance? . . ."

"No, I'm afraid not. As I told you the other day, I'm not really a practicing witch, so. . . ."

"I just thought," interrupted Mrs. Trueglove, "well, I'm sure other boys have had this problem."

"Yes, I'm sure, too. But, you know, most boys—and their mothers—just wait for time to solve it. Boys grow, eventually. It's just that some get their growth spurt later than others."

"Yes, but some have problems. They need growth stuff. I've read about it in magazines. My Bert's almost sixteen and is still just five-four. That's cruel hard on a boy."

Carrie looked at Mrs. Trueglove's squat figure and debated telling her maybe five-four was what Bert was meant to be.

"Perhaps if you approached your doctor again?"

Mrs. Trueglove pursed her mouth. "That man! Goes on about how Bert's a fine specimen. Probably because he's just as short himself. Doesn't want Bert to be taller. No, I've come to you. Now, I'll just come in and wait while you go through those books or whatever of yours."

"Mrs. Trueglove," Carrie said through her teeth, silently cursing the age-old code which said that a witch must aid whoever comes to her for help. "I have over fifty books that have come down in my mother's family. All of them are handwritten, some of them in foreign languages such as Latin and Greek. Most are brittle with age. Finding one specific spell is not the work of an afternoon. Plus, I do have other things to do. I'm a mother, myself, you know. I am working on it. As I said yesterday, I'll call you as soon as I find something."

Mrs. Trueglove's face fell, and she twisted the short black straps of her purse. "His school prom's coming up in two weeks."

Carrie saw red, took a deep breath, and told herself the woman was ignorant, that was all.

"Mrs. Trueglove, these things take time, as I explained to you when you first came. Like every other science, witchcraft has changed through the years and we have found that 'presto, chango' instant spells are not as long-lasting and are more injurious than ones that work with nature. Even if I found a spell that suited your son's needs, it would take more than two weeks to make a noticeable difference in his height."

Mrs. Trueglove looked as annoyed at Carrie as she undoubtedly had at her doctor. Maybe she was annoyed enough to take herself away and never come back?

Mrs. Trueglove admonished Carrie five more times to find the spell as quickly as she could. Her parting words were: "I'll check back tomorrow, just in case."

Carrie shut the door, bolted it, and leaned against it wearily. She was going to kill Sylvia!

Two long hours later Carrie was sitting on an upturned fruit crate in the basement, thumbing slowly through old books and mentally upping Mrs. Trueglove's bill. Witches might be oathbound to help those who came to them, but they weren't bound to do it for free. In the mood she was in, she'd see that Mrs. Trueglove paid through her pudgy nose.

Before she could feel more vindictive, she shut the book, put it firmly away, stood up, and stretched, her hand rubbing the small of her back. When she noticed what her hands looked like, she frantically twisted around. Oh damn! She'd gotten black book-mold all over her blouse!

She stomped up the steps and scrubbed her hands so hard they stung. She was still stomping as she went up to the small bedroom under the eaves. She changed her blouse. When she glanced at the clock, she moaned. Four o'clock already? She had to get to the supermarket, and if the shipyard traffic in Kittery reached Route 236 before she did, she'd sit there for half an hour trying to turn onto the highway. Then she'd have to skip the groceries or be late picking Melanie up.

As she drove fast down the highway, she justified her pique, muttering aloud that she wasn't really a witch. Well, she *was*, of course: trained, initiated, and confirmed. But she'd never charged money before, or cast a spell for anyone but her family since she'd passed her "practical." Indeed, if it hadn't meant so much to her mother, she never would have done that. She hadn't wanted to hurt her mother's feelings by telling her that professional witchcraft, in today's technological world, was embarrassing and anachronistic. Now, here she was, with three or four people each week coming to her for spells. . . . Thank you, Sylvia.

Over the next three weeks, Carrie combed through every book in her collection.

"I don't know, Sylvia," she said one afternoon over a cup of tea. "There just doesn't seem to be a spell for making a young boy grow. It does seem odd. There's two for making adult men grow taller, but for some reason both are forbidden for anyone under twenty-five. There must be fifty for making specific features, such as noses, chins, ears, and eyes grow large or smaller or just change shape. Spells for growing thinner, spells for growing heavier . . . even a spell for *thwarting* another's growth, but nothing to fit Mrs. Trueglove's son."

"A spell for *thwarting* growth! Do you think someone else could have put a spell on him?" whispered Sylvia, wide-eyed and enthusiastic: Witchcraft, alive and real in the 1980s, had gripped her as if it were a fever.

"I don't think so, Sylvia. Witches don't really turn up everywhere in York County, you know, and those that exist have better things to do with their time than thwarting one unremarkable boy's growth. Like pulling ragweed out of their garden before they have to run their son and daughter over to the allergist for more shots. Or getting their cats to the vet to be dipped before the fleas take over the house. Anyway. . . ."

"Can't you just do spells for the ragweed and the fleas?" interrupted Sylvia.

"Oh, Sylvia," Carrie groaned. "Life isn't one spell after another. It's easier to do things the normal way, honestly. And much more fun. And it doesn't get your hands filthy and smelling of must."

"Oh, come on, Carrie. You must admit it's exciting."

Carrie stared at her friend and realized she'd never make her understand. To Sylvia it was all a big game, a new enthusiasm, like mah-jongg had been a few years back. To Carrie, witchcraft was a quiet part of her life, something she used occasionally, with love and nostalgia for her family's origins, much as she used her mother's recipe for Christmas fruitcake.

"Well, it's certainly not exciting having Mrs. Trueglove descend on me every other day," Carrie grumbled.

"*I think you're up against another witch,*" Sylvia cried with the fervor she used in describing a new Stephen King novel.

"No, Sylvia," Carrie sighed. "As I was trying to say, I used a spell to lift other spells, just on the off-chance, but there's nothing at work on that boy except nature. I'll just have to keep plugging away."

"Oh." Sylvia was disappointed. She was not as interested in

witchcraft when it was a dull search through books instead of lightning and curses made at midnight.

That day Carrie came to a conclusion. She had felt she was falling behind in everything else that was important to her. She was getting irritable with her family, and she was in danger of disliking her best friend. It was time to do something about her burgeoning reputation as a witch.

First, she did something about Sylvia's mouth. It took her a while, because the spell had to be precise. Otherwise, Sylvia might never talk again. . . well, Sylvia *did* talk too much.

That taken care of, she proceeded to turn all newcomers away from her door.

"Oh, yes," she'd say. "I do have a collection of memorabilia, mainly books, about witchcraft. I really have to do something about sorting them out and donating them to the local historical society or something." She'd smile blandly when the person stuttered out his or her confusion. "Oh, no, you must have me confused with someone else. I don't read the Tarot or anything else."

She'd send them on their way and then have to avert her eyes from the photographs of her mother, grandmother, and great-grandmother. She was afraid their images would come alive in the frames and berate her for breaking the code.

Carrie tried to excuse herself with the thought that few, if any, of these people truly needed witchcraft: Modern medicine, fast airplanes, and telephones took care of most of the needs people a hundred years ago had gone to witches for. And as long as she hadn't agreed to help them, she was within her rights, as spelled out by the oath she had taken.

Finally, Carrie was left with Mrs. Trueglove as the only outstanding responsibility on her books. She had agreed to help her. And Mrs. Trueglove had her stumped. Carrie had been through every last page of all the books, giving herself headaches from reading the crabbed script and difficult language. She hadn't been so immersed in antiquity since her practical. Still, she had found nothing, except possibly something in her Great-Aunt Trudy's personal book.

She didn't want to think about using any spell from that. She went over to Sylvia's instead.

Sylvia bustled about, making a pot of tea with some gourmet blend she had picked up down at one of the outlet malls. "You know, the funniest thing happened the other day. I was just about to tell Jo Ann—you know, my friend up in Wells—about your being a witch. I had my mouth open to tell her, and I got distracted and the thought went clean out of my mind. I never did tell her."

"That's strange?" asked Carrie, with a smile. "I get distracted all the time. I think it's a virus that comes with motherhood."

Sylvia laughed. "Talking about motherhood. . . ." She was off and running, spending the next twenty minutes talking about her five-year-old. Carrie smiled behind her teacup. The spell was working. Eventually Sylvia wouldn't even remember her urge to tell about Carrie's status as a witch.

Knowing that the spell was working well gave Carrie the incentive to wrap things up with Mrs. Trueglove. She decided to go ahead and use the spell from Aunt Trudy's book, but not without trepidation.

Her mother had always said Great-Aunt Trudy was a little weird. Or, as her mother had actually put it: "Aunt Trudy's sense of humor always had an extra kick."

Her mother had told her the one time she had used a spell from Trudy's book to de-flea a cat: it had been de- flea'd all right—by virtue of being de-furred. Have you ever seen a furless Angora? Or its irate owner? Her mother, twenty years after the event, had finally laughed about it. Carrie wondered what Mrs. Trueglove would say about, say, an eight-foot-tall son. That was the risk, she thought.

Still, it was the only spell she had found which might solve the problem. "Spell To Cure Any Male Problem." Carrie didn't care for its ambiguity, its all-purpose billing, but. . . .

She summoned Mrs. Trueglove and her son. Once they arrived, the process took only thirty minutes, about twenty of which were show. Mrs. Trueglove left, wheezing happily. Her son followed, walking as tall as he could. Carrie was left biting her lips. She shook off her uneasiness and bustled Melanie and Jason out of the house and down to Route One for some back-to-school clothes shopping.

By October she had relegated Mrs. Trueglove to the back of her mind, and no alarms rang when Sylvia asked about her.

"She's fine, I guess," Carrie answered easily.

"It's funny," Sylvia said. "I'd almost forgotten about her, until I saw her knocking on your door the other day."

Carrie did feel a faint unease then, but she remembered Mrs. Trueglove still owed her part of the large sum she had charged for her services. She must have come in person to pay.

Sylvia was going on, cocking her head and looking at her friend. "In fact, I'd practically forgotten about your being a 'witch.'"

"It's just a few things handed down by my mother. It's not that important," Carrie said soothingly.

"No, I suppose not. Not in this day and age. I mean, you're certainly not teaching Melanie and Jason that nonsense."

"No," Carrie agreed. She raised the teacup to her lips and sipped. Actually, she should be. She pushed the thought out of her head. "How's Andy coping with kindergarten?"

Sylvia embarked on her favorite topic, and Carrie sat back with relief. That was all she needed, for Melanie to be labelled a budding witch. She would be called a freak by the other kids and teased as she herself had been. "How come you don't live in Salem?" "Better watch out for her on Halloween night!" Or worse.

When Carrie returned home, Mrs. Trueglove and her daughter were waiting on her doorstep.

The woman stood and glared as Carrie walked up the driveway. Her purse jerked with the twists she was putting into its short black straps.

"I've heard about people like you," the squat woman started in, tears at the corners of her angry eyes. "But I didn't ever think I'd meet one. What did my Bert ever do to you? That's what I want to know."

"Mrs. Trueglove, I don't know what you're talking about. What's wrong?"

"What's wrong! With my Bert standing right there you ask

me what's wrong?"

Carrie took a closer look at the somewhat muscular girl, and her heart sank to her toes. She should have known better than to use a spell from Aunt Trudy's book. It had solved a male problem all right. By making it a female problem!

Carrie hustled Mrs. Trueglove and her "son" into the house. Her brain raced frantically. The first step would be to lift the spell. But then what?

She muttered some nonsense about a tea ceremony to create the necessary atmosphere and made it sound good. While the Truegloves sat and sipped in the absolute silence she had decreed, Carrie nipped down to the basement and attacked her books. Thanks to her recent session with them she was able to quickly put her finger on most of the spells. She didn't really like the thought of using the one she found. But it was necessary unless she wanted police screaming down on her home, rocks thrown at her children, and maybe even lawsuits.

Carrie hurried back up the stairs, her fingers clutching several of the old books and marking the places in them.

"Now, Mrs. Trueglove, we'll get right down to work and correct this problem. We must have worked under the wrong atmosphere the last time, but this tea ceremony will correct that." She continued her patter as she set up the first spell, the one to remove her initial damage. Quickly she triggered it and moved right on to the next: a "glamour" to restore Bert's features and chest and everything else to its former appearance until nature took over the job in its more time-consuming way.

Carrie watched carefully as Bert's brown hair tightened into a more springy texture, and his features lost their rounded softness, regaining the mismatched, long-jawed look of male adolescence. Even his shoulders seemed to straighten and broaden a bit. And his chest, thank God, lost the small peaks that had been forming. She breathed a sigh of relief. The ironic thing, Carrie thought, checking Bert over for anything she had missed, was that he seemed to have grown.

She had him step over to the wall. She measured him. Sure enough, one and a half inches in as many months. Maybe the change in hormones had shaken up his pituitary, because it certainly hadn't been the spell — female hormones were more apt to suppress growth. Carrie shrugged and went on with her work.

She finished by casting spells for forgetfulness of the past, six weeks' worth, and for the substitution of false memories. It was tricky, with her lack of practice, to set them up to ripple and affect everyone who came into contact with Bert. The goal would be to have them all forget his unfortunate period of gradual feminization.

She watched the spells take effect. Mrs. Trueglove's face smoothed out and lost its bulldog suspiciousness, and her hands loosened their grip on her purse. Bert, too, lost his expression of bewilderment.

Carrie felt a worm of guilt—what had she done to this family, all because this woman had annoyed her! If she had been less wrapped up in her own feelings and more concerned with the principles her mother had tried to instill in her, this never would have happened.

Again and again her mother had preached: "Never use a spell you're not familiar with." But Carrie had so seldom used her craft, she was unfamiliar with most of them.

As the workings of the spell ground to an end, Mrs. Trueglove started to look around. Carrie put a cheerful smile on her face and tripped into happy conversation.

"I'm so glad you stopped over, Mrs. Trueglove, to show me how Bert is progressing. One and a half inches! I'm glad the spell is working so well."

Mrs. Trueglove stared at a now-masculine Bert, looked confused for a moment, and then beamed at Carrie. "Yes, he looks good, doesn't he? I'll tell everyone what a good witch you are."

"You want to be careful about that, Mrs. Trueglove. People, especially kids, can be very cruel. I'd hate to see Bert laughed at, especially now when his new height will give him a better chance with the girls. You wouldn't want them all turning him down for a date because they thought there was something peculiar about him."

"Yes, that's true," Mrs. Trueglove agreed thoughtfully.

"We'll just keep it our secret," Carrie emphasized, backing it up with a quick little obedience spell, one of the few she had used over the years—with her kids, this little extra push did wonders.

Mrs. Trueglove and her son left happy and thinking nothing had happened in the last six weeks except Bert's gradual growth. Carrie watched them go, knowing she, not Sylvia, had brought this all on herself, by neglecting her heritage in the first place. By allowing herself to get rusty, and a little desperate, she had nearly ruined the lives of two people.

She went down to the basement and stayed there all afternoon, diligently reviewing the primers and relearning some of the meditation exercises.

Her daughter banged in from school and not finding her Mom in the kitchen or upstairs, clattered down to the basement.

She stuck her head around the corner. "What'cha doing, Mom?"

Carrie smiled, taking a close look at Melanie's thirteen-year-old legginess and approaching beauty. There was a look about her eyes that reminded Carrie a bit of her own mother.

"Come here, Melanie, and I'll show you."

THE AUTHORS

Edith Wharton

Edith Wharton (1862-1937) was born in New York City, but spent much of her adult life in Europe, where she was a close friend of Henry James. The winner of the Pulitzer Prize in 1921, she was an extremely perceptive writer who excelled at short stories ("Xingu") and novellas (*Ethan Frome*). Throughout her career, she wrote about a dozen science fiction and fantasy stories. "All Souls'" first appeared in her posthumous collection, *The Ghost Stories of Edith Wharton*, 1937.

Joseph Payne Brennan

Born in Bridgeport, Connecticut, Joseph Payne Brennan (1918-) was a decorated veteran of World War II. He has spent much of his life working in the Yale University Library, and is the author of several books of poetry and macabre short stories. "Canavan's Back Yard" first appeared in his collection *Nine Horrors and a Dream*, 1958.

August Derleth

August Derleth (1909-1971), born in Sauk City, Wisconsin, wrote regional fiction, poetry, and short stories of mystery and the fantastic. Perhaps his most noteworthy accomplishment was founding Arkham House, the twentieth century's leading publisher of horror fiction. "The Night Train to Lost Valley" first appeared in *Weird Tales*, January, 1948.

William Lee

William Lee is the true mystery man of this collection. He authored ten science fiction and fantasy stories from 1962 to 1972. He is deceased, but neither his agent nor the magazines he wrote for know anything about his life, and repeated attempts to contact his widow, check obituary columns, phone libraries, and get in touch with possible places of his employment have failed to unearth anything about him. "A Message From Charity" first appeared in *The Magazine of Fantasy and Science Fiction*, November, 1967.

Howard Pyle

Howard Pyle (1853-1911) was born in Wilmington, Delaware, and attended art schools in Philadelphia and New York City. A popular illustrator, he also wrote and illustrated more than twenty books of his own including the *Merry Adventures of Robin Hood of Great Renown in Nottinghamshire*, *The Wonder Clock* and *Men of Iron*. "The Salem Wolf" first appeared in *Harper's Monthly Magazine*, December, 1909.

Shirley Barker

Shirley Barker (1911-1965) was born in Farmington, New Hampshire, and educated at the University of New Hampshire, Radcliffe College, and Pratt Institute Library School. The author or editor of approximately fifteen books, she spent much of her career working in the American History department of the New York Public Library. "The Fog on Pemble Green" is an award-winning story which first appeared in *Ellery Queen's Mystery Magazine*, May, 1955.

Alice Morse Earle

Alice Morse Earle (1853?-1911) was a native of Worcester, Massachusetts. She became an expert on colonial social customs, clothes, and antiques, publishing such works as *The Sabbath in Puritan New England* (1891), *Two Centuries of Costume in America, 1620-1820* (1903), and *China Collecting in America* (1903). She also wrote several fantastic stories for the leading magazines of the day. "Witch Sheep" appears to have been first published in her collection, *In Old Narragansett*, 1898. The version used here has been edited slightly.

Mary Wilkins Freeman

Mary Wilkins Freeman (1852-1930), born in Randolph, Massachusetts, became noted for her short stories of New England small-town life, such as are found in her collections *A Humble Romance* (1887) and *A New England Nun and Other Stories* (1891). She also wrote a number of fantasy stories, most of which appear in *The Ghost Stories of Mary Wilkins Freeman*. "Silence," which is based upon an actual incident, first appeared in *Harper's Monthly Magazine*, July, 1893.

Ogden Nash

Ogden Nash (1902-1971) was born in Rye, New York, and attended Harvard University. After a brief stint in advertising and publishing, he became a full-time writer, producing more than fifty books. Many consider him to have been "America's most popular and most frequently quoted contemporary poet." His little-known story "The Three D's" first appeared in *Harper's Bazaar*, April, 1948, as "Victoria."

John Cheever

John Cheever (1912-1982) was born in Quincy, Massachusetts, and spent much of his life as a full-time writer. Noted primarily for his short stories, he received many awards including The National Book Award in fiction for *The Wapshot Chronicle*, 1958; an honorary doctorate from Harvard University, 1978; and the Pulitzer Prize in fiction, 1979. Most of his short fiction appears in *The Stories of John Cheever*, 1978. "The Music Teacher" first appeared in *The New Yorker*, November 21, 1959.

Mrs. Volney E. Howard

Mrs. Volney E. Howard (1816-18??) was born Catherine Elizabeth Gooch. Although she published two stories in the 1840s, much more is known about her husband, whom she married in 1837. A Maine native who became a Mississippi state representative, Texas Congressman, and Los Angeles district attorney and superior court judge, Mr. Howard died at the age of eighty in 1889. It is not known whether Mrs. Howard survived him. "The Midnight Voyage of the *Seagull*" first appeared in *Godey's Lady's Book*, July, 1842. The version here has been edited.

Seabury Quinn

Seabury Quinn (1889-1969) was born in Washington, D.C., and studied medicine and law. The author of the notable Jules de Grandin psychic detective stories, he was the most popular contributor to *Weird Tales*, the seminal magazine of the horror genre. Much of his best work appears in two collections: *The Phantom Fighter* (1966) and *Is the Devil a Gentleman?*; "Is the Devil a Gentleman?" first appeared in *Weird Tales* on January, 1948.

Stephen A. Rynas

Stephen A. Rynas (1921-   ) is a native of New York City and graduated from City College of New York with a degree in English. He served as an officer in the Air Force during World War II, briefly published about a dozen fantastic stories in the early 1950s, and then moved on to a career in publishing and advertising. "The Apprentice Sorcerer" initially appeared in *Fantasy Fiction*, November, 1953, and is reprinted here for the first time.

H. P. Lovecraft

H. P. Lovecraft (1890-1937), of Providence, Rhode Island, is considered the twentieth century's most influential horror writer (at least until Stephen King). Lovecraft's "Cthulhu Mythos," which provided a scientific explanation for his stories, and his encouragement of young writers such as Robert Bloch and August Derleth, were among his greatest accomplishments. He died in virtual poverty, earning very little during his lifetime. "The Thing on the Doorstep" first appeared in *Weird Tales*, January, 1937.

Patricia B. Cirone

Patricia B. Cirone (1952-   ) was born in Chicago and graduated with a degree in biology from Notre Dame University. A resident of Maine, she is a full-time writer, specializing in fantasy and poetry. "Just Another Working Mom" appears here for the first time.